I0835546

LIFE'S SECOND JOURNEY
BOOK 4 in the SHOW ME SERIES
Published by Anne Stone

ISBN: 978-0-9997860-3-1

This is a work of fiction. Names, characters, places and incidents are either the product of the author's imagination or are used fictitiously, and any resemblance to actual persons, living or dead, business establishments, events or locales is entirely coincidental.

Printed in the USA.

Cover Design, Editing, and Interior Format

The ShowMe Series
BOOK 4

Life's Second Journey

Anne Stone

I'd like to thank my editor, Barb, from the Killion Group. My writing is so much better because of you!

To my sister, Isabel, who never let me give up hope that my dream could become a reality.

And as always, to you Dad. I wouldn't be on this journey without your encouragement.

Prologue

MELANIE CLENCHED THE ARMRESTS AS the plane pitched wildly through the clouds and lightning as they neared the airport. On top of her current air sickness, Melanie woke that morning with a migraine to beat all headaches. She'd barely been able to see as she drove herself to the airport. Her temples still pounded as the plane continued its bumpy ride into the San Antonio International Airport. She was a nervous flier to say the least, but add turbulence and it never failed to send her over the edge. All she wanted to do was call it a day and return to bed.

As the plane flew through the clouds, the stewardess came across the speakers indicating they were preparing the cabin for landing. They should be at the gate momentarily. Momentarily couldn't come fast enough for Melanie. A fine sheen of moisture had broken out across her brow when the plane rocked violently as it approached the tarmac.

The plane bumped along as they landed. She rested her head against the back of her seat, thanking the gods for a successful landing. Melanie took a deep calming breath as the plane made its way to the gate. She'd made it. Now she needed to compose herself before she claimed her luggage, and headed to the hotel.

Melanie was ready to stand when the stewardess once again came across the intercom. "There are severe thunderstorms in the area and the airline is not allowing anyone to disembark at this time. Please sit tight and as soon as the storm passes, we'll allow departure."

Melanie didn't like the sound of that. Her anxiety ramped up again as she wiped the moisture from her palms against her slacks. She wanted, no, needed to get off this plane and get to her hotel. Her migraine had worsened. She needed to take her medicine and go straight to bed. It was three o'clock in San Antonio and sleep was her cure.

After waiting twenty minutes, everyone was cleared to disembark. Melanie hurried as quickly as her worn out legs would take her and somehow made her way to baggage claim. She hailed a cab to take her to a bed and breakfast located just a short walk from the convention center where the Mortgage Bankers Association's annual conference was being held.

Melanie was the vice president in charge of acquisitions at Parklayne Bank in St. Louis. It was a relatively small bank privately owned by the Parklayne family. The family was considered old money having settled in the St. Louis area in the late eighteenth century. They started in the fur trading business and eventually got into banking.

Melanie had been on pins and needles since the last remaining member of the Parklayne family involved in the business was lost in a horrific boating accident. She attributed her migraine to the latest rumor she'd heard just as she was preparing to leave for her business trip to

San Antonio. Her source told her that they were almost positive that the bank was being sold to Amcrost Bank.

She rubbed her eyes hoping to ease the pain. From the first moments after his death, rumors floated about that the bank was up for sale. Nothing had been confirmed, but Melanie believed the end was near and that she was about to lose the only job she had since high school.

Melanie had started as a teller sixteen years earlier and worked her way up to VP of Acquisitions. They gave her a scholarship to one of the area universities, and she'd graduated at the top of her class. Her nerves were getting the best of her. She had to stop worrying about the possibilities of the bank sale and just move on until it was confirmed.

She often traveled to San Antonio, and Night's Landing was the only place she stayed. Over the years, she'd become friends with the owners. Due to the uncertainty of the sale, her trip was last minute and she'd been lucky to secure the last room at the inn. They'd had a cancellation only that morning. The Mortgage Bankers Association annual meeting was being held at the convention center, and all of the hotel rooms had been sold out for months.

Melanie lumbered her way into the foyer of the renovated house. The inn had only ten rooms, but each room was uniquely decorated. Melanie was staying in the Lavender Room. It had a huge canopy bed and was decorated in, what else, all lavender. It was her favorite color and she always tried to stay in it.

Pulling her suitcase behind her, she practically collapsed inside the door. "Welcome, Melanie," Eleanor Budke greeted her as Melanie managed a weak nod.

"Oh dear, are you unwell?"

"Migraine," Melanie barely uttered.

Eleanor swiftly handed her the key to her room. "We'll settle up later. Here's your key. Do you need help to your room?"

"Thanks, but no. I know the way." Painfully she smiled.

"I see that you're in town for five days. I have to run over to Austin for the next couple of days. We're renovating another home into a B&B. I'll be back Friday before you check out. I hope you feel better and enjoy your stay." Melanie hugged her friend and turned away. All she wanted to do was fall into bed and sleep away her headache.

Melanie had started down the hall when Eleanor called out, "We're expecting some severe storms later on. I wanted to let you know there's a chance we could lose the power. If we do, we have a back-up generator so there's nothing to worry about."

"Thanks for the heads-up, Eleanor." Melanie made her way to her room. She undressed and didn't even take the time to locate her nightgown. She stripped down to her underwear and slid under the covers. Before she knew it, sleep had claimed her. It was only five o'clock. She planned a quick nap to rid herself of her headache, then she'd have dinner. She needed to get up early in the morning as the conference began promptly at eight, and she didn't want to be late to her first meeting. Melanie closed her eyes and fell right to sleep.

James Samuels couldn't believe his bad luck. His cab pulled away from the airport terminal just as the worst of the storm hit. Torrents of rain were falling. He held on for dear life as his cab driver negotiated the rapidly flooding streets of San Antonio.

James reached for his carryon as the driver pulled up in front of the inn. Draping his coat over his head to prevent the wind-whipped rain from soaking him, he ran for the entrance. Thankfully, the door wasn't locked.

As he closed the door behind him, he heard a voice call, "Welcome to Night's Landing, that's quite a storm out there." The room was barely lit by a sole candle.

He made his way to the desk and was greeted by a young man. "Hi, there. You must be James Samuels. My name is Elijah Metcalf and I'm the night manager. I apologize for our lack of electricity. Our generator just went down a few minutes ago."

James shook his raincoat and rested it atop his suitcase. "I thought when I pulled up there were more lights on."

"Yep, it just went out. Not sure what that's all about but I'm going to check into it. At least we have actual room keys and not the electronic ones like the major hotels do. Thankfully, you can access your room without issue." Elijah reached in a drawer and withdrew his key. "Eleanor, our owner, is in Austin right now so it's just me. Since it's late, I'll check you in tomorrow. Here's your key. You're staying in the Lavender Room. Here's a flashlight for you. I'll show you to your room."

"That's not necessary, just point me in the right direction."

It had been a long day for James. After his three-hour delay at the airport in St. Louis because of the storms, he'd arrived in San Antonio at eleven o'clock. It was close to midnight when he headed off in the direction Elijah pointed him in. With flashlight in hand, James located his room and inserted the key into the lock. As soon as he opened the door, he threw his bag on the floor, turned off the flashlight, and made his way to the bed, falling hard onto the mattress. Sleep instantly took over.

Melanie drifted in and out of sleep. She was half-awake and realized something wasn't right. Sometimes her medicine affected her senses. She felt like she was moving and that's when she discovered a weight pinning her to the bed. Her heartbeat sped up. She needed to open her eyes but was too afraid. Then she felt the pressure. Her legs were trapped. Something was squeezing her. What was it?

Slowly she cracked open her left eye. It was dark in the room. She trembled. No lights. How could that be? She'd turned on the lights, hadn't she? She hated to sleep in the dark and always went to sleep with the lights on. She eased open her eyes and let them adjust to the darkened room. Her breathing sped up. She realized she wasn't alone. A leg was draped over hers and an arm surrounded her waist. She was going to hyperventilate she just knew it. And then, she turned her head to the right and let out on ear piercing scream.

A gravelly voice eeked out, "What the hell?" The body moved and then she was immediately blinded by a bright light. She blinked once, twice, clearing her vision. Melanie was sitting in the dark with a man she didn't know. Or did she?

Chapter One

Six months later…

JAMES STARED OUT THE WINDOW of his twentieth-floor office, his chin in his hand and forefinger resting against his temple. His mind kept drifting. He closed his eyes against the loss consuming him. He couldn't focus. Couldn't put his mind on work. Couldn't do anything. He felt useless. He looked down at the picture frame he held in his hand. A huge smile adorned their faces. He and Elsa had been at his sister Angelina's house celebrating his niece, Angel's, christening. He pressed his finger against the glass wishing things had turned out differently, but they hadn't. He took once last glance at Elsa and turned over the frame. Opening his briefcase, he slid the photograph inside closing it soundly.

Elsa Daniels had been his fiancée until last night. They'd been together forever, dating in high school and all through college and graduate school. He'd proposed the day they both graduated with honors from graduate school. She with an advanced degree in engineering and he in business. James' path to success had been secured from the time he was born. His father, Ben

Samuels, was the president of Amcrost Bank and he'd been employed with the bank since high school. Now, at the age of thirty-three, he was the vice president of acquisitions.

James and Elsa had been engaged for what seemed like a lifetime— almost seven years—but kept postponing a wedding date, blaming it on establishing their careers before settling down. They'd been comfortable with that decision. Every time they revisited setting a date, they always walked away from making the all-important decision. He was thankful they never got that far.

As time passed, their lives started going in different directions. They rarely saw one another and when they did, they often argued about everything and anything. They still loved one another as friends, but not as lovers. And definitely not as husband and wife. He made the decision to call off their engagement after returning from his trip to San Antonio. There, he realized that he and Elsa just weren't going to make it. They'd drifted apart over the years and really didn't see eye-to-eye with their future goals. It was best to just break things off and remain friends before either one of them said or did something that would ruin their friendship.

When James had told Elsa that they were over, she shed a few tears, but that was it. He knew by her reaction that he'd made the right decision. James would always hold a special place in his heart for Elsa. They'd been through so much together. He hoped they'd remain friends.

As he returned to staring out the window, his thoughts swept back to San Antonio. That trip had been a nightmare from the outset. From his flight delay to the horrible storms, the mix-up with his room...

He had a hard time putting his head around his roommate. If he could have chosen anyone to share a room with, it wouldn't have been her. He was pulled from his thoughts when he heard a tap against his door. He spun his chair around as his father sauntered in.

His father slid into the chair directly in front of his desk. Generally, he only visited James's office when he had a new venture for the bank. He and his father were close but didn't let their familial relationship enter into their work environment. "James, what happened? You look awful."

He hadn't slept well the night before after he dropped Elsa off at her house. He ran his hand along his chin and rubbed the stubble discovering he'd forgotten to shave that morning. He was a mess inside and out. In fact, he'd been lucky to dress in a suit and tie and get to work on time. He rubbed his temple and sighed. He had to tell someone, so it might as well be his father. "Dad, Elsa and I broke up last night."

"What?" His father eased to the edge of his seat with a surprised look on his face.

"Yeah, we parted ways." James stood and came around the front of his desk to sit in the chair beside his father. "We were going in two different directions. She's on the road, I'm on the road. We hardly ever saw one another and when we did, we often fought." Taking another deep breath, he added, "It's for the best, Dad. Neither one of us believes in divorce, and we'd have been miserable married. I know it, she knows it. I just hope we can remain friends."

"I'm sorry to hear this, son." He shook his head worry creased his forehead. "Are you okay? I realize it's your life and if you think it's best."

"I'll be okay, in time, but yeah, I think it's best. We were both miserable."

"Your mother will be devastated." Ben waved a dismissive hand, hesitated and then continued. "I have some news for you. The board has just decided to make a play for Parklayne Bank. With the passing of Ralston Parklayne, the family has finally come to an agreement to sell the bank. It's been over six months in the making, but I think they'll take our offer. In fact, they came to us. The family thinks our bank is the best fit for them. Being local and all, they want it to stay that way. They want to still be a presence in the community."

"That's good." James stood. "What's our next step?"

"Since they are only considering us, I told them we needed to come in and evaluate everything, then make a formal offer. They're okay with that. What's currently on your plate? Since we just finished the Fireside acquisition, I would think you're looking for something to sink your teeth into."

"Actually, I am. This has come at the right time. I needed something new to focus on. When are they expecting us?"

"I just spoke with Saxson Ulrich who is heading this up from Parklayne's side. I told him we'd be getting back with him this afternoon. Are you free for dinner tonight? Maybe we can meet and start laying the groundwork for our review."

He frowned. Of course, he was free. He'd just broken up with his fiancée. "Tonight's good, Dad."

Standing, Ben looked closely at his son. "I'll get back to you about tonight. Why don't you go home and try and get some rest? I'll call with the time and place."

James knew he must look a fright if his father was

sending him home. Clicking the locks in place on his briefcase was the beginning to closing off his heart to Elsa. He'd take her photograph home and put it in a drawer. He didn't want to get rid of it. She was a big part of his past. He was freeing himself of her presence from his office.

With this new project on the horizon, he'd focus and get his head on straight. Put her into his past and move on. He grabbed his briefcase and stepped from his office. A huge weight lifted from his shoulders. And in that moment, he felt free. Freer than he'd felt in a long time. He'd made the right decision. It was time to move on and focus his efforts on something new.

Melanie had heard the rumors that only intensified since the MBA conference six months earlier. Every day she waited for the shoe to fall, waited for that call to come from Saxson Ulrich's office informing her of the bank's sale. Her waiting was over. As of five minutes ago, she got the call to meet with Saxson directly.

Melanie's anxiety picked up as she made her way to Saxson's office on the tenth floor. She couldn't wait to get off that elevator as her ride was much longer than usual. She chastised herself for not taking the stairs. The exercise may have calmed her nerves. She stepped from the elevator and her pulse rate climbed. For the first time in a long, long time, she was scared. Scared of the unknown. Her palms began to sweat and she feared she might hyperventilate. She just needed to take a deep breath and calm herself.

Saxson's administrative assistant wasn't at her desk, so Melanie approached his partially opened door. Softly knocking, she stuck her head around the edge. He was waiting for her and waved her in. He stood as she approached his desk. Motioning for her to take a seat across from him, he reclaimed his office chair. Melanie eased herself onto the high back leather chair and sat on the edge, clasping her shaky hands in her lap.

"I guess you've heard the rumors," he said.

"Yes. Is it true? Has the bank been sold?" She clenched and unclenched her hands, awaiting his answer.

"Not officially it hasn't, although, I'm pretty sure that it will happen in time." Melanie nodded. She stiffly sat in the chair waiting for him to share the news with her. "That's what I wanted to talk to you about. I have a dinner meeting planned this evening with the potential buyers and wanted you to join us since you are head of our acquisitions department. They will be working closely with your department, and I wanted you to get to know their people before they burst onto the scene. Are you free?"

Whether she had plans or not, Melanie must go. She had to make a good impression to hopefully keep some type of job with the bank after the sale. Hell, she'd change departments. She just wanted to stay safe in the secure world she'd established for herself. "I'm free."

"Good, then meet us at seven at Steeltown Inn on Sixth Street."

"May I ask who the intended purchaser is?" Before he could answer his phone rang.

"I'm sorry. I've got to take this call."

Melanie made her way out of the office. She somehow found the door to the stairs and hurried down them to her office. She was too riled up to be confined to the elevator. Not with how anxious she felt. She didn't like change and feared the unknown.

It was just after two in the afternoon. She had almost five hours to wait to learn who she was dealing with. Time moved slowly. At six-thirty, she decided to leave the office and head over to the restaurant. She was filled with uncertainty unsure what the night would bring.

As she handed her keys to the valet, she caught sight of the back of a man as he entered the restaurant. His stature looked familiar. The color of his hair, his height—all too familiar. She shook her head realizing a lot of men looked the same from behind. Again, she chalked it up to nerves and made her way to the entrance of the restaurant.

The doorman held open the door. Just as she crossed the threshold, the man who'd preceded her stood just off to the right of the doorway. She kept trying to place him when he turned and she immediately recognized him.

Her head dropped. Never in her wildest dreams did she think Amcrost Bank would be the buyer. They were local and she assumed a much larger bank would be a player. Not Amcrost.

James Samuels stood right before her. She had her answers.

For a split second, she felt the room spin. She took a deep breath to right herself and calm her nervous stomach. Her bank, Parklayne, was being sold to Amcrost Bank. It was being sold to her nemesis and she knew in her heart of hearts that this was the beginning of the end. She was definitely going to lose her job.

Chapter Two

MELANIE TOOK ONE LOOK AT James and almost walked out the door. Then, she remembered why she was there. She was all too familiar with how mergers were handled. Very often the employees from the selling bank lost their jobs. Her future success stood right before her. He'd more than likely be the one to recommend her firing and she couldn't let that happen. It never entered her mind that Amcrost would be the buyer. She and her counterpart, James Samuels, had a history, one that she wasn't proud of. They ran in the same circles at conventions and on occasion when there was a potential acquisition in the works. Occasionally, there was a bidding war and companies would go in, do their due diligence, and then leave. Their paths crossed too often in the past year, and she wasn't proud of how she handled those meetings.

Melanie wanted to slink into a hole. She could only imagine the expression on her face when she'd seen him across the lobby. She didn't like him and after San Antonio, liked him even less. They hadn't seen one another in several months and now the time they spent together in San Antonio came crashing back to her. Her anxiety increased and she didn't know how to stave off the pounding of her heart, her shortness of breath. She was seriously in trouble.

Melanie caught James' concerned look as she reached for the wall. She tried to steady herself when he came to her rescue, wrapping an arm around her waist. "Hey, are you okay?"

Melanie chewed on her lower lip. Trying to calm her breathing she glanced at the floor. Raising her gaze, she focused on the plant just over his shoulder. "I'm fine," she barely whispered as she continued to calm herself. James stepped away. Whatever she was doing seemed to work as her heartbeat slowed, and she was able to breath normally again. "Are you meeting someone?" she asked, almost assured as to what her answer would be.

"I am. I'm having a business meeting with my father."

"You are?" Melanie tried not to sound like she knew the answer.

With that, Saxson walked into the restaurant, flanked by Ben, James' father. "Ah, Melanie. I'm glad you made it. I see you've caught up with James." Raising his hand to James, Saxson shook his hand. "It's good to see you. I wasn't the least surprised when your father told me you were joining us. Is our table ready?"

James glanced in her direction then he returned his attention to Saxson. "I'm glad I was free this evening too. I'm not sure if our table's ready or not. I just got here right before Melanie. We'd barely said our helloes when you arrived."

"Let me see, then." Saxson approached the hostess.

James' father approached with a relaxed smile on his face and extended his hand. "You must be Melanie Holmes. I'm Ben Samuels, president of Amcrost Bank."

She shook his hand. "It's nice to meet you, sir. I've heard a lot about you."

He laughed. "I'm not sure if that's good or bad."

Saxson returned indicating their table was ready. James walked behind Melanie, guiding her with his soft touch.

He held her chair as she sat, surprising her with his manners. He settled right beside her.

Saxson started off with some small talk while they waited for their waiter to arrive. Once their drink orders were placed, he thanked James and his father for arranging their evening so quickly. "I'm glad that you are taking this merger seriously."

"Merger," Ben squawked out. "This is not intended as a merger. We will be outright purchasing Parklayne, and Amcrost will be totally, one hundred percent in control."

"Ben, I misspoke." Saxson nervously apologized. "I know this isn't a merger. The Parklayne family has decided it's in their best interest to sell. No one in the family is presently in banking. In fact, they've wanted to get out of it for some time."

Melanie clasped her trembling hands in her lap. She didn't want to react in any way that would affect her future employment.

The waiter returned with their drinks. Saxson then took over the conversation once the waiter left with their dinner selections. "I realize that this is pretty much a done deal as long as you don't find anything during your due diligence that would prevent the sale." Nodding, Ben listened. "I've asked Melanie to join us for dinner since she heads up our acquisitions department. James, you will be working directly with Melanie both during the due diligence and transition phase."

Turning to Melanie he added, "Melanie, you will be our point person. I expect you to coordinate all aspects of this transaction—dealing with the various department heads, answering and coordinating all responses to Amcrost's due diligence questionnaire. You will be the face of Parklayne in regards to the sale. Understood?"

"Yes, Saxson, I understand." The reality of the sale was upon her. Tonight, it hit home. Melanie's anxiety ratcheted up again. She was starting to have a panic attack, she just knew it, and needed to do something to waylay it. She needed to control her racing heart, her shortness of breath, and her sweaty palms.

Just as she made the decision to leave the table, she again felt James' eyes on her as she took quick short breaths. She had to escape and calm herself. She was assured he saw her quickness of breath; then he moved his eyes to her hands, catching their trembling just before she clenched them tightly.

When there was a pause in conversation, Melanie took her chance. They couldn't witness her while she had a full-blown panic attack, they just couldn't.

"I'm sorry gentlemen, please excuse me. I must visit the ladies' room." She reached for her purse slung across the back of her chair, knocking into James in the process. She apologized as she fumbled with her purse strap. James quickly stood to hold her chair and then announced that he too, needed to use the facilities.

James followed her as she hurried to the ladies' room. He stood guard outside the door. While he waited, he thumbed through his phone. He came across an email from Elsa. She was missing him and wanted to talk, try and make things right between them. She'd even called twice since he'd turned off his phone for dinner. He elected to ignore her for the time being. Deep down, he knew he'd done right by breaking off their engagement. Yes, he missed her; she'd been a part of his life for so many years. He missed their friendship and their ease with one another, but he also knew that wasn't enough to build a marriage on and he was going to stick with that decision.

Minutes passed and James saw several women come and go from the restroom and still no Melanie. Just when he was about to enter himself, the door slowly opened and she sluggishly came through the door. She looked beaten almost like she'd been involved in an argument. James reached for her hand, steadying her as the door closed behind her. "Mel, are you feeling okay? You look a little…"

He surprised her because she jumped when he clasped their hands. Before he could utter another word, she stopped him. "I'm fine, just a little headache. Nothing to worry about."

Nevertheless, he knew something was wrong but chose not to draw attention to it.

Melanie didn't want him to know about her near panic attack. She'd been under so much stress lately worrying about the pending sale and then rehashing James in her mind and their time in San Antonio. She had to let it go and do her best to avoid being a casualty in the merger. She needed to realize she couldn't control what may happen and swallowed deeply reminding herself that she'd come far in life. If she fell, she'd pick herself right back up again just like she had as a child.

She'd begin preparing for her future and the possibility that Parklayne may not be in it. Her job track record was good and she could count on references in the event she needed them.

Pulling her hands from his, Melanie gave James her best smile. "We better get back to the table. I'm sure our dinner's waiting."

As they ate, Melanie secured a smile on her face as she listened to Ben and Saxson carry on how banking had changed over the years. They rehashed all of the new regulations that had been enacted since the global crisis in 2008. Melanie sat in an almost trance-like state, nodded when appropriate, but didn't say a word. James interjected on occasion, but kept a watchful eye on her. She had a feeling he knew something was afoot with her but didn't want to cast a light on it. She gnawed on her lip, worried that he'd want to address her nervousness from earlier. She took another deep breath, pushing all of those thoughts aside. She needed to concentrate on the other men's conversation in case she needed to add something noteworthy.

As the evening wore on, Melanie forced herself not to look at her watch. It had been a stressful day all around. She needed to get home as she couldn't sit listening to Ben and Saxson carry on with their conversation. They decided to move their party into the bar when James turned to her, "Are you ready to call it a night?"

Sheepishly, she nodded. "I am, thank you." Rubbing her forehead, she said, "This headache came out of nowhere. Thank you, I would like to call it a night."

"You should have said something earlier," Saxson said. "Ben and I were just reminiscing of old times."

"I enjoyed listening to your stories. I think I learned a few things this evening." She reached for her purse again, but it slid through her hands dropping to the floor.

James immediately retrieved it. Their hands touched and their eyes met. He smiled down at her as she pulled both her hand and purse from him. She reacted too quickly. She felt the spark just like she did in San Antonio. He smiled. "Thank you for dinner this evening."

As his dad and Saxson headed towards the bar, James again placed his hand on her lower back and escorted Melanie from the dining room. It felt right to him, guiding her along. He'd sensed her anxiousness and felt a need to protect her. They each waited while the valet went to claim their cars. James stood in front of Melanie, gazing directly into her hazel colored eyes. He noticed brown flecks that he hadn't seen before. She'd also added blonde highlights to her light brown hair that softened her face. He didn't know why he was taking the time to really see Melanie, but he was. It's not like this was the first time he'd been around her. In fact, it had been countless times, but tonight there was something different about her. Maybe a loneliness, a sense of loss, or even vulnerability that wasn't present before.

"How do you want to handle this?" he asked. "Since this is still in the initial stages and Saxson isn't planning on announcing it to the staff until Friday, do you want to come to my office or shall I come to yours? Or maybe we could meet somewhere else?"

She shook her head. He imagined she didn't want to do any of the above but knew she had to since she was spearheading the sale. She tipped her head. "Let's meet somewhere. I really don't want any of my employees to get wind of this until Saxson announces it. I just don't think it would be right."

"That's why I asked. Where would you like to meet? The weather's been really nice lately. After the long winter, I'd hate to be locked up in a stuffy office. Are you up to meeting outdoors? Maybe a park? Somewhere where we can concentrate and not be bothered." She thought for a moment when James suggested, "How about the Botanical Gardens? We can find a bench where no one will interrupt us. We can work and enjoy the weather at the same time."

"I've never thought about not working in the office."

"Mel, sometimes we do off-site meetings." Smiling at her he continued, "Come on now, doesn't the Botanical Gardens sound like fun? Say yes. I'll come by and pick you up and we can even have lunch there. We'll make it our little office. What do you say?" She chewed on her lower lip, weighing what to do then sharply nodded her head. "I'll phone your office tomorrow morning say around nine or so. Just tell your staff that you have an outside appointment. I'll bring the questionnaire that we use and we can go from there. Sound like a plan?"

"It does, but I'm still not too sure about this off-site excursion."

"Ah, don't worry about that. Live a little." And with that, the valet pulled up with Melanie's car. As she climbed in and pulled away from the curb, he wondered what was going through her mind. She was going to be a hard one to figure out. Yes, they had a history they had to deal with, between what happened in San Antonio and their past business encounters. Maybe they should let the past be just that—the past. Maybe they'd discuss their differences, maybe not. Right now, they had to work closely to ensure a seamless transition occurred when Parklayne Bank ultimately merged into Amcrost Bank.

Chapter Three

MELANIE HAD BARELY FALLEN ASLEEP when she woke with a fright. She'd encountered another dream. A dream she'd had many times since she was a little girl and often resurfaced when her anxiety levels rose. Her dream was always the same. A dark closet. The rapid beating of her heart while she waited, waited for release.

She knew she wouldn't get an ounce of sleep the remainder of the night, so she put the covers aside and swung her feet onto the floor. Leaning over her knees, she wrapped her arms underneath her legs and curled into a ball. Closing her eyes against the soft light from her bedside table, her mind drifted back to the conversation at dinner. Melanie knew the sale was the right decision for the Parklayne family. The bank hadn't grown much over the last several years, and with Ralston's illness and sudden death in a boating accident, acquisitions had been placed on hold. Her department still bid on portfolios but never aggressively, knowing that ultimately the deal would never come to fruition.

She pulled herself up and headed to her home office where she made a list of everything she anticipated needing for her meeting with James. Before she knew it, a legal sized pad was filled with titles of various reports she knew James would want to review. With that, she threw on some lounge pants and logged on to the system so she could begin generating those reports.

Four hours later, she looked at the clock. It was nearing 5 a.m. Time to shower and dress for the day. She logged off the system and headed to her bathroom. She took one look at herself in the mirror and moaned. Dark circles had developed underneath her red-rimmed eyes along with the bags that she often fought against when her dreams resurfaced. There was absolutely nothing she could do except try and cover her smudges with concealer.

She wasn't quite sure what to wear. She needed to remain professional and decided to wear one of her conservative suits. By the time she finished showering and dressing, it was a little after six. Just as she grabbed her purse, her thoughts returned to the evening before when James retrieved it from the floor. She remembered the feeling that coursed through her body when her hand brushed his. Just that brief touch reignited the spark she first felt in San Antonio. She needed to get that thought out of her mind. She and James were colleagues and nothing more.

She tucked her purse onto her shoulder and almost ran out the door. She stopped at her local coffee shop, Mochas and Coffee, and purchased the largest cup of coffee they had, along with a bagel and cream cheese. She pulled into her parking place in the Parklayne garage at nearly seven o'clock. She practically ran through the revolving front doors, signed in with the guard, and then made her way to her office.

The reports she generated from home were sitting

on the printer outside her office. Grabbing them she stopped momentarily to take in the view. *Where will I be this time in six, nine months?* She wasn't going to go there. She'd let whatever happened in her job happen. She couldn't get herself all riled up about it, she just couldn't. If she did, her anxiety attacks would consume her and she couldn't let that happen. Wouldn't let that happen.

James had difficulties going to sleep after their dinner. His mind wouldn't shut down. He kept rethinking what was said and not said during dinner. Melanie sat through much of dinner with a frozen smile on her face. Something was bothering her physically—from her initial sighting of him when she entered the restaurant, all the way through dinner. She agreed to the Botanical Gardens, but he decided they'd need a backup plan in the event of rain.

His house was warm and inviting. He'd bought it a few years earlier right after he and Elsa had become engaged. He had a beautiful sunroom that looked out over his expansive backyard. He lived alone as he and Elsa never found the time to move in together. That should have been a clue to him but it hadn't registered until just recently.

In that moment, he decided to bring Melanie to his home. He'd order out lunch. They'd have the privacy they needed to discuss not only the impending sale but also address their relationship. They needed to put everything out on the table and learn to get along, especially if they'd eventually work together at Amcrost.

James grudgingly pulled himself out of bed and showered. The warm waters sliced across his back and helped wake him. By the time the shower was over, he was ready to take on Melanie Holmes.

James dressed in his usual attire— suit with long sleeved white shirt and a green and blue striped tie. He always dressed professionally while others in the office took the casual route. He took his job seriously and always played the role of a banker.

James grabbed a cup of coffee from his single serve machine and headed out the door. His mind was still running at lightning speed. He couldn't stop thinking about Melanie and what her role would be at Amcrost. They were peers and both held the same job. How would his father see both of them in this position? Either one of them could be demoted, or moved to a different department, or heaven forbid lose their job altogether. He most assuredly wouldn't lose his job; after all his father was the president of Amcrost. He wouldn't fire his son, or would he? James knew the outright answer to that question. And maybe that's why Melanie had been so disturbed the night before. Maybe she believed she'd lose her job. He wouldn't let that happen. He knew her skills and work ethic. She'd add so much to Amcrost that James wouldn't let his father lose her in the sale. Someway they'd both remain employed at the bank. He'd figure out a way.

James pulled up in front of Melanie's office at ten thirty. It was a little later than he'd originally planned, but his lack of sleep and his need to locate all of the files he needed for their initial meeting took him longer than he'd anticipated.

James rang Melanie's cell phone and she answered almost immediately. "Hey there, Mel. Sorry I'm a little later than I'd planned, but I'm outside in the visitor parking lot. Are you ready to get started?"

"Um, sure. Give me a few minutes and I'll be down."

Just as she hung up the phone, raindrops pelted his windshield. Soon, the rain fell heavier. *Well, that sure decided it.* They were definitely going to be holding their meeting at his house. He was glad he carried in the door of his car the carryout menu for the pizzeria that was around the corner from his home.

James didn't want Melanie walking across the parking lot in what was now pouring rain, so he started his car and pulled up to the front doors of the building. He watched as she approached the revolving glass doors. Her arms were laden with what appeared to be reams and reams of paper. As she started through the doors, her purse caught and she lost everything she was carrying. Papers went flying everywhere. She pressed her hands to her eyes in frustration. He started to get out of the car, but the security guard came out of nowhere and helped her retrieve all of her reports. Melanie aligned the papers before standing.

James jumped from the car when she finally came through the doors. He didn't want to draw attention to her clumsiness and nervousness. He remembered her fumbling with her purse the night before and made note to say something about her purse getting in the way too much lately. Maybe a stupid joke would calm her nervousness.

"Here, let me get the door for you," James called out as he opened her door. Melanie continued to fumble with her reports as she eased her way into the car. "What do you have there, a book?"

She pursed her lips at him. "No, I have a few reports

for you to peruse."

"A few," he commented as he closed her car door. "That'll take all day and night by the looks of that stack."

Melanie shook her head as he entered the car. "I wanted to be prepared..."

"And by the looks of things you are." His automatic wipers took that as the cue to swish across the windshield. "I have a back-up plan for the Botanical Gardens since it's now raining." He handed the pizzeria menu to her. "Decide what you want and I'll place the order."

"You mean we're holding our meeting at the pizzeria?"

"Silly. No, we're not. I thought we'd pick up lunch and then head back to my place. We can spread out there plus it's private. No one will overhear our conversation."

"Your place?"Wide-eyed she questioned as he handed her the menu.

"Yep. I think that's our best choice since it's raining, and we want to keep this meeting between us."

She gnawed on her lower lip. She really didn't want to be alone with him. Her stomach was beginning its roll. She'd had issues with her stomach for as long as she could remember dating all the way back to her childhood and it only reared its ugly head when the rumors began. She'd hadn't suffered from her anxiety for some time and it generally acted up in conjunction with her stress levels. She wasn't sure she could drink a soda let alone eat pizza.

James stared at her as she looked at the menu he was handing her. "Is there something wrong with Pizzas, Pie & More? I thought everyone loved their thin-crust pizza topped with Provel cheese. It just melts in your mouth, that oozy, gooey cheese."

On a normal day, it was her favorite restaurant. She loved everything on the menu and normally had carryout from them at least once a week. She knew the menu backward and forwards. "Order what you want. I'm fine with anything but pepperoni."

He tapped his fingertips on the steering wheel. "I thought everyone loved pepperoni."

She looked at him. "I'm not everyone, am I?" she replied, then turned away.

"No, you're certainly not." James grabbed his cell phone, ordering their deluxe pizza without pepperoni, a chef's salad, and chocolate chip cookies for dessert. "It'll be twenty minutes. I'll take my time driving over. And with the way the rain's coming down it will probably take us at least twenty minutes."

She pursed her lips and stared out the window. She didn't like the idea of being alone with him at his home especially after their incident in San Antonio. She knew, in time, they were going to have to address that along with the other business run-ins they'd had over the years. They had to put the past aside if either of them planned on making this relationship successful. She wasn't going to lose her job, that was for sure.

Chapter Four

JAMES CAREFULLY MANEUVERED HIS CAR through the rain slogged streets of St. Louis and a half hour later he was pulling up at Pizzas, Pie & More. "I'll be right back," he said as reached for his umbrella in the back seat.

Sarcastically she said, "What, you think you're going to melt?"

He smirked. "I'm sure you're wishing for that to come true." With that he opened the car door and pushed the button on his umbrella to deploy it. With a loud whooshing sound, the umbrella popped open, sheltering him from the rain.

Melanie watched James as he hurried into the restaurant. Shaking her head, she told herself she needed to behave.

She had drifted into her own little world and wasn't aware of James' struggle with his umbrella and the car door until she heard him yelling. Reaching across the seat she pulled the handle and pushed the door open. "Didn't you see me struggling with the pizza and salad while trying to hold onto the umbrella?" He chuckled. "If I didn't know better, I'd think you were hoping that our meeting was over before it began."

Struggling to speak, Melanie reached for their food while James closed the umbrella and threw it into the back seat, flinging water about the car in the process. "They just took the pizza out of the oven, so the box is pretty hot. Be careful," he said as he started the car.

"It is hot," she added doing her best to ignore his comment about their meeting. In silence, they made their way through the flooded streets to James' house. Flicking the garage opener, he waited as the door raised then pulled his car into the oversized garage. He put the car in park and turned to Melanie. She sat stiffly beside him staring straight ahead.

"The smell from that pizza box has been driving me crazy. Come on, let's go. Don't worry about your stuff; I'll get it after we eat." He opened his car door then reached for the food.

She was lost in thought when she felt his touch. "Did you say something?"

"Here, let me take that," he grabbed their food from her lap and exited the car.

The warmth of his hand pulled her from her thoughts. She didn't know what was going on with her. Actually, she did. It was her anxiety ratcheting up. She couldn't focus but then she also realized she'd had little to no sleep the night before after having gotten up at one o'clock after another disturbing dream. She shook her head trying to clear it. When she got out of the car, James was standing, holding their food and watching her closely. "You okay?"

"I am. Sorry about that. I guess I zoned out from lack of sleep. Between my headache last night and..." She thought briefly and realized; she didn't know him well enough to go there with him. She hurried to his side. "Can I help?"

"Yeah, you can get the door. It's open."

"You mean you don't lock your doors? That's pretty stupid on your part." Brows raised. "I… I mean in this day and age you can never be too careful."

"Normally I do, but today I didn't. Why should it bother you anyway?"

"It shouldn't, should it?" she muttered under her breath. He led her through the mud room into the kitchen. She was surprised with her first impressions. The room sparkled. The granite counters were barren except for his single serve coffee pot. A tea kettle also sat on the stove.

"You drink tea?"

Setting their food down onto the counter, he turned towards her. "I do. I find it relaxing after a long day. Come sit down and I'll grab us some plates and silverware. What do you want to drink? Coffee, tea, water, wine…"

"Wine? We're on the clock. How could you think about having a drink?" When she was working, she always toed the line—never drinking while on the job. In fact, rarely drinking at all.

Shaking her head in disgust, she reached for the bag that contained their salad and cookies. Surprised with the abundance of crackers included, she grabbed one and tore open the packaging. She hoped it would settle her stomach which was rolling with every breath she took. From the moment she sat in James' car, her stomach had bothered her. She needed to get her anxiety under control before the symptoms consumed her. She'd come so far from the childhood that had shaped her into the woman she was today. Melanie downed the crackers and reached for a second pack.

"Wow, you must really be hungry with the way you're scarfing down those crackers." She didn't respond instead she reached for the plates he'd grabbed from the cabinet and set them along with the silverware onto the kitchen table. She turned back toward the counter and discovered a napkin holder that contained brightly colored napkins. She was surprised by the bright green color let alone that he had a holder to neatly organize them. Grabbing two, she placed them besides their plates.

James filled two glasses with ice and retrieved a pitcher from the refrigerator. "How about iced tea? I made it yesterday after work. It's plain so if you need to add sugar or lemon..." He pointed towards the sugar bowl. "I can slice a lemon if you'd like that."

"I'd love some lemon." Melanie stood at the table as James grabbed a lemon from a bowl on the counter. He appeared comfortable in the kitchen as he set the lemon on a cutting board and skillfully sliced it into equally sized wedges. Arranging the slices onto a plate, he made his way to the table. He quirked a smile as he pulled a chair from the table, offering her the seat. As she sat, he slightly pushed in her chair. She welcomed his manners. James was a gentleman through and through. But why hadn't she noticed this on their previous encounters? She didn't know. Maybe it was because there was always tension in the air when they were together, either attending a conference or on a due diligence trip. But now, she was seeing a different side to him and work had nothing to do with his behavior. She had to believe this was the true James Samuels. One not influenced by work or his peers. He was himself and she was beginning to like what she saw.

James threw open the pizza box. The spicy aroma hit her nose. She wasn't quite sure her stomach had settled and decided the tea might help. She grabbed a slice of lemon. She hadn't noticed the lemon seed, but as she squeezed the ends together, the lemon seed shot out across the table hitting James squarely on his forehead. "Hey," James flinched. "Watch what you're doing."

"Huh? What are you talking about? I'm just squeezing my lemon."

"And that's the problem." He scooped a lemon seed off his plate and showed her the evidence.

"I did that?" she asked with a surprised look.

He chuckled. "Um, do you see a lemon in my hand or in my tea?"

"No, I don't." Melanie giggled. "Sorry about that. I guess I wasn't paying attention. Normally, I hold my hand over my lemon but…"

"You didn't this time."

"No, I guess I didn't." Melanie stirred her glass so the lemon flavor would disperse. Taking a sip of her tea, she focused her eyes on her drink.

He raised his brows. "Is there a problem with your tea?"

"Ah, no there isn't. In fact, it's really good." Her stomach was still rolling; the first two packages of crackers hadn't done a thing to settle it. She tore open another packet.

"Melanie, is there something wrong? That's the third package of crackers you've eaten in a matter of minutes." She crumbled the cellophane packaging. "Are you not feeling well?"

"No, I'm fine." She fiddled with her silverware, clearly

lying.

"Really, now?"

Melanie clutched her stomach and took another sip of tea. He reached for her hand, brushing his fingers across it. "If you're not feeling well, we can call it a day. I can take you home."

"No, I'm fine. I just need to sit here for a minute. You go ahead and start eating. My stomach's a little upset after taking my migraine medicine. Don't worry about me. I'll be fine."

James took his first bite of pizza. The gooey cheese fell off as he savored his first taste, sliding onto his plate. Melanie took one look at it at grabbed her stomach. "Is there a bathroom nearby?"

"Yeah, sure." He pointed towards the hallway. "First door on the left."

"Thanks." She practically ran from the room. He sat at the table for a few moments then made his way outside the bathroom. He wanted to be near in case she needed anything.

James stood there for a few minutes. He didn't hear her getting sick but was worried just the same. "Mel? Do you need anything? Are you okay?"

Slowly the door opened and an even paler Melanie appeared. He reached for her hand and drew her to his side. "Sorry about that. I took one look at the cheese…"

"Don't worry about it. Would you rather go into the family room and rest while I clean up the kitchen?"

Stammering, she said that she was okay. "You go ahead and eat. I should be better shortly. I think the crackers are starting to kick in."

"Why didn't you tell me you weren't feeling well?

We could have gotten something else for lunch, or even postponed our meeting for today."

"We can't do that. Saxson is counting on me to make this sale happen. Not tomorrow or in the future but today. Now."

"Mel, you know that's not going to happen. We have to do our own due diligence, and that's gonna take some time. One additional day isn't going to make or break this deal. Why don't you go lie down and I'll clean-up? If you're feeling better, we can continue, otherwise, I'll take you home and we can try another day. No one's going to fault you if you're sick." Nodding approval at his suggestion, he led her to the couch in his family room. "Why don't you lie down here and I'll be right back."

Melanie took his suggestion and grabbed the throw folded across the arm of the couch. She laid down and covered herself. Almost as soon as her head hit the couch, her exhaustion took over, and she was out like a light.

James had been clueless to Melanie's condition. He felt awful that he hadn't recognized her state. He finished his lunch and cleaned up the kitchen. He checked on Melanie and discovered her fast asleep. He decided to let her rest and elected to retrieve her reports from the car. He could at least begin his initial review.

When he opened the car door, he was surprised with how much paper she'd generated in the short time from their initial meeting the night before. There had to be at least three reams of paper. She'd neatly stapled each report together. So as not to disturb her, he set up his office at the kitchen table. It would be easy to find him. Normally, he would have worked in his expansive home office, but Melanie didn't know where that was and he didn't want her to feel abandoned when she woke.

James was impressed with the reports she'd run. Not only did she have various bank level reports suggesting the number of account holders and deposits, she also had mortgage level reporting too. At first glance, he knew Parklayne was in great financial shape, even better than he ever thought. It was a shame that Ralston had died. Everyone in the banking community had known he'd been sick, but his sudden death in a boating accident took everyone by surprise.

James lost track of time. When shadows from the setting sun crossed the kitchen floor, he realized how late in the day it truly was. He hadn't heard from Melanie and was actually a little concerned. He stood to check on her when he heard her stir. As he neared her, he heard her moaning. And then, she bolted upright on the couch. Throwing her legs over the side, she hugged her sides and leaned over her legs. James reached for her running his hand along her back. At first, she didn't react, and then she turned her head, looking back at him.

"Hi," he whispered. He didn't want to frighten her. "Feeling better?" He sat down beside her. Again, he reached out his hand, smoothing her hair down her back as she calmed her breathing.

He decided not to comment on whatever had happened as he walked into the room. He surmised she'd been having a dream but he didn't want to call attention to it. "Hey, I went through those reports you pulled. You were quite thorough. I can't believe you were able to generate such an extensive amount of information in such a short period of time. You must've been up since before dawn."

She ran her hand through her hair. "Try since one and you'd be close."

"You've been up since one this morning? No wonder you're exhausted. Mel, these reports could have waited. We could have discussed things and come up with a preliminary listing of what we needed. You didn't have to lose sleep over this."

She raised her gaze. "I did. It's my job to make sure you receive everything needed to make a decision on whether or not to purchase Parklayne. I'm just following Saxson's orders and I'm not going to fail."

Melanie systematically discussed each report. James got tired of listening to her rattle everything off. Raising his hand, he stopped her. "Enough. I've heard enough. I don't want to discuss Parklayne anymore right now. What I want to discuss is you, us." He pointed back and forth between them.

She drew her lower lip in, biting it. Staring at the floor she didn't know what to do. She didn't want to talk about them. It was safer to stay on point, discussing Parklayne. And since he didn't want to focus on that, she knew the only way for her to get out of this conversation was to lie. So, she did. "James, I'd like you to take me back to the office. I'm not feeling well and I just want to go home."

James wasn't surprised with her request. He knew how apprehensive she'd be in discussing what happened, what was happening between them. Whatever it was, he felt it and it was ongoing. He needed to address it sooner rather than later before they'd be entrenched in negotiations. He didn't want that to interfere with what he wanted to discuss.

James would leave it alone, for now. "It's getting late. I'll just take you home."

"But my car's at the office."

"Don't worry, I'll pick you up tomorrow and take you in. We can get back to what we'd intended on doing today— discussing the sale." James stood and reached for her hand.

Melanie definitely didn't react the way he intended and shied away from his touch. "Don't look at me that way. I'm just trying to help you from the couch." James smiled and shook his head at her. He didn't know what her problem was with him, but he was going to find out. When she didn't give him her hand, he walked away and headed off towards the kitchen. "I'm going to keep these reports here and look through them in a little more detail. Come on, let's get you home."

Chapter Five

JAMES DROPPED MELANIE OFF AT her home and returned to his office. She had insisted he take her back to her office but he refused because he knew she wouldn't go straight home like she'd promised. His gut told him she'd return to her office and work until God knows when, trying to keep Saxson from being disappointed in her for not accomplishing more during her day.

James believed there was more going on with Melanie than met the eye. It was clear she didn't want to disappoint Saxson or anyone that mattered. He knew of her anxiousness surrounding her job. He'd seen it firsthand when they'd been reviewing a failing bank for purchase almost a year ago.

To expedite the sale, four companies had been called in at the same time to review the bank. Each had their own conference rooms where they went over all the necessary reports, met with the bank's key staff members, and did whatever they needed to determine if their respective company would be making an offer. Several times, James had witnessed her tearing into one of her staff members for not being thorough enough in their analysis. Melanie, while performing her own research, uncovered something that hadn't been disclosed. James hadn't been sure what the issue was but he'd witnessed her displeasure with her findings.

When the four leading representatives from each bank met with the selling bank's head officer, she lit into him. asking extremely pointed questions. When their officer became evasive with his answers, Melanie walked out of the room never to return. She, in fact, had pulled her entire team and left the facilities.

Melanie had a reputation for being hardnosed but after that incident, he believed there was more to the situation with Parklayne than he knew. And in all actuality, there was. James discovered that Ralston had recently disclosed his illness. Everyone at the time had been on pins and needles because they knew he was the last of the Parklayne family involved with the bank. They all worried that the bank would be sold. And then, Ralston's health had improved only to have him taken from them in a boating accident.

James had also seen another side to Melanie while they were in San Antonio at the MBA conference. One that intrigued him. He saw how she interacted with her peers in a different light. She was supportive of their ideas and genuinely kind. She knew a lot of people and was excited to touch base with them again oftentimes inquiring about their families. She smiled a lot and appeared relaxed and comfortable in the conference setting, that was, until they were back at Night's Landing. Then, a much different personality appeared. One where she was aloof, fidgety, almost scared of her own shadow. She withdrew and stayed to herself, refusing his offers for dinner.

He'd mentally filed away her different personalities

waiting for this moment to begin dissecting them. Now he had the opportunity to get to know her, really know her. He wanted to discover who the real Melanie Holmes was. Now that he was free of Elsa, he could do that. Deep down, he knew the reason for breaking up with Elsa. And that reason was tied up in one word—Melanie.

James reviewed the extensive personnel files that Saxson had sent to his father. James was willing to bet Melanie had even considered where the personnel side of the sale would fall. She was well aware of her own situation, especially since they shared the same title—Vice President of Acquisitions. James decided he was going to keep his review of the personnel part of the sale a little secret from her. He hoped he'd be able to use the information to uncover who the real Melanie Holmes was. James immersed himself in the files and didn't realize the time until he heard the cleaning company vacuuming his outer office. That's when he decided to call it a day. It was almost eight o'clock.

James locked up his office and waved goodbye to the cleaning staff, then made his way to the elevator. His stomach growled and he realized just how hungry he really was. It had been almost eight hours since he'd last eaten. His mind drifted back to Melanie. She hadn't eaten a thing at his house except for those three packages of crackers she downed. As the elevator doors opened on the garage level of Amcrost's parking facility, James had a bright idea. At least he thought it was… He decided to grab dinner and take it over to Melanie's. He'd make sure she ate, but in all honesty, he wanted to make sure she was taking care of herself. He was worried about her and how she was taking the news of the sale.

He jumped into his car and headed off to Pedals Diner. He would pick up something light for Melanie. He knew the owner, Gus, quite well. He phoned ahead and ordered a club sandwich and chips for himself while he got a bowl of chicken noodle soup for Melanie. If she didn't want it, she could throw it away. He just wanted her to know that he was concerned about both her physical and mental health. Of course, he wouldn't come right out and say he was concerned about her mental health… Hell, he didn't know what he'd say, he just hoped she'd open the door and let him in.

James hoped to forge a friendship with her. They were both bright people, having successfully run their own departments. Somehow, this would all work out. He had faith in the process and knew his father and the board would make the right decisions for both companies.

James pulled up at Melanie's; he wasn't sure how he would be greeted but he didn't care. He marched up to Melanie's door and rang the doorbell, waiting patiently for her to answer. After three times Melanie still hadn't answered the door. She was home, he could hear the television through the partially opened window.

Melanie hadn't been feeling well earlier and James became concerned. He went around the back of her house and looked in the windows. The whole back of her house was lit-up like a Christmas tree; she was definitely home. He couldn't understand why she wasn't answering. He tried the doorknob on what he believed to be her kitchen. Surprisingly, it turned. He opened the door and walked in. Nothing looked out of the ordinary. He set their food down on the kitchen table and called out her name. No response. He became more worried as he wandered through her home.

James meandered through her house continuing to call out her name. He didn't want to frighten her. As he approached her bedroom, he heard her scream. He ran into the room to find Melanie thrashing about on her bed, apparently having a terrible dream.

He vividly recalled her dreams while they shared the same room at Night's Landing. Over and over again, she'd moaned, "Don't touch me. Stop it." He hadn't questioned it then just chalked it up to a nightmare. But now, it appeared to be the same dream. He approached her side cautiously. He feared he was going to startle her but he also didn't want to see her putting herself through the throes of another nightmare.

He ran his fingertips along her forearm. His touch settled her, but she was still in the midst of her dream. James drew his hand along his jawline, unsure what to do next. Clasping her hand in his, he lightly squeezed. She calmed almost immediately and mumbled his name. Had he heard her correctly? As he watched her sleep, he knew he wasn't mistaken. She'd called out his name.

"Melanie, hey, Mel, wake-up. It's me, James."

She took a calming breath and slowly opened her eyes. They grew as big as saucers and she attempted a scream but not a sound left her.

"Mel, please don't be frightened. I brought you dinner but you didn't answer the door. I came around the back and found your kitchen door unlocked. I was worried that something happened..." James closely watched her. "Please say something. Are you feeling better?" She swallowed and wet her lips. He realized she was still waking up and taking everything in including his presence.

Once again he squeezed her hand. Clearing her throat, she tried to sit, so he wrapped his arm around her shoulders and helped her upright.

Calmly, she began to speak. "Please tell me again why you are here. Why you're in my house, let alone my bedroom." The tone of her voice amped up as she got her bearings. "Now," she yelled. "I want to know, what the hell are you doing in my house?"

James stepped away from her bed. he didn't want to upset her any more than she already was. "I—"

"Out with it, James. Why are you here?"

Spinning around he ran his hand through his hair. He took one of several deep breaths before he turned back towards her. What he saw before him took him all the way back to San Antonio. The look on her face, her posture. She was frightened. Should he approach her or stay at a distance? He did what he thought best—he neared her again and opened his arms. He wasn't sure what her reaction would be but to his surprise she practically threw herself at him. She wrapped her arms around his neck and held on for dear life.

She trembled under his hand rubbing up and down the length of her back. After only a few moments she pulled away. Melanie closed her eyes, covered her face with her hands, and then ran her long fingers through her hair. "I'm sorry. Thank you for coming and checking on me. I'm perfectly fine. As you can see, after you dropped me off earlier, I followed your instructions came home and took a nap. Could you give me a moment?"

"Sure, whatever you need." James retreated to the kitchen. While he waited, he took the food from the bag and checked all of the drawers until he came across her utensils. He grabbed a spoon for her soup and returned to the table. A few minutes later she joined him. She'd thrown on a sweatshirt and had run a comb through her hair.

"Feeling better?"

"I am. Thank you for your concern." She grabbed two bottles of water from the refrigerator. Handing one to him she unscrewed her lid and took a deep swallow. "Did you do this?" She said pointing towards the bag of food.

"Yeah, I did. As I said, I was worried about you and decided to bring you dinner. I hope you like the Pedals Diner."

"Of course I do." A smile crossed her face. "Gus and I go way back. I eat there all the time. Is this soup for me?"

"Yep."

"Thanks, their soup is the best." She reached for the spoon and sat. "James, sit down. Please, stay and eat."

He reached for his sandwich. "Would you like half? It's a club sandwich."

"No, I'm good with just this." She took the top off her soup; steam rose from the cup. "Gus's chicken noodle soup is one of my favorites." She stirred the soup and raised her eyes to him. "This was extremely thoughtful of you. Thanks again." James took a bite from his sandwich as Melanie slowly sipped her soup.

She set her spoon down and gazed at him. "James, really, why are you here? I have to say you scared the living daylights out of me." She tucked a strand of hair behind her ear. "I can't remember what I did. Did I scream, or what?"

"No, you didn't scream. I guess I really should apologize. I overstepped my bounds by entering your house. But Mel, I was worried. The lights were all on. I could even hear the television. When I found your door unlocked, my fear for your safety took over and I rushed in." He reached across the table and placed his hand over hers. "I hope you believe me when I say I truly was concerned about your wellbeing."

She smiled at him and nodded her head. "I do believe you." She pulled her hand out from under his and went back to her soup. They ate the remainder of their meal and when she finished, he stood and washed her soup spoon off and set it into the dishwasher. He leaned against the counter and crossed his arms. "We really need to get organized before I bring the remainder of my team in to review Parklayne. Do you think you'll be up to it tomorrow?"

"I have to be." She ran her fingers across the placemat on the table. "Can you come over here so we can finish ironing out our game plan? If we work from here, I can download whatever additional reports we may need. That would probably work out better especially if you want to run further analysis."

"That's a good idea. What time would you like me here?"

"Seven?"

"You want me here that early?" James thought she was crazy.

"Well, why not? That's when I normally start working. In fact, that's late for me as I generally get into the office around six each day."

"You're definitely a work horse. I think we'll compromise and I'll be here at eight."

"You call that a compromise?"

"Yeah, I do since that's when I generally start to work."

"Ok then, I guess I'll see you at eight."

"Yep, and I'll bring the breakfast. I'll stop by Coffees and Mocha and pick us up something. How do you like your coffee?"

"With cream. Four to be exact."

"On that note, I guess I'll be going. It's getting late. I'll see you tomorrow bright and early at eight o'clock with breakfast and one coffee with four creams." He headed towards the door before turning back to her one more time. "You sure you're okay?"

"James?" she questioned with a slight smile.

"I just wanted to be sure, that's all. I worry about you, Melanie."

"Again, thank you for your concern and I'll see you tomorrow." She walked him to the door. He hesitated. "Yes, I'll lock the door."

"How did you know that I was going to say that?"

She laughed. "Intuition?"

Pointing back at her he smiled and added, "If that's what you want to call it." James waved and headed around to the front of her house. He paused and saw her through the window, leaning against the door. He was pleased that she'd been receptive to his presence.

For some reason, he felt protective of her and felt something was brewing between them. Whether it was appropriate or not considering their positions was another story. He needed to be careful as they moved forward.

Chapter Six

JAMES WOKE EARLY THE NEXT morning and headed off to Coffees and Mocha. He decided to not only grab breakfast but lunch too. He had no idea what Melanie preferred so for breakfast he ordered a variety of bagels and cream cheese and a couple of Danish pastries. For lunch he selected an Asian chicken salad and a chef salad. He threw in a couple of shortbread cookies for dessert. After yesterday and her lack of appetite, he wanted to make sure she ate well and stayed healthy. They'd be putting in long hours in the coming weeks and he didn't want her getting sick. Lastly, he ordered himself a café mocha and her coffee with four creamers. He was looking forward to his first sip; he hadn't slept well the night before and needed that extra jolt of caffeine to get him moving for the day.

James pulled up in front of Melanie's at seven thirty. He was early but he wanted to also let her know he heard what she'd said about compromise and he figured this was his way of doing it.

He ambled up the sidewalk outside her house with his shoulder bag briefcase and their food. He struggled to ring the doorbell and almost lost their coffee in the process. He was just righting the drink carrier when she answered. "You're early."

"I am," he said as he made his way through the doorway. "I'm calling it compromise." Melanie chuckled at his comment as she closed the door. James made his way into the kitchen, setting their food and drinks down on the granite counter.

Grabbing her cup from the carrier, she flipped up the lid and took a sip. "Ahh," she sighed swallowing the warm liquid. "You remembered...four creams."

"Of course, I did. Didn't you think I was listening to you?" he teased.

Melanie eyed the huge shopping bag filled with food. "What's all of this? Did you buy out the store? Are you expecting to feed an army?"

"No, just us." Grinning at her he added, "I guess my eyes were bigger than my stomach. What's the old adage? Don't go grocery shopping when you're hungry. Well, I'm starved and everything looked and smelled so good. I also brought us lunch. Thought we could work through without stopping and having to go out." He handed her the salads and she placed them into the refrigerator.

She frowned. "It's not like I don't have food in the house."

"I know. I just thought I was being gentlemanly." He chuckled.

"That's one thing I can definitely say you are, James Samuels." Melanie fished a bagel from the bag. "You are a gentleman through and through."

"Well, if that's a compliment, I'll take it." His coffee and briefcase in hand, he motioned towards the table. "Are we working in here?"

She hurriedly swallowed a bite from her bagel to

answer. A chunk became stuck in her throat. She coughed as she tried to clear it. James rushed to her side and slapped her on the back. Once she cleared her throat, she turned. "What was that for?"

"I was trying to help. You alright now?"

"I am, thank you." She sipped her coffee. "Let's work in my office. It'll be easier." She reached for her coffee and the bagel she'd been eating and motioned for him to follow her. He swung his briefcase back onto his shoulder, grabbed his coffee and bagel and followed.

Melanie climbed the stairs, turned down one of the hallways and headed to the back of the house. When he walked into the room, he was taken aback by its size. The room was lined with windows that overlooked her pristine backyard. The lawn was bright green after the recent rains. A bird sat on the edge of a concrete bird bath, sipping from the waters. Flower containers lined the patio area, adding bursts of color. Her yard was immaculately maintained likely by a landscape company. "You have a beautiful yard. I didn't realize it was this large."

She joined him at the window. A broad smile lit her face. "Yep, that's what attracted me to this house. I wanted my own yard that I could have both flowers beds and a vegetable garden. I so missed that growing up."

"What do you mean?"

"Never mind. Now, let's get to work." Melanie sat down at her large executive desk. She booted up her desktop and set her coffee cup down on her desk. She took another bite of her bagel, stood and retrieved a wing-backed chair from the corner that she often used while reading one of her favorite novels or dreaming of the childhood she never had.

"Here, I'll get that." James grabbed the chair and set it across from her. He opened his briefcase, pulling out the multitude of reports she'd provided the day before.

Over the next several hours, they went through the reports. Melanie made a list of the additional information James needed then logged onto her office computer. While she requested the reports, James pulled out his phone and reviewed his email. He'd received one from his father so he excused himself to make a call.

Since he wasn't sure what his father wanted, he headed outdoors and to the safety of his car. "Hey, Dad. What's up?"

"I thought I'd check in and see how you and Melanie are faring."

"Melanie pulled quite a few reports yesterday that we are reviewing. I've also requested some more information which she's compiling. In fact, we're working from her house to remain out of sight until Saxson makes his announcement."

"Are you finding any deal breakers?"

"None so far. Everything looks pretty clean."

"Good, that's good. What are you doing this evening?"

"Working, more than likely. We didn't get too far yesterday as Melanie was still suffering the after effects from her migraine the night before. I think she had some kind of reaction to her medicine." James wasn't going to go into detail with his father. "We've made good strides today. Why?"

"How about you and Melanie come over to the house for dinner? Your mother would like to catch up with her again. She hasn't seen Melanie since your sister Kelly's and Alec's barbeque. She really likes Melanie and wants to begin welcoming her into the family."

"Dad, really? Do you think that is wise? She works for a competing firm. We haven't locked down this sale. I don't think it's appropriate."

"I'm overruling you, son. From the little I know about Melanie, I think family is just what she needs. Will you ask her, or shall I?"

"I'll talk to her but I don't think she'll accept. I don't think she's into family and I really think this is inappropriate."

"It's not like we haven't socialized with her before."

"You haven't."

"Well, maybe I haven't but your mother has and she wants this, so make it happen. You know how your mother can be."

"I know, I know." Pausing he added, "If that's all you needed, I'll let you go."

"Your mother's expecting your call. James?"

He pinched the bridge of his nose, trying to stave off a headache. "I heard you. I can't guarantee that she'll agree to come."

"It's in your best interest to convince her to."

"Dad?" James started to say something else when he heard a click and then the dial tone.

James couldn't believe his father. They shouldn't be socializing with Melanie now, especially with the impending sale of Parklayne. He knew what her answer would be but he still had to ask.

Pausing outside Melanie's office, he watched as she concentrated on reading her computer screen. When she smiled, her eyes lit up. She had a cute nose and when she was uptight, he realized she gnawed on her lower lip. She had long flowing light brown hair that curled on the ends and long eyelashes that emphasized her whiskey colored eyes. He hadn't realized before just how beautiful she truly was. In fact, she took his breath away. Shaking his head to clear it, he reentered her office.

"Everything okay?" she asked as her fingers sped across the keys of her keyboard. "I'm just about to email the last of these reports to you." She groaned and stretched her back. "I think I need to take a break and move around." Rolling her head back and forth, she closed her eyes until the ding on her computer indicated the export was complete. After a few more keystrokes, she pushed her chair away from her desk. Before she could stand, James was right behind her pushing her back into her chair.

"Sit there for a minute while I try and loosen up the kinks in your neck." He massaged both sides of her neck. He could feel the tightness in her shoulders.

She dropped her head forward while he continued with his ministrations. "That feels so good," she uttered.

James leaned closer and whispered into her ear. "I'm glad. You're awfully tense. You need to relax."

Melanie jerked away, nearly knocking him over as she stood and rushed from the room. *Now what did I say?* Whatever had caused her to run had broken their magical moment. And now he knew she'd never accept his invitation to dinner.

He found her sitting on the patio, staring out across the backyard. "Mel, did I do something wrong? Why'd you run?" He sat in the chair next to her and reached for her hand. Surprisingly she allowed him to hold it. "Please let me know, so I won't do it again."

Chewing on her lip, Melanie withdrew her hand from him. "I can't do this now, okay? I need to stay focused. Focused on the sale."

He stared across the yard. "I'm sorry for whatever I said to upset you." She incessantly flicked her thumb against the nail of her middle finger. He'd noticed this behavior before and realized she must do this when she was nervous or upset about something. "I spoke with my dad."

Upon hearing those words, she stopped flicking her thumb against her finger and glanced up at him. A look of pure fear etched across her face. "Hey, you don't have to be worried. He wants me to ask you… No, he practically ordered me to ask you to dinner." Now, she was starting to panic. Her eyes grew larger and she began to take quick, short breaths. "Actually, it's my mother who wants you to come to dinner."

"Dinner, where?"

"At my parents' house."

Her hands started to sweat. "Why?" She rubbed her palms against her thighs.

"Just because. My dad told my mom we went to dinner the other night and she felt left out. She loves to entertain and…" He watched the emotions cross her face. "Mel, what's wrong?"

"Ah, nothing. I'm just surprised, that's all."

"You have to say yes or my mom will kill me. She really wants to see you again. I know she enjoyed your company at Kelly and Alec's Memorial Day party. Please, you have to say yes because I definitely don't want to be in the doghouse with her."

Melanie chuckled. "I really don't think it's a good idea with the sale and all—"

"That's what I told my dad, but he insisted. His take on the matter is you had a relationship with the family before this came up." Melanie's sister Janet taught with James' sister Angelina and her best friend Gabriella at St. Margaret's.

"I really didn't."

"Of course, you do. Your sister taught with Angelina and still teaches with Gabriella. We see you whenever they have parties. I know my dad didn't meet you until the other night because he'd left the party before you came..." He didn't want to beg and plead but he was getting there.

"If your mom is going to cause you so much angst, I guess I'll have to attend."

He sighed. "Thank you. I didn't want to face my mother's wrath. You have no idea how she can be when she wants something."

"What time?"

"I have to call her and confirm. In fact, I'll do that right now." James whipped out his phone and pressed the speed dial assigned to his parents. His mother picked up on the second ring.

"Well?" she asked.

"Don't you even say hello?"

"Why should I when I know why you're calling. Did she say yes?"

"She did. What time should we be there?"

"Oh, you're going to bring her." Jackie shrieked. "Perfect. That's just perfect." James knew what she was up to but wouldn't confront her in front of Melanie. "How about six-thirty. That'll give your father ample time to come home and relax for a few minutes. You know he's been working so hard lately."

"Mom?"

"Okay, I'll stop. I know I can ramble when I'm excited. Tell Melanie I can't wait to see her again."

"I will." And on that note, James ended the call.

He gave Melanie a sheepish grin. "Please don't disappoint her and back out at the last minute. She's thrilled that you're going to join us."

She shook her head, her brow furrowed. "Where would you get the idea I'd back out? If I say I'll come, I will. What time should I arrive? I'll need directions too."

"She's expecting us at six thirty and I'll drive you." Melanie's eyes grew huge. She probably feared this was a date.

"I'm going to head on home and change. I'll stop back by around six to get you."

"See you in a bit, then." Melanie watched James walk down her sidewalk. She needed to remain polite and not do or say anything that would hurt her down the road. She did like James' mother and deep down she was really looking forward to having dinner with her.

Chapter Seven

JAMES WENT HOME AND ATTEMPTED a quick nap after having a sleepless night the evening before. He was unsuccessful as his mind wandered back to Melanie. Throughout their day he had witnessed various expressions and mannerisms he hadn't noticed before. From the way she scrunched her nose when deep in thought to the gnawing on her lower lip and the flicking of her fingers when she was nervous. He knew little about her background just that she had a sister that his sister Angelina had once taught with before marrying and having a family.

She was tight-lipped regarding her personal life. What he knew was her job was extremely important to her. It seemed to be her life. It almost consumed her and he wondered if that's why she became anxious in certain situations. She was thorough and expected excellence in all aspects of her job. He'd witnessed these characteristics first hand, on the road, and in the last few days since the sale was announced. He was cataloguing all of her idiosyncrasies as he got to know the true Melanie Holmes.

Almost as soon as James left, Melanie became troubled with why Jackie Samuels would be asking her to dinner. She didn't really know her at all only having been in her presence a few times at her daughters' homes. Melanie couldn't relate to Jackie's meddling into her children's lives. She didn't know or remember too much about her own mother. And what she remembered, she had pretty much locked away only to revisit during her nightmares.

Her memories were scarce. Melanie had been placed into foster care when she was six years old after her mother's death. Her mother pretty much drank herself to death after having lived in an alcohol induced state after her father's death when Melanie was just a baby. Her mother had never recovered and used the bottle as her escape. Janet, her sister, being six years older, wasn't matched in the same homes as Melanie, and they'd temporarily lost track of one another until Melanie was in high school. Thankfully, Janet had found her and they'd remained close since.

After a warm, relaxing bath, Melanie applied a thin sheen of her favorite peony scented body cream as she dressed for the evening. She didn't want to dress too casually so she pulled a nice pair of black dress pants from her closet. She topped it off with a fuchsia colored blouse and a white cardigan.

Before she knew it, her doorbell rang. Her eye caught the time. James, of course, was early. *I guess I'll have to get used to that. Compromise, is that what he called it?*

Melanie answered the door and was completely surprised by his relaxed state as he rested his hand on the door frame. His eyes shone brightly and he quirked a smile at her. He was dressed casually in a pair of khakis and a yellow polo shirt. She took one look at him and was lost. She'd never really taken the time to look at him before. Maybe it was because he was casually dressed and not wearing a stuffy suit and tie which seemed to be his choice of attire. He appeared at peace without a worry.

She didn't know why, but she was shocked with the change in him.

"Are you going to let me in?"

"Oh yeah, sure." Melanie moistened her lips almost embarrassed for gawking at him. She stepped aside. "Let me grab my purse and we can head out." She retrieved her purse and slowed her step as she neared him. "Are you compromising again?"

Looking a little flummoxed, he asked, "What do you mean by that?"

Pointing at her watch she said, "You're twenty minutes early."

"At least I'm early and not late." He chuckled. "If you want to call that compromise, so be it."

He leaned closer and pushed a strand of hair behind her ear. "You look nice and smell good too. Is that peony you have on?"

"Why it is. How?"

"It's Angelina's favorite flower."

She blushed. "You look pretty good yourself. I like the casual dress."

"Thanks. Well, let's go. The sooner we get started, the sooner we'll be able to call it a night."

Melanie didn't like the sound of that. *Did he or didn't he want to do this?* As far as she was concerned this definitely was not a date. He was only trying to please his mother. She realized she'd misread his earlier advances.

James was a peer and maybe would someday be a good friend, but that was all. He started down the stairs while she locked her front door. Yes, he was right. The sooner they got this evening underway the sooner they'd be able to draw it to a close. And that was one thing she looked forward to. She didn't need to get too close to the Samuels family.

She met James at the passenger door. She jumped in while he held it for her. As he walked around to enter the car, she kept telling herself this was only one evening and it would be over in the blink of an eye. At least that's what she hoped for. She reminded herself that she couldn't get too close and she didn't do family.

James pulled up at his parents' house. Melanie had been to his sisters Kelly's and Angelina's homes for parties. She was nervous but it was a different kind of nervous than what she experienced with her anxiety. She knew the family and had socialized on a few occasions with his mother but nothing to write home about. She didn't understand why his mother was so interested in seeing her again. She decided to take one minute at a time and see where the evening went.

Melanie got out of the car and proceeded around to the front where James waited. He gave her a half-hearted smile and led her into his parents' kitchen where Jackie stood over the stove stirring a pot. "Mom, we're here."

Jumping in surprise, Jackie clutched her chest. "James, why do you always do that? I think you enjoy scaring the living daylights out of your mother." Turning towards Melanie, she approached her with her arms held wide and hugged her. "Melanie, thank you for coming on such short notice. I'm so glad you could join us."

Melanie thanked her for the invitation. The butterflies took over and she clasped her hands in front of her. She didn't know what to say. "I'm sorry, Jackie. Are we early?" Looking back and forth between mother and son she added, "Can I help you with anything?"

"Oh no dear, everything's right on schedule. And no, you're not too early. I halfway expected it since James is always prompt, never late to the party. In fact, he was three weeks early when he was born. So, I guess this trait of his started at birth." Laughing it off, Jackie returned to her pot. "James, why don't you get Melanie something to drink? I have wine, beer, iced tea, whatever you prefer."

James raised his eyebrows in question. "What would you like?"

"Oh, um, I guess I'll have an iced tea."

"You know we are off the clock."

"I know, I just prefer the tea." He filled a glass with ice from the refrigerator and poured the freshly brewed tea over the cubes.

In jest he said, "I guess you'd like lemon, too. I think these lemons are seedless so I don't have to worry about being pelted with a lemon seed." He winked.

Giggling, Mel reached for her glass. "Thank you." She caught Jackie's quick glance at them; a winsome smile lined her face.

James poured himself a glass of wine and took his first sip. "This is a good wine. Mom, did it come from The Vineyard on the Hill?"

"Isn't it divine? So smooth. Melanie have you ever been there?" Jackie turned back to the stove.

"Where?"

"The Vineyard on the Hill. It's a lovely restaurant. Both Alejandro and Alec proposed to Angelina and

Kelly there. It's simply magical. James, you need to take Melanie there sometime. Maybe after the sale is complete. You can celebrate."

James shrugged. Jackie had a reputation for matchmaking and he quickly skedaddled from the room. "Is Dad around?" he called over his shoulder.

"I believe he's in the family room watching the news. Melanie why don't you join them while I finish up in here?"

"I'd rather stay here and help you." She did like Jackie and hoped to garner the motive behind the dinner invitation.

Melanie shook her head at James' quick departure and inhaled deeply. She stood alongside Jackie as she finished her preparations. "Whatever you're cooking sure smells good."

"Thank you, dear. It's just roasted chicken, macaroni and cheese, and my peppers and tomato dish. I hope you'll like it. It's my own recipe."

"Really? I wish I was that adept in the kitchen." Laughing she said, "I can barely boil water and warm something in the microwave."

"Well honey, I'd love to teach you. That is an open invitation. Come over anytime and I'll give you lessons."

"That's so kind of you, Jackie, but I'd hate to intrude."

"Intrude? Where did you get that idea? I'd love to teach you. Angelina barely gets by. Alejandro is really the cook in that family. Kelly does pretty well according to Alec, although they're still really in the honeymoon phase and I think he'd compliment anything she did."

"Now, Jackie, why would you say that?"

"Because I've seen the two of them together. He

idolizes everything she says and does. Young love—that's all I can say. Anyway, back to my offer. Why don't we schedule something? We could start small and go from there. Is there anything that you'd like to learn to make? Surely you watched your mother in the kitchen when you were growing up."

The conversation needed to move on. She wasn't going to go there with Jackie. She didn't want anyone to know about her childhood— what there was to it. No, she needed to change the direction of their conversation, but instead of doing that, she took the cowardly way out. "Thanks for the offer. I'll think about it."

Melanie noted the disappointed look that crossed Jackie's face. She was doing her best to get Melanie to talk about her mother but she refused. "I'm going to go check on James, that is if you don't need any help." Yes, she shied away from talking family and she would continue to do so.

"Oh no, dear. You go on and relax."

Dinner was definitely a family affair. James' younger siblings Colleen and Wyatt were at the table as well. Wyatt went on and on about the colleges he was looking into. He was going into his junior year of high school and had so many scholarship offers Melanie's mind spun listening to him. What she would have done to have the same opportunities when she was his age. Instead, Melanie worked hard at the bank. She did get a scholarship from Parklayne, but it was only to a local school. To travel out of state to another college or university would have been a true dream. Instead, she stayed in St. Louis and made it her home. She wondered if the nightmares would have continued if she weren't still living here. If she'd moved out of state, maybe the memories would have disappeared and she'd be able to happily live her life. Instead, she was consumed by her dreams.

James placed his hand on her arm. "Mel, where'd you just go? My mom was asking you a question."

"Oh, I'm sorry, Jackie. What was it you asked?" Melanie couldn't let the what-if's infiltrate her thoughts any longer and she joined in the conversation.

"I asked where you went to school."

"I went to the University of Missouri. I won a scholarship from Parklayne and was fortunate to continue working for them while attending school."

Somehow, Melanie made it through the evening. She did her best to smile and her cheeks ached from the effort. Melanie said her goodbyes thanking his mother for a lovely dinner. What she would have done to have grown up in an environment like that. Parents asking how their children's day went, discussing whatever came to their minds. *That is what family's all about.* She would have given her last dollar to have grown up surrounded by love.

She started for the car leaving James to say one last goodbye to his mother. "Thanks, Mom, for dinner. It was fabulous as always."

"Thank you, James, for bringing Melanie." She hesitated until Melanie was far enough away that she's couldn't hear her words. "James, Melanie is special. She needs you, us, in her life. I think she's lonely…"

"Enough, Mother. Please. I don't need you interfering in my life like you did with Angelina and Alejandro. I just broke up with Elsa. I need some time to myself." He was completely aware of what she was doing—she was trying to set them up. Well, he was going to have nothing to do with it. If he chose, in time, to ask her on a date that would be different, but right now it wasn't in the cards for him.

"Okay, James, I hear what you are saying but I still believe—"

"Mom."

"Alright, son. I'll stay out of it. Take Melanie home now, she looks tired." Jackie kissed James' cheek. "And please don't be a stranger."

James waved to his mom as he strolled down the sidewalk. Melanie was leaning against the car with her eyes closed. He wondered if tonight had been too much for her.

He unlocked the car and Melanie practically fell in. He trotted around to the driver's side and slid in.

"Mel, thanks for doing this for my mom. She really enjoyed seeing you. She told me she wants to teach you to cook. I thought you knew how."

She rolled her eyes at James. "If you call cooking opening a can and heating it up in the microwave, then I can cook."

"I gathered you cooked when you said you had food in the house."

"Yeah, microwave dinners and canned soup!"

"Oh, I see. She was serious when she offered to teach you. Maybe you should take her up on her offer."

Melanie nodded. "She's a great cook, but I'm so busy right now. I'll give it some thought." All too soon, James had her home. "Thanks again for the ride. I had a nice time."

"Me, too." He suddenly wanted to have dinner with her again. But without his folks.

"When do you want to get together again? I really need to go into the office tomorrow as I have a few things that I can only handle there."

"How about late tomorrow afternoon? With Saxson making the announcement on Friday, I think I need to do a little more work to ensure that Amcrost is going to make that offer." Startled concern flashed across her face. "Don't let your mind go there, Mel. I just need to tie up a few things and then pass my recommendation onto the Board."

"But today's Wednesday."

"Don't worry, we'll work it all out. And what if Saxson has to postpone his announcement? Isn't it just the two of you that know about the sale?"

"I guess you're right. I think he pulled Friday out of the air just because…"

"So, I'll pick you up at the office. Say, two o'clock. We could go for a late lunch and then head back to my house and finish up."

"Great. I'll see you at two."

James jumped out to open her door.

Melanie took his proffered hand and stepped out of the car. "I bid you good night, Mr. Samuels."

He chuckled and watched her saunter up the sidewalk. At her front door, she turned to wave goodbye. She waved one more time before closing the door. His stomach fluttered. The night turned out to be pretty great, after all.

Chapter Eight

JAMES WOKE SURPRISINGLY EARLY WITH more energy than normal and got into the office before seven. He felt like he was keeping Mel's hours as he grabbed his first cup of coffee. He was in a good mood and looked forward to working with her later in the afternoon. He'd just finished his coffee when his cell phone rang. He was surprised to see his mother's name pop-up. It was too early in the morning to deal with her shenanigans. He rolled his eyes before answering, thinking that he didn't need her interfering in his life like she did with Angelina and Alejandro's.

"James." He heard the panic in her voice. Immediately he feared something horrible had happened. His thoughts went to his sister Collen who'd undergone a life-saving liver transplant three years earlier. She repeated his name. "James," the tone in her voice then led him to believe that something happened to his father.

"Mom, what is it? Is something wrong with Colleen, Dad?"

"No, son. It's Kelly. She's at the hospital. She's gone into labor."

"What did you just say? She's not due for—"

"Ten weeks. Alec rushed her to the emergency room early this morning. He's frantic with worry. I've never heard the panic that I heard in his voice, not even when Kelly went missing. Alec is beside himself, so we're going to the hospital to sit with him. Your father has cleared his calendar for the day, so he won't be in."

James ran his hand through his locks with concern, stood and began pacing. "What about Angelina? Does she know?"

"Alec phoned Alejandro on his way to the hospital. I worry about Angelina getting too upset over this. We can't afford to have two premature births."

"Mom, Angelina's a little farther along than Kelly."

"I know. I just worry. I'm just thankful both of their husbands are physicians. I'd better go, so I can get to the hospital. Maria and John are already there supporting Alec."

"Can I help?"

"We may need to call you in for babysitting duty. I'll let you know if Angelina needs help with Angel and Matthew. More than likely she's got that taken care of. I hope she stays home but knowing your sister she'll be right there with Kelly and Alec."

"Keep me apprised of her situation. I'm supposed to meet with Melanie this afternoon, but if I need to postpone it, I will. Family comes first, isn't that what you and Dad say?"

"Absolutely."

"Mom, tell Kelly I'm thinking about her and let Alec know if he needs anything to not hesitate to call."

James was beside himself. He ran his hand across his jaw. Kelly didn't deserve this. She was happy now that she and Alec had married. She'd gotten pregnant shortly after their wedding. He recalled the days when Kelly had first returned home from Knoxville after being fired from her job at Lattice Works. Alec had rescued her after her car slid off the road into a snowbank. He had also been there for her as she dealt with the aftermath of being sexually harassed by her boss. She had gone through an extremely emotional time and Alec was there for her—every step and every minute of the day. She'd recovered and was happier than James could ever remember. He hoped and prayed nothing happened to her or the baby.

James tried to focus on the Parklayne deal but his mind kept wandering to his sister. He phoned his mother around noon to discover that Kelly's contractions were under control, at least for the time being. James was thankful for the good news but Kelly and the baby weren't out of the woods yet. After getting off the phone with his mother, he spun his chair around and stared out across the skyline, watching the clouds.

James was lost in thought when his assistant tapped him on the shoulder. He slowly raised his eyes. "I'm sorry, did you need me, Ophelia?"

"Your phone has been ringing off the hook, and your calls keep bouncing to me."

"Sorry about that. I was lost in thought worried about Kelly."

"I understand, but I have a Melanie Holmes on the line for you. She insists she needs to speak with you. Something about a missed meeting."

James glanced at his watch. What happened to the time? Sighing he said, "Yeah, put her through."

James' phone rang and he reached for the handset. He took a deep breath as he answered not sure exactly how Melanie would take the news that he needed to put their meeting on hold. He couldn't concentrate on anything except for his sister. "Hi, Mel."

"Is everything okay? You were supposed to pick me up a half hour ago."

"Yeah, about that..."

"Is it the sale? Do I need to get you more information? Please let me know what you need..." Melanie kept rambling, no doubt thinking his no show was a message to her that the sale was off.

"Mel, slow down and let me talk, okay?"

"Sure." Melanie waited for James to explain.

"Sorry about not calling you. I've been a little preoccupied. My sister Kelly was rushed to the hospital early this morning. She was having contractions and is only thirty weeks."

"I'm sorry to hear this. Is she okay?"

"Two hours ago, she was holding her own. I'm sitting here waiting for the day to end, so I can run by the hospital. I'm worried about her."

"Of course, you are. Is there anything I can do?"

"In fact, there is. Are you still in the office?"

"I am."

"How about I come by and pick you up. I'd like to run by and check in with my family and then I'll take you to dinner and we can further discuss the sale and the additional information we need." James expected a response but all he heard was silence. "Mel, are you still there? Did I lose you?"

"Ah no, I'm still here."

"Are you okay with going to the hospital?" He heard a distinctive change in her voice and wondered if she was okay with hospitals.

"I'm sorry, James, I heard you. Yeah, that's fine. What time?"

"It's almost three right now. Let me try and wrap my head around a few things here. How about I pick you up around four-thirty? Five at the latest. I'll call you when I'm in front of the building."

"Um, yeah, that's good for me. I guess I'll see you then. Is there anything that you need me to bring?"

"Just yourself and maybe your planner. I thought we'd start drafting the tasks needed for our project management listing. We track everything under the sun to make sure we don't miss anything. I guess you do the same at Parklayne."

"We do. I'll bring an example of our plan when we perform an acquisition. We haven't had the need to use it in a while, but it will at least give you an idea of what's important to us and what we track."

"I'd better let you go so I can finish up here. I'll see you shortly." He wasn't exactly sure why he'd asked her out. He ultimately blamed business on their date, but in all actuality, he wanted someone by his side when he went to the hospital. He knew his family would be there, but for some reason he also needed Melanie there.

He did nothing to speak of for the remainder of the day. He did locate Amcrost's latest project plan on its most recent merger. In addition to the plan, he added a legal pad to his briefcase to take notes during their dinner meeting. He glanced at his watch. It was almost five and he'd promised Melanie he'd be there by now. He grabbed his cell phone and briefcase and headed out the door. Dialing Melanie's number, he headed for the elevators. Just as the doors whooshed open, he got her voice mail. "I'm on my way. I got delayed. I'll phone when I arrive." Short and sweet. He didn't want her to think that he forgot about her a second time. She seemed awfully nervous about the sale, in general, and he didn't want her to think his delay had anything to do with it. He chalked her nervousness up to dealing with change and knew most people disliked major changes in their lives.

Surprisingly, he made it to her office in record time pulling up at the front doors at five-thirty. He threw the car in park and started to dial her number when out of the corner of his eye he caught someone with brown hair making their way towards the doors. Just as he was about to hit send, he realized Melanie was approaching his car. He reached over and threw open the door.

Bending over, she looked inside. "I thought I'd save us some time and meet you in the foyer." She eased her way into the passenger's seat. James was taken by her. He didn't notice anything different other than the fact her hair seemed curlier than normal. She turned to him with a bright smile that practically took his breath away. She looked absolutely beautiful. *Where had that thought come from?*

"Ah, hi. Thanks for meeting me." He looked over his shoulder as he pulled away from the curb. "I appreciate you doing this. I really need to see Kelly, if possible, and today was an absolute waste. I got nothing done. With us going to dinner, at least I'll accomplish something from my to-do list for the day."

"How is Kelly? Any news since we last spoke?"

"They're going to keep her overnight. Her contractions have stopped and that's a good sign, from what I understand. My parents are with her along with Alec's. I think Angelina made her way to the hospital, but Alejandro was concerned about her and sent her home. She's due in about six weeks, and he didn't want her getting too upset or tired."

"That's understandable."

"I think Gabriella and Ashton are due to drop by, too, so it may be a little crowded. Gabby was coming right from school while Ashton was going to meet up with everyone after he completed his rounds for the night. I don't think a night goes by that one of my brothers-in-law isn't at the hospital late checking on patients. They all work so hard and are so conscientious of their patients and families."

"From what I understand, their practice is well known. Didn't Ashton join it when Alec's dad retired?"

"He did and I think he's turning into an Alvarez, himself. They have a certain culture in that practice. Family is first and foremost."

"That's nice to hear."

James pulled up at the hospital right at six o'clock, surprised to immediately locate a parking spot. He put the car in park and turned to Melanie. Placing his hand on her forearm stopping her from exiting the car he said, "Thank you for coming with me. We won't stay long, I promise." James exited the car and met up with Melanie. He placed his hand under her elbow as he escorted her into the hospital.

As they waited for the elevator doors to open, he smiled broadly at her. He was ever so thankful that she was by his side. He couldn't explain why he felt that way, but he did.

Chapter Nine

MELANIE HATED HOSPITALS. SHE DISLIKED the smells, the sounds, and the bright lights that seemed to follow her everywhere. She didn't understand why the lights bothered her as she hated the dark, but for some reason she detested the fluorescent lights in a hospital.

They turned a corner and Melanie immediately spotted Gabriella standing beside Alec inside the waiting room. It was filled with the Samuels and Alvarez families.

Ben and Jackie sat huddled together while John, Alec's father, nervously scrolled through his phone. Maria, Alec's mother, was nowhere in sight.

Alec looked exhausted. Dark circles lined his eyes and his face was drawn with worry. Gabriella pulled Melanie into a tight hug, making her feel as though she were a part of this family. "I'm so glad you came, Melanie. I'm dying for some girl talk. Angelina left right as I came and there's only so much I can take listening to Alec." Gabriella laughed, playfully punching her brother's arm. Most everyone knew Alec and how he liked to ramble when he was upset or bothered by something. "I'm just kidding and he knows it."

"How is Kelly?" Melanie asked.

Alec ran his hand through his already rumpled hair. "She was given an IV of magnesium sulfate which thankfully stopped the contractions. I'm hoping she can come home tomorrow although she's not going to like being on bed rest for the remainder of her pregnancy."

"Wow, that's a long time, but if it prevents her from going into labor."

"That's what I say, Melanie." Turning to James, Alec shook his hand. "Hey, James, thanks for coming. I really appreciate it and I'm sure Kelly does too."

"I wanted to come earlier—"

"Especially since you weren't very productive today," Melanie interjected in a teasing manner.

James smiled at her. "Melanie's right, there. We had a meeting I completely forgot about. So to make it up to her, I'm taking her to dinner." Jackie's head spun in her direction, a huge smile crossing her face. Melanie wondered why the expression of sheer happiness lit the woman with her daughter lying in the hospital. Jackie was a complex person and Melanie was aware the matriarch liked to stay involved in her children's lives. She'd have to keep an eye on her, especially since she wanted to give her cooking lessons. Now that she thought about it, was there an ulterior motive to Jackie's offer?

Melanie watched James interact with his family. He was a concerned brother who listened carefully to Alec and his description of the events that led to his and Kelly's arrival at the ER. "I grabbed for her suitcase, since she packed it weeks ago, only to find myself hurrying out of the house with my briefcase. I ran back in and snapped up her bag. I jumped in the car but didn't have my keys, so I had to race inside again, all the while Kelly's writhing in pain. I finally started the car only to discover that I was still dressed in my lounge pants with no shirt. Back in the house I went and then realized I didn't even have shoes on. By the time I was ready to head out, Kelly was between contractions and she was laughing hysterically. When I look back on it, it was pretty funny. So much for being in control all of the time."

By the time Alec finished his story of their journey to the hospital in the early morning hours, Melanie was laughing so hard tears ran down her face. "I didn't think you'd be so rattled especially with your training."

His brows raised with concern. "When you see the love of your life clutching her stomach like Kelly was, all your training leaves you."

"I'm glad to hear she's doing better," James said. "Any idea what caused it? I thought her pregnancy was going pretty well."

"It was, but last week she had a urinary tract infection and a high fever. It just lasted one day, but I would presume that's what precipitated today's events."

"I didn't realize she was sick."

"I'm not even sure she told your mom. She didn't want to worry her. But it's all behind us now, and we can hope that she continues to hold onto the baby a little longer before delivering. That's our ultimate goal right now. Melanie, maybe you could visit her while she's home. I'm sure she would love it."

"I will, of course, when she's up to it." Melanie clasped her hands in front of her. She was getting nervous. She wanted to visit with Kelly but she was uncomfortable being around pregnant women. People always wanted to know when she was going to get married and have children. Most of the time, she was able to fend off the conversation just by changing the subject. So far, no one was the wiser. When it came down to it, Melanie never planned on getting married *or* having children. Never—too much childhood baggage on her part. She was thirty-two years old and had made it this far without a serious relationship and she didn't intend to ever have one.

Maria joined everyone in the room. "Ah, James, you came, and Melanie too. I'm sorry you didn't get a chance to see Kelly but she just fell asleep."

"I'm sorry to hear that. Alec, please let her know that Mel and I were here to see her. I'll catch up with her when she returns home." Maria nodded and James went to speak with his mother. Gabriella began rambling to Melanie about her latest class field trip. Melanie plastered a smile on her face and clasped her hands in front of her, shifting her weight back and forth. She could feel moisture pooling between her shoulder blades. She felt like the walls were closing in and she was more than ready to leave.

After a few minutes, James returned. "Ready?" she asked hoping he was.

"Yep, let's head on out. Since Kelly's asleep, there's no reason for us to stay." They said their goodbyes and headed back down the hallway. Each step towards the elevators brought her closer to the front door. She couldn't wait to get back in his car. Standing there listening to Gabriella made her nervous. She didn't know why her heart rate was increasing. She wasn't upset over anything other than standing in the middle of the hospital and she hated hospitals. She knew that was the reason for her angst, but she couldn't show her fear to James or his family. Too many memories is all she thought. She took a deep breath as they walked out of the hospital to the parking lot.

As she waited for James to open her car door, she took a deep cleansing breath.

He rested his hand on her shoulder. "Hey, are you okay?"

"Just fine." And she was just fine because she was outside of the hospital away from the sights and smells that brought back way too many memories.

She rode quietly as James talked about his sister. "I'm so grateful that she has Alec in her life. Listening to him earlier brought back memories of when they got married, and he couldn't remember Kelly's name when he went to say his vows. Alec is so serious most of the time but seeing him in these situations makes me realize he's just like any of us. He loves his family and they definitely come first in his life."

Melanie didn't want to hear any more about his family. Family was a sore subject with her. She wanted to just get to the restaurant and start their meeting. She needed to know what else he required to recommend the sale of Parklayne to Amcrost.

She sat in silence as James pulled into the valet service at Steeltown Inn. "I hope this is okay since we just ate here recently. But it was close, and I knew we'd have privacy."

"It's fine." The valet opened Melanie's door and she hopped out with her file in hand. James met her at the sidewalk with his briefcase. Placing his hand upon the small of her back, he ushered her to the door held open by another valet. "Thank you," she said as they walked through. James' hand brought her comfort after dealing with the emotions she felt in the hospital.

The restaurant was busy and since they didn't have a reservation, they had a half-hour wait. James led her to the bar where they grabbed a table and both ordered wine. White for Melanie and red for James. "Since we have a wait," she said, desperate to avoid the dinner become a date, "shall we start in on business?"

"Let's just sit here and relax a minute. We can talk business after dinner."

She nodded not sure where he wanted the conversation to go. In the end, she just wanted to get in and get out, talk business and go home. She didn't want to be rude but she needed to be alone. Tonight, being in the hospital had brought back too many painful memories. She'd never had a relationship before. But being in James' presence affected her; she didn't understand why. It just did.

They enjoyed their glass of wine and by the time the hostess had seated them at their table Melanie was exhausted. Between the wine and the stress of her day, she could barely keep her eyes open.

"Hey, are you okay over there? You look like you're about ready to fall asleep on me."

"I forgot to eat lunch, so I guess my wine's going to my head."

"How about we eat and I take you home? We can talk business tomorrow. In fact, I don't feel up to it right now myself." She played with the stem of her wine glass as she listened to him rehash his grueling day. "Let's just plan on tomorrow. I'll pick you up since your car is still at the office and we can go over the project plan then. Okay?"

Melanie surprised herself and agreed to his request. The more time she spent around him, the more she liked him and that wasn't a good thing, in her opinion.

They ate their dinner and while James paid the bill, Melanie visited the ladies' room. She needed to splash some cold water on her face, or she'd fall asleep on the ride home, she just knew it. She patted her face with cold cloths and then made her way from the room. James greeted her just outside. He reached for her hand and she didn't think twice. She grabbed onto it and he led her from the restaurant. "I don't know what hit me, but I can hardly stand up I'm so tired."

"Let's get you home, then." He had called for the valet while she was in the ladies' room so when they walked out of the restaurant his car was waiting for them. He helped her into the car and before he knew it, he was pulling up in front of her home. She'd fallen asleep. In the glow of the street light, James looked at her. He watched as she breathed in and out, contemplating their future. He had no idea what his father's plans were for her in the bank once their companies merged. He expected to remain in his position, but what about her? She'd grown up with Parklayne just as he had with Amcrost. He had his father behind him, but who did Mel have? He knew she had a sister, but was there anyone else in her life that would support her during this time? He'd be by her side, but in the end, he was her competition and he didn't know how she felt about that.

Reaching over, he caressed her cheek. She looked tense and so alone as she slept. He wondered who the true Melanie really was. He knew her business persona.

Knew she could be cruel and ruthless in her pursuits. From what he could see in their business dealings, she either got her way or got out. They'd had their own verbal altercations at times too, the last one being Alec and Kelly's Memorial Day party.

James had just returned from a business trip from hell. The last thing he wanted was to go to his sister's holiday picnic. When his mother discovered he wasn't attending the family gathering, she'd called him and berated him into attending. Elsa had been visiting friends and he'd had to attend it by himself. Tired from his trip, he planned to stay for an hour before going home and sleeping the remainder of the day.

He'd been at Kelly's only a few minutes when she'd seen him across the room. He couldn't believe how nice she seemed, so unlike the person he'd seen only days before yelling at a low-level manager about something that had actually been done by a vendor that represented the bank.

In mid-sentence, Melanie stopped speaking. He approached his sister, giving Melanie a stern look while he kissed Kelly's cheek. Moments later, Kelly was called away and he and Melanie had been left alone.

Before he could utter a word in his defense, Alec had called out to him, requesting his help. James spun away and didn't face Melanie again until later in the day in the kitchen.

"Melanie."

"James," Melanie had responded. She eyed him closely. He felt his blood pressure rise and could feel his temple pulsing thinking back to their run-in at the bank.

He'd been in California on business for the last two weeks burning the midnight oil. He'd had little sleep and while on his trip he'd encountered Melanie. She'd been visiting the same bank, auditing some loans for purchase. An issue had arisen with the underwriting of a group of loans and he'd raised it to the seller. At the same time, he was raising his own issues, Melanie was dealing with a completely different issue. Hers had something to do with unpaid homeowner's insurance and delinquent property taxes. He was mortified listening to her yell at the representative from the bank. Too many delinquent taxes resulted in unnecessary penalty and interest expense on top of risk of loss due to potential homeowner claims on expired insurance policies. Escrow issues were her forte and got on her last nerve.

After her verbal assault, he ran into her in the hall. He couldn't hold back and said a few things that right now he wished he'd kept to himself. Surprisingly, she'd listened to his advice and then she hightailed it off in a completely different direction, not to be seen again until he walked into his sister's home and saw her laughing with Kelly.

"I guess it's my lucky day having to deal with you again so soon," he said. "I still can't believe you spoke to that escrow manager the way you did. That was so unprofessional of you. Yes, things happen and slip through the cracks, but you didn't need to yell at her. It wasn't her fault." He gazed at her. "If you plan on making a name for yourself in the mortgage industry, you need to have a little more couth and know how to address an issue in a different manner. Yelling isn't going to fix it." She slinked back into a corner. "You're lucky you don't work for Amcrost because we definitely wouldn't tolerate your behavior, Ms. Holmes."

That's not how you run a business, Ms. Holmes, he'd said

to her. He had quite a few more choice words for her and then had walked from the room. He hadn't seen Melanie again until their dinner at the Steeltown Inn when he discovered that his father intended to buy Parklayne Bank.

He'd often wondered why she was the way she was in business. So far, he hadn't experienced that wild Melanie again, but they'd just begun this process and he was almost certain that the witch would rear her ugly head again. He wondered if her nervousness around him stemmed from that discussion all those months ago. Even though she hadn't said it, she must be concerned for her job.

Melanie slowly stirred awake. When she opened her eyes, James was leaning over her with his hand stroking her cheek. She smiled briefly and when she realized where she was, she pulled away. "I guess I fell asleep."

"You could say that."

She immediately reached for her purse and folder. He could tell by the way she quickly gathered her things that she wanted to run from him. "I guess I'll see you tomorrow. How about nine?"

"Not earlier?" James raised his eyebrow and gave her a half-smile. "Nine's fine."

She opened her door and jumped from the car. He watched as she walked up the sidewalk to her front door. She waved upon entering her house. There was more than met the eye to her. She was hiding something.

He couldn't get involved with her. His breakup with Elsa was still so new. But in his gut, he knew something wasn't right. He intended to find the real Melanie.

Chapter Ten

JAMES HAD JUST GOTTEN UP from bed when his phone rang. He glanced at the caller ID. "Hi, Mom." He knew what she wanted and didn't want to deal with her this early in the day. He'd dropped Melanie off at her home around ten the night before and went directly home where he went through his Parklayne files in detail. Falling asleep around three in the morning, James barely got three hours rest. He was tired and not in the best of moods.

"James, dear, how are you this morning? How was your dinner with Melanie? It was so good to see you two together last night..." Silence. "James are you there?"

"I'm here, Mom." He didn't want to address the topic of Melanie so he changed subjects. "How's Kelly?"

"I just got off the phone with Alec. He spent the night at the hospital. Alec's a tremendous husband..."

"I asked about Kelly, not Alec."

"That's right, son. Sorry, you know how I can get. Kelly's doing well. She wants to come home today, but Alec thinks she should stay another day in the hospital. I'm sure Alec will get his way."

"I'm glad she's okay. I don't have time to shoot the

breeze. I've got an early morning meeting."

"Oh sure, James, I understand. I wanted to let you know that I'm calling Melanie and inviting her for her first cooking class." He rolled his eyes and listened, not wanting to misspeak and say something his mother would grab onto to. "I hope she'll come over this weekend. How about you come too?"

"You need to stop. Stop trying to match us up. We're working together only because of business. Understand?"

"I do." His mom sighed. "I just want you to be happy, James. Elsa—"

"Enough Mom. Please, it's too early to be addressing this. I've got to go."

"James."

"Yes, Mother?"

"I love you."

"I know you do but please stay out of my personal life."

"I will, I promise." His mother never kept her promises. Jackie had her nose in Angelina's relationship with Alejandro and would have been more involved with Kelly and Alec's if she'd lived in St. Louis. James needed to find his way since breaking up with Elsa. One day, he'd be ready to date again, but today wasn't that day.

James elected to dress casually in a pair of khakis and a polo shirt— so unlike his usual suit and tie. He and Melanie wouldn't be going into their respective offices. He'd decided they'd return to his house after he took her out for coffee. He needed a good cup of caffeine to jump start him after his sleepless night.

He rang Melanie's doorbell promptly at nine. Not even two seconds elapsed before she opened the door.

"I guess you were standing at the door waiting."

"No, I wasn't."

James knew better. Starting her day at nine was too late for her and he knew it. She liked to begin work at the crack of dawn and work until well past dark. He too, worked those hours when necessary, but not daily.

"I thought we'd run by Coffees & Mocha and grab a cup of coffee and a muffin and then head back to my house to work. Sound like a plan?"

"That's fine. I could use a good cup of coffee."

Thankfully the coffee shop drive thru wasn't crowded so they went right through. Large coffees with cream and two blueberry muffins later they arrived just before ten at his place and started working immediately. They worked well together and by one, they'd completed their review of the project plan and James was ready for lunch. "Hungry?"

"Surprisingly, I am," Melanie said as she organized her files.

"I could order a pizza and we could finish going through these reports."

"Deep dish from Pizza, Pies & More?" she asked as she reached for her phone. He agreed and then headed off to his kitchen where he grabbed two bottles of water. Melanie ordered their pizza. "What's your address?" she called out to him as he rejoined her. James recited his address and then left her alone again while he ran to his home office.

Melanie decided to check her phone and noticed she had two missed calls, but also had one voice mail. She checked the calls, didn't recognize the numbers, and then listened to the voice mail. Jackie. Melanie sighed and raised her eyes just as James walked back into the room.

"From your look, if I had one guess, I'd say my mom called."

Surprise crossed her face. "How did you know?"

"Because she called me way too early this morning and told me she was calling you today. I told her not to, but you can't tell my mom no."

"I figured that out. James, it's really nice of her but I—"

"You don't have to explain yourself, just don't do it."

"But?"

"No buts. That's the only way she's going to learn. If you don't want to do it, don't. End of story." Melanie smiled. It was one of the first real smiles he'd seen cross her face.

"Thanks." With that the doorbell rang and he headed off to get their pizza.

Even though she would decline the invitation, she decided to return Jackie's call. Jackie answered on the first ring. "Melanie? Thank you for returning my call so quickly…"

She didn't even have the chance to say hello. "Jackie, yeah, hi. Thanks for reaching out to me."

"Oh honey, I'd love to teach you to cook. How about Saturday morning at nine? We can make something for lunch and then start on dinner."

"Jackie, I—"

"We'll have a blast. Kelly's a good cook, I taught her, but Angelina, well that's another story…"

"Jackie, I…"

"You know Alejandro's really the cook in that family. He almost always cooks for us when we come over…"

"I really…"

"How's a quiche sound for lunch, maybe a salad too? Dinner, I'm not sure. We can decide when you get here. If we have to, we can run by Schulers and grab whatever sounds good for dinner. I'm so looking forward to this after Kelly's scare and all…"

Melanie couldn't get a word in edgewise, so she decided to just give in and say yes to Jackie's request. She was still listening when James reentered the room. He chuckled as he set their lunch down. "Nine sounds fine, Jackie. What can I bring?"

"Just yourself, dear. I've got it covered."

"I'll see you then." Melanie ended the call and loudly set her phone down.

"I knew you'd give in."

"Give in? I couldn't get a word in. Once your mother gets something into her head, she doesn't give up, does she?"

"Nope." James held open the pizza box for Melanie to select a slice. They enjoyed their lunch and began working again. Time got away from them and Melanie glanced at her watch. She jumped up. "Look at the time. You need to take me home. I need to go."

"Ah, Mel, what's wrong?"

"I need to be somewhere. I'm going to be late." James acknowledged her request as she gathered her files.

As he drove her home, she kept wringing her hands back and forth. He reached over and placed his hand against hers. "Would you please stop that. You'll be home in five minutes."

"I realize that, but I'm going to be late. I hate to be late."

"Where do you need to be?" She didn't answer as he'd just pulled into her driveway. She was holding her files and fled out of the car. James rolled down the passenger side window. She hadn't even said goodbye. "Mel?" he called out as she raced up the sidewalk. She waved and yelled bye over her shoulder and ran inside.

Melanie threw her files down and rushed to change into jeans and a t-shirt. She never wore her finest clothes when she volunteered. That way, if she got paint all over herself, she didn't care.

She grabbed her purse and ran to her car. If she were lucky, she'd be there by five. She volunteered at least twice a week at her local YMCA art therapy program. In addition to a business degree, she'd also pursued an art degree.

Unfortunately, her bank job didn't afford her the time or money to complete a full art degree, which included a thousand hours of practicum experience. So instead she had to fulfill her love of the subject by volunteering in a program to help children overcome their fears.

She made it to the Y with five minutes to spare.

She rushed into the room, brushing her hair out of her eyes, only to discover she was alone. She looked at her watch, glanced at the clock on the wall, and yet no one was present. She sighed, wondering where everyone was. As she backed out of the room, she ran smack into Madeleine Jensam, the director of the program. "Oh, hi, there Mel, didn't you get my message?"

Melanie had no idea what Madeleine was talking about. "By the look on your face, I can tell you didn't," Madeline said. "We had to cancel. I can't go into the details, but we won't be having classes for a few weeks."

"Okay. Since I can't ask why, may I ask if you plan on continuing the program? It's so—"

"I hope we can." Madeleine's comment took the

wind out of her sails. Melanie stood in the middle of the room with her shoulders slumped and feeling forlorn. The program meant a lot to her. In her heart, she believed if only—if only she helped one child overcome their fears, she'd have done her job. "I'll call you in a few days with an update. I'm sorry."

"Don't worry about me. I'm worried about the kids, especially Monica and Jared. They were making so much progress. I don't want to abandon them."

"We won't if we can help it. I'm trying to work this all out…"

"I understand." In just a moment in time, Melanie's world was thrown upside down. Her volunteer work kept her whole. It was the one thing in her life that she looked forward to. She was giving back to society and didn't know what she'd do if she lost this one outlet that made her feel good about herself.

Somehow, Melanie made her way to her car. She sat down, gripped the steering wheel, and stared straight ahead. Her vision fogged and the tears that she'd been holding at bay began to spill. One of her purposes in life had been robbed from her, at least momentarily, and she didn't know how she would fill her days until she could start up again. She didn't want to think this was over. She just wouldn't. She needed to move on and that's what she'd do. She jammed the keys into the ignition, started the car, and drove home—to the only other place that she now felt safe and secure.

Chapter Eleven

SEVERAL DAYS HAD PASSED SINCE the program had been canceled at the Y. Through her own investigation, Melanie discovered that funding for the art therapy program had been lost. She wished she had the money to keep the program up and running but she didn't. She'd just have to wait and see if Madeleine got everything under control.

She prayed nightly for Monica and Jared. They had come to mean so much to her in the time they'd been attending the program. Both of them were in foster care and had endured traumatic experiences in their young lives. Several of Jared's issues had been buried so deep in his subconscious that the therapy enabled him to unleash on therapists the pain and hurt that he'd endured in his family before becoming a ward of the state and entering foster care. No one had a clue what he'd been through until he began drawing what was troubling him; none of his hurt or anger came out while talking. His drawings revealed the pain he was internalizing towards both of his parents. Once he got his hand on a crayon, everything flowed and became clear. Shortly after beginning his art therapy, in combination with another incident that landed him in the hospital, he was removed from his home.

Late Friday evening, after Saxson had announced the sale to the staff, Melanie sat alone in her office. She was lost in thoughts about Jared when she felt a presence. She looked up to James in her open doorway.

"May I come in?"

She nodded and he made his way to the office chair in front of her desk. "You look like you've lost your best friend."

She shrugged off his comment. It had been a rough few days between the announcement and losing her outlet at the Y.

"I was meeting with Saxson and decided to drop by. Ask you to dinner. It's been a long week and I just wanted to chill out, and thought about you."

Melanie raised her gaze to him. "Please don't let your mother know about this." James laughed hysterically.

The previous weekend, Melanie had experienced her first cooking lesson. The entire time she was there, Jackie kept bringing up James' name. It was clear what she was doing and Melanie couldn't listen to her any longer. So, Melanie being Melanie, didn't hold back. She threw her thoughts out there to Jackie.

"Jackie," Melanie had said. "I need to be blunt with you." Jackie paused while rolling the pie crust for the apple pie they were making for dessert. "James and I are not a couple, nor will we be. We work together right now and that's it. In fact, we might not be working in the same circles once the sale goes through. So please, stop trying to push us together. It won't work." Jackie probably hated her for it and more than likely wouldn't want to see her again. But she did what she had to do.

Jackie had been thoughtful for a moment before she

smiled at her. "Thank you for your honesty, Melanie. I do apologize for rambling on about James. I worry about him since his break-up with Elsa. I know I'm a meddling mother and I thank you for calling me on it. I promise to stop. I am enjoying our time together too much to lose our friendship. Can you forgive me?"

"I can. I'm sorry I was so blunt, but I just needed you to know that we won't happen. And I'd like to say I am enjoying our time together too. Thank you for this." At the end of the day, she hoped their cooking lessons continued as she'd thoroughly enjoyed their time together.

"Yeah, Mom can be a little too much… Enough about her. So, are you up for it? Dinner out? No business."

Just hearing the words *no business* put a smile on her face. For some reason she couldn't explain to herself, she was tired. Tired of working and trying to be perfect. Perfect so someone would accept her. In that moment, she decided she'd take him up on his offer. She'd go to dinner with James. "I'd like that. Thank you."

"Where shall we go?"

"I don't care. Anywhere so I don't have to think about work. This has been a trying week to say the least." Since Saxson had announced the sale, her office had been flooded with anxious staff fearful of losing their jobs. Melanie tried to lay their fears to rest, but who was there for her? In a matter of weeks, the end was in sight. She didn't know how she would face it, but she'd do her best to hold her head high and make it through the trying days ahead.

Melanie reached for her purse. "Shall I meet you somewhere?"

"Go home, change into something comfortable, and I'll come by in an hour. Let's relax and enjoy the night."

Melanie drove home, her thoughts never far from James. Why? Why did he want to go out? The questions ran through her mind as she pulled into her driveway. She knew she didn't have much time to dawdle, so she hurried inside and ran to her bedroom where she exchanged her suit for a pair of well-worn jeans and a lightweight sweater. She was glad to get out of her business clothes and let her hair down. She needed this night after her week and was going to enjoy it.

She heard James close his car door and ran to the front door. She was looking forward to their evening. In the last few weeks, she'd really grown to like James. He was down to earth and extremely bright. He was close to his siblings which is something she wished she'd had with Janet growing-up. Her heart ached every time he mentioned Angelina and Kelly and their pregnancies. He was a family man through and through and that wasn't something she was looking for. She relied only on herself and no one else. Life was simpler that way.

She'd enjoyed working on the project with James. When she got past her nervousness, she discovered how sensible he was. She hadn't felt that before when he'd confronted her during one of their run-ins or during their time in San Antonio. He was her friend now and she hoped he'd remain one after the sale was complete.

Melanie opened the door before James could ring the bell. "Ready?" he called out as she reached for her purse that was sitting on the floor besides the door.

"I am." Side-by-side they strolled to the car.

He rested his hand on the roof of the vehicle. "How about barbeque? Or maybe Chinese?"

"Whatever you're in the mood for. I'm starved."

James made sure she was settled in the car and then

closed the door.

Soon he pulled into the strip mall that held his favorite Chinese restaurant.

"We're going to Imperial House? Oh my, gosh. I love this restaurant."

"It's nice to know we have something in common outside of banking because it's my all-time favorite restaurant."

Melanie hopped out of the car meeting James at the doors. She preceded him inside where Debbie Yan greeted her. "Melanie, it's so good to see you. It's been a while." Then, Debbie pointed at James. "Are you two together?" Melanie smiled. "My two favorite customers. Any particular table in mind?"

"How about the one in the back near the screen?" James responded, "It's more private."

"You're on a date... That's wonderful."

Melanie immediately chimed in. "No, we're not dating, just friends having dinner."

James grinned at her quick reply. *Friends? I guess that's what we are.* Deb led them to the one and only secluded table in the back of the restaurant.

"We're a little short on help tonight. Yan'll be your waiter and possibly your chef too," Deb said snickering. Yan was Deb's husband and they just knew him by his last name. Everyone knew how much Yan loved to cook but most days didn't have the time with running the restaurant. "Enjoy." Deb laid the menus on the table and hurried off to seat another customer.

"I've never sat here before." Melanie unrolled her silverware and set her napkin on her lap.

"I thought you'd enjoy a little more privacy. It's definitely quieter and after the week you've had, I'm sure you're in need of it."

"I am."

"Do you know what you want?"

"I do. I know the menu by heart. Depending on my schedule, I come here sometimes twice a week. I'm going to have Yan's special beef."

"Good choice. I really like that dish. Do you like cashew chicken?"

"One of my favorites."

"That's settled. We'll share if you're up for that." She smiled when Yan appeared.

"Melanie, James, it's so good to see you. I didn't know you were dating. Small world."

"We're just friends" James said. "This isn't a date."

"If that's what you say, my friend." Yan glanced back and forth between the two of them. "Ready to order?"

"We are," James gave Yan their order. He even added crab Rangoon, one of her favorites too. "Would you care for soup, Mel?"

"Oh, I'd love a cup of hot and sour. You have the best."

"Make that two cups, Yan. You know I never come here without your soup." Yan finished up their order and scurried to the kitchen.

Since James had stressed no business for their evening, he asked about her cooking lesson. "I really learned a lot from your mom. I surprised myself that I had such a good time except for..."

"Except for what?"

"Well, I kind of told her off."

"You what? I didn't hear anything about that."

"Every other word that came out of her mouth was James this and James that. I felt like she was trying to set us up." She paused, then continued. "So, I had to reel her in. I told her we weren't a couple now or in the future. She worries about you since your breakup with—"

"Elsa."

"Yeah, that's right. Anyway, she just wants to see you happy."

"I know she does. My mom wouldn't be my mom without her incessant meddling. Hopefully, you've put a stop to it."

"I hope so because I have another cooking class with her on Sunday."

He raised his eyebrows in surprise. "I didn't know that."

"She called right before you arrived at my house. She said she was going to be alone and wanted the company."

"She is. Dad's taking Wyatt to hockey camp an hour away. Mom didn't want to go and I think Colleen is babysitting for Angelina so she and Alejandro can have a day to themselves before the new baby arrives."

Yan appeared with their soup. Soon their meals arrived. James stabbed a piece of chicken with his fork and offered it to Melanie. "Here have this."

"I have some on my plate."

"I know, but this piece looks so succulent."

She took the piece of chicken into her mouth. "Mmm, that was good, but I do have my own."

"I know you do." They enjoyed the rest of their meal exchanging small talk about nothing in particular. When they'd finished the last of their dishes, Yan appeared clearing the table, leaving their bill and fortune cookies. "Good to see you both. I hope to see you two soon, yes?" They thanked him for dinner, but neither addressed Yan's last comment.

James held up a fortune cookie. "I love these. They're the best cookies around. Take one and let's see what our fortune tells us."

"Yes, the cookies are good, but the fortunes are nonsense. Who makes up these stupid fortunes, anyways?"

"I haven't a clue but they're fun nonetheless."

Melanie chose her fortune and cracked open her cookie. She shook her head at the saying.

"What's it say?"

"Life's path doesn't always lead you in the right direction. Follow the stars and take that second journey. My magic numbers are 3,27,30,75 and 2."

"I guess there's some insight in that." James broke his cookie and popped the flavorful sweet into his mouth. Slowly chewing it, he read his fortune. He folded it without reading it aloud.

"What's it say?"

"Nothing but gibberish."

"If I had to read mine, you must read yours, so out with it." Wide-eyed, James threw his onto the table. "Since you won't read it aloud, I will." Melanie opened the small piece of paper and understood why he chose not to read the words aloud. "Love is in the air, staring you directly in the face." She chuckled and gazed at him. "I can understand why you threw it down, it's nonsense."

"If you're ready, let's go." James stood and reached for the check while Melanie grabbed both of their fortunes. She didn't believe in the words but she did believe in the magic numbers. Maybe one day, the numbers would come in handy.

Melanie stopped by Laketown Bakery on her way to the Samuels' house. She wanted to do something nice for Jackie since she was spending what should have been a quiet day teaching her how to cook. Melanie chose their famous gooey butter cake. As she drove the rest of the way to her cooking class, she rehashed her and James' Friday night dinner. She had a good time. Learned a few things about him— first, that he loved what she called her restaurant and second, that he wasn't over Elsa. By the way he reacted to his fortune cookie, she knew he still loved her. They'd been together since high school and one didn't get over their first love that easily.

She pulled into the Samuels' driveway and grabbed the cake from the back seat. She had never had Laketown's famous cake and she was anxious to try it. Jackie opened the door before she made her way up the sidewalk. She smiled. "What do you have there?"

"Something special from Laketown Bakery."

"Is it their gooey butter cake?"

"What do you think?" Melanie chuckled as she entered the house. She followed Jackie to the kitchen where Jackie immediately sought out two plates and a knife to cut the cake.

"This is such a treat, Melanie. I love this cake but I always seem to be watching my diet and rarely have it."

"You're in fabulous shape, Jackie. You don't have a thing to worry about."

"That's because I stay away from Laketown. If I went in there, I'd gain ten pounds just looking at the lusciousness."

"I feel the same way. Everything in there is mouthwatering good." They chitchatted about Angelina and Kelly's advancing pregnancies, the weather, and Wyatt's hockey camp as they snacked on their cake. "So what are we making today?"

"I thought we'd make one of James' favorites." Melanie glanced at Jackie. "Before you get started, I'm not trying to set you up. This is an easy dish for a cold wintery night. Plain and simple. I don't even know why I said that about James, but it *is* one of his favorites."

Jackie gave her the easy recipe for beef and wine— a couple of cans of soup with some seasoning, wine, and bake it forever. "Three hours is a long time to cook this, isn't it?"

"It seems like it but this cut of meat needs to cook slowly to break down the connective tissues. When it comes out of the oven, it will melt in your mouth, it's that tender." After preparing the main dish, she set out to show her how to make a creamy macaroni and cheese dish. "Now this is all about the béchamel sauce pairing it with the cheese, onions, and mushrooms. This is easy and a rather tasty dish, if I say so myself. For our vegetable, I thought we'd have wilted spinach, especially since it's in season. Are you okay with that?"

"That all sounds wonderful. I hope I can recreate it myself at home."

"Easy-peasy. I guarantee you won't have any problems. After you perfect the béchamel sauce, everything goes downhill from there. I think that's the hardest thing—keeping the lumps out."

Melanie listened while Jackie taught her the simple steps behind the béchamel sauce— and then she continued talking non-stop. It was near five when the kitchen door opened and closed. In walked James. "Oh honey, what are you doing here? Not that you're not welcome. It's just—"

"I thought I'd rescue Melanie."

"Rescue Melanie from what?"

"You, of course."

"Melanie, do you need rescuing?"

"Not today, but maybe I did last week." Jackie laughed at her remarks.

"Since Mel doesn't need rescuing, I'll stay for dinner. It smells wonderful in here. I'd have to guess beef and wine with macaroni and cheese. Am I close?"

"How did you know?" asked Melanie. James pointed to the mac and cheese that sat on the stove.

"I know my mother too well." He brushed his mother's cheek with a kiss. "Can I help?"

"No dear, we're about done. We still have to wilt the spinach, but that won't be for some time. I think we have about an hour left on the main dish. Melanie, would you mind putting the macaroni in the oven?"

Melanie grabbed the baking dish, sliding it into the oven.

Before they knew it, dinner was served. Afterwards, James said, "That was a fantastic meal, Mom."

"Don't thank me alone. Melanie helped too." Melanie shyly looked up at him. It was an odd feeling to be complimented.

Chapter Twelve

MELANIE GOT HOME AROUND NINE-THIRTY Sunday evening. She'd enjoyed her time with Jackie so much, they planned another class for the following Saturday. She knew she'd need it after her business trip that week. She was flying to California to look at a block of loans for Amcrost. Even though the sale had yet to be finalized, James' father wanted her to analyze this special group that had just popped onto the market. They'd made an offer and needed either her or James' approval from the Acquisitions Department to go through with the sale. She hoped the trip was a good sign she'd retain her job.

Melanie had packed the night before and was all set for the trip. She needed to be at the airport bright and early. She crawled into bed with her copy of the seller's due diligence questionnaire to review it one last time before going to sleep. She needed to ensure she was on top of her game—make a good impression, one of perfection for James' father.

Melanie slept fitfully and groaned as she got out of bed. Nervous flier that she was, she knew she'd be even worse today with the little sleep she'd gotten. Somehow, she showered, dressed, and made it to the airport with plenty of time to spare. After checking in at the gate, she sat with laptop in hand, again reviewing the questionnaire she'd developed for this trip. She decided to try something new, hoping that she'd get in and out with all of the answers she needed.

Melanie boarded the plane and quickly found her seat beside the window. Enveloped in her own world, she watched the bag handlers load the luggage onto the plane. She wasn't paying attention until she felt a breeze as someone dropped something onto the seat next to hers. She wasn't in the best of moods due to her lack of sleep and just wanted to ignore whoever sat beside her. In fact, she hoped to sleep on the four hours-plus flight.

As the person sat down, they bumped into her. She glanced over to discover James beside her. Excited to see him, she spun in her seat. "What are you doing here?"

"What do you think? I'm heading out to California."

"I gathered that, silly. I mean I thought I was traveling alone."

"Last night after you left, my dad received a call from Maxwell Dalton. They have another pool of loans to sell and my dad wanted me to look at them." She was surprised and immediately felt as though Ben didn't believe she had the skill to review both pools of loans. "Stop fretting, Mel. My dad's not questioning your abilities. He thought with the two of us we'd be able to get through this more quickly than if you had to do it alone. Hey, look at it this way— at least you'll have someone to go to dinner with."

"Just what I wanted, a dinner companion," she teased.

"I thought you'd be happy that I was going with you. I guess not." he frowned.

"It's not that at all." She stopped and something caught her eye out the window. The baggage handlers were retrieving a bag that had fallen onto the tarmac. Between lack of sleep and the long-anticipated flight, her anxiety was starting to rear its ugly head again. And one thing was for sure, James didn't need to witness her in another meltdown.

She felt James' eyes upon her as she focused her attention out the window. Her hands began to shake. *I don't need this now.* She pursed her lips trying to stay in control when all she wanted to do was curl into a ball against the airplane and put her fears to rest. She knew he was speaking to her. She saw his lips moving but she couldn't hear him. He placed his hand on her leg and squeezed. His other hand brushed aside her hair from her face caressing the side of her cheek. He clasped her jaw and forced her head in his direction. Ultimately, she didn't want to hear what he had to say. She wanted to fall into her own world where she could protect herself from everyone and anyone. A world where she often found herself when she was a little girl, where she protected herself from all the evils that seemed to find their way into her life.

"Mel. Hey, is something wrong? Are you not feeling well? You've zoned out on me for some reason."

Melanie licked her lips and clasped her hands together. She didn't want him to see how fragile she was. She hated flying and absolutely hated the feeling of being completely out of control. She felt crowded as soon as James sat down beside her. Out of nowhere, all of her childhood fears came crashing down on her.

Over the years, she'd dealt with so much. She'd overcome more than any person should ever have to, but lately those fears were smacking her in the face, right this very moment, and she felt like she was going to have a panic attack. She'd had them before when she faced her past, and hadn't had one in a while, but she knew the signs.

Melanie's heart rate climbed. Her fingers tingled. Chills spread across her body and she was short of breath. She knew the signs and she knew she must overcome them. Her attacks generally lasted less than ten minutes but those ten minutes were filled with terror.

James moved the arm rest up and pulled her into his arms. "Breathe, Mel, just breathe. Everything is going to be fine." She nodded, then rested her head against his shoulder while she listened to his calming voice.

As soon as her attack started, it was over. The flight attendant came over the airwaves indicating they were preparing the cabin for departure. Mel pulled away from James. "I'm okay now." James gave her shoulder one last squeeze and settled back into his seat. He took her hand and held it securely in his. She clutched it tightly as the plane backed away from the gate. She closed her eyes and knew James continued to watch her. He ran his thumb in circles over the back of her hand. His touch was comforting and eased her fears.

"Keep breathing, Mel, and we'll be airborne soon." She realized that for the first time in her life she had someone to lean on. Someone recognized one of her fears without her having to say a word. James was in tune with her. She was grateful he'd appeared on her flight, sitting next to her. She didn't know exactly what brought on this attack other than the fact that he appeared and her self-confidence took a direct hit, tossing her into the throws of this attack.

She closed her eyes and took a deep breath. "Thanks," is all she said. James tightened his hold on her hand.

"Everything's going to be just fine. I'm here and I'll make sure nothing happens to you." With that, he raised her hand to his lips, placing a soft kiss on the top. "Lean on me. I'm here for you." She smiled up at him. She felt a closeness with him that she'd never felt in her entire life. She didn't know her father and her mother was not someone she wanted to emulate. In fact, she wished she never had to lay claim to her mother. She hated the woman with a passion.

Mel was secure, wrapped in James' arms.

"Mel, what just happened?"

"Nothing."

"Don't tell me nothing. Did you just have a panic attack?"

"Nah, what are you talking about? I'm fine." She didn't want to show weakness.

"Don't lie to me. I know what just happened isn't normal. Are you afraid of flying?"

She sat momentarily and then nodded her head. She didn't want to explain why she felt the way she did. She felt trapped when the doors shut on the plane, locked in a tiny space, unable to get out, which, of course she couldn't, but she didn't know how to explain her fears without revealing them in full. She needed to keep them close to her chest as few knew of her past life.

No one could know what she went through. Absolutely no one. If James discovered what she'd endured, he'd think she was damaged and ultimately unable to perform her job. In fact, often, when she flew off the handle, she blamed her temper on her childhood. Something little and innocuous would set her off. That's when she revolted and that's when she found herself in the middle of an attack. Some would classify her with a panic disorder while others thought she suffered from an anxiety disorder. No matter how she was classified, Melanie had definite issues and they all stemmed from her traumatic childhood.

Melanie had drifted off to sleep once their plane hit cruising altitude. James had been excited to join her on this trip. They'd spent time together mainly dealing with business but now they'd have some time alone without having to interact with others. He realized while sharing dinner at his parents the night before that he wanted to get to know her. Really know Melanie Holmes. What he did know was that she seemed to appreciate his mother and knew when Jackie was trying to interfere in both of their lives to put her in her place. Melanie didn't think twice about telling Jackie if she were right or wrong about a situation. He had witnessed Melanie dealing with his mother and was refreshed seeing someone tackle her so openly without repercussion.

Elsa had never been able to do that. She put up with his mother's antics, but once they were alone complained until he agreed with her opinions. Looking back, he should have never spoken or had those thoughts about his mother. He should have stood up to Elsa, and when he believed she was wrong, he should have told her. In the end, he was glad that he'd broken off their engagement because, in time, he more than likely would have hurt his mother some way or another.

James knew Melanie had been in the throes of some

type of panic attack earlier with the way she held her shaking hands. He'd noticed her unease and watched as she took short breaths, saw the sheen of moisture as it dotted her forehead. He didn't understand what she'd gone through because he'd never had a panic attack or whatever it was she'd endured. He just wanted to help her. James guessed she feared flying once the doors were closed and the flight attendant had indicated they were ready to get underway. That's when she started to fall apart and that's when he reached for her.

Melanie was a complicated woman. She was shielding herself from something but he didn't know what. What he did know was that he wanted to be by her side and help her overcome whatever was causing her to come apart.

James held her hand as they flew through the skies. When she became unsettled, he squeezed her hand and she seemed to relax. He decided that he was going to determine what was behind her fears and try and help her put them to bed.

He thought back to the times he'd witnessed her attacks and hoped to be able to discover a common element. The Melanie he'd been working with the last few weeks was kind, thoughtful, but also feared for her job. He hoped this trip would open his eyes to see who the real Melanie Holmes was—the good and the bad.

This would be the first time traveling as colleagues. He wanted to know if traveling alone caused the behaviors that he'd witnessed on his past encounters with her. Those run-ins shaped his beliefs of who Melanie was, but maybe there were extenuating reasons for her behavior. He wanted to find the answers because in the end his recommendation of her talents would go a long way with his father in her securing a job with Amcrost after the sale was culminated.

James dozed off himself and when he woke the plane had begun its decent. They were scheduled to arrive around eleven-thirty California time. They had about a three-hour drive to Monterey where they would stay at Monterey Lights Bed and Breakfast. The inn was situated right on the bay. James had stayed there several times both on business and on pleasure. When traveling he preferred to stay in bed and breakfasts because they were quiet and offered him the privacy he enjoyed. Often times, the accommodations were in line and often cheaper than the hotel chains found in large cities. He'd never been disappointed.

Melanie still slept. She looked relaxed unlike the moments she encountered prior to falling asleep. On top of everything else, he'd seen the tension that lined her face. That tension was gone for the present and he hoped would remain that way during their trip. He wanted her to have a good time. They'd be busy, but he also wanted to explore the area at night and really get to know her. They'd be exclusively tied to one another the entire week and what better way to learn a little more about her

The flight attendants cleaned the cabin before landing and stopped at their row. "Sir, please make sure your wife's seatbelt is securely fastened for landing."

James chuckled and started to reply that Melanie wasn't his wife but decided to leave it alone. "Sure thing."

He checked her seatbelt when she began to wake. He cupped her jaw as she opened her eyes. "Mel, we're getting ready to land." He reached for her hand again and clasped it resting it against his thigh. Squeezing her hand, he looked her directly in the eyes. "Better?"

She nodded having lost her voice. Swallowing deeply, she whispered, "Thanks." No additional words were spoken as the plane cut through the low-level clouds, finding the runway, and touching down with a slight bump along the way. James watched as she calmed before his eyes. She was definitely a nervous flier.

When they received the all clear to depart the plane, James stood and reached again for her hand, helping her stand. She stumbled, but he caught her before she fell into the aisle. "I need to get my balance," she said as she looked into his eyes and smiled. He felt something this time that he hadn't felt before when holding her hand. She needed him.

They secured their luggage and car and before they knew it were on the road. "Do you know anyone at the bank?" she asked. "I have to say I've never had dealings with anyone at Dalton Bank and Trust. I certainly hope their records are up to date and we don't have to wait on reporting. That always drives me crazy. These lenders know we're coming and should have everything waiting for us… How do you want to go about this? What do you want me to handle?"

"Melanie, would you please stop and take a breath? I don't think you've stopped talking since we got in the car an hour ago."

Melanie stopped and swallowed her words. "I guess I'm anxious to get started. What time did you say we're meeting their team tomorrow?"

"Nine."

"Nine?"

"Yes, nine. You do realize we're in California and not

Missouri. Things move a tad slower out here."

"But?"

"No buts, Mel. We're meeting them at nine." She sighed. "Will you please relax? You're wound tighter than..." He stopped, not wanting to upset her. He wanted her to stay calm and get to know her in a different light.

They drove for another ten minutes in silence when he informed her of their dinner reservations. "I thought we'd eat early and take a drive along the coast. Chill out some. Relax."

"We're here for a job, not to play."

"I understand that, but you can have some fun while you travel. Our entire trip doesn't have to be all business."

"But it needs to be. We can't afford any issues with this. We have to analyze all of their reports, conduct department interviews. There's so much that must be done. We don't have to do it all at their office. I plan on taking the reports back to the inn and reviewing them at night, so I can be prepared each morning. This is how I operate. I'm constantly reviewing all of the material to be sure we make the right decision."

"And maybe that's your problem. You work too hard and don't stop to have a little fun. Maybe that's why you tend to get out of control and verbally attack when things don't seem to go your way. Amcrost doesn't operate in this manner. We treat people with respect and that's something you need to definitely work on." She jumped almost as though she'd been slapped in the face. She opened and closed her mouth then turned away to look out the window.

James knew he'd hurt her but what he said was the

truth. He'd witnessed her in several situations verbally assault her peers. Melanie needed to realize her counterparts had feelings and berating them wouldn't provide them with the results they needed. He was beginning to witness the side of Melanie that he didn't like. One where she took charge and needed everything to go her way—fall into her prescribed calendar whether necessary or not.

From what James could see, she was consumed, with what he didn't know. Something drove her to these ends and he was going to discover what because if she didn't change, he wouldn't be able to recommend her continued employment. She flew off the handle too easily and his father didn't put up with that. Amcrost had a stellar reputation in the banking industry and they couldn't risk losing that if Melanie stayed on. He hoped it wouldn't come to that and wanted to believe her change in demeanor resulted from whatever happened on the plane before takeoff. He believed that in their time together he'd be able to determine what caused her anxiety. He admired her determination and work ethic. Maybe he could make a difference in her life and help her forge a path that allowed her to deal with the demons that seemed to surround her.

Chapter Thirteen

SO MUCH FOR A RELAXING dinner. Once they checked into Monterey Lights, Melanie came down with a migraine. James wasn't sure he believed her. He left her at the door to her room and headed out himself. He wasn't going to allow her to put a damper on his evening. He'd been looking forward to his dinner and he was going to enjoy it.

He sat at his table overlooking the bay, recalling the events of the day. He replayed Melanie's behaviors while on the plane and in the car. She was a difficult person to figure out. He'd thought he was beginning to know her, but realized that he didn't.

It was almost ten. It would be midnight at home. He should be exhausted, but he wasn't. As he strolled along the boardwalk, he thought about his sister, Kelly. She'd come home from the hospital and was on bed rest. She hated being confined to her home, but also knew how much this baby meant to both her and Alec. Kelly had been through an ordeal before realizing that Alec was the love of her life. And then, he remembered that Alec had hired Jonas Sounds, a private investigator, to look into her boss, Ken Jones, when she worked for Lattice Works. Ken had a past that few people knew about. It was his past, in addition to the assault of both Kelly and a co-worker, that led to his arrest.

James thought about looking into Melanie's background. He'd talk to his dad about it and maybe use Jonas to uncover her past. Often times, Amcrost ran background checks on their high-level employees and maybe he'd recommend that if they decided to keep her on. He didn't want to invade her past, but something wasn't right with her and her need for perfection. He wasn't sure that perfection was the right word, but there was definitely something that caused Melanie to need the approval she sought.

He returned to Monterey Lights and sat on the wraparound porch that overlooked the water. It was a perfect evening and the overhead ceiling fans on the porch moved just enough air around. He was comfortable as he watched the moonlight cast a glow across the water. He sat there for a few minutes when he heard a door close. He looked up as Melanie stepped outside. The moonlight silhouetted her, the rays of light filtering over her shoulders. She looked like an angel. She quietly sat beside him on the porch swing.

"Feeling better?" He stared straight ahead into the night.

"Yes, thank you, I am. Sorry about earlier. I guess I should have told you I was a nervous flier. Today was worse than normal. I was running on practically no sleep."

"How come no sleep?"

"I guess I was anxious for the trip knowing that this was a purchase being funded by Amcrost and not Parklayne. I need to prove my abilities to your father."

"I'd say your record working for Parklayne speaks for

you." By her annual performance reviews, Saxson had no issues with her; in fact, she'd received glowing marks. Again, James' issues with her were her explosive temper and how she treated her co-workers including peers in the industry. He didn't want to bring up past experiences, but felt he needed to set some boundaries with her. "From where I stand, the issues you have are how you interact with your colleagues, especially when you travel. I've witnessed too many times where you've verbally attacked for no reason at all. If you have something to worry about, it's that. I just know what I've seen as an outsider. I certainly hope you don't treat your own employees in that manner." Melanie gnawed on her lower lip as she shook her head. "I don't know what happens to you when you travel. You seem unsettled. Any little mishap sends you over the edge and that's definitely something you need to work on especially if you become an Amcrost employee. My dad doesn't put up with that type of behavior at all."

She clenched her fists in her lap, not uttering a word. She was listening to him because her whole body tensed. The saying what goes around comes around crossed his mind. He still didn't know what his father's plans for Melanie were. Maybe his father was using this trip as an audition for future employment with Amcrost. But there was only one VP of Acquisitions at Amcrost and the job currently belonged to him.

Melanie couldn't deny his allegations as they were all true. She was unsettled when she journeyed out of her comfort zone. She was a hellion when she traveled and she owed it all to her mother. She hated flying and not knowing what her accommodations would be when she arrived at her destination. She didn't want to be closed in— in a small hotel room with little light. She needed lots and lots of light.

Often when she traveled, she was a nervous wreck. She knew her job inside and out but her anxiety always ramped up and she just didn't know how to control it. Her medications helped but not always. She wanted to tell James but was afraid. Afraid that her past would somehow enter into the decision on whether or not she'd be offered a job when the sale was complete. So instead of telling him everything about her childhood and how it shaped her into the woman she was today, she remained silent on the topic.

"Well, I guess I'll head on in…" Melanie stood. "Thanks again for your hand today. I hope I didn't squeeze it too hard." James chuckled at her reference.

"You didn't do any damage. I hope you sleep well."

"You too. Is there a particular time you'd like to meet? I know we're not scheduled to arrive until nine."

"I'll be down here around eight for breakfast if you'd like to join me. Otherwise, I'll see you at the front door at eight forty-five."

"'Night." Melanie walked away. How she wanted to tell him…tell him everything, but now was not the time.

She went directly to her room and prepared for bed, thankful she had lamps not only on her end table but dresser and desk as well. She turned them all on so her room was brightly lit. She'd get a good night's sleep and prove to James that she wasn't the woman he inferred her to be. She'd be an asset to Amcrost and she'd show him just how talented she was.

Melanie's wish came true when she slept through the

night. She jumped out of bed at five, dressed casually, and headed out for an early morning stroll along the bay. The water gently lapping the boardwalk relaxed her even more. By seven-thirty she'd showered and changed into her power suit. Next, she was off to the restaurant where she grabbed a table, beating James in the process. He joined her moments later.

"Still on St. Louis time?" James smiled at her as he poured half-and-half into his coffee.

"I am. I did sleep in for me, but I was still up at five and decided to take a stroll along the bay. It was so peaceful. I really enjoyed myself. I'm all ready to start my day."

She had time to peruse the morning paper and relish her breakfast. She glanced at her watch. "It's almost eight-thirty. I'm going to run up to my room and grab my briefcase. I'll meet you in a few."

Promptly at nine o'clock they walked through the doors of Dalton Bank and Trust. James took control of their meetings. She was calmer today than she'd ever been when traveling and first meeting her counterparts. She assumed it was because James was there and she could lean on him for support. As she sat listening to him while he addressed Dalton's key staff, she realized for once in her life that she could rely on someone. He was taking full ownership of their initial meetings and she was thankful for that. She could be herself and hopefully not screw up.

When Melanie broke off to begin her part of the due diligence, she had a sureness about herself. As VP at Parklayne she was confident but for some reason she felt different, lighter today and she owed it all to James' presence.

Their day went well and Melanie felt extremely comfortable with everyone she met. The reports she requested were ready and waiting for her to begin her analysis. In a surprise to herself, she was able to comb through the voluminous amount of paper before lunch and was satisfied with her findings. She just needed one more day to write up her findings and they'd be able to go home as long as James' review was going as well as hers. It was the first time she'd ever been able to complete a due diligence in less than two days and she was ecstatically happy about that.

They broke for lunch and she advised James that she could be done with her review the following day. "Surprisingly, my review's going just as well. Let's play it by ear since we don't have to be back until Friday." Melanie felt like James was gearing up to take Thursday off and for once she kept her mouth closed on that subject. She'd sit back and wait and see.

They left the office at five and returned to the inn where they changed into casual clothes for dinner. Melanie had suggested a drive before deciding where they'd stop for dinner. It was a gorgeous day and she wanted to make the best of it. She met James in the sitting room at six. They drove along the coastline, discovering a quaint little Mexican restaurant. They chose to sit outside for their meal where they were surrounded by heaters that took the early evening chill out of the air.

Casa del Sol was an ideal spot for a romantic evening. The patio overlooked the cliffs that protected this part of the town from the bay. The lighting was dim and provided the perfect ambiance for their meal, soft music played in the background— nothing too loud to overshadow their conversation. The setting alone was a ten in her book and she couldn't wait to try the food. If the aromas coming from the kitchen were anything close to what their meal would be, she would definitely classify this as a five-star restaurant.

James decided on his selection almost immediately while Melanie couldn't make up her mind. "Do you like tacos, burritos?"

"I do."

"Is that one or both?"

"Both," she laughed, "but I just can't decide. Why don't you choose for me?"

"You're sure about that?"

Smiling at him she nodded. "Of course, I am or I wouldn't have suggested it."

James chose a burrito for her. "Chicken or beef?"

"Chicken."

"The lady will have your chicken burrito with rice and a garden salad on the side. I'll have the taquitos and the same sides. And make it the salsa-ranch dressing?"

Melanie nodded her approval. She rested her chin on her hand and looked at James with a huge smile on her face.

"What's the smile for?"

"I had the best day."

"I'm glad to hear that. And what do you attribute it to?"

"You?"

"Me?"

"Uh huh."

"Why's that?"

Melanie didn't want to tell him why—that his presence calmed her nerves and let her self-confidence shine.

"Just because, that's all." They enjoyed a little chit chat before their salads were served. "When's Angelina due, again?"

"I think she has five or six weeks to go. I've never seen her so happy outside of the last time she was pregnant and, of course, when she married Alejandro. I'm really looking forward to two new babies in the family. My parents are overjoyed, as are the Alvarezes."

"I gather you're the doting uncle."

"I am and enjoy every last minute of it. I can't wait to have children. What about you?"

Melanie didn't want to ruin their evening. She didn't want children or a family. She'd come to that conclusion before she was ten years old. Thankfully, she didn't have to answer his question because their salads were served and they moved onto another topic.

The entire evening was relaxing for both of them. Just as she predicted, James broached the subject of taking Thursday off to play. He checked off what he'd like to do before returning to St. Louis. "I guess we can decide what to do if everything falls into place and we can complete everything tomorrow." After James finished off his glass of wine, she asked, "Are you ready? I have a few things I'd like to review before I go to bed."

"Yep, I'm done here."

"Thanks for a nice dinner." He stood and helped her with her chair and as they walked to the car, he placed his hand along her back. She felt special and for once in a long while she was happy.

Later that evening, Melanie's happiness came to abrupt end. While she was reviewing her reports, the lights went out. Her room was completely dark. She froze in place. She was in a situation that she could do nothing about and it brought her to her knees. She couldn't move. The darkness enveloped her and she soon found herself back in a small, stuffy locked room trying to get out. Her fears overcame her and she started to hyperventilate. As quickly as the lights went out, they came back on, but Melanie was affected by the loss of electricity the remainder of the night. She feared going to sleep. She sat on her bed with her lamp clutched between her hands, as if holding the lamp would prevent the lights from going out again.

Melanie was ever-thankful morning was on the horizon. She decided she'd take a quick snooze and be ready for James at nine. She'd forgo breakfast for a little sleep.

The next thing Melanie was aware of was a heavy knock on her door. Her alarm clock blinked. Darn it. She'd forgotten to reset it when the generators had kicked-in. She was clueless as to the time. "Mel, are you in there?" James. It was James at her door. She jumped from her bed and caught her reflection in the dresser mirror. She was a tireless mess. Her hair stood on end, she had dark circles underneath her eyes, and her face was puffy. She didn't want him to see her this way.

"Mel, are you up?"

Melanie couldn't let him think something had gone awry. She cracked the door open. "James, hi. Um, I'm sorry, but I guess I overslept. My alarm didn't go off." *Yep that's a good excuse.* "I guess the power went out during the night and my clock didn't reset. I'll be ready in fifteen minutes, okay."

"Sure thing." He winked at her and walked away.

Melanie hurriedly dressed and made her way to the

dining room where James sat drinking a cup of coffee. She knew she looked a fright and did her best to conceal the tiredness from her face and eyes. She was surprised when he didn't comment on her appearance, but instead ordered breakfast. "You waited for me?"

"I did and then I got worried when you didn't show up. I'm glad nothing was wrong.'

She knew that James knew something was wrong, but he didn't say a word. Instead, they ate their breakfast, ran into the office, and finished up their review by five. As they made their way to the car, she stumbled catching herself before she fell. "Everything alright over there?"

"Fine."

"You look exhausted, Melanie. Didn't you sleep last night?"

"Oh, I did." She didn't want him to know that she sat on the edge of her bed clutching her bedside lamp praying that the lights would remain on. Somehow, she made it through dinner and when James advised her that they'd be returning home the following day instead of staying over she was thrilled. She needed to go home and get herself back under control. She hoped that Madeleine had gotten some good news about the Y's program so they could resume the art therapy group. Right now, she needed it more than Jared or Monica. Painting would put her in a good place and she needed that right now.

Chapter Fourteen

DUE TO A TRAFFIC TIE-UP on the highway, they missed the one and only direct flight to St. Louis for the day. The airline tried to route them through Denver but the plane was filled to capacity. Their only alternative was to spend the night in San Francisco and fly on as intended on Friday.

James secured them a hotel room in the heart of downtown San Francisco. It was a high rise with their rooms on the thirtieth floor. Melanie stood ramrod straight and nervously chewed on her lower lip as the elevator climbed to their floor. Surprisingly they rose to their floor without stopping and when the doors opened, he heard her breathe a sigh of relief. Fortunately, James' room was right across the hall from hers.

"Do you think you can be ready in a half-hour? I thought we'd head down to Ghirardelli Square, grab something to eat, and sightsee."

"That's sound nice, yeah, I'll be ready. I'll meet you in the lobby."

"Let's take a ride down to Fisherman's Wharf. Maybe we'll be able to take a cruise around the bay. It's a gorgeous day."

"That sounds like fun." Her eyes lit up with the mention of Fisherman's Wharf.

They met in the lobby and a short walk later boarded a cable car to the Wharf. Melanie's eyes sparkled with wonderment, a good look for her, as they rode along the hilly streets of San Francisco. She was so beautiful and he couldn't help but brush aside her hair whipping in the wind. She smiled at him as they traveled along and hopped off the cable car when the line ended.

They walked a short distance to the Pier where James was lucky enough to purchase tickets for the San Francisco Bridge to Bridge cruise. He got caught up in Mel's excitement as she snapped photographs of the Golden Gate Bridge as they passed underneath. He'd never seen her so relaxed and filled with joy.

They grabbed a snack as their boat toured San Francisco Bay passing by Alcatraz Island. "I wouldn't have wanted to live there," Melanie said pointing to Alcatraz Island. "It gives me the chills just looking at it." James reached over wrapping his arm around her shoulders.

"Better?"

"Yeah, thanks." They listened to the narration on the cruise that gave them a much deeper understanding of San Francisco's history.

It became chilly and James felt her tremble slightly. "Are you cold?"

"A little. It's quite windy out here." James stood holding out his arm to her. There was easy comfort between them as James wrapped his arm around her shoulders drawing her close.

"How about a hot chocolate?"

"That sounds wonderful." James returned with their drinks and sat beside her. She sipped her hot chocolate carefully. "Oh my gosh, this tastes like heaven."

James always seemed to laugh at something she said—that is when she was in a good mood. Melanie seemed to have two distinctive personalities— one at work where she seemed tense and the other outside it where she was relaxed and at ease. He watched the swells in the bay and tried to decipher why that was. James surmised the more he was around her he'd uncover why.

Before they knew it, their cruise was over. Hand in hand, they walked along the pier towards Ghirardelli Square. James loved the area. It had transformed itself over the years and was registered as a National Historic Site. He thought they'd visit the well renowned soda fountain after dinner. There Melanie could shop for all forms of chocolate till her heart was content. They perused the various shops along the way and found themselves at McCormick and Kuleto's Seafood & Steaks restaurant. They had to wait for their table, so they ended up in the bar where she got a white wine and he had a beer.

She fingered the stem of her wineglass and smiled at him. "Thank you."

"For what?"

"For today. I've had a fabulous time. I've never ridden on a cable car before and that cruise was something I'll always remember." She looked down at her hands. "This has been a really good trip."

"It has, but why do you say that?"

"I don't know. Maybe it's the company." Shyly she looked away from him taking another sip of her wine and changing the subject. "So, what's good here?"

"Everything. Be sure and leave room for dessert because we're going to Ghirardelli's for that." They enjoyed their view of the water and decided to have their meal in the bar.

When their waitress asked about dessert, Melanie smiled again at him. "I've been told we're going to Ghirardelli's for that. Something about chocolate there." The waitress roared with laughter.

"Yep, I'd say they have chocolate." James paid the bill, stood, and again reached for her hand. It felt right holding it in his.

They walked around a little more and ended up at the chocolate shop where Melanie shopped for various chocolates from bars to chips and cocoa. James laughed to himself as he watched her stock up on the various items. "Wipe that smirk off your face. This isn't all for me. I have a nice selection for your sister that's on bedrest too." Holding up a chocolate bar, "I definitely think this will cheer her up."

"I would have to agree with you. Kelly does enjoy her chocolate." They paid for their purchases and made their way to the soda shop.

Melanie couldn't stop smiling. "This all looks so good, but I think I'm going to have the Treasure Island. I love brownies, hot fudge, and vanilla ice cream, and who doesn't love whipped cream too?"

"After my dinner, I should go light, but I'm not. I'm going all in with Crissy Field. I love cookies 'n cream ice cream. I've never had this sundae before, but I've had what you're having and there are no words for it." James knew Melanie was seeing a different side to him, but he wanted her to. She seemed so much more relaxed and he wanted her to stay that way.

Melanie's eyes about popped open wide when she saw her dessert. "I'll never be able to eat all of this."

"Do you want to bet on that?"

"No, because I'll probably lose." He smirked and grabbed a spoon to dig into his own.

"This is heaven— even better than that hot cocoa we had earlier." Licking the fudge off the back of her spoon, she moaned with pleasure. "I wish I could package this up and take it home, it's that good. Maybe Amcrost could open a satellite office out here." Taking another bite, she said, "But that wouldn't be good for the waistline, would it?"

James took another spoonful of his dessert, watching Melanie. She was definitely in pure heaven. "You're not going to lick the bowl?"

Raising her gaze to him, he knew she was happy. He'd never seen such a look of elation from her. "I definitely thought about it, but sadly no." She wiped her lips and smiled back at him. That's when he realized that he loved her smile and the way she scrunched her eyes when she did. He was glad they'd missed their plane because today he put that winsome smile on her face. She was happy and he was glad that he'd given her this day.

Instead of returning to their hotel via the cable cars, they grabbed a cab. It was getting late and he wanted to get back. They needed to get up early to make their flight. James held her hand as they rode up the elevator to their rooms. She was more relaxed than the last time they'd ridden the elevator up. Hand-in-hand they walked to their rooms. She withdrew her key card from her purse and he reached for it. He inserted it into the reader and opened her door. "Have a good night, Mel." He felt the need to kiss her but didn't want to take advantage of the situation.

Instead, it was Melanie that rose to her toes and kissed

his cheek. "Thank you for a wonderful day."

He clasped her jaw and looked her directly in the eyes. Smiling at her, he didn't know what to say or do, so he did what his heart told him. He placed a soft kiss on her lips. He didn't linger and pulled away. "You're welcome, Mel. See you at six." With that he turned and walked across the hall to his room.

Melanie touched her fingers to her lips in completed surprise. James kissed her. Really kissed her. She was pulled from her thoughts when his door loudly closed behind him. *Wow.*

Still in a state of shock, she entered her room and flipped on all of the lights. She slept well and met James in the lobby promptly at six. When they checked in at the airport, they were surprised to see that they'd been upgraded to first class. Looking at her boarding pass, "I'm in first class, what about you?"

"I am too. I wonder how that happened, but I'm not going to question it." He reached for his bag and they headed off to the gate. Both were seated in the third row. James, being the gentleman he was, put her carryon into the overhead bin. She made a mental note to tell Jackie that she'd raised her son well.

"Thanks for that. Somehow my luggage got heavier. I don't know why."

"Well, I do," James chimed in. "It's all that chocolate you bought."

"Oh yeah, I forgot about that." She giggled into her hand. They settled into the flight when she nudged his arm. "Are you going to your mother's tomorrow?"

"I wasn't planning on it, why?"

"I have another cooking class with her."

"I think I'll stay away. You do a good job at handling her."

"What do you mean by that?" She tipped her head.

"Ah, nothing," he replied. Melanie thought back to last week's class. She guessed he was referring to the way she put Jackie in her place when she tried to impress James onto her. *I'm sure that's it.*

Upon returning home, Melanie checked her voice mail to discover that Madeleine had phoned. "I have terrific news, Melanie. We're starting back up next week. If you have any questions, let me know. Otherwise, I hope to see you Tuesday."

Melanie was elated with the news. She couldn't wait to see Jared and Monica. She hoped they hadn't regressed in the time without their therapy. They'd been making great strides and it wasn't as if the center had been closed down for months— only a few short days. Melanie needed to be at the Y amongst the kids. It was her outlet as well. She needed it almost as much as the children did.

Melanie was tired after their flight. She decided to postpone her review of her files until Sunday. That way, everything would be fresh in her mind, not that it wasn't already. She grabbed a quick bite to eat, ran a couple of loads of laundry, and headed off to bed.

As she got into bed, she was smiling and had been for days now. In fact, her cheeks ached. She raised her hand to her lips remembering the way she felt when James kissed her. The slight brush of his lips turned her world upside down. She needed to move on, though.

She was afraid she was getting in too deep with him and she could not afford to do that. She sighed and rolled to her side. She had to be at the Samuels' house bright and early and needed her sleep.

She slept fairly well and headed off for her cooking class. Before leaving the house, she grabbed the specialty chocolate chips that she purchased for Jackie as a thank-you for teaching her how to cook.

As usual, Jackie was all smiles when she answered the door. She pulled Melanie into a tight hug. Melanie wasn't used to all of the hugging as she'd never had that physical type of relationship with her own mother. It comforted her knowing Jackie enjoyed her presence.

"Melanie, it's so good to see you. Come on in." Melanie followed Jackie to the kitchen. "I've got bagels and coffee and I thought we could chat for a bit before we get started." Melanie set her purse and bag down in the living room and followed after Jackie. "So how was your trip?"

"Oh, you know how a business trip goes. I hate traveling. By the time I get used to my surroundings, it's time to come home."

"That's so true."

Melanie reached for a bagel and the cream cheese while Jackie poured her coffee. Melanie wondered if Jackie knew James had traveled with her. She assumed she did but was pleasantly surprised that she didn't ask. Melanie instead decided to bring him up. He'd been so good to her and she wanted Jackie to know that she raised a true gentleman.

James' name was on the tip of Melanie's tongue when Jackie started up again. "Did you have a chance to do any sightseeing? I know you were there for work, but

San Francisco is such a fun place to visit. I visited with Ben a few years ago. He was there for a conference and while he attended his meetings, I toured the city. Did you have a chance to go to Alcatraz, or better yet, Ghirardelli Square?"

"Oh my, wait a minute." Melanie jumped from her seat and went into the living room to retrieve her bag. She'd completely forgotten Jackie's surprise. Rushing back into the room, she pulled the bag from behind her back. "Here, this is for you."

"Oh dear, what did you get me?" Jackie peered into the bag and saw the specialty chocolate. Her eyes lit up. "Melanie, you didn't have to do this. Thank you." Again, Jackie pulled her into her arms. Melanie decided she better get used to this because Jackie was sure a hugger. "I love these, how did you know?"

"I didn't know. James and I went there after dinner at McCormicks."

"You and James?" she asked.

"Oh yes, James went on the trip with me." Melanie caught Jackie's smile as she reached into her bag. "I thought you knew that he went with me."

"I know his father talked to him about it after you left last week, but I didn't think he went."

"Why's that?"

"I don't know. Anyway, enough about James. Let's get started." Melanie realized that Jackie didn't want to upset her talking too much about her son.

"So, what are we making today?"

Melanie listened while Jackie instructed her on how to make a cake from scratch. Melanie had never made a box cake before, let alone one from scratch. "Now, I hate the icing that comes in a can, so we're going to make our own seven-minute icing and put our twist on it."

"Seven minute? Does it take that long to make it?" Jackie nodded her head as she grabbed the ingredients. She needed sugar, cream of tartar, salt, water, egg whites and vanilla. Jackie also grabbed some chocolate squares, placed them into a pan, and set them on the stove to slowly melt.

"Now, I'm going to show you how easy it is to separate an egg." Melanie watched as Jackie skillfully separated the egg yolk from the egg white. Then, she placed all of the ingredients except the vanilla into a pan over a pot of boiling water. She beat the mixture with a hand-held mixer for seven minutes and then added the vanilla. "See, it's nice and fluffy. Now, I'm going to carefully fold in the cooled chocolate."

"Oh my, that looks really good."

"Here, taste it." Jackie held a spoon out for Melanie to taste the luscious frosting. Melanie rolled her eyes when it hit her tongue. "Isn't it good?"

"I've never tasted icing like this. It's wonderful."

Melanie watched as Jackie began to ice the cake and then she turned over the spatula to Melanie. "Go ahead and try. It won't break."

"But what if I mess up?"

"How could you mess up? This is just a cake and it's not rocket science.'

"I don't think I should. You finish."

"How else are you going to learn than by trying? After all, you need to know how to ice a cake for when you have a family— children." The color drained from Melanie's face. "Melanie. Hey are you okay? I'm sorry if I said something wrong. I know I get talking sometimes and don't know when to stop."

Melanie swallowed deeply and got a hold of herself. She'd made a solemn vow to herself. After the childhood she had, she never intended to marry or have children. She didn't have the best of role models growing up and was afraid of passing her DNA onto a child. "No, I'm fine. I'll try, but make sure I'm doing it correctly." She hadn't a clue as how to respond to Jackie and froze. She took a moment then began spreading the frosting.

"You're doing a fabulous job." Melanie heard Jackie's reassurance as she finished frosting the cake.

As they were washing the dishes, Jackie reached for Melanie's hand. "I'm sorry for making you uncomfortable." Melanie wasn't sure what she was talking about and looked at her strangely. "I know how it feels when you can't have children. Angelina, for a time, thought she'd never be able to have a family of her own. That's one of the reasons why she and Alejandro adopted Matthew. And then, out of the blue she became pregnant. So don't worry your little heart. One day you might be able to have that family."

Melanie pulled away. She wasn't sure what the right thing to say or do was in this very moment. She didn't want to think she was heartless for not wanting a family, but then, again, Jackie had no idea what she'd endured as a child. She hoped no one ever had to experience what she did. Those experiences had shaped her into the person she was today, and she didn't like it. Melanie also knew that she could change, if she wanted to, but that was the problem, she didn't think she wanted to.

She responded in the only way she knew how. "That's alright, don't worry about it." She went back to washing the dishes and changed the subject altogether.

Melanie knew Jackie would think twice before speaking the remainder of her class. They reaped their rewards and ate roasted chicken and mashed potatoes for dinner. Melanie couldn't wait for a slice of cake. "This is the best cake I've ever eaten. It's so moist, delicious."

Melanie called it a day at around seven-thirty. She was tired from traveling and just wanted to go home and put her feet up. "Thanks again, Jackie. I can't believe how much you've taught me already."

"Are we on for next week?"

"I'm sorry but I have plans with my sister, Janet. We're going to a festival."

"Let me look at my schedule and I'll call you and see when you have some time. I'm really enjoying our time together."

"I am too." Melanie was truly enjoying her time with Jackie. She had taught her so much, the simple things her own mother should have taught her. Instead, her mother had been the mother from hell and Melanie didn't want to go down that road. She needed to point her thoughts in a different direction before they started to consume her again and cause her endless nights of horrific dreams that sent her spiraling into the anxiety filled attacks she feared more than anything.

Chapter Fifteen

MONDAY WAS UPON HER AND Melanie couldn't wait to get into the office. Everything she'd been told pointed to the sale of Amcrost being completed by the end of the following month. There was so much she needed to do to insure a smooth transition. There was also the fact that she'd know soon whether or not she was losing her job.

She'd barely made it into the office when her phone rang. She wasn't familiar with the number. "Good morning, this is Melanie Holmes, how may I help you?"

"Let's see, how can you help me?"

"James. Oh hi, how are you?"

"I'm good. Do you think you can make a nine o'clock over here? My dad wants to go over our due diligence."

Melanie's heart dropped. He was all business. She hoped she hadn't done something wrong and wasn't in trouble. Was Mr. Samuels mad they stayed over? It couldn't have been helped, could it? They should have found a way to get home on Thursday. Melanie's heart rate picked up. She was worried.

"Mel, hey are you still there?"

"I am."

"Well, can you make it?"

"Ahh, make what?"

"The meeting."

"Oh yeah. Certainly, I'll be there."

"Is something bothering you?"

"Why would you ask that?"

"You did spend time with my mother."

"Oh, that was a lot of fun. We made a cake."

"I know. I had a sampling and it was fabulous."

"Don't think I had anything to do with it because I didn't."

"Don't say that when I know you did. I'll see you in a little while."

"Thanks."

"And Melanie?"

"Yeah."

"You have nothing to worry about, so quit chewing on your lip and relax. Alright?"

She hung up the phone. *How did he know I was nervous and chewing on my lip?* As she drove to Amcrost she couldn't help but wonder if she'd done something wrong. She pulled into the parking garage and into a reserved visitor's spot. Checking her face in her mirror, she reapplied her lipstick and brushed powder across her forehead and cheeks. She wanted to look perfect for her meeting.

Melanie grabbed her briefcase and turned to open her car door and that's when she saw him. Holcomb Newson. *It can't be him. No, I'm just seeing things.* And then he turned more in her direction and that's when she threw herself onto the floor of the passenger side of her car. *He can't see me.* Melanie flew into a panic attack.

Her vision tunneled and everything around her spun

wildly. Her entire body shook violently. Her heart was racing as a sharp pain seared her chest, taking her breath away. She feared she'd faint but thankfully she couldn't fall since she was already scrunched up on the floor of her car. She felt like she was having a heart attack. She prayed he wouldn't find her, drag her from the car. Fear paralyzed her. She didn't know how long she lay there when she heard a knock against her window. She was afraid to move. Afraid to look up for fear he'd see her.

"Mel, are you alright?" *James. Thank goodness.* "Can you open the door?"

A look of fear crossed his face as Melanie eased her way off the floor and pressed the button to unlock the car doors. James opened the door and crouched beside her. "What happened? Did someone hurt you?"

She couldn't speak, couldn't communicate until she calmed. *What would James think seeing her like this?* He opened his arms for her as she threw herself at him. He held her close, rubbing his hand up and down her back. "Hey, hey, what happened? Are you hurt?"

Melanie found her voice and spoke. "I'm okay, really I am." She was trying to convince herself that she'd never seen Holcomb. She hadn't laid eyes on him in years. Why now? Why when her career with Parklayne was on the line? "Let me sit here for a minute and I'll be just fine. Why did you come looking for me?"

"It's almost nine-thirty and I was concerned. I phoned your office and your secretary said you'd left almost an hour ago. I phoned your cell and you didn't answer, so I thought I'd take a walk and see if something was wrong and that's when I saw your car. I was even more concerned, then. When I approached, I saw you lying on the floor, I thought you'd fainted or something worse had happened."

Melanie tried to stand. "I'm fine. I just had a little scare but everything's good now." She reached for her briefcase. "I hope your father isn't too upset that I delayed the meeting."

"Don't worry about him. I'm just worried about you."

"Never better," she said in a pitched voice. She closed her car door, locking it behind her. She even checked to make sure because she didn't need Holcomb waiting for her in her car. She smiled at James as though nothing had happened and started towards the entryway. Melanie caught a glimpse of him in the mirrored door shaking his head as he followed her. She could only imagine the thoughts that were going through his mind.

What the hell just happened to her? James was more than concerned about Melanie as he followed her into the building. When he'd approached the car, she was lying in almost a fetal position shaking uncontrollably. Someone or something had upset her, and he needed to know who and why.

James escorted her to his father's office. "Why don't you freshen-up and I'll make sure my dad's available."

James watched as Melanie headed off to the ladies' room. Should he be concerned about her mental stability? Something had definitely spooked her. James waited for her as she freshened up. He knew his father was available so whenever she was ready, so was he.

Within minutes she rejoined him and they headed off to his father's office. "Melanie, it's good to see you." James' father shook her hand, welcoming her. "By the way, that cake you made was out of this world."

"Don't compliment me, it was all Jackie's doing. I pretty much just watched."

"I find that hard to believe. I'm sure she had you working right alongside her. Please be seated." James' father held her chair for her as she sat. "James, here, tells me you were in and out of Dalton B&T in two days. That's something you should be proud of. What were your findings? Should we go through with the purchase?"

James listened as Melanie went through minute details of what she thought were the positive aspects of the sale along with the negatives. "From what I could see, they have some escrow issues that need work: a few unpaid homeowner insurance premiums and delinquent taxes, but with a purchase of this size, I'm not too concerned. We'll just make sure they clean up the issues before the sale goes through. There were also a few delinquencies but since it's not even the middle of the month, I don't think there's too much to worry about there, either." Ben nodded approvingly at her.

"James, what about you? Are you satisfied with your findings?"

"I am. I have to concur with what Mel just said. There were a few issues that can be quickly resolved. I think we should go through and purchase both portfolios."

"That was easy," Ben stated. "It seems you're both working well together, complementing each other's strengths as well as weaknesses. Work together and finalize the deal. If that's all you have, I have a conference call in a few minutes. Melanie, thank you for coming all the way over here on such short notice. Why don't you stay a while and James will take you to lunch for your troubles?"

"Sir, that's not necessary. I have quite a bit of work back at the office."

"I insist. James take her to that Italian restaurant down the street. You know which one."

"Sure thing, Dad." Turning back to Melanie, "Follow me to my office and we can iron out the remainder of this purchase agreement."

Melanie thanked Ben, grabbed her briefcase, and followed James to his office. He stopped at the coffee bar on the way. "Coffee?"

"I'd love a cup."

James poured them each a cup then led her down a long hallway to his office. He showed her to a small conference room table that sat in the corner. "Let me get the purchase agreement and we can start there."

Melanie sat down and sipped her coffee. With his focus on her, he lost sight of his files, dropping them all over the floor. An expletive slipped from his lips, causing Melanie to laugh.

"Having problems over there?"

"Just a few." He laughed at himself as he crouched down to pick up the files. "I can't believe they stayed all intact."

He set them down and returned to his desk where he grabbed a tablet of paper— all the while keeping an eye on Melanie. She seemed alright, almost as if nothing had happened. He didn't understand. Was she psychotic? After witnessing her on the floor of her car, he decided to speak with his dad about having Jonas perform the background check. If she had a past of mental health issues, Jonas would definitely discover it.

He was well known for uncovering the smallest piece of information that would make or break a case. Hopefully he'd discover who the real Melanie Holmes was.

James joined her at the table and they worked through the purchase agreement. "I'll submit it to legal for review and if they're in agreement, we'll send it over to Dalton today. I'll let you know where we stand."

She glanced at her watch. "I think I'm going to head back to the office. I appreciate your invitation to lunch, but I have so much work to catch up on with being out of town last week."

"It can sit for another hour or so. If we leave now, you can be back in your office by one." He reached for his coat. "I'd really like to get out of here for a little while. I think I was spoiled last week especially with the cruise of the bay."

She smiled broadly at him. "Yeah, that was nice. Alright, let's go. I am hungry."

They headed off to Mamas Italia. It was a small hole in the wall and if you didn't know it was there, you'd pass it by. They were greeted by Theresa Rossi the owner of Mamas. "James, how are you? It's been awhile."

"It has, Theresa. I've been busy traveling. I'd like you to meet Melanie Holmes, a colleague."

Theresa showed them to a table. As Melanie took her seat the woman leaned into him. "Colleague, my eyeball, James Samuels," Theresa stage whispered. "Not once have you brought a female here. Melanie is more than that and you know it." He gave her the evil eye and knew Melanie overheard as she raised her menu to cover her face, her shoulders quaking. Was she laughing? As Theresa walked away, James reached for Melanie's menu. "Quit hiding," he said laughingly.

"Hiding, who me? What do I have to hide from?" She lowered her menu and her eyes were shimmering. "Who was that, anyway? Your mother?"

"No, and you stop it over there. I thought you were the one that wanted to eat and run."

"I do."

"Then let's order and get the hell out of Dodge." Melanie chuckled aloud this time. They placed their order and James got serious. "Mel, about this morning. Finding you in your car and everything..."

Panic crossed her face. He reached for her hand. "You can tell me what happened. Maybe I can help you."

"Nothing happened."

"Come on, Mel. You had a look of sheer terror on your face and when you discovered it was me knocking on your window, you immediately relaxed. You can tell me what happened. I won't tell anyone."

Her eyebrows furrowed and he knew she was contemplating what to say. He hoped she'd feel comfortable enough to share what happened.

"I thought I saw someone that I hadn't seen in a long, long time. Someone who wasn't very nice to me. I panicked and threw myself to the floor. That's all, nothing else."

"Who was this person? Are you sure it was him? Would I know him? Maybe he was just a customer."

"I'd rather not say other than I thought I'd never have to see him again in my lifetime. In all honesty, I could have been wrong too. You know, everyone has a double somewhere."

"That's what I've heard." James changed the subject knowing everyone could, in fact, have a double. "We need to set up a meeting to go over the project plan with everyone. How does tomorrow at three sound?" He could see the wheels spinning in her head.

"Why three? can we make it earlier?"

"That's the only time I have available."

"Well, if that's it then I'll make it work."

They finished their lunch and James walked Melanie to her car. "I guess I'll see you at three then."

"Yep, tomorrow at three."

Melanie was getting antsy sitting in an Amcrost conference room. It was almost four thirty and they weren't even halfway through the project plan. She had to leave by five to get home, change, and get to the Y in time. She needed her art for her own sanity, especially after seeing Holcomb yesterday. Her anxiousness ramped up. She was sure James noticed as he kept glancing at her.

Finally, he said, "Let's call it a day. We can finish this up tomorrow. Mel, what works best for you?"

"How about right after lunch? Does that work for everyone?" There was a consensus of approvals to meet promptly at one. Upon everyone's agreement, she grabbed her things, threw them into her briefcase, and blazed a trail to her car. She felt James' eyes on her and thought she'd heard him call out her name, but she ignored him. She had to get to the Y. She needed it more than anything.

Melanie surprised herself and made it there in plenty of time. She ran into Madeleine as she walked through the doors.

"Mel, I'm glad you got my message. I apologize for the mix-up these last couple of weeks, but we temporarily lost our funding. I think it was more of an accounting issue, but either way, we're back up and running. Jared and Monica are already in there waiting for us.

Melanie hurried into the room. She knew they didn't like to be hugged, but she was more than surprised when Monica ran up to her, throwing her arms around her legs. Melanie squatted down and pulled her into a hug. "I missed you so much, Miss Melanie. I can't wait to paint again."

"Me either, Monica. I've been waiting for this day since Miss Madeleine called me letting me know we could get back together." Monica pulled away and went to her easel where she grabbed her brush and started painting stick figures.

"See Miss Melanie...You, me, and Miss Madeleine. See we have smiles on our faces."

"I see that."

"We're happy today."

"Yes, we are." Melanie reached for a sketch pad and started sketching. This was one way for Melanie to get her emotions out. She often sketched when she was in a bad place. She realized she hadn't sketched in a while. Maybe if she had, she would be in a better place. Maybe her mind wouldn't have played tricks on her yesterday. Maybe she wouldn't have thought she saw Holcomb Newson. It was just her imagination, that's all.

Monica pulled Melanie out of her thoughts, drawing the attention back to her. "Miss Melanie, I got to see my mom while we were away."

"You did?"

"Yep, I did. The mean man wasn't with her. I was so glad about that." Melanie listened as Monica shared with her. This was the first time ever that Monica spoke about her mother or stepfather. She generally spoke with her art, drawing pictures that depicted the turbulent life she'd led so far. In her four years, she'd been horribly abused by her stepfather resulting is his being sent to jail for child abuse. Her mother was a drug addict and was in rehab. Monica was in foster care waiting for the day she could return to her mother. Melanie didn't know if that day would ever happen, but what she did know was she would be by Monica's side, be her advocate until a decision was made on her behalf. If it were up to Melanie, Monica would never return to her mother's care. She'd be adopted by a loving family.

Melanie got more than she thought out of the art therapy session. She felt in charge again. She'd sketched the Golden Gate Bridge. Those were happy memories for her. Ones she needed to hold close in the coming weeks as the decision about her career was just around the corner.

She hadn't even thought about a resume. It was the farthest thing from her mind. She told herself if she rewrote her resume it would jinx her chances of staying with the bank. She would do her best to remain positive and hope for the best, although she wasn't too sure how James perceived her. He'd not only seen her at her best but also her worst.

Chapter Sixteen

MELANIE WOKE LATER THAN NORMAL Wednesday morning. She didn't feel well. She had a sore throat, earache, and when she checked her temperature, discovered it was slightly elevated. She'd slept well, but felt like she hadn't slept a wink. She was barely able to drag herself out of bed, grab aspirin, and something cool to drink before heading back to bed for a few moments. She wanted to call in sick but knew she couldn't. She had too much to do. She had a meeting scheduled with her staff at ten. There was something else on the agenda but for the life of her couldn't remember what it was.

Melanie dozed off only to be awakened by the ringing of her cell phone. She could barely speak. "Hello," she said, her voice gravelly.

"Mel, hey it's James. I tried calling you at the office and just kept getting your voicemail. Are you in?"

"No, I'm home right now. I had something come up." *That's a good excuse.* "I'll be in shortly, why?"

James went through a list of tasks that needed to be completed as soon as possible. Groaning, she told him she'd meet him at one for the meeting he'd scheduled on the fly. Melanie dressed and made her way into the office. She felt worse by the minute but couldn't let that stop her from getting done what she needed to accomplish for the day.

Melanie somehow made it through her first meeting and out of the blue, the meeting James scheduled was canceled. She was more than happy when she made her way towards her car. It was three and Melanie was leaving the office before seven for the first time in a long time, except for the days when she had her art therapy classes. Generally, on those days, she left at five.

Melanie went home and changed into her comfy lounge pants and a t-shirt. She'd gotten a second wind and was feeling a little better when her doorbell rang. She wasn't expecting anyone and glanced through the side-window. *James. Why is he here?*

Melanie pulled open the door and greeted him Leaning against the frame, he said, "I went by the office and you were gone. I ran into one of your co-workers who said you weren't feeling well. Is that true?"

Melanie stepped away from the door allowing his entrance. She led him into her family room, grabbed a blanket and sat down, covering herself in the process. "Yeah, that's true."

"Then why were you in the office today? You should have told me when I spoke with you earlier. Mel, it's not going to do any of us any good if you get sick."

She swallowed with difficulty and cleared her throat. "I know but I had so much to do. With the sale and all—"

"The sale's pretty much in the bag. We just have a few, no, more than a few, tasks that need completing, but we've got it. You need to take care of yourself. Have you eaten?"

Melanie shook her head. He jumped from the couch, exiting the room. The front door opened and he returned within seconds holding a bag from Schulers. "What's that?"

"This is what you call dinner." James pulled items from the bag. "I've got us some chicken soup," he said pointing to the container. "Sandwiches and even brownies," he added, raising the dessert from the bag. "Now, point me to your pots and pans and I'll have this warmed up in a jiffy."

"James, you don't have to do this."

"I want to. Plus, I'm saving you from the wrath of Jackie. If my mom knew you were sick, she'd be over here in a heartbeat. So, you either have me or her."

Melanie smirked. "I'd rather have you." She led him into her kitchen and deposited herself at the table while James warmed their meal. As he moved about her kitchen, she realized this was the first time she'd ever had a man cook for her, albeit just to warm food. She felt warm inside, like someone could really care for her aside from her sister.

Janet and she had a rough childhood; in fact, they'd lost touch for several years before finding one another again. Melanie was only six at the time they were separated in foster care and had no way of finding her sister. She'd never been exposed to love and really didn't believe it existed. Yes, she'd seen it with her friends but she was damaged and had no room to ever love, or commit to having a family.

Melanie was in her own world and didn't hear James until he placed his hand on her arm. "You doing okay?"

She smiled. "I am, and thanks for doing this. I was sitting here thinking that I've never had a man cook for me."

"Never?"

"Nope, never."

"Well, then I feel honored, although I don't really call this cooking." He flashed her a swoon-worthy smile.

"It is to me." Melanie needed to speak with Jackie. She wanted to tell her that she'd raised a kind, caring, and overall wonderful son. She'd forgotten to tell her the last time they were together; she definitely wouldn't forget the next time.

James carefully poured her soup into a bowl and then added her sandwich. "I hope roast beef is okay with you. That's all they had."

"It's perfect. I can't believe you did this for me. I've never had someone show me such kindness, outside of Janet that is. It means a lot." Melanie slid her spoon into her soup catching a noodle in the process. "Your mom should be proud of you."

"Why's that?"

"Because you're kind and caring." She paused. "I hope you've forgiven me for San Antonio. I wasn't the nicest person back then. I said some awful things to you, and honestly, I'm ashamed by my behavior. I sincerely apologize that it's taken me this long to tell you."

"You thought you had a room to yourself and then you wake to a stranger in bed with you. You were scared—that's what I chalk it up to." He rested his hand atop hers. Her voice was waning and she didn't feel up to dragging up those emotions. Melanie knew they had to further discuss that time in their lives, but she guessed now wasn't the time. They were growing closer but nothing could come of it. "James, I want you to know that I really like you, as a friend, but nothing more. I have no plans of ever entering into a serious relationship." And there she said it.

"What are you talking about?" A puzzled look crossed his face.

"Well, I thought with your kindness and all you were expecting more, especially after our kiss."

"That kiss, it was just as a friend…" He squinted and ran his hand along his jaw.

"I get it." She tipped her head. "I guess I misread it. Anyway, let's put it aside. We have to concentrate on the sale and thereafter."

James cleaned up after dinner, rinsing the dishes, and placing them into the dishwasher.

"I'm going to head on out and let you get some rest. Call if you need anything." He started to lean in and place a kiss on her cheek, but stopped himself. "I'll call you tomorrow, and, Mel, if you're not feeling better, stay home. You're only hurting yourself."

Melanie stood and walked him to the door. "Thanks, James. Thank you for everything." She rested her hand on his forearm. "You're a good friend." With that, James walked out the door. Melanie stood watching as he got into his car and started to back out the driveway. She waved as he headed off down the street.

Melanie was lucky to have James as a friend. If she were any other woman, she'd be hoping for a long-term relationship. But she wasn't. She was Melanie Holmes. Damaged to the core. And when she added her mother and Holcomb Newson into the mix, she became the person she was this very moment—lonely, unforgiving, and irreparably marred.

Melanie woke feeling much better. She made it into work at her usual hour and her day flew by. She was just getting ready to leave for the night when she heard a knock on her office door and looked up. James stood before her. It was almost five and she couldn't be delayed as it was Thursday and she needed to be at the Y.

James sauntered into her office and sat in the chair across from her desk. He looked like he planned on staying awhile.

"What's up?"

"I was going to ask you the same thing, but first how are you feeling?"

"Better, much better."

"I'm glad to hear that. So, what are you working on?"

"I'm just finishing up the mapping of the data to board the loans from Dalton B&T. We're on schedule to make this happen. I have to say, Parklayne moved a little slower with its acquisitions. I can't believe we're going to board these loans in just a few short weeks. That's a record."

"We do work pretty fast here, but this was a relatively clean portfolio with the exception of the escrow issues, but that's nothing new. What's on the agenda for you this evening?"

She glanced at her watch. "I've got to be out of here in fifteen minutes. I have somewhere I need to be. Why?"

"I was going to ask you to dinner. I've got nothing going myself and thought I'd ask."

"I'll take a raincheck, if that's okay, but James, I really need to get going." She reached for her briefcase. James stood. "I'll talk to you tomorrow, then."

"Yep, tomorrow." James walked out of her office, not looking back. She had been short with him but she needed to get to the Y.

Melanie had just walked into her house when her

phone rang. She answered without looking at the caller id. It was Jackie. "Melanie, dear, how are you feeling? James told me you weren't feeling well."

"I wasn't, but I'm much better today."

"Glad to hear…I know you told me you had plans with Janet this weekend, so I was wondering if you were available next week for our next lesson. Wyatt has another hockey clinic, this time out of state, and I'm going to be all alone again. I hate it when that happens. Before I know it, Ben and I will be the only ones living here. The kids will have all left the nest."

"I think that'll work. Can I call you early in the week? I'm heading out the door."

"That's fine, dear."

Melanie hurried to change her clothes and left. The parking lot seemed pretty empty as she pulled up at the Y. Madeleine greeted her at the door.

"Melanie, I'm sorry I didn't get a chance to phone you but we had a little incident and the automatic sprinklers went off flooding the facility."

"What happened? Is everyone alright?"

"We're fine. Just a little misunderstanding about this being a non-smoking facility. One of our older clients came in and lit up a cigarette. The smoke detectors sensed it and the next thing we knew the fire alarms were ringing and the sprinklers were going off."

Disappointment resonated in her voice. "You think they would have known better."

"Yeah, unfortunately, it was one of our clients that has a bit of dementia and thought they were at home. All is good, but we have a lot of clean-up. I'm hoping we can get back up and running in the next few days. I promise I'll phone you."

Melanie needed to paint tonight; she just did. So she went home and pulled out her paints and a canvas. Before she knew it, she'd painted a landscape of the Golden Gate Bridge. It was her safe haven right now. She was at peace and needed to stay that way.

Just as she finished cleaning-up, her sister called. "I can't wait for this weekend," she told Janet. "I've been looking forward to the Apple Butter Festival all week long."

"That's why I'm calling… I'm sorry to ruin it for you, but I can't go. I tripped while on a field trip today and sprained my ankle."

"Oh no. Is there anything I can do? Are you in much pain?"

"The pain is manageable. The doctor said I needed to keep it elevated and stay off it. I really wanted to go. I look forward to this every year. I just love the apple butter."

"I know you do. Do you want me to go and pick you up some? I can."

"I'd hate to trouble you. I'll make do without." She wished her sister well and without another thought dialed the one and only person she'd ask to attend with her.

Melanie wasn't the least bit surprised that Jackie answered her call so quickly. Melanie didn't think the phone rang even once on her end. "Melanie, hello dear. How are you?"

"I'm doing well. I was wondering what you were doing this Saturday."

"Well, nothing, why?"

"I was supposed to attend the Apple Butter Festival in Kimmswick this weekend, but my sister sprained her ankle and can't go. She loves apple butter and I thought I'd go and pick her up some. Are you interested in going with me?"

"I'd love to go. What time shall I pick you up?"

"I asked you to go, so I'd like to drive, if that's okay with you." Melanie wanted to do things right, please her, gain her approval even more than she already had it.

"That's fine, honey. Oh, I can't wait to tell the girls. They always attend but with both of them pregnant and with Kelly's recent scare neither Alec nor Alejandro are letting them step too far from home."

"It sounds like a date. Would you like to go to breakfast beforehand and fortify ourselves?"

"That's a fabulous idea."

"Is seven too early for you? We can stop at one of the restaurants along the way. We need to get there early, so we can get a decent parking place. Those fields they use as parking lots fill up so quickly and I'd hate to have to take a shuttle in."

"I know. The last time I did that I was on a school bus. And honestly, I don't know how the kids ride them. The seats are so close together. I barely had room to scrunch my legs into the seat. Melanie, you made my day. Thank you for thinking of me."

Melanie felt good about inviting Jackie to go. She was looking forward to Saturday.

Friday seemed to drag on. She found herself looking at the clock more than anything and when five o'clock rolled around she bolted for the door. Normally, she stayed till seven on Fridays and often times worked a full day on Saturday, but not this weekend. She had plans and she was going to enjoy every minute.

She stopped by Schulers to pick up something quick

for dinner and ran into Gabriella. "Oh hi, Gabby," Melanie said approaching the counter. "Fancy meeting you here."

"I guess great minds think alike, huh?" Gabby grinned. "It's been a loooong week and I didn't feel like cooking. Ashton's been on call all week, so I thought I'd do something quick and easy. What about you?"

"Same here. I feel like this year has dragged on. With the impending sale of Parklayne to Amcrost, I've been working nonstop. I decided to take the weekend off for a change, and I invited Jackie to go to the Apple Butter Festival. Janet injured her ankle."

"Yeah, I know. I guess it happened on her field trip."

"That's what she said."

"Did you just say that you're going with Jackie? That's surprising."

"Yes and no. Did you know she's been giving me cooking lessons?"

"I heard about that through Angelina. But with Jackie, really?"

"You know, Gabby, she's really not that bad. Yes, she loves her children, but through this I've found someone that I really like. She is caring and thoughtful. Even though she did try and set James and me up… I put her in her place and she's been fine with that since. She wants her children to be happy, and she'll do anything that a mother would do to see that. Enough of me, how's Kelly? I haven't had a chance to catch up with her. In fact, I was ill earlier this week."

"I'm sorry to hear that. I hope you're feeling better."

"I am thank-you.'

"In regards to Kelly, I just got off the phone with Alec. She absolutely hates being confined to the house, but in the end, she knows its best. In fact, that's one of the reasons why I am here. I'm taking them dinner. Alec hasn't had time to shop and he's been working pretty late every day. Jackie and Maria have been taking turns staying with her, supplying them with meals, but I thought I'd give them relief and drop off dinner. Something simple like chicken pot pie. It's quick and easy for them to warm up in the oven."

"That's what I'm getting too. It just sounds good for a change."

Melanie said her goodbyes to Gabriella and picked-up a few additional groceries before heading home. She was more than excited for her outing the next day.

Saturday morning dawned with the most beautiful sunrise Melanie had seen in quite some time. Generally, she was up early to take in the view and today's was extra special. Melanie believed it was the omen of a good day to come.

On the way out the door, Melanie grabbed her go to bag for festivals and craft fairs. It was reinforced and held a lot. She never knew what she'd purchase. Outside of apple butter, she hoped to find a new fall display for her front door.

She hopped into the car and pulled into the Samuels' driveway promptly at seven. Before she could get out of the car, Jackie was bounding out of the house with Ben alongside. "Morning, Melanie," Jackie called out as she opened her car door. Ben stood at the driver side of the car. Melanie rolled down her window.

"Good morning, Ben."

"Melanie," he said. "I hope you're ready for hurricane Jackie, at least that's what I like to call her. Just prepare yourself because she will want to see every single exhibitor there whether it's a crafter or used car salesman."

"Now Ben, that's not true." Jackie caught her husband's eye. "Well I guess he's right. I do love a craft festival."

"Enjoy your day, and, Melanie, plan on staying for dinner. Jackie already has something cooking in the crock pot. I'm not sure what it is but I know it will be wonderful."

"Ready to go, dear," Jackie said to Melanie as she waved goodbye to her husband. "Be sure and check on Kelly today."

"You worry too much. I already told you I will. Have fun and don't drive Melanie crazy."

"Never," was Jackie's response as Melanie put the car into reverse and headed down the driveway.

Chapter Seventeen

MELANIE AND JACKIE ENJOYED A scrumptious breakfast eating in less than forty-five minutes so they could get right back on the road.

As Melanie drove down the highway listening to Jackie ramble, she realized this is what her life should have been like. Sitting side-by-side in the car with her mother going to festivals, movies, or even shopping. Melanie became a little despondent as Jackie went on and on about her children, grandchildren, and what she missed now that all her children were practically grown. Wyatt was the only one living at home, Colleen was in college. Angelina and Kelly were married with families while James was languishing with presently no one in his life.

As she'd grown up, Melanie had compiled a list of the characteristics she would have loved to see in her mother and her foster mothers. Her own mother was a wasted cause, but Melanie had found some redeeming qualities in a few of the families she'd lived amongst.

She'd had learned a lot from two particular foster moms: Althea Monsook and Karen Jaynes were the only two that had treated her as one of the family. Althea loved to cook but Melanie had been so young at the time, just seven, and she didn't have the chance to pick up her skills before being transferred. Althea loved to bake and she made the best sugar cookies. Unfortunately, her husband had been killed and she had to quit being a foster parent.

Then there was Karen Jaynes. Melanie lived with her when she was ten. Karen loved to do arts and crafts and Melanie owed her love of painting to Karen. Melanie lived with her the longest— almost a year; then, the Jaynes' started having financial problems and couldn't afford to care for Melanie, so she was placed back into the system.

There were more than enough subpar families that took her in. One of them was Holcomb Newson and his wife June. She did everything to get out of their house. At the age of fourteen, Melanie had even run away. In time, Social Services discovered what was truly going on in the household and removed her. She would never forget what he did to her. He was partly responsible for her panic attacks.

Holcomb had abused her. When she didn't respond quickly enough to his questions, he'd grab her by the arm and throw her down making her promise to listen. Several times, he'd slammed her into the wall. She ended up in the ER one too many times. The last, after one of his rages, required stitches to her forehead. She was pulled from their clutches and never returned to the home.

Melanie didn't even want to think about her own mother and what she did to her that caused her to enter foster care. Melanie just listened as Jackie went on about a scholarship Wyatt had just been offered for hockey. She was filled with joy as she recounted all of his accomplishments.

Melanie needed a mother like Jackie. Someone whom she could go to and share her hopes and dreams with. Someone who would help her put her past behind her. Someone that would aide her with moving on. All the wishing would never bring back the kind, loving mother she knew before things went bad or fix her childhood. She'd have to move forward and hope to continue to forge her relationship with Jackie. She was a role model that Melanie definitely needed in her life.

They arrived on the festival grounds just before nine and were able to park in a prime location. "Good job, Melanie. Fantastic parking spot. This is perfect in case we need to bring some of our larger purchases to the car."

"Are you planning on buying a lot?"

She winked and smiled. "You never know."

Their first purchase was apple butter. Melanie wanted to be sure and buy some before they ran out. Even though Janet had told her she could do without, she wanted to surprise her since she wasn't able to attend.

They walked the grounds, checking out the various fall and holiday crafters. Jackie paused at one booth that sold lighted displays she could put on her front porch. She circled the display, taking her time choosing the perfect one. "Melanie, which do you think?"

"I like the one with the pumpkins, gourds, and the stuffed Pilgrims and Indians. That would look really nice on the front porch."

"Well that's it, then. I'll take this one." She pointed to the crafter to unplug the display she'd chosen. "This qualifies as a return to the car, don't you think?"

"I do. I can't see you lugging it around the rest of the

day." Jackie paid for the display and they returned to the car to drop off all of their purchases and start out again.

Four hours later they returned to the car. Dropping her bag into the trunk alongside Jackie's display, she turned and looked around. "This was the perfect day. Thank you for coming with me."

"Anytime, dear. I enjoyed being here with you. I wish the girls could have come too, but at least I picked up a few things for them. I think they'll be happy."

"I'm sure they will."

Jackie had purchased Kelly and Angelina Christmas ornaments that read "Baby's first Christmas." They were uniquely quilted and embroidered. It was timeless, something she knew they'd both enjoy.

"I have to say, I'm tired. What about you, Melanie?"

"A little. It felt great being outdoors and enjoying this fantastic fall weather. I sure hope I sleep well."

"Do you have problems sleeping?"

Melanie had said too much. "I have to admit I do sometimes." She quickly came up with an excuse. "You know when your mind just won't stop spinning, well that's me. I'm always planning out my day, making sure I get everything I need to done."

"Honey, you need to relax. You do what you can and what doesn't get accomplished will be there the next day."

"I know, but it's easier said than done." Melanie needed to get over her hellacious dreams but doubted she ever would since many of the memories had been with her almost her entire life.

Before they knew it, they'd arrived back at Jackie's. Melanie popped her trunk and grabbed Jackie's display while she gathered the remainder of her things.

"You are staying for dinner."

"I appreciate the offer but—"

"Not buts here. You are staying. You said so yourself today that you wanted to have fun and relax. I've got plenty and as you already know dinner should be about ready. We really have nothing to do but set the table and make a salad. We'd love for you to stay."

"I thought you were planning on staying." Melanie turned around at the male voice. James. "Did you two have a good time? You must have by the looks of your purchases." He pointed to his mother's bags. "I saw Dad over at Kelly's and he said to come over for dinner. I hope that's okay, Mom."

"It's perfect. Would you mind taking this inside while I convince my driver to stay too?"

Melanie stood with her hands at her side while Jackie placed her hands together pleading her to stay. She knew Jackie would begin begging and already knew she'd say yes. "Now, Melanie. I'd planned for you to stay. I love it when you join us. It's like I have another daughter that I can share things my own daughters don't particularly like. So please, end your day amongst friends."

Melanie knew her answer before listening to Jackie. She enjoyed being in her company and for the first time didn't want to go home to a quiet empty house. "I'll stay."

"Wonderful," She clapped and reached for the crook of Melanie's arm. She escorted her into the house in the event she decided to change her mind. Melanie crossed into the kitchen to the most delicious smelling aromas. "Dinner smells like it's coming right along. It won't be ready for a couple of hours yet, so let's sit down and take a load off our feet. Mine are killing me.

Are yours too?"

"They are a little tired."

"Well, then, kick off your shoes and make yourself at home. James, can you get us both an iced tea?"

"Sure, Mom," he said with a lop-sided grin.

"And while you're at it, pull out that cheese tray I have in the refrigerator and grab the crackers. I'm starved."

In just those few minutes, Melanie felt like a member of the Samuels' family. Jackie was so endearing, making her feel right at home. Melanie enjoyed not only their snack but also their dinner. Jackie served noodles with the pot roast, a tossed salad, and brownie sundaes for dessert.

"Oh my, am I full," Melanie said, patting her stomach. "That was fabulous, Jackie, and so easy to make. I think I could even make that."

"Of course, you can, dear. Easy-peasey."

Melanie and James cleaned up the kitchen while Jackie looked on. "You know you don't have to do that. I could just as easily do the dishes."

"You invited me and it's the least we could both do." She wagged a finger between her and James. "He's a third wheel too."

"Yes, he is as I hadn't counted on him. I knew Wyatt was going to be at a friend's house. Changing subjects, how was Kelly?"

"She's antsy." Grinning, James said, "Wants to get out of the house. In fact, she tried to escape, as Alec terms it."

"She did?"

"Yep, but Alec came home from work and surprised her just as she was grabbing her car keys. According to her, he scared her to death. She was surprised she didn't go into labor right then and there." He chuckled.

"She sees the doctor this week. Maybe they'll lift her restrictions and let her go, at least for a drive. I know it's difficult being confined to the house. I don't know how she's doing it."

And neither did Melanie. She hated being confined. She disliked elevators with a passion and every time she rode one prayed that she wouldn't get stuck. She didn't know what would happen if she ever did.

Melanie was tired but also wanted to check in with her sister. "I hate to leave such good company, but I need to head on out. I'd like to stop by Janet's and see how she's doing."

"Yes, of course. Please send her our prayers for a speedy recovery."

"I will. Are you up for another craft fair?"

"Anytime, dear, anytime. I just love them."

Melanie stood and pulled Jackie into a hug. "Thank you for going. I had the best time."

"I did as well. Now what about our cooking lesson next week? Is Sunday good for you?"

"It certainly is. I'll see you then." Melanie started out the door.

"Noon?"

"It's a date." Melanie opened the door only to discover that James was right alongside her. "I think I can make it to my car."

"I know you can. I'm just trying to be a gentleman."

"That's one thing I can say about you, James… You are definitely a man someone could fall in love with." Melanie clasped her hand over her mouth. She didn't know where that thought came from and she definitely couldn't take it back.

"That's nice of you to say, Mel. My mother would love to hear that coming from you."

"I'm sure she would." Melanie hopped into her car, waving goodbye to James as she backed out of the driveway. She'd stuck her foot in her mouth, but she knew that what she said wouldn't hold true for her.

James went back inside. He finally decided to talk to his dad about Melanie. He felt it was only right for the bank to perform a background check on her if she was going to be offered an officer's position for the bank. "Dad, do you have a moment?

"Sure, son, what is it?"

"In private please." His mother gave him the once over. "Mom, don't get upset, I need to speak to dad about an issue with the bank."

James followed his father to his home office where he closed the door behind him. "Dad, I didn't want Mom to overhear what I have to say."

Ben sat on the corner of his desk. "Okay, son, what is it?"

"I want you to know that I have the bank's best interest at heart."

"I realize that." Ben clasped his hands together.

"I think, if you plan on hiring Melanie, you should perform a background check." James caught the surprised look that crossed his father's face. "I think there's something not quite copasetic with her. I've seen her in many situations over the years. How she's acting today is not what I've seen in the past. She's the complete opposite. I just want to set my mind at ease that there's nothing in her background that could come back to haunt us."

Ben seemed concerned and stood. "What aren't you sure of?'

James detailed the numerous outbursts that he'd witnessed while performing due diligences. "From what I've seen, she has a short fuse. I just think we should check her out—that's all. It's not like you haven't run background checks before."

"I realize that and I have. I was planning on offering her a job within the bank. Where? I'm not sure yet. She does have glowing reviews from Saxson, but if you think we should, then I will."

"Good. I'm glad you agree. I think you should use Jonas Sounds."

"Sounds? Why him and not the firm we currently use?"

"I just do. Look what he discovered when Alec used him to uncover Ken Jones. Don't forget, he also found Ashton's half-brother, Duncan. It took him some time, but he did."

"If you think he's the man then I'll phone Alec and get his number. I hope you're onto something because I'd hate for her to discover that we're looking into her background."

"I know there's something there and I wouldn't feel right vetting her for a job at Amcrost if we didn't look into it. I'm concerned about her. I hope I'm wrong, but I don't think I am. Don't get me wrong—she's done an amazing job with the sale and these acquisitions. I enjoy working with her but I think you should dig a little deeper before making an offer."

"All right then. I'll take your suggestion."

James stood alongside his father while he phoned

Alec. "Jonas is a one-of-a-kind private investigator. If there's something to find, he will. It may take him some time, but his efforts are well worth it."

Ben secured Jonas' number and phoned him. James thought he'd have to leave a message but was more than surprised when Jonas answered. "Jonas, this is Ben Samuels, I'm Alec's father-in-law. I'm placing you on speaker. My son, James, is beside me."

"Oh hi, James. How's Kelly?"

"She's doing as well as can be expected after experiencing premature labor. Thankfully, the doctors were able to stop it and she's on bedrest."

"And driving Alec bonkers?"

"How did you know? Anyway…The reason for my call. I'd like you to investigate a potential employee. Her name is Melanie Holmes and she currently works for Parklayne Bank. She's their VP of Acquisitions."

"Are you looking for anything in particular?"

"Whatever you can find— if anything. She's received stellar reviews but I need to know if there's something in her background that would interfere with her holding an officer's position in the bank. I know of nothing but just thought I'd be safe rather than sorry."

"I understand. If you could send me all the pertinent information that will assist me, that would be great."

"I appreciate it, Jonas. I want to reinforce that I'm not aware of anything, but just thought we'd check it out."

"I totally understand. I'll get started right away."

James wasn't sure he believed in questioning her background but he wanted to know what fueled her change of behavior.

"Thanks, Dad. I hope he finds nothing because I think she can add a lot to Amcrost in whatever capacity you assign her." James and his father discussed the sale and the boarding of the new portfolio from Dalton B&T. It was getting late, so he decided to call it a night. "I guess I'll head on out. It's getting late."

"That it is, son. I hope by performing this background check we're not going to open a can of worms, because if we do, your mother will never forgive us. She's become quite fond of Melanie."

James didn't want to hurt either one of them, but he needed to stifle his own curiosity before he acted on his feelings. He was ever so slowly falling for her. He needed to be careful before he made his first move. He wasn't sure how accepting of him she'd be, but he'd try anyway.

Chapter Eighteen

MELANIE WENT STRAIGHT HOME, DECIDING to visit Janet the next day. Calling ahead to make sure Janet was home, she stopped by Laketown Bakery where she purchased a coffee cake. Her sister's eyes got big when she met her at the door and saw the box from the bakery.

"Tell me you didn't."

"Sorry, but I did. It's a butter crumb cake and it looks delicious."

"Follow me." Janet hobbled to the kitchen and plopped into a seat at the kitchen table. "This is about as far as I can go. You know where the dishes are—hurry, I'm starved."

Melanie placed the coffee cake down along with her bag full of goodies and grabbed plates and silverware.

"I just made that pot of coffee. Oh boy, will it go good with this cake." Melanie set the plates and silverware down and then poured them each a cup of coffee then grabbed the half-n-half. Janet watched the steam rise from the cup. "I thought my coffee pot was going out, but look at that steam. I guess it was just having a bad day." She took a sip. "This is hot for a change. I'm glad I didn't buy a new pot yet." Janet picked up the knife and sliced into the cake. "This looks and smells like seventh heaven. You know you shouldn't have done this. I'm watching my diet."

"Aren't we all," Melanie chimed in and reached for her slice.

Janet took a bite and closed her eyes as she swallowed. "I'm going to have to be extra careful this week. I think I'll gain five pounds just eating this one bite."

Out of nowhere, Melanie stopped and dropped her fork to her plate. "I almost forgot." She rummaged around in her bag then pulled out several jars of apple butter. "Here you go, sis. Since you couldn't join me yesterday..."

"You went."

"Yep. I took Jackie Samuels with me. I really enjoyed myself."

"Every time I've been in her company, I've always thought she was super nice."

"She is. In fact, I think I forgot to tell you but she's teaching me how to cook."

"Really now?"

"Yeah. I've learned quite a few things from her—unlike from our own mother." Melanie stopped and thought for a second. "She's the type of person you'd want for a mother. I am so comfortable around her. I kind of wish she could have been our mom."

"Melanie, let's not go there, okay. She can't be. We had what we had. We both know she wasn't the best of influences."

"The best? She was no influence. She was a nightmare from hell and never should have been allowed to be a mother. I just wish Dad would have lived. Maybe things would have been different."

"From what I remember, she was different when he was alive. She changed after his death. I'm sorry about that."

"Hey, it's not your problem. It was hers and hers alone. She didn't want us and it definitely showed— at least where I come from." Bygones should be just that, bygones, but from where Melanie stood, they weren't. She'd carry all that pain and anger the rest of her life.

Melanie shared with Janet all of the various crafters she saw. "I bought a few things but Jackie bought this huge display with pumpkins and stuffed Pilgrims and Indians that's lighted. She put it on her front porch. It looks really cute."

Melanie looked at her watch. "I hate to eat and run but I've got laundry and a little work to complete before school starts again tomorrow." Melanie always referred to work as school when she was around her sister, especially since Janet was a teacher.

"I'll check on you later in the week. You stay off that foot." She leaned over placing a kiss on her sister's cheek. "I can show myself out. Take care," she called out as she walked out the door, softly closing it behind her.

Melanie spent the remainder of her day doing tasks around the house. She went through a few reports, checked on her project tasks and was pleased with the status of the overall project plan. She made a quick dinner and for once in a long while sat down and watched a movie. At ten she went to bed only to be confronted with dreams.

Melanie clawed at the door. She couldn't get out. It was dark. So dark. Her mother cackled. Then, the silence. The deafening silence that went on forever.

Melanie's legs cramped from squatting on the floor. Her hands were clammy and her heart rate intensified. Her chest ached from its rapid pounding. She might never be able to escape the small closet. She whimpered, could barely breathe. Then, suddenly a bright light blinded her.

Melanie woke. Her dreams always ended with a bright light shining in her face. Her heart hammered against her chest, tears streamed down her face, her hands were shaking. She took several deep breaths before her breathing was back under control.

She wouldn't sleep the remainder of the night so she threw her legs over the side of her bed and slowly stood. Her balance was slightly off and she grabbed onto the wall. It took her a few seconds to steady herself before she headed to the family room where she turned on the television and channel surfed until it was time for her to get dressed for work. Melanie glanced at the clock, realizing she only had at best two hours of sleep. She ran her hand through her hair and sighed. It was going to be a long day.

James was on pins and needles when he went into the office, Monday. He didn't know how long it would take Jonas to complete Melanie's background check. James felt as though he should remain as close as he could in case she got wind of it.

He was busy the entire day and lost track of the time. He'd wanted to run by Parklayne before the close of business but decided he'd stop by the following day.

Early Tuesday morning, he went into work, much more at ease. He'd called Melanie but she'd been in a meeting. Another day flew by and before James realized, four o'clock was upon him. He grabbed his things and drove over to Parklayne to not only see Melanie, he also had a meeting with Saxson.

He'd pulled into the parking garage and almost ran into one of the pillars as a car came out of nowhere speeding down the ramp. The driver didn't notice him, but he noticed her. It was Melanie, racing out of the office like she had a place to go. As he walked inside, he realized she'd left the office early the last several Tuesdays and Thursdays. He wondered what that was about. Was she meeting someone? A therapist maybe? His thoughts were all over the place as he entered Saxson's office.

"James," Saxson called. "Come right in." They shook hands and Saxson led him to a small conference table in the corner of his large office. "How are things going with the transition? From what Melanie tells me, we're right on schedule for the sale to be completed."

"That's right. In fact, I was coming over to see her and she almost ran me over in the garage."

"Oh really? That's so unlike her. She's normally here late every night, going home well after I do."

"That's what I thought too, but I also noticed that she's been leaving early on Tuesday's and Thursday's."

"What do you call early?"

"Around five."

"That's her normal quitting time, so I wouldn't make anything over it." James thought the same but his gut told him something else. He knew she was nervous about the sale and worried about her job. If she were so worried, in his estimation, she wouldn't be leaving early— she'd be working late. James thought about it and decided to see if she left early on Thursday. If she did, he'd follow her and see exactly where she was headed.

Melanie was fixed on making it home and to the Y. After her nightmare early that morning, she'd been unsettled all day— barely able to concentrate. *I need my outlet tonight. That's for sure.*

Lately it seemed as though she was barely making it home, changing, and arriving at the Y before the session began. Tonight, she was late and hated the thought of interrupting everyone as she entered the room.

She wasn't feeling quite herself and noticed Jared seemed off as well. He was more withdrawn than normal. Madeleine was trying to get him to use his crayons to draw what he was feeling. He gripped the crayons with such intensity that one snapped in his little fingers. She could tell by the way he held his jaw that he was doing his best to get his feelings down but they just wouldn't come. She decided to let Madeleine handle him while she helped out Monica.

Monica had taken out the paints and was painting a picture of stick people. "This is Mommy, me, and Daddy." Melanie wondered where "Daddy" came from as she thought he was out of the picture. Then she realized Monica was reliving the past when things were half-way right in her family. Her heart went out to the little girl because she, herself, didn't know what a good family was all about.

Melanie wanted to draw so she pulled out a sketch pad and sat next to Monica. Melanie chose to draw from memory riding the cable cars in San Francisco and the area where they got off. She sketched it in charcoal, adding two people. The couple was holding hands as they looked across the bay. This was her happy time and she needed it to help her overcome the memories from the night before.

Melanie helped Madeleine clean up after Jared and Monica left for the evening. "Jared looked like he was having a difficult day."

"He was. From what I gather, his father tried to contact him and it didn't go well at all. It brought back all of the bad memories and emotions he is trying to overcome. Hopefully, things will be better Thursday. He was making such great strides and today I feel like he's regressed to where he was when he entered the program."

Melanie grabbed her sketch pad and headed on home. Her heart hurt for Jared and what he must be enduring. She'd been there herself and knew what it felt like to be out of control and not able to share with anyone what was troubling her. That's when she really discovered her art. She could draw. Put her feelings onto paper. It helped her overcome so much as a child and still helped her today. When Melanie felt out of sorts, she painted or sketched and seemed so much better.

She did her best to put Tuesday's incidence with Jared behind her when she went into work the next day but wasn't able to. She had flashes of watching him drawing the scene and then remembered seeing the crayon snap in his little hands. She wished she could do something— anything to lessen his pain. In her own world she didn't realize James was in her office until he stepped into her line of vision and she practically jumped out of her chair.

"Ah James, hi there. You scared me to death. Why didn't you knock or let me know you were here?"

"I did. I knocked, called your name, and when you didn't respond I came right in. Is everything alright?"

"Yeah, why would you think it wasn't?"

"Because you were sitting here staring at nothing…"

Melanie wasn't going to share with him where her thoughts had been. "So, what brings you here?"

"I thought I'd take you to lunch. I was in the neighborhood. In fact, I came by last night to see you, and you practically ran into me when I drove into the garage."

"Really? I didn't see you."

"Wherever you were headed you were definitely in a hurry."

"Sorry about that. Lunch. Let's see." Melanie checked her calendar. "Yep, I can go. I'm free the rest of the day. No meetings, thank God. I'm getting tired of spending the majority of my days sitting listening to others ramble when I should be here in my office getting things done."

"I hear you, but sometimes meetings are necessary. So where would you like to go? My calendar's free as well for the remainder of the day."

"You know what sounds good…Imperial House. I have a taste for Chinese."

"Sounds like a plan. Grab your things and let's go. I'm hungry."

"Isn't it a little early for lunch?"

"Live a little, Mel. We'll find something to do along the way." Melanie grabbed her purse and coat. James placed his hand on her lower back and escorted her to the elevators. "Maybe we can play hooky the rest of the day."

"There's so much to do."

"And it will be here tomorrow too."

They were greeted by Debbie Yan at the doors of Imperial House. She looked back and forth between the two. "James, Melanie, it's great seeing you again. Same table?" Melanie looked at James as he nodded his head.

"Yep, I think that's going to be my new table of choice."

Debbie seated them. "I'll be your server today and Yan's your chef. Would you like a pot of tea?"

"I'd love it," Melanie said. "Can you bring us both a cup of hot and sour soup? James says he's starving."

"I will. Would you also like egg rolls and crab Rangoon too?" Melanie looked at James who smiled broadly at her. "That too, but you can start with the soup."

Debbie returned with their pot of tea and cups of soup. "Have you decided on an entrée?"

Melanie ordered lemon chicken while James ordered boneless hot braised chicken. "That's sounds good," claimed Melanie. "I haven't had that in forever."

"We'll share then." They started in on their soup. "So, where were you off to last night? I thought you were headed to put out a fire."

"I'm sorry about that. Honestly, I didn't see you." She wanted to change the subject and not tell him about her art therapy session. "I'm cooking again with your mom this weekend."

"That's becoming a regular event."

"It is and I really enjoy it." *Good, I got him off where I was going.* They took their time eating their lunch. Melanie looked at her watch. "It's almost two. I've got to get back to the office."

"Like I said, live a little, Mel. We'll call this a working lunch."

"But, James—"

"Not buts. Let's see what our fortunes say this time. The last time we were here they made no sense."

"Are they supposed to?"

"I see your point. I guess not."

Melanie cracked open her cookie, pulling out her fortune. As she read it, she scrunched her face.

"Is something wrong?"

"We thought the last fortunes were odd, this one's really out there. It reads 'Be careful of those around you. Trust no one as they're not who you think they are.'"

"That is strange. Let me read mine." He pulled his from the side of his cookie. "Take one day at a time. There's light at the end of the tunnel..." He threw his down onto the table. "Who writes these, anyway?"

He reached for the bill. "Ready?"

"I am." James headed off to pay the bill while Melanie grabbed up their fortunes. She kept all of hers, marking the date on each slip of paper. "Maybe these magic numbers will pay off someday." She joined James at the cashier and reached for his hand. Clasping it in hers, he looked down at her in surprise. She smiled at him as they headed for the car. She didn't know why she reached for his hand, but she did. *It feels right,* she reasoned as she got into his car.

"It's a beautiful day. Let's go to the park and take a walk. Get some fresh air." She surprised him when she nodded in agreement.

"Why not since the day's just about over."

James drove to a nearby park. As he helped her from

the car, he reached for her hand. Hand-in-hand they walked along the park trails. She felt him squeeze her hand and stop. She almost tripped but he caught her. "Sorry about that. But I want to ask you a question. You can say no and it won't hurt my feeling, but I need to do this. Will you go out with me? On a date, a real date?"

"James, we work together. We shouldn't."

"It happens all of the time." He reached for her face. Cupping her jaw, he looked her directly in the eyes. "Mel, I don't know if you feel it, but I do. I have feelings for you. Real feelings. I want to explore them, but only if you want to."

She looked away. How did she tell him? She didn't want to break his heart but she needed to be honest. "Yes, I have feelings for you, but I need to be honest. I can't let this go anywhere. I'll go out with you but I want you to know that I'm not looking for something serious— now or ever. If you're okay with that then fine, I'll go out with you. Otherwise, I'd have to say no. I don't want to hurt you."

James believed he could convince her otherwise but didn't want her to know that, so he agreed with her demands. "I understand. Anyway, it's too soon for me to get serious after breaking up with Elsa. I just want to have someone to go out with. Enjoy a nice meal, a movie. I guess that's what I'm really looking for."

"Okay then. You have a dinner partner."

He pulled her into a friendly hug and brushed a kiss on her cheek. "Thanks, Mel. You're just what I need." They continued walking along until he realized how late it was getting. "I'd better get you back to the office or everyone will think we're both missing in action."

Melanie chuckled. "We wouldn't want that, would we?"

"Certainly not."

He dropped her off just before four. She'd had a good day, better than she'd imagined when she woke up. She realized she needed him in her life. He made her laugh, smile and relax— and that's what she needed most of all to keep her panic attacks at bay.

Chapter Nineteen

JAMES BELIEVED HE COULD CHANGE Melanie's mind and convince her that they could be something more than just friends. *It'll just take some time.* She'd gotten under his skin. He sensed her issues and hoped someday she'd feel comfortable enough to share them. Whatever they were affected her deeply. He wanted to protect her and help her find her way. He knew his mom was beginning to break down some of her walls. If only he could too.

He stopped by his parents' house and visited with his mother. "So, what's new, Mom?"

"Nothing really. Melanie's coming over this weekend again." She turned to him and smiled brightly. "I so enjoy her. She's a breath of fresh air. She knows when to put me in my place, that's for sure. And you know what? It doesn't bother me in the least. It feels like she's becoming a daughter. I know it sounds crazy, but I feel like I've been put into her world for a reason. I don't know what it is yet but I'll figure it out. I watch her and she sometimes gets this faraway look in her eyes. It's almost like she's taking her experiences in for the first time. Hopefully, I'll be able to get her to open up a little more— tell me about her childhood." James nodded in agreement. "It's as if she's holding back a huge piece of herself. I know she has a heart but I think she's afraid of sharing it. It's almost like she's afraid of it breaking."

"I know what you mean, Mom. I see it too. When we've traveled, she's a completely different person. Nervous, agitated. What I do know is she's definitely afraid of flying and seems to almost be claustrophobic at times. I'm trying to get to know her. Can you keep a secret from her?" Jackie nodded. "I asked her out on a date." Jackie's eyes grew big. "Don't get your hopes up, because she told me she's not into relationships. I'm hoping that in time I'll be able to break down her walls." He shrugged. "If not, then we'll just be good friends. But I am definitely going to try. I know it's too soon after my break-up with Elsa to go into a relationship, but there's just something about her. She seems so lost at times, but I'm going to work on that with her. Maybe in time, who knows?"

"I see the same in her. I'm afraid something happened to her when she was growing up. I know she and Janet seem to be close, but I don't know. I can't put my finger on it but I just feel like…"

Wyatt entered the room. "Hey James, how's it going?"

"Good, Wyatt. I heard about your latest scholarship. That's, wow, is all I can say. You're going to have a hard time deciding where to go to school."

James was excited for his brother. He was a hockey phenom. While Wyatt discussed his next hockey clinic, James recounted his mother's earlier conversation concerning Mel. His eyes opened even further. At least he wasn't imagining his concerns for her.

Melanie left work a little earlier than usual for a Thursday. She wanted to make sure she got to the Y before any of the children arrived. She was still worried about Jared and hoped she'd find him in a better frame of mind.

Art therapy had aided Melanie through the rough times. She used art then and now as a way to express herself. As she got older, it was the coping skills she learned when she was a child that strengthened her and helped her through the dark days, allowing her to deal with life's various challenges. She hoped in time Jared would learn these skills too.

She wanted to work with kids like herself— those who were in the foster care system. Like Monica and Jared, many of them had behavioral and emotional needs that stemmed from being abandoned or neglected by their families. Some children had been impacted by domestic violence while others were in the system due to an illness or death.

Melanie aspired to do good and help these children heal and move on with their lives. Art for her gave her the freedom to help bring these emotions out and hopefully allowed the child to recognize them and begin the long process of healing. Through this process, she hoped the children learned to strengthen themselves and to develop coping skills that would allow them to lead a better life.

When Melanie pulled into her drive way, she noticed a car pull to the side of the street a few doors down. She quickly changed and hurried to the Y. She parked and as she ran into the building, she dropped her keys. When she stooped to pick them up, she thought the car that she'd seen earlier had pulled into the parking lot.

She grabbed her keys and went on her way deciding too many cars looked alike.

Melanie's happiness at seeing everyone came to screeching halt when she took one look at Jared. He had a scowl on his face and she immediately knew that he didn't want to be there. She eased her way over to the table where he sat with cups of paint. She presumed that Madeleine wanted to try another medium with him. On Tuesday, he'd broken almost every crayon he'd held. She hoped Madeleine hadn't made a wrong decision with the paints but instead of questioning her choice sat beside him.

When Melanie sat Jared reached for a paint brush. "So, Jared, what are you going to paint for us today?" Jared, who was usually talkative, uttered not a word. She smiled at him and flipped open her sketch pad to look at her last drawing. The cable cars. She wanted to draw him out. "Jared, what do you think of this?" He raised his shoulders. "Do you know what this is?" Again, no real response. "Have you heard of a cable car?"

"No," he finally whispered.

"Would you like me to tell you a little about them?"

"Sure."

"I was on a trip not too long ago. Have you heard of San Francisco?" He nodded. "Well, one of the ways to get around the city is by taking one of these cars. They have them because of the huge hills." Melanie gestured with her hands the size of some of the hills. "In the day of horse and carriages, it was difficult for the horses to go up these hills, so they invented these cars. You can ride on them seated or standing, holding onto these poles." Melanie gestured to the poles. "It was a lot of fun. My friend and I..."

"Is that him?" Jared indicated pointing to her picture where Melanie had sketched them walking along the wharf.

"Yeah. His name is James. We were there on business."

"Why were you holding his hand?" Melanie wasn't sure why he asked that and didn't know how to respond. "Are you married?"

"No, Jared I'm not."

"Why were you holding his hand?" The boy became more agitated. She didn't know what to do so she tried to refocus him onto his own painting. She pointed to his artwork and he let out a yell and flung his hand against the paint cups. The paint splattered all over Melanie and her sketch book. Before she could say anything, Madeleine had intervened, trying to calm him. Melanie took that as her signal to begin cleaning up the mess. She moved her sketch book aside and set the paint cups upright then, reached for some cleaning cloths. She had the mess cleaned up in no time. Madeleine had calmed Jared and he approached her.

"Melanie, I'm sorry I messed up your sketch book." In her urgency to clean-up the mess, she hadn't taken the time to look at her book.

"That's okay, Jared. I know it was just an accident." He moved onto another activity in the room and that's when Melanie took the time to look at herself. Paint was all over her clothes. She tried to wipe it off, only causing it to smear even more. She couldn't even begin to look at her book. Her heart and soul were in those sketches. She'd worry about that later.

The rest of the night passed in a blur. While the children were dismissed to their guardians, Melanie glanced through her sketch book. It was ruined. Her sketch of San Francisco brought tears to her eyes. She'd been so proud of it. It had made her feel happy and now it was destroyed.

She slowly made her way to her car. She'd grabbed a plastic trash bag to sit on so she wouldn't get paint on her seats. Setting her sketch book down on another trash bag, she closed her car door. She wanted to cry. She grabbed onto her steering wheel and laid her head against it. The tears flowed. *Why didn't I see that he was upset? Why, why, why?*

She wiped her eyes and that's when she saw the shadow. At first, she was scared and then she heard the voice. "Melanie, are you alright?"

She looked up at James. He motioned for her to open her window. She rolled it down and he leaned inside. "What happened?"

Finding her voice, she said, "Nothing, why?"

"I can tell you've been crying. And look at yourself, you're covered in paint."

"I was taking a class and accidentally spilled some paint. Everything's fine."

"But the tears."

Melanie didn't know where he'd come from and why he was asking her questions. How strange that he appeared when she needed him the most. She really needed a hug. "What are you doing here?"

She could see the wheels spinning. "I was driving by and saw your car."

"Lame excuse James, and I don't believe you for a minute. I'm going home. I'll see you later." Melanie started her car and James moved aside as she pulled away.

❦

That was strange. What was up with her? He should have never approached her but she seemed upset. He wanted to yank open the car door and pull her into his arms. She'd been crying, he was sure of it. He wanted to protect her from whatever upset her. He ran his hand along the back of his neck in thought, then decided to head inside. Maybe he could figure out what happened to upset her.

He walked inside and looked at the bulletin board for a calendar of events. Maybe he'd find a clue as to why she was there every week. Scanning it he saw classes for swim aerobics, yoga, step aerobics, and then he saw it or at least he thought he found his answer. Art therapy. That had to be it. James sauntered up to the receptionist. "May I ask you a question?"

"Sure."

"What is the art therapy class?"

"Well, sir, it's for kids that are having some issues. We use art to help them express their feelings."

"Who can attend?"

"Anyone really, but this specific class is geared towards children that are in foster care. The majority of the children have been taken away from their parents. Some, however, are in foster care because of a death. There's just so many reasons…"

"Oh no, I completely understand. I just saw it on the bulletin board and wondered what it was for. Thank you and have a nice evening." James turned and left the complex. *Foster care. I wonder if that's our answer.*

He grabbed his cell phone as he made his way across the parking lot. Punching the number assigned to Jonas Sounds he left a message. "Jonas, this is James Samuels.

I need you to see if Melanie Holmes was ever in foster care." He jumped into his car and headed towards home. He wondered if that was the answer— foster care. *Maybe that's why she's always seeking acceptance.*

He wasn't sure what he should do. His first thoughts were to go home, but instead, his heart told him to find Melanie. He pulled up in front of her home but there were no lights on. He hoped she'd made it home without problems and, if she were home, was resting. He didn't want to disturb her, so instead he decided to go on home and face her the next day, hopefully after she'd calmed down from whatever had upset her.

Chapter Twenty

MELANIE HURRIED HOME, CHANGED HER clothes, and went right to bed. She was mentally and physically exhausted after witnessing Jared's meltdown. What set him off, she hadn't a clue. She fell asleep almost right away and then found herself in the middle of another dream. This time Holcomb had just come home from work. Melanie had been sitting in the kitchen doing her homework. She'd accidentally knocked a few papers on the floor and as soon as he saw them, he came unglued.

Melanie didn't have time to react as he grabbed her long hair from behind and pulled. Her head shot back and she was forced to look into his evil eyes. "Do you think you live in a barn, little girl? Pick up that mess."

Melanie chewed on her lower lip and he reached down and slapped her across the face. "That is so unbecoming. Stop that. Now pick up your mess." Holcomb had yanked her chair out from the table so quickly she flipped over backwards slamming her head into the floor. He grabbed her by the shirt and dragged her to the three pieces of paper that were on the floor. "Pick it up now!" She fumbled for her homework and tried to stand but was unsteady on her feet. Somehow, she'd set her homework down and reached for the fallen chair.

She woke, her heart was beating erratically. She sat up in bed and recalled the rest of the incident that had caused her to be taken to the ER.

Holcomb had come at her again after she'd sat down. "What do you say, little girl?" She remembered looking at him unsure what she was to say.

When Melanie hadn't responded, Holcomb yanked her from the chair. He spun her around and she flew into the corner of the door, cutting her forehead and cheek right below her eye. Blood spurted everywhere.

It was the blood that brought him around. Reacting almost instantly he rushed to get a towel to stop the flow of blood. Holcomb got ahold of himself and called for his wife. June threw her hands up to her face screaming at him.

"What did you do?"

June had come to her side helping her apply the towel to stop the blood. She took one look at the injury, grabbed Melanie and headed for the car. She'd rushed her to the hospital and that was the beginning of her many trips to the ER.

That first incident was explained away and somehow slipped through the cracks.

She healed from that and had grown afraid of him. Over the course of several months, Holcomb's anger worsened. Melanie somehow took the brunt of his outbursts. Oftentimes, the damage she'd incurred was hidden beneath her clothes. He was smart in his attacks and no one was the wiser.

Each time he beat her, Melanie fell deeper into the darkness. The episodes increased in intensity and piled one upon the other. She never forgot. She lost all sense of self-worth. Holcomb instilled perfection and if she stepped outside those lines there was always some type of repercussion.

Thankfully, in time, and after several attempts at running away, Melanie was pulled from the household and forced into another foster home.

She got up and went to her office where she mindlessly perused the internet. She searched a favorite clothing site, looked at various art supplies, and ended up looking at Amcrost's website. She read all about the company and Ben Samuels' tenure as CEO. Next, she searched a recipe website looking for something easy that she could try her hand at.

Before she knew it, the sun had risen. She made her way to her bedroom to prepare for work after another sleepless night.

Melanie arrived earlier than normal with a headache that matched all others she'd had in the past. She surmised part of it was from her crying the night before and the other stemmed from her sleeplessness. She logged into her computer and tried to focus on the day ahead.

Her cell phone lay on her desk beside her and she heard an incoming text. It was from Jackie reminding her about their cooking lesson that weekend. She read that and then heard another beep. Another text. This time Jackie asked her if she wanted to go to bingo that night. St. Margaret's, the parish where Janet taught, was having a fundraiser. Melanie had only played bingo a handful of times in her life. *What the hell. I'm not doing anything.* Melanie texted back: *I'd love to go. Haven't been in years. What time?* Ten seconds later: *Six. Dinner too.*

Melanie responded: *See you then.* Jackie's thoughtfulness to include her marked a change in Melanie's day.

She had something fun to look forward to.

At lunchtime, Melanie phoned Jackie. "Jackie, I'm glad you answered. Thank you for thinking of me."

"Dear, it's not a problem. I forgot this was a fundraiser until Angelina reminded me last night. She's going to be there, as is Gabriella. I'm not sure if Alejandro and Ashton are planning on coming, but Kelly and Alec are definitely out. Wyatt's coming, as is Ben."

She didn't mention James. I wonder if he's coming. "How does this work?"

"They're offering food as part of the fundraiser so plan on eating there."

"I'm so glad you invited me. I need a night out." *Especially after last night's fiasco at the Y.* "I guess I'll see you at six."

Melanie ended the call with a smile on her face. Things were looking up. She grabbed her purse and reached into the pocket for the fortunes she'd saved of late. She reread several of them not understanding at all what hers meant: *Life's path doesn't always lead you in the right direction. Follow the stars and take that second journey.* And then there was her latest one: *Be careful of those around you. Trust no one because they are not who you think they are.*

Melanie shook her head and then focused on her magic numbers. She wrote some of them down, hoping she could find some lucky bingo cards using them. The rest of the day flew by with the promise of going out that night.

James was sitting at his desk when his phone rang. His mind had been on Melanie and he wasn't paying attention to the caller ID and answered automatically. "James, do you have plans this evening?"

"Well, hello to you mother. Why?"

"All of us are getting together for a fundraiser at St. Margaret's. It's bingo tonight and I thought you might like to join us. Have a little fun after a long work week."

"Mom, I don't know." James thought for a second and decided what the hell. "Okay, I'll go. After all, it's for a good cause. What time?" Jackie filled him in on the particulars leaving out one key point. Melanie.

James left work a little earlier than normal for a Friday. He ran home, changed into casual clothes, and stopped by the ATM machine on the way over to St. Margaret's to grab some cash. He hadn't attended a bingo at St. Margaret's in years and hadn't a clue how much money he needed.

As he walked into the gymnasium where the fundraiser was being held, he saw Janet Holmes limping along. He wasn't surprised to see her since she taught there but he *was* surprised to see Melanie. He lost focus and almost ran directly into his sister, Angelina, as she waddled towards a table at the back. "James, follow me. Mom texted me where we're sitting." He grabbed his sister's elbow and escorted her to the table. "Gabriella's joining us too. Ashton's on call and can't attend."

James came upon his mother who was organizing snacks in the center of their table. "I thought they were selling food."

"Well, they are," she said, pointing to the area where food was being served. "I decided to bring some snacks too. Not everyone buys their food."

"Didn't know," James said. "I would have stopped by Schulers and picked up something, if you would have told me."

"Don't worry about it. You know how I am."

"Yes, Mom, I do. So where do we buy our bingo cards?" Jackie pointed across the room to the table in the corner. "Do you want me to pick you up some?"

"Already got mine. You know I had to find the cards with my numbers."

"I know." James headed over to the table. He stood in line and glanced across the crowd. He looked down momentarily and when he looked back towards the table to see if Alejandro had joined them, he noticed her. Melanie. James shook his head. *Mom duped me. She's at it in her own way. She set us up.* He decided not to say anything and just let the evening play out. He grabbed a fistful of cards, paid, and returned to the table where Melanie was just getting ready to head over and purchase her cards.

"Fancy meeting you here," he said, surprising her.

"Ah, James, I didn't know you were coming. When Jackie called, I thought it was your dad coming— not you."

"Well, I'm not quite sure how to take that."

"Oh, no, I don't mean any ill will by it, I just didn't expect you." She looked down at his hand filled with cards. "I see you've already secured your cards. I need to head over there." She reached into her purse and pulled out a piece of paper.

"What's that?"

"Oh, it's my lucky numbers from our fortunes."

"You mean you kept those silly fortunes?"

"I did. I hoped the numbers would be lucky someday. I guess we'll find out if they are."

Melanie made her way to the table to purchase her

bingo cards. He eased his way over to his mother, whispering in her ear. "I'm onto you. I can't believe you asked her."

"Why not? I thought she'd have a good time."

Shaking his head, he said, "Mom, I know you, and I know you have an ulterior motive."

"Maybe, maybe not. I guess you'll have to see." Jackie turned away from her son and focused on Angelina.

It seemed like it took forever for Melanie to choose her cards. She scanned through pile after pile, often referring to the list she held. After almost twenty minutes, she finally returned to their table. "What took you so long?" James asked. "They're about to begin. Let's go grab something to eat."

He led Melanie over to the food booth where they each decided on a sub sandwich and chips. He paid for both of their meals.

"You didn't have to do that."

"Of course, I did."

"Are you saying this is our date?"

"No. Just being a gentleman."

They'd just returned to their seats when the caller started announcing the numbers. Melanie had so many cards she could barely keep up. "After all the time spent selecting your cards, I'd have thought you'd have them memorized," James said.

She gave him a sideways glance as she placed a chip onto her card. "Look at that. I almost have bingo. One more number…"

Melanie lost the first, second, and third rounds. "I thought you were going to win. Didn't you say you only needed one more number?"

"I did, but someone beat me to it."

"Three times?"

"I guess so. You need to congratulate your sister over there. If Angelina gets any more excited, she's going to go into labor."

He lowered his voice. "Don't say that too loud or you'll upset my mom."

"Why? Isn't she about due?"

"Yeah, but still." They played another round of bingo and this time James won. "Bingo," he shouted.

"Ah, come on now, really? I needed..."

"One more number..."

"Well, I did."

"Mel, each time you've just needed one more number. I find that hard to believe."

"You saw it."

"Well, I did, you're right. But still..."

"I can't help it. Now go collect your winnings." James had won a gift card to Pedals Diner.

Melanie sat watching Jackie interact with everyone. She was a true mother hen making sure Gabriella had covered all of her numbers. Each time Angelina had won, she jumped from her chair shouting, Bingo. That made everyone uneasy considering her condition.

Finally, Alejandro had to say something. "Angelina, you don't need to get so excited. This is just bingo."

"I know, but you know how I can get."

"That I do. Let's ramp it down a little, okay. I don't need you going into labor right here in the middle of St. Margaret's."

The callers took a break so everyone could get a snack and use the restroom. They announced there would be five more games for the night. Melanie was still winless. "I see those magic numbers aren't so magic."

"We'll see. We still have a few more games, and I think the prizes only get better." She popped a grape into her mouth.

No one near them won the next three games. The second to last game went on forever. It was a coverall where everyone needed to cover their cards. Melanie and Angelina only needed one more number to win. The prize was a gift card to The Vineyard on the Hill. "I'd love to win that," Angelina said, smiling at Alejandro. "That's our restaurant."

"Yes, it is," he said.

James leaned over to Melanie. "That's where they got engaged, or at least it was the second time."

She looked at him not understanding his comment. "They got engaged on the spur of the moment at the Botanical Gardens and then Alejandro surprised her at The Vineyard with her ring."

They all sat waiting impatiently for the next number. "B-12" was called. Barely a second elapsed before Angelina screamed and jumped up and down. "Bingo," she yelled out. "Bingo, I won." Alejandro tried to calm her but it was too late. The look of elation changed in a heartbeat. Angelina grabbed her stomach. "I think my water just broke." Alejandro looked down and sure enough there was a trickle of water right underneath her.

"See, I told you not to get so excited." Alejandro said as he wrapped his steadying arm around his wife.

Jackie ran to her side. "Angelina, remember to breathe. In, out, in out."

"Mom, will you stop. It's not like I need to worry about that right now."

"Listen to your mother. You need to get to the hospital," Alejandro said in a calming voice.

Angelina turned to Alejandro. "Alejandro, the baby's not going to come right this minute. Let's stay for the last game."

James hurried over to the caller, asking them to stop for a minute while Alejandro worked to get her out of the gymnasium.

The ever-calm Alejandro raised his voice. "Angelina. We're going to the hospital. Now..." With that she was gripped with a contraction.

She paused and sucked in her lips as she made her way through the contraction. "I think you're right. We'd better get to the hospital." They started to leave when she turned back to her mother. "The kids. What about the kids? Eliza, the sitter, needs to be home by ten."

"Don't worry, Angelina. I'll go stay with them," James said. "You go have that baby." He hugged his sister. "Now go."

"Okay, okay."

"Angelina, I'm behind you... Oh, but first I need to clean up the table."

"Don't worry about it, Jackie. I'll take care of the table." Melanie said.

"Wait. I'm coming too," exclaimed Gabriella, as she hurried behind the couple. James watched the expression on Melanie's face change from happiness to one filled with concern. He wondered what was going through her mind.

"Is it alright if we stay for the last game? I just know I'm going to win."

"We can stay if you promise me one thing."

"What's that?"

"Come with me."

"Where do I need to go?"

"Weren't you listening to anything that was being said?"

"Of course, I was. Why?"

"I volunteered to take care of the kids. Will you sit with me? They should be fast asleep by the time we get there."

Melanie thought about it and nodded. *Why not?* "Okay, I'll come. I'm really not good with kids, babies especially."

"You have nothing to worry about. I just want the company. I'll take care of everything else."

As luck would have it, Melanie carried away the final prize. "See, I told you I'd win."

"Yeah, okay. I'm glad you won the coveted prize— a weekend getaway to Chicago."

"I am too." She smiled at him. "And if you're a good boy maybe, just maybe, I'll ask you to go with me."

"I'm glad my mother's not here to hear you say that. She'd be all over us to make sure it happens."

"It's not like we haven't shared a hotel room before."

His eyes darted to hers. "No, it's not, but that couldn't be helped."

Chapter Twenty-One

JAMES WAS TAKEN ABACK BY Melanie's comment. Yes, they'd shared a room in San Antonio but it wasn't as if they'd been amenable with it. It had been the only room available when they'd attended the MBA conference. He still wanted to discuss that with her and would in time.

Melanie cleaned up the table after Bingo. It had only been a half-hour since they left for the hospital, but he kept checking his phone to see if he'd missed a message.

"We've got to get going. I promised we'd be there so Eliza could be home on time."

"Ready."

"How about you drop your car off at your house and ride with me."

"I appreciate it, but I think I'll drive."

James wondered if she wanted to drive so she could leave at a moment's notice. James had seen the look on her face when he asked if she would go with him to Angelina's. As the kids slept, maybe they'd have the chance to have a real conversation— with no interruptions.

He escorted Melanie to her car and followed her to his sister's home.

James had phoned Eliza as he drove to the house to let her know that Angelina had gone into labor and he was going to relieve her. He didn't want to surprise her when he showed up at the house.

Ten minutes later, James and Melanie pulled into the driveway. He escorted Melanie through the back door where he found Eliza watching a movie in the family room. "Eliza? Hi, I'm James, Angelina's brother and this is my friend, Melanie."

"Hi, James. I appreciate you phoning. Wow, I can't believe Mrs. Alvarez went into labor. That's so exciting."

"It definitely was. My sister knows how to bring excitement to the table that's for sure. Can I give you a ride home?"

"Oh no, thank you for the offer. I called my dad and he's coming to get me." Not five minutes later Eliza was heading out the door. "Be sure and tell Dr. and Mrs. Alvarez congratulations. I can't wait to see the baby."

"Yeah, neither can we." James closed the door and headed off to the kitchen. "Melanie?"

"I'm in here," she called from the kitchen. He found her sitting at the table.

"I'm going to get something to drink and then check on the kids. Would you like something?"

"Water's fine."

"Water it is, then." James checked the refrigerator and located a pitcher of water. He also grabbed himself a cola. "Angelina always keeps filtered water in the refrigerator. I hope this is okay."

"It's fine." Melanie watched him move about the kitchen. She'd gone quiet and he wondered what was going through her mind.

"Would you like to come with me when I check on the kids?"

"Ahh, no thanks. I'm afraid they'd be frightened seeing a stranger."

"They should be sound asleep."

"Yeah, I know. I realize that, but I think I'll just stay here."

He left Melanie sitting at the table while he checked on Angel and Matthew. They were both sound asleep. When he returned, Melanie seemed deep in thought.

"Follow me… Let's sit in the family room. We can watch a movie if you'd like." James led the way. "What would you like to watch? Or we could just chat."

"It doesn't matter to me. Whatever you'd like is fine."

"You know, I don't think I could begin to concentrate on the television right now. I keep checking my phone to see if Mom has texted me. I'm so excited for Angelina and Alejandro. I hope she has a boy. She wanted it to be a surprise. She and Alejandro don't care what they have. They pray that it's healthy. I think this pregnancy was a surprise…" James stopped talking realizing he wasn't giving her a chance to speak.

"Sorry about that, Mel. You didn't come here just to listen to me ramble." He watched her sip her water. "You know all about my family. What about yours? I've never heard you speak of your life growing up."

Her face paled and she looked away. "There's not much to say. You already know Janet."

"I do. But what about you? Your mom and dad? What did you like doing as a child? I went into the bank with Dad on Saturday's. I loved pretending I was him running the bank. Did you role model your parents?"

"No, I didn't." Her shoulders slumped and she nervously moistened her lips.

"How come? Most kids do."

"I just didn't. Can we move on?"

James reached for her hand but she pulled away.

"You never speak of your parents. Are they alive?"

"No, they're both dead," she said with anger.

"I'm sorry. Has it been long since they passed?"

She crossed her arms in front of her. "My dad died when I was a baby. I never got to know him and my mom died a few years ago." She was nervous speaking about her parents, so he decided not to press her. Maybe in time he'd learn a little more about them.

"Ok. You don't want to talk about your parents. Was there something that you liked doing while growing up? Did you play sports? Any hobbies you enjoy?" He believed he knew the answer to that. *She must like art if she helps out at the Y's art therapy class.*

"I enjoy reading when I have the time."

"That's all?"

"I like to draw."

At least I got her to open up about her art. Their quiet was quickly disrupted with Angel's crying. James went into the nursey to find tears streaming down Angel's face. He really didn't know what to do with her. He'd never babysat a baby before. He'd watched Wyatt and Colleen when they were younger, but they hadn't been babies like Angel. He picked her up and checked to see if she needed a diaper change, which she didn't, and then carried her to the kitchen, unsure of how to quiet her. *Mel will know what to do, Angel. She'll be able to help you.*

"She won't stop crying." James kept rubbing her back.

Wide-eyed with fear in her eyes she said, "What do you want me to do?"

"Calm her."

She shook her head. "I can't do that. I've never held a baby." James approached her but she raised her hand. "Don't hand her to me, James. I'm serious. I haven't a clue." And that's when her anxiety picked up. She jumped up from the table and eased towards the corner of the room. He could tell she was closing off. *From what, a crying baby?*

"She won't bite, I promise."

"Stay away from me. I mean it. I can't do this. I can't." And with that, Melanie grabbed her purse and ran out the door. His head spun—*What the hell just happened?* He couldn't think about Melanie. He was worried on how he could calm Angel without waking her brother.

Time passed ever so slowly. Somehow, he'd gotten Angel to sleep and he too dozed off. He was awakened when his phone rang. He immediately answered. "It's a boy."

"Really?"

"He's precious and healthy, and—" James interrupted his mother as he knew she'd go on and on about the baby.

"How's Angelina?

"She's doing just fine. A little tired. What about the kids? I know Angelina's concerned."

"Sleeping." Changing the subject, he went on. "I'll stay here the remainder of the night, but I will need relief. By the way, have you heard your granddaughter cry? She certainly has a set of lungs on her."

Jackie laughed. "She does, doesn't she?"

"I feel sorry for Angelina and Alejandro. Having to deal with her and a newborn…"

"You're just not used to it, James. What about Melanie? I'm sure she's been a big help."

"Ah, she went home." The line was quiet. Clearly his mom was waiting for an explanation. "As soon as Angel started in with her crying fit, Mel bolted. It seemed as though she'd never been around a baby before. She became anxious and ran. That pretty much sums it up."

"Huh, that's unusual. I'll have to talk to her."

"Mom, don't. Just leave it alone. She had her reasons."

"Alejandro said he'd come home once Angelina and the baby were settled for the night. She needs her sleep and Alejandro wants to be there when the kids wake up."

James was excited for his sister. She had a boy. While he sat on the couch, he recalled the look of fear that had crossed Melanie's face when he tried to hand her Angel. Her eyes got as big as saucers. She'd freaked out. He wasn't sure what he should do when he saw her next.

Melanie couldn't get home fast enough. She was still rattled by the effects of Angel's crying. *Who in their right mind would fall apart at a baby's cry? I've got to get a handle on this.* Her hands were still shaking. She curled up into the corner of her couch with every imaginable light on in the house. The brightness would help calm her. As she sat there, she realized that Angelina's house was dark. James had very few lights on turning off many of them as he'd made his way through the house when he went to check on the kids. *Maybe that's what set me off? It was dim in the house. Not bright like I need it at night.*

Melanie wasn't sure if it was a combination of the low-level lighting or Angel's screams that threw her over the edge. Her mind drifted back to a time when her cries reverberated through the darkened room. She'd been scared. She feared no one would open the door to let her out and that's when she started crying, screaming at the top of her lungs. The memories were too much for her… She needed to do something, anything, to get her mind off of them.

By the time Melanie came to grips with the fact the she needed to do something to calm herself, it was almost two in the morning. She grabbed her sketch book and started drawing. She really wasn't paying attention to what she'd drawn until she completed it—a sketch of Angel being held in James' arms. *Where did that come from? Me drawing James, yes, but he and a baby?*

She liked what she'd done and decided to finish it off. She'd frame it for Angel. A good memory of the night her baby sister or brother was brought into the world. Melanie's eyes grew heavy. She closed them for just a minute. That minute turned into hours of uninterrupted sleep. Melanie woke when she heard a knock on her door. She set the sketch pad down, swept her hair out of her eyes, and made her way to the door. She glanced at her watch. It was just after eight. Who'd be at her door this early on a weekend? She didn't have friends that just popped on by. Janet and she always planned their visits.

She opened the door and wasn't too surprised to see James standing before her in the same rumpled clothing he wore the night before. "Can I come in?"

"Sure." Melanie gestured for him to enter. "I guess Angelina had the baby."

"She did. A little boy. I don't think they've named him yet." James swept his hand across his face. He looked exhausted. "I hope it's okay that I stopped by. I was concerned with the way you ran out of the house last night. I wanted to check to make sure you got home alright."

"I did. Thank you for checking." She didn't know what to say. When she thought about it, she was a little embarrassed by her behavior. No words. Nothing. She just took off. "So, are you coming from Angelina's?"

"Yeah. Alejandro wanted to get home before the kids woke. He didn't want them scared not knowing that she'd gone into labor. He came home around five. I decided to stay so he could catch a little sleep but he'd barely drifted off when Angel started crying. I have to say, he has the magic fingers. Angelina has talked about how Alejandro can calm Angel in a matter of seconds. I didn't believe her, but she was right. Alejandro had barely picked her up and she settled back down. Supposedly that's true of Alec as well. I guess Kelly will find out if that's true or not in time."

"How is Kelly? I need to stop by and say hello."

"She's doing fine. Anxious to get this pregnancy over with."

"I'm sure she is."

"Are we just going to stand here in your foyer or can we sit down?"

"Oh, yeah, sorry about that. Follow me." Melanie had forgotten about the sketch and led him into her family room. Her sketch pad lay open on the table. Before she could grab it and close it, James' eye zeroed in on it. He walked over and picked it up.

"Did you do this?"

"Uh, yeah, I did."

"When? Is this me holding Angel?" Shyly she nodded her head. "Mel, this is outstanding. But why? You were barely there long enough to take one look at the baby. And yet, you captured this image to perfection. You're good."

Melanie sat down and her gaze drifted to the carpeting. She couldn't look at him. She was embarrassed with her behavior. He skimmed his fingers across the sketch then squeezed her leg. When she didn't react, his hand grazed across her cheek. "Mel, please look at me." She didn't respond but when he brushed his thumb across her cheek, she raised her gaze to his.

"What happened last night, Mel?"

She scrunched her face, closed her eyes, and chewed on her lower lip. A nervous habit that she'd had since she was a young child. She clenched her hands into tight fists. James noticed it because he grabbed her hands in his and held them. She felt herself begin to relax and then she opened her eyes and looked at him.

"I want to help you. Please let me."

His wanting to help her lay her fears aside brought tears to her eyes. She did her best to prevent them from escaping but one fell and then another.

James pulled her into his embrace. He held her and gently rubbed her back— trying to sooth her. She felt him reach up and brush her tears from her face. "Mel, please look at me. Tell me what happened to make you this upset. I want to help you. Let me."

A sob broke out and she wrapped her arms around him. She'd never had someone want to help her put her fears to rest. Her foster parents generally just left her alone, letting her cry until her tears were spent. They didn't know what to do for her. Her only outlet had been her art but at times that wasn't even enough to put her demons to bed. James had no idea what she'd been through, and she was doing her best to keep her secrets from him.

"Just hold me, James. That's what I need most right now." In the last few weeks, even though she didn't want to allow herself, she'd grown close to James, something she'd never once thought possible. He was supportive and caring and she needed that the most right now. Too much was going on in her life. The sale of Parklayne, the temporary loss of her art therapy, and the addition of Jackie into her life. All of these changes were resurrecting the memories she'd tried so hard to tuck away in the recesses of her mind.

He held her until she calmed and brushed the last of her tears from her face. "Melanie, I want to help you, but if I can't, please let someone. Whatever's got you this upset you need to deal with— you can't go on this way."

He was right, but she didn't want to face all of the memories. They were too much for her. She couldn't have another breakdown.

Seven years ago, when she was twenty-five, she had a breakdown of sorts. During an intense thunderstorm, she'd been in the bank vault when the lights went out. The door automatically slammed closed with a loud bang. She'd been transported back to that closet. She pounded on the steel door but no one heard her. The power outage lasted only a few minutes but that short time sent her over the edge. She'd walked out of the branch and took a leave of absence to deal with the memories.

It was as a result of her breakdown that she'd been forced to sleep with all of the lights on. Prior to that, she'd slept with a single light.

She'd been lucky that her manager was understanding and put her on a temporary leave of absence. Her job had been waiting for her when she got her head back on straight.

Melanie hadn't had any episodes like that until now, and she definitely didn't want to return to that state again. She'd worked to pull herself back up but she was afraid she was headed down the rabbit hole again and she couldn't let herself.

"I'm okay now. Thanks." She pulled away and eased down the couch a bit. She didn't want to talk anymore about her mental state. "So, tell me about the baby." He shook his head, probably in confusion, but in the end, he dealt with her change in conversation. She listened as he told her the little he knew of his nephew. "I'm glad Angelina's okay. I can't even imagine being pregnant and giving birth."

"Give it time. I'm sure you'll find out soon enough."

"Not me," she pointed to herself and stood. "Coffee?"

"Thanks, but no. I think I'm going to head on home and try and get some sleep."

She followed him to the door. "Thanks for coming by."

"Yeah, no problem."

She watched as he walked out the door. She'd stayed strong and true to herself. She hadn't divulged her past. She was proud of herself because at one point she thought she was going to lose it and spill everything to him. She was stronger than she gave herself credit. She'd made it through another painful episode and had kept the truth secured tightly in the closet of her memories.

Chapter Twenty-Two

JAMES DROVE HOME UNSURE OF what he'd just experienced. All he knew was that Melanie side-stepped him again. *Why won't she tell me?* He decided to check in with his dad. He hadn't heard if Jonas had uncovered any of Melanie's past in the background check and he wanted to make sure his dad was still on top of it. He showered, changed, and headed over to his parents' house.

He surprised both of his parents when he flew into the house.

"What are you doing here?" Jackie asked.

"Thanks for the welcome, Mom. I thought I'd stop by and hear all about my new nephew."

"You could go see him."

"I know but I thought I'd go later after Angelina's had time to rest. So, tell me all about him. Does he have a name yet?"

"Not that I know of. I think they're still working on it." Jackie grabbed a cup of coffee and sat down while his father snatched a donut from the box on the counter.

"Donut, James? We picked them up on the way home from the hospital. I had no idea Laketown Bakery opened at six."

James grabbed one from the box his father extended to him. "Mmm, this melts right in your mouth."

"Yep, those glazed donuts are the best in town."

"So, James, what's the real reason why you came by? I know it's more than asking about your nephew because you would have just phoned." James reached for a second donut. "Could it be about Melanie. I know you're concerned about her. I can tell. So out with it."

James stood and retrieved a mug, poured a cup of coffee, then turned back to his parents. "I'm going to be quite frank here. I think Melanie's been through something traumatic in her life. I don't know what it is, but whatever happened to her, she's still affected by it."

Jackie took a sip of her coffee. "I know she's reserved at times. She definitely doesn't like to talk about her childhood."

"Or her parents," James added.

"I've tried several times to get her to open up but she never bites. You'd think she'd relate some type of memory with cooking, but she doesn't. She always changes the subject when I get too close."

"She's good at that too. Before you know it, you've forgotten what you were originally talking about. Dad, may I speak with you privately?"

Jackie's eyes rose at his request.

"Sure, son." James followed his father to his office and closed the door behind them.

"Have you heard from Jonas? Has he completed the background check on Melanie?"

"He has."

"And?"

"Everything checks out. She's clean."

"What about her childhood?"

"James, I don't think how she was raised should enter into our decision on whether to hire her or not. She's an exemplary employee and earned her place at Parklayne. And in the end her childhood doesn't affect her job status."

"I realize that. I was hoping that you'd uncover something, anything that would help me understand her. Dad, I'm going to be honest with you. I really like being around her. I'm trying to figure out who she is and what she's all about." He crossed the room and gazed out the window then turned back. "I knew everything about Elsa and we didn't make it. I…I know I shouldn't feel this way and definitely know I shouldn't be talking about this with you, but I think I'm falling for her."

"James?" His father's voice raised.

"I know I just broke up with Elsa but Melanie's different. When I'm with her I just want to protect her, from what, I haven't a clue. I feel like she needs me to help her with something that she's been put in my world for a reason. Six months ago, my life was all set. I was going to marry Elsa and have a family with her, but then it all fell apart and Melanie entered my world. I don't know why. What I do know is there must be a reason that we're purchasing Parklayne and there must be a reason why I'm having to work with her to pull this off. You know how I am… I always feel like there's a reason for everything."

"I know, son. What I can tell you is that she didn't have a normal childhood. If she wants you to know about it, she's going to have to be the one to tell you, not a private investigator. It wouldn't be fair to her if you knew about her background first before she wanted you to.

"In regards to her employment with us, I hope we can work something out, but there's always the chance that we won't be able to. I don't want you involved in any of this. It's my decision based on what I've seen as you've worked together. If you two do enter into a relationship, you shouldn't be involved with deciding whether or not to hire her. That would ruin anything that you could have together."

"I fully understand where you're coming from. I just hope that she'll feel comfortable enough with me to share whatever shaped her into who she is today."

"I do too, son. From what I know, she needs someone like you in her life. She needs to know there are loving, caring people in this world. Enough of this, I'm sure your mother is chomping at the bit to see your sister and our new grandson again. What do you say we head off to the hospital so you can meet him?" His father slapped James on the back and opened the door to find his mother standing with what appeared to be her ear glued to the door. "Jackie," Ben scoffed at her. "Did you hear what you wanted to?"

"I don't know what you're talking about, dear."

"Of course, you don't," he said as he headed off to the bedroom. "I'm changing, taking a shower, and returning to the hospital. You're welcome to join me. James is already on board, and I'm sure Wyatt will be more than happy to meet his new nephew." He walked off leaving James and his mother standing in his wake.

"What was that all about?" James inquired. "Were you listening to our conversation?"

"I tried my hardest, but you two didn't speak loud enough. I only got a few words, nothing I could make heads or tails out of."

"That's good. Mom, you need to stay out of this."

"But James?"

"No but James me. This is my life and I have to live it without interference from you. Got it? If I fall flat on my face, I did it myself without anyone else's help." He paused. "Tell Dad I've headed off to the hospital. I guess I'll see you there." He didn't want to discuss this any further with his mother. He had a lot of thinking to do himself.

James and Alejandro arrived at the same time, meeting on the way to Angelina's room. A few steps ahead, Matthew was pushing Angel's stroller as they traipsed down the hall. "Thanks again, James, for taking care of these two. Matthew could hardly contain himself when he heard about the baby. He couldn't wait to meet his new brother."

Matthew called over his shoulder. "James, did you hear that Mom had the baby?"

"I did. That's why I'm here."

"Yep, a brother. I'm so happy. I'll have someone to play catch with…"

"Matthew, you already do."

"I know, but Angel's a girl."

"So?"

"She can't play ball."

"Why not? Your aunt Colleen plays. From what I hear, your mother played too but wasn't very good at it."

"I know. But a brother. I wished for one, and I got my wish."

"I guess you did." James rumpled Matthew's hair. "Now, let's go see that brother of yours." James followed Alejandro to Angelina's room entering right behind her family.

"Oh, James, you're here. Thanks again for watching the kids for me. I still can't believe my water broke right in the middle of bingo."

"The way you jumped up and down I'm surprised he didn't pop right out there on the gym floor."

"I wasn't that bad."

James scrunched his face up. "Not that bad, huh?"

"Okay, I guess I did get a little excited."

"Mom, where's my brother?"

"The nurses took him to the nursery while I showered. I was just about ready to ring for them to bring him back."

"Can I push the button?"

"Sure thing. Go ahead."

Matthew rang the button. "I can't wait to see him." Looking back and forth between his parents he asked, "What's his name?"

"I was wondering the same thing," James interjected.

"We're still working on it." With that, the nurse returned with the baby. Alejandro passed Angel off to Angelina while he reached out. James watched the expression on Alejandro's face change as his son was placed into his arms. James imagined he was reliving a time during his first marriage when his son had been placed in his arms. Unfortunately, he and his mother had been swept away in a flash flood. Alejandro was still living with their tragic deaths, but he'd also moved on and now had a beautiful family with Angelina.

James saw the love emanate from Alejandro. He was sure Alejandro was making plans for fishing trips and Boy Scouts. James hoped that one day he'd have the same expression on his face. "So, when are you going to name this little one? I'm sure Mom can't wait."

"She was already harping on us last night," Angelina commented as she watched her husband fall more in love with his son. "We're working on it. He has to be named before we can leave the hospital, so by sometime tomorrow, he'll definitely have one."

Matthew sat on the bed besides his mother and held his new brother. Angelina set Angel alongside her brothers. Alejandro scrunched on the bed beside his wife and James, using his cell phone, took their first family photo.

"Now it's your turn James to hold your nephew." Alejandro removed the baby from Matthew's arms, passing him to James.

"You know what I realized last night?" James said as he took in his nephew.

"No, what?" commented Alejandro.

"I've never babysat the kids before. That is something that I definitely want to change. So anytime you two want to go out, please let me know. I need to spend more time with my niece and nephews."

"At least something good came out of last night—that is, outside of our little miracle."

"Don't make fun of me, sister dear. I mean it. I need to find more time for family. You going into labor really opened my eyes. I plan on making a concerted effort to be around more. I promise."

On that note, the door opened. In walked not only Ben, Jackie, and Wyatt, but also John and Maria. It was the first time that Alejandro's parents had the chance to meet their new grandchild.

"Look at him, John. Isn't he precious?" Maria held out her arms as James passed the baby to his grandmother. John reached in and the baby grasped his finger. James quickly snapped another family photo.

"I'll send you these photos." He shot a few more of his parents and Wyatt with the baby. "It's pretty crowded in here, so I think I'm going to head out."

"Thanks for coming, James. I'm sure Kelly's not too far behind, that is, if Alec allows her to leave the house. I spoke with Gabriella and she and Ashton will be here this afternoon."

"I think I'll wait until you come home to visit again. You've got way too many people that want to see him and you." James reached in and kissed his sister's cheek. "Congratulations, again— he's definitely a keeper." He shook Alejandro's hand and walked out of the room.

James leaned against the wall waiting for the elevator. He ran his hand across his face thinking of the family he'd just left and the one he hoped to have someday. He'd given up on that dream when he'd broken up with Elsa. But as the elevator doors opened, he realized that his dream might not be that far off. Maybe, if he played the cards just right, he'd have that family sooner rather than later.

Chapter Twenty-Three

MELANIE SPENT THE ENTIRE WEEKEND painting. She needed the relief after Friday night's bingo and the incident where she practically fell apart at the sight of a crying baby. She wrapped herself in her art.

She detested feeling the way she did. Memories cropped up making her feel lost and alone. The time she'd spent with James had made her feel more alive than she'd ever felt, but then, somehow, her ancient fears always found their way back. By Monday morning she was back on track, ready to move into the final stages of merging the banks. She still didn't know whether or not she'd have a job once the sale was complete. Anything could happen. She could have a job one minute and the next find herself in a job consolidation. She knew there was absolutely nothing she could do, but she still worried.

When she rounded the corner to her office that Monday morning, she was taken aback by not only James' presence but also Ben's. In her surprise, she almost dropped her cup of coffee.

"Melanie, how are you? Did you have a good weekend?" Ben greeted her with a bright smile. "I guess you heard the news. Angelina had the baby."

"James told me. What did they name him?"

"Christian Patrick Alvarez."

"I like that. A nice strong name. Has Angelina come home, yet?"

"She comes home today. All I can say is they are definitely going to have their hands full trying to manage two under two. Matthew's a big help but it's definitely going to be crazy at first."

"Once Angelina gets settled, I'll have to go visit her." James cast a sideways look at her. She could only imagine what thoughts were racing through his head, especially after the way she handled herself when he was babysitting. "So, what brings you gentleman into my neck of the woods?"

"I have a meeting with Saxson and James, here, thought he'd check on you."

"Oh, okay. Have a good meeting, then." Melanie started for her office with James on her heels. She guessed why he was there and didn't quite know how to address his questions on why she ran away from him. Thankfully, he was all business.

Melanie closed her office door behind him and sat at her desk with coffee cup in hand. She needed something to do with her hands so she just held onto her coffee. James remained standing and looked out her office window towards the arch grounds. She knew he wanted to ask her again about her behavior, but was pleasantly surprised when he discussed business.

"We just bid on another group of loans. We'll hear today whether we've won or not. If we win, we're headed on another trip. Be prepared to leave next Monday."

Melanie sat wide-eyed listening to James, surprised they'd be traveling together so soon. "Where's the portfolio located?"

"New York City. I'm pretty sure we're going to win this so you might as well start preparing."

New York City. That was one place she'd never been. She hoped they could complete their due diligence quickly because she'd love to visit the Empire State Building, Statue of Liberty, and the National September 11th Memorial Museum.

"It's going to be the two of us, and if we handle this like we did Dalton B&T, we should have a little time for sightseeing."

"I want to make sure we do a thorough job, but yeah, sightseeing would be fun since this would be my first trip to New York City."

"Let's hope we win it then."

She was becoming in tune to his facial expressions and the way he held his body. He wanted to ask her something so she reversed course and came right out and said what was on her mind. "Is there something else, James?"

He raised his gaze and pursed his lips. "How do you know me so well?"

"We've been spending an awful lot of time together lately. I can always tell when something's on your mind."

James stood and walked about her office then leaned against the side of her desk. He raised his hand, running it along the side of her face, brushing a wisp of hair that had broken loose from her bun behind her ear. "You asked for it. I know we've discussed this before but... Mel, will you go out with me? Really go out on a date. I know you said you didn't want a relationship, but I feel like there's too much going on between us not to try for one."

Melanie looked away from him. She felt it too but she also wanted to remain true to herself. She'd promised herself not to get serious with anyone. Based on her childhood, she didn't think she had what it took to be in a true relationship. To be part of a family. *Should I give in and try?*

"I promised myself a long time ago that I'd never get serious with anyone."

"Who said this has to be something serious? At least not right away..." James slid his hand along her jawline. "I'm going to be really honest here. I shouldn't feel this way, but I do. After my breakup with Elsa and all… But I can't help it. I have real feelings for you. I know you say you'll never feel the same for me, but you might surprise yourself. And in the end, you might decide to forgo that promise you made to yourself and learn to live a little. Live outside of your comfort zone for once."

Melanie wanted to try, she really did, but she also feared that somehow, he'd discover her past. It was a past she wanted to leave behind but couldn't. If she did decide to get serious with James, she knew she needed to be honest with him. A real relationship did not work with half-truths. She'd have to tell him everything. Tell him about her father, her drunk of a mother, and the hells of living in foster care.

She had so much baggage. Baggage that affected her almost every day. But then again, maybe he could help her. Maybe with James by her side, on both the good and the bad days, she'd learn to live. Learn to deal with horrible memories that followed her everywhere.

"I think you're thinking too much here. Will you or won't you give us a try?"

"There's so much you don't know about me. I'm afraid when you learn about my past you'll want to walk away. I can't live with that. I can't start to have real feelings for someone that will leave me in the cold."

"Mel, I'd never do that to you."

"I'm not so sure."

"Then, I guess you don't know me too well." He started to pull away. She couldn't let him. He was the best thing that had ever happened in her life. Ever. She couldn't let the feelings she had for him walk out the door.

She grabbed for his hand, halting his movement. "Don't leave me," she shyly said. Swallowing loudly, she looked up at him. Tears started forming in the backs of her eyes. She was having a hard time controlling them from falling. She knew James. She knew he was aware of her emotions. Before she could swipe at the first tear, James beat her to it.

"Don't cry."

"Just please don't leave me. You're all that I have now." The tears she'd been doing her best to control released one right after the other. She turned her head but he didn't let her pull away. Instead he reached down and pulled her into his arms. "James, I have so much baggage— more than you'll ever know. I can't expect you to sign up for it."

"It's in your past, right?" She nodded into his shoulder. "Then, what I can promise you is we will deal with it together, okay? I'd do anything to have you in my life. Absolutely anything." He ran a comforting hand along her spine. "I don't want to see you sad anymore. I want to see a smile on your face. I've only had glimpses of your beautiful smile but it's something that I hope I can put there all the time. Please let me in. Let me help you deal with your past. We can face it and at the same time make a future for ourselves."

"James?"

"I know I'm pressing you, hoping for a future. But can't I hope for that too?" He pulled back slightly wiping the last remaining tears from her face. "Melanie, I know we can get through this, together. I want to be there for you. I honestly do." Raising his hand in the Boy Scout salute he added, "I promise you Melanie Holmes, to never walk away from you. Ever. I want to be by your side in both good times and bad. Please will you give us a try? Go out with me?"

Melanie nodded her head. "Before I answer your question, you have to realize that I have to tell you about me in my own time. Please don't rush this."

"Anything, sweetheart. Anything. I'll wait forever if that's what you need. I just want to be able to hold you freely, knowing that you're in my life because you want to be. Take all the time you need."

"Okay, then. James, yes, I'll go out with you." Melanie was drawn into his tight embrace. It felt wonderful having someone that she could confide in. *If I share my past, maybe my demons will be forever released.* She could only hope.

Their special moment was interrupted by a knock on her office door.

James tapped his index finger against her nose, "We're not finished here."

He took his seat as Melanie wiped the few remaining remnants of tears from her face.

"Just a second," she called as she made her way to the door. She opened it to discover both Saxson and Ben standing before her. "Melanie, is James still here?"

She opened the door wider. "He is, do you need him? We were just discussing the possible acquisition."

"That's why we're here. James, I just got the word that we won the bid. White Donegal Community Bank wants to wrap this up immediately. You and Melanie need to get on a plane as soon as possible. They want our final decision by Wednesday of next week. I realize this is unheard of and you may be required to work the weekend, but this is an important deal for Amcrost. I have Delia making arrangements as we speak. Can you be ready by this afternoon?"

"I can," commented Melanie.

"Pack for at least a week and a half because I think you won't be back until next Wednesday, maybe Thursday at the latest." Saxson motioned to Melanie. "And Melanie, don't forget to use your new questionnaire. It seems like it paid off in the Dalton B&T deal."

"I will." Turning to Ben she asked, "Do you know when our flight is?"

"Delia's working on that right now. You'll be on the first available. We need to leave so you both can prepare for your trip. We'll be in touch I'm sure," Ben added as he headed towards the door.

Saxson and Ben left James and Melanie in her office. "James, we have so much to do. I don't know if I can be ready to leave in a matter of hours."

"We'll be okay. I have a list of all the reports we ran on the Dalton acquisition. You have the questionnaire. It's a piece of cake. Just grab your laptop and we'll make do." She knew James could see the fear cross her face.

She'd started biting her lip and then felt James' hand on her arm. "You're not alone. We're in this together."

"I know. You'd better get going so you can gather your things. I need to pack. Oh my gosh, I hope my dry cleaning is ready. I'm supposed to pick it up today. What if it's not?"

"Melanie, stop for a minute and take a deep breath." Melanie followed James' advice and took a deep breath. "Feel better?" She nodded her head. "Another."

"I don't have time to sit here taking deep breaths. We have too much to do. Go, get out of here. I'll see you at the airport."

"No, you won't."

"What do you mean by that?"

"I'm taking you to the airport. Give me an hour and I'll meet you at your house."

"An hour? I need more than an hour." She stopped and looked at him. "We don't even know when our flight takes off."

"I know but I'm coming over if not to do anything but try and calm you."

"I need more than an hour," she repeated.

"One hour," was his reply.

Melanie went crazy trying to get out of the office. She had to notify her staff of her last-minute trip, gather documents and make sure she had all of the appropriate files on her laptop. She hurried out the door a half-hour after James left. She ran by the dry cleaners. Thankfully, her clothes were ready.

As she drove home, she realized she needed to pick up a few items at the store. She'd run out of toothpaste just that morning and didn't have a spare tube in the house. She'd just put a run in her last pair of panty hose and needed to grab a couple pair of them as well. But at her local pharmacy that carried all of these sundries, she got stuck in a long line. By the time she made it to her house, the hour was up. James' car sat in front of her house and James stood leaning against the passenger door. When he saw her car, she noticed that he began tapping at his watch.

"Ready?" he called out as she pulled into her driveway.

"Do I look ready? I had to stop and get a few things. I haven't even begun to pack." She paused and looked at him. "How come you're ready so fast? Didn't you need to pack?"

"I pretty much keep a go-bag ready for last minute trips. Maybe you should think about doing that yourself."

She felt like he'd just chastised her. "I guess I just don't travel as much as you do. In general, I have more than a moment's notice before I have to get on a plane." She threw open her door and ran inside, James following.

"Is there something I can do to hurry you along?"

"Stop, please stop. First of all, do you even know when our plane leaves?" Melanie checked the clock as she walked into the house. It was just after eleven.

"I think around four."

"Four? You've got to be kidding me. We have plenty of time."

"I know." Snickering he added, "I just wanted to make sure we had enough time for you to pack. I know what girls are like. It takes Kelly hours just to put her make-up on and fix her hair. Angelina's a whole other story. But now that she has children, I think she's whittled down the time. And Colleen—she's a breeze. She can be ready faster than I can."

"So why are you lumping me in with you sisters?"

He chuckled. "Because."

"Because why?"

"Just because. Now go get your things together while I sit patiently waiting for you." He threw himself down on the couch. "Go. I want to be at the airport by two."

"Two? That's two hours before our flight."

"And two hours where we can get something to eat, go through security and relax before our plane. Hurry up," he called out as he shooed her towards her bedroom.

Melanie needed the time to mentally prepare for this trip. She led James to believe she didn't have a go-bag at the ready, but she did. Her toiletries were always packed and her suitcases were always at the ready. She just had to grab a few casual outfits, in case they had the opportunity to sightsee, throw in her shoes, and grab the dry cleaning she'd picked up. She had a combination of five suits and dresses. She could always use the dry cleaner at the hotel, if needed. In a record fifteen minutes she rejoined James with suitcases in hand.

"Ready?"

James looked up from the magazine he'd been reading a look of shock on his face. "You can't be ready already. You haven't been gone for more than twenty minutes."

"Fifteen to be exact."

He stood and walked towards her. "You were pulling my leg, weren't you?" He pointed to her suitcase. "You had a go-bag packed, didn't you?" She smirked. "Melanie Holmes, you had me going. I thought I was going to have to wait for hours while you packed."

She laughed. "I guess I surprised you then."

"You certainly did. Now, since you were so quick about packing, let's grab something to eat before we hit the airport. Airport food is not one of my favorite things."

"Mine, either."

They arrived at Lambert International Airport with plenty of time to spare, made it through security and were one of the first to board their plane. Somehow Delia had worked miracles and they'd been booked into first class. "I love traveling with you. Nothing but first class, huh?"

"Not always. I think my dad felt guilty about dropping this trip on us with little time to prepare. By the way, Delia was only able to book us a suite, so we're going to have to share our living space again. At least this time, we'll have separate beds."

"Why a suite?"

"She said there's a conference in town and all of the rooms near White Donegal were filled except for this one. It's a good thing, though, because we can work as late as we want and then head off to bed."

"James?"

"I don't want to imply anything with that comment, but it will be easier since we didn't have any time to prepare. We can't take the reports back to St. Louis to analyze them. We have to do this on the fly, per se, so we're going to have to make the best of a bad situation."

"I wouldn't necessarily call this a bad situation. It's just not your run of the mill trip, that's all. We'll make it work."

Chapter Twenty-Four

AT FIRST MELANIE STIFFLY SAT in her seat as the remaining passengers boarded. She knew James watched her. She could feel his eyes on her, then, the next thing she was aware of was his hand clasping hers. She half-cocked her head towards him.

"Just hold on. I won't let anything happen to you." And with that, she felt a sense of calm overcome her. For once, she wasn't facing a panic attack as the flight attendants closed the doors and prepared the cabin for takeoff.

James told her about all of the attractions they could visit while in New York. He talked about going to the Statue of Liberty and Ellis Island. She had no interest in learning about her roots but James went on and on about how his family immigrated from Ireland. And he described how he hoped to search the database to see if he could find his relatives when they crossed into New York.

Melanie discussed her desire to see the Empire State Building and the 9/11 Memorial. He was doing a phenomenal job keeping her mind off flying and on something that she was interested in. Before she knew it, they were getting ready to land. It was evening as they flew over the city. She leaned over James and took in the lights.

The next thing she knew, the wheels touched down onto the tarmac. She smiled. "Thanks."

"For what?"

"For keeping my mind off of flying. This is the first time I didn't have a near panic attack." She brushed a kiss onto his cheek.

"What was that for?"

"For being you. For knowing what I needed today." Minutes later they were deplaning. James led her to the baggage claim. From all of the horror stories she'd heard about flying into New York, she was surprised they only had to wait a few moments before their luggage was coming off the plane. *So far so good,* Melanie thought as they made their way to secure a cab.

It was almost nine-thirty by the time they arrived at their hotel. Luckily, the restaurant was still open so they hurriedly checked-in, dropped off their luggage at their suite, and made it to the restaurant just before it was ready to close. They both ordered a cup of soup and the special of the day. They figured they'd get their meal quickly and head off to bed.

Melanie was a people watcher and enjoyed the views from their table. Even at the late hour, people were bustling along the streets. She couldn't wait to see the city during the day. She hoped they'd have some time at night to take an evening tour of the city. Seeing it during the day was one thing, but at night she was sure it would look completely different.

By the time they finished their meal, she was exhausted. They entered their suite where Melanie headed off to bed. James grabbed his laptop. Knowing him, he'd be reviewing the agenda for the following day. "I'm off to bed," she said. "I can't keep my eyes open."

"Good night then, Mel. Let's plan on breakfast for eight. White Donegal's office is just two blocks over. We need to be there by nine."

"Thanks. See you in the morning." James walked towards her. She wasn't sure what he was going to do, then he reached out, drawing her into a hug.

"Sweet dreams." He leaned in and kissed her softly on the forehead. He pulled away and she watched him as she walked towards her room. If she didn't know better, James was her knight in shining armor. He'd kept her mind busy and for once she wasn't out of sorts when she traveled. She hoped it continued because she wanted to enjoy this trip.

Morning brought clear skies and a beautiful day. They ate a quick breakfast and made their way to the White Donegal offices where they were pleasantly surprised with the preparedness of the staff. The entire list of reports James had requested were waiting for them when they walked in. He'd even had the foresight to email a copy of the questionnaire that Melanie had created and they'd completed that as well.

James took one look at Melanie and smiled broadly. "This should be a piece of cake. They must really want an answer quickly."

"They must. I thought Dalton B&T was prepared but White Donegal's beat them hands down."

Even though they had all of the reports they required, analyzing them was still a time-consuming process. "I think we can relax tonight, Mel. I don't think we'll have any problems working through this. Let's take it one day at a time, okay? Hopefully, we won't need to work in the evenings."

"I hope not. There's so much to see and do here—not that I'm here to sightsee but I'm just saying."

"I know. Let's take advantage and see everything we can. How about we go to the Empire State Building tonight? It's a clear day so we should have a good view."

That night, they ate in a well-known Italian restaurant then headed off to the Empire State Building. James noted that the observation deck was on the 86th floor. They'd have a panoramic view of up to five states. With the recent restoration of the building, they'd also be able to take in the art-deco lobby and murals along with several exhibits.

James couldn't wait to get Melanie up to the observation deck. He figured they could tour the lobby on the way out, paying tribute to its designation as a historical landmark.

James could feel Melanie's anxiousness pick up when they entered the elevators that would take them to the observation deck. He reached for her hand. She held on tight as the elevator climbed. Before they knew it, the doors opened. The deck wrapped around the building's spire and provided one-of-a-kind views. "I can't believe we can see Central Park from here. Well not really, since it's dark but that's remarkable. Look over there, I can see the Brooklyn Bridge."

"And look, the Statue of Liberty." They peered through the binoculars and couldn't believe how far they could actually see.

A couple caught James' attention. Before he knew it, the man was getting down on bended knee to propose.

James nudged Melanie so she could witness the event. When all was said and done, he approached the couple. "May I take your photo to commemorate this?" The couple was delighted. James learned that a lot of people became engaged there. In fact, during the weekend, a saxophonist played to set the stage for couples just in case someone decided to propose. "Can you believe it? That couple will always remember where they got engaged."

"They certainly will." Melanie reached for James' hand. "Shall we go up to the top deck?"

"Only if you want to."

"I do."

Melanie and James completed their tour of the building and headed back to their suite. "Let's get a bottle of wine."

"That sounds lovely," Melanie said reaching for his hand. He purchased a bottle of wine at the corner store just a block from their hotel. He couldn't wait to sit down, relax, and have a conversation with her. Their entire day, with exception of their tour, had been all about business. He just wanted to have some time alone getting to know her better.

Just as they arrived at their suite, James' phone rang. "Hey, Dad, what's up?"

"I just wanted you to know that your sister, Kelly, just went into labor."

"What did you just say? I thought she was doing alright."

"She was but Kelly's water broke a short time ago and Alec rushed her to the hospital. That's where your mother and I are right now. Just say a few prayers."

"We will. Please tell Alec and Kelly we're thinking of

them. Text me when the baby's born and let me know how it is, rather how they are."

"I will, James. It might be awhile." James hung up the phone. He was speechless.

"Is Kelly in labor?"

"Yeah, and this time she's definitely having the baby." James sat on the couch. He propped his hands on his knees and combed his hands through his hair. "Mel, it's too soon. I think she still has eight weeks to go."

Melanie sat beside him and placed her hand on his thigh. He reached for her hand. "Everything has to be alright for both the baby and Kelly. Mel, she's been through so much in the last few years. She was happy. She found Alec—"

"Stop it. Both she and the baby will be just fine."

"How can you be so optimistic? I'm really worried."

She squeezed his hand. "You've got to think positively, James."

"Where did this Melanie come from? Think positively?"

"I guess I've been around you a little too much," she chuckled. James released her hand and draped his arm around her shoulders, pulling her close. "Kelly's where she needs to be. She's surrounded by doctors who are giving her the best possible care. Alec's there and I'm sure John is too. Most likely Joe and Ashton are there as well. She'll have so much knowledge surrounding her that everything will be just fine."

"I wish I were there."

"What could you do? Are you a doctor?"

"I could offer moral support."

"I think she has that between your family and Alec's. Think about it, how many people could possibly be there right now? Between your family and Alec's, it's quite overwhelming on a good day. Add in everyone's nervousness and I can't imagine…"

"You're right, Mel. Thanks for talking me down." They fell asleep in one another's arms and didn't wake until James' cell phone chimed an incoming text. James fumbled for his phone while Melanie did her best to wake up.

"It's my dad. Kelly had the baby. A little girl. She's on the small side. They're taking her to the NICU but think she's going to be fine. Kelly's doing well although she's exhausted."

"I can imagine. From what I've heard, labor is not a piece of cake." James smiled at her comment. "Hey, it's almost six. Let's get started early. The sooner we get through everything here, the sooner we can go home."

Melanie stood and made her way to her bedroom. He knew she was happy for him but he also saw a look of sadness cross her face. He wondered if she were having second thoughts about developing a true relationship with him. Only time would tell as they delved a little further into them as a couple.

James was thankful they were able to complete their review by Friday. He couldn't do anything for Kelly so he decided they'd stay in New York for the weekend. Take in the remaining sites they wanted to see and fly home Monday morning.

By the time Sunday evening rolled around, they'd gone on a bus tour of the city, traveled by ferry to see the Statue of Liberty and Ellis Island. James had been able to locate his grandfather's name on the list of immigrants that had come over from Ireland. He was thrilled that he'd be able to share the news with his mother. They walked along Wall Street, visited Rockefeller Center, stopped in St. Patrick's Cathedral where they lit a candle for Kelly and her newborn daughter.

One of the last things they did was rent bikes. They'd had marvelous weather and decided to take advantage of it and pedaled through Central Park. They'd just finished their ride as the sun began to set over the city, putting an end to a beautiful day and an unforgettable trip. "I like traveling with you."

"Why?"

"Because I haven't felt like I should be working… I mean I never allowed myself to have fun and enjoy myself when I traveled. It was always work, work, and more work."

"Mel, you have to have some fun in life."

"I realize that now."

They finished their sightseeing with a stop at the iconic Loeb Boathouse in Central Park. The weather wasn't warm enough for the boats to be out but they enjoyed taking in the lake at sunset. It was the perfect end to their stay in New York.

They purchased a bottle of wine, returned to their hotel and were surprised to find the lobby empty. They also had the elevator all to themselves. As the elevator climbed, it lurched and came to an abrupt halt. James immediately recognized the look of panic on Melanie's face.

"Did we just stop?" Before he could say anything, she panicked. "James, do something. We're not moving." She started to pace in circles. "We've got to get this moving. Do something."

"Mel, calm down. Let me see if this phone works." James retrieved the phone and after a few moments someone answered. "Ah, hello. We're in the elevator and it stopped moving."

"Yes, sir we are well aware of it. We've called for our technician but it may be a little while before we get it moving again."

"What do you call a little while?"

"Can't say for sure." He noticed the longer they didn't move the more upset she became. Her hands shook and she was taking short breaths. As soon as he hung up, he pulled her close.

"James, you've got to get this elevator moving. Please." A fine line of moisture had broken out on her brow. "I've got to sit down. I'm dizzy. I feel like I'm going to faint."

James eased her to the floor. Sitting beside her, he pulled her into his arms. "Take a deep breath, Mel." He knew she was listening to him because she did as he asked. "That's right, slowly release it." He ran his hand gently up and down her arm. "Take another deep breath..."

"We're going to die."

"Sweetheart, no we're not. We're going to be just fine." He didn't think she believed him. "They have a technician on the way. They'll get us out soon. Why don't you close your eyes?"

"Close my eyes? I can't. It'll be too dark in here. No."

"Close your eyes and focus on my voice." He watched her as she took deep calming breaths. "I wonder what my mom's doing."

"Why are you talking about your mother at a time like this?"

"I'm sure she's having a blast. Two grandchildren in

just a matter of days. I bet she's driving both Kelly and Angelina crazy. I wonder what they'll name the baby. I can't wait to see her." As he spoke, he could feel Melanie calming. She didn't seem to be trembling quite as badly as when he first pulled her into his arms. Her breathing seemed under control. He just needed to keep talking until they got out of this mess.

"I bet Maria's having the time of her life too. She took the death of Alejandro's first wife and son pretty hard. I know she was ecstatic when he and Angelina adopted Matthew. Matthew was lucky he didn't have to go into foster care. Angelina and Alejandro were pretty much his foster parents until they adopted him."

Upon hearing Matthew had been in foster care, albeit in Alejandro and Angelina's care, she'd tensed again. James knew his father didn't want him inquiring into Melanie's background, but he had to know if she'd ever been in foster care. With the way he felt her body tense with just the mention of it caused him to believe that she had. He knew of her involvement in the art therapy program at the Y. He wondered if her childhood had anything to do with that.

James decided as he sat on the floor of the elevator that he was going to contact Jonas and determine if his gut was right. He believed Melanie had spent part of her life in foster care. He wanted, no, *needed,* to know if that were true. If he had that knowledge behind him, maybe he'd be able to address some of the concerns he had with her.

He continued to talk doing his best to calm her. She sat listening to his soft, smooth voice when all of a sudden, the elevator lurched and they started to move again. He pulled her to her feet and before either one of them could react any further the doors opened. She ran off the elevator, James following right behind. They were immediately greeted by the hotel manager who apologized profusely for their inconvenience.

Melanie didn't hear a word he said. She was elated to be out of the confines of the elevator and on firm ground. James wrapped his arm around her as he listened to the man. He had forgotten all about his bottle of wine until the technician pointed it out. James grabbed the bottle, reached for Melanie's hand, and vaulted for the stairs. Thankfully, they had only two flights to climb before they reached their floor.

By the time they reached their suite, Melanie was better. As soon as he opened the door, he made his way to the kitchenette where he grabbed the bottle opener, deftly removed the cork, and poured them each a glass.

"I really need this," she called as she sat down, taking a swallow of her wine.

He sat beside her and reached for her hand. "What happened?"

"I hate elevators."

"I realize that. What really happened? Did you have a panic attack?" She couldn't look at him. She kept her head lowered. "It's alright if you did. We all have something to fear." His thumb softly stroked her palm. "Mel, please look at me."

When she didn't automatically react, he raised his finger to her chin, edging it slowly upwards so that her eyes would meet his. "Melanie, lean on me. I'll help you through this. I understand that you were scared. In fact, I was a little scared myself." She started to chew on her lower lip. "I'm here if you need me. I'm a good listener, I promise."

"Thanks, but I'd rather not talk about it right now. I'm okay and that's what matters."

James held her and spoke softly, doing his best to further calm her. By the time they'd finished their wine, he knew she was better. He hoped in time she'd learn to trust him and share what was on her mind. If they were to have a relationship, she needed to know he'd be there for her in good times and bad. That was important for him because he'd fallen off the wagon when it came to Elsa. Somehow, in the end, they'd lost that sense of bonding, making him realize neither of them had truly been there for the other. He wanted to be there for Melanie. Help guide her along a path filled with honesty, support, maybe even love and a sense of forever.

Chapter Twenty-Five

JAMES AND MELANIE FLEW HOME bright and early Monday morning. Melanie was surprised that she had another uneventful flight. James sat beside her holding her hand the majority of the way home. Unlike their flight to San Francisco, she was more at ease. She smiled at him and carried on a pleasant conversation about his mother. James still couldn't believe how well they got along.

Jackie drove her kids crazy on a normal day but Melanie took it all in stride. If she didn't like something Jackie said, she matter-of-factly told her straight out. James believed her openness with his mother aided with the success of their relationship. Melanie wanted to learn and Jackie was more than willing to teach her the craft that she so enjoyed.

As soon as they deplaned in St. Louis, he hurried her through the airport. He couldn't wait to get to the hospital to see both Kelly and his new niece. Melanie was reluctant to go with him, but she agreed since she was pretty much at his beck and call. They arrived shortly after noon at the hospital.

Not only did they run into his parents as they made their way down the hallway towards Kelly's room, they also rode the elevator with Alejandro and Ashton. They both were visiting patients in the hospital and decided to check in on Kelly while they were there. "See, what did I tell you?" Melanie practically whispered to James as they neared Kelly's room.

He looked at her, confused. He had no idea what she was referring to. "Remember I told you that Kelly was probably overwhelmed with all of your family? We're here at the hospital not even five minutes and run into your parents and your brother-in-law and Ashton. Kelly must be going crazy with all of this attention."

James glanced at her perplexed. "What is it with you and family? I can't help it that we're all so close. I think you need to get used to it." He grabbed her hand and walked into Kelly's room where she was surrounded by her parents, Alec and Gabriella. James wasn't the least surprised when his mother's eyes honed in on their clasped hands. *She doesn't miss a thing.*

He knew Melanie was a little overwhelmed. Kelly's hospital room wasn't one of the largest but it was still good sized. He could feel her tense when they walked into the room. She'd done her best to hide it but he knew she was out of sorts with so many people.

Alec sat beside Kelly on the bed. He was holding her hand and had a winsome smile on his face as he glanced at his wife. "James, glad you could finally make it," Alec called out. "At least you're here when we make our announcement." He paused and looked lovingly at his wife. "Kelly, do you want to do the honors or shall I?"

"Let's do it together."

"First of all, Kelly and I appreciate everyone's concerns. I'd like to say that she and our daughter are doing quite well. Kelly's coming home later today. I am definitely thankful for that." Alec leaned over and brushed a kiss on his wife's forehead. "Now, for the news you've all been waiting for." Alec looked at Kelly. "Our daughter's name... This was a hard decision. We've been working on this from the moment Kelly discovered she was pregnant. Thankfully we had a girl because we were nowhere near deciding on a boy's name. We decided to call our daughter," he paused again, winked at Kelly, and in unison said, "Abigail Elizabeth Alvarez."

"It's a beautiful name," Maria said as she hugged Alec.

Jackie joined in. "It's perfect for that precious little bundle," and turned to hug both Alec and Kelly.

"I love it," called out Gabriella. "James, have you seen our niece yet?"

"I literally just got in from New York. Melanie and I came straight from the airport. I think we're going to head up there and see our little Abigail, then, I'm going to drop Melanie off at work and head into the office myself. We've got a lot to do today, especially with the sale just around the corner."

"James, both you and Melanie work too hard. You should take the rest of the day off," Jackie said. "Enjoy the day. After all, you have been traveling."

Ben eyed his wife. "There is work to be done."

"Lighten up. Let them play a little. You know how tiring it is traveling."

Ben gave his wife a look of disgust but agreed with her. "Take the rest of the day off. I'll see you both tomorrow. We have a meeting with Saxson at ten."

James and Melanie said their goodbyes and made their way to the NICU. Alec accompanied them. James could feel Melanie begin to tense up as they made their way down the hallway towards Abigail.

"I think I'll wait here." Melanie paused at the waiting room adjacent to the NICU. She half-smiled at him and took a seat.

He wasn't the least bit surprised by her behavior. Alec took it in stride. They cleared security and approached little Abigail's incubator. She was sleeping soundly. "She's beautiful, Alec. Precious. I'm thankful that she is going to be okay."

"Yeah, she needs to put on a little weight but all in all we were pretty lucky. I'd have to say your sister added ten years to my life when she told me her water had broken. Being a doctor, you're prepared for things to happen but when it's your wife, the woman you love, everything changes. Kelly's a real trooper. She didn't get upset. She kept telling me everything was going to be alright, but the possibilities of a premature birth kept running through my head. All I could think of was the worst-case scenarios but thankfully everything turned out in the end. We have our precious Abigail and Kelly's going to be just fine."

James and Alec stayed with the baby for a few more minutes. "I'd better get back to Kelly. I don't want to leave her too long with all of those visitors. I don't want her to overdo it. She's still pretty tired."

"Tell Kelly I love her and that I'll come by to visit her in a few days." They walked out of the NICU, stopping by the waiting room to get Melanie.

"Melanie, thanks for coming. I know Kelly was glad to see you."

"Not a problem, Alec. Tell Kelly I'll come by soon."

"Sure thing." Alec returned to Kelly's room while James escorted Melanie to the elevators. As he had stood over Abigail's incubator, he decided he wasn't even going to confront Melanie on her decision not to see the baby. He'd pretty much dragged her along and didn't even give her the chance to say no. He knew how she reacted to babies and didn't even take into consideration how she would feel. He was glad that he took her but also was a little disturbed by the fact that she couldn't take the time to visit an innocent newborn. Melanie did have a lot of baggage and after today he was more than ready to contact Jonas to learn a little about her background.

He dropped Melanie off at her house and headed home. He had a lot to do before returning to work. He'd barely closed the door behind him when he phoned Jonas. Jonas answered almost immediately.

"It's James Samuels, here."

"Hey, James, how goes it? I heard that Kelly had the baby. I hope everything's okay with it being premature and all."

"I just came from the hospital. Both are doing great. Abigail's going to be in the NICU for a little while so she can gain some weight. Otherwise, mother and daughter are doing wonderfully."

"I'm glad to hear. So how can I help you?"

"I'm calling about Melanie Holmes. I know you performed a background check for Amcrost and I have a couple of questions for you."

"James, I was contracted by your father, not you."

"I realize that. I've grown quite close to her of late. I know there is something significant in her childhood that still affects her today. Am I wrong?"

"No, you're definitely onto something."

"Let me ask you this, was she ever in foster care?"

"Why do you ask?"

"Was she?"

"Okay James, I really shouldn't be discussing this with you. Let's just say she had a difficult childhood and leave it at that."

"I'm right, aren't I?"

"I won't confirm or deny but what I can say is she's lived a life most people wouldn't dream of living."

"Thanks for the information. I owe you."

"I didn't provide you with anything."

"You said enough."

In so many words, Jonas confirmed James' beliefs. She had been in foster care, but what happened to her family? James decided to call her sister. Janet and he were friends. She'd worked at St. Margaret's with Angelina for years before she quit to concentrate on her family. Maybe he'd be able to get some information out of her.

Janet answered as St. Margaret's had an early release for the day. "Hey, James, I heard you and Melanie were in New York. I bet you had a blast."

"We did have a good time. We were lucky that we were able to see the town at night. This wasn't as difficult a trip as I'd previously imagined. The bank we dealt with had been through quite a few acquisitions and knew what they were doing. It made our trip so much easier."

"I hope Mel enjoyed herself. She's so uptight sometimes. I wish I really knew why."

"She wants to do a good job."

"Yeah, it's that and more. She always wants to please everyone and when she can't she falls apart. I tell her to just chill out and everything will be alright but she doesn't listen to a word I say."

"I hear what you're saying." He paused. "One of the

reasons I called is because I really like your sister."

"Wow! That's great. I can definitely see you two together."

He sighed deeply. "I can too, but I can't seem to prove that to Mel. She keeps resisting me. Apparently, she doesn't believe she's capable of having a relationship. I'm hoping to convince her to give us a try."

"Melanie and I didn't have the best time growing up. She's kept a lot of what happened bottled up. For some reason, she won't let go. I know she had it much worse than I did, but I just wish she'd put it all behind her and realize that she owes herself to take that chance."

"May I ask what happened?"

"I'll be quite honest with you. Melanie and I were separated when I was twelve and she six. A lot happened to her in the time we weren't together. I had no idea where she was. I was lucky to find the perfect family that loved me unconditionally."

"Where was Melanie at the time?"

"I really shouldn't tell you this, but I will because I know you care for her. We were placed in foster care. I won't go into the particulars. I'll let her tell you if she so chooses, but from what I know she was constantly moved about. Never had time to build a life with a family." She paused then said, "I think she may have been abused. I can't say for sure but my gut tells me she was."

James gasped.

"I hope someday she'll confide in you what happened to her because she certainly won't tell me."

"Janet, I appreciate you telling me this. I guessed that she'd been in foster care, but I never realized what a horrific experience it was for her." Being constantly moved, never having a sense of family. Now, he understood her aversion to family.

"Yeah, a lot went on in the time we were separated. Now, when something comes up and she begins to share her time growing up, I just listen to her. It's a rare occasion. Just be there for her, listen, and don't pass judgement. I know whatever she went through shaped her into the person she is today."

"I realize that too. Janet, thank you for sharing this with me. I plan on being by her side through thick and thin. I hope she'll feel comfortable enough with me to share her ordeal soon. Whatever she's gone through is eating her up inside. If she won't talk to you or me, maybe she should see someone."

"Don't go there with her. That's a sore subject with her. I'm just warning you—"

"I hear you, Janet. I appreciate your time. Let's make plans to go out for a drink sometime."

"Sounds good to me."

James ended the call and stared at the phone for a moment. His instincts had been right on. Now, he had to convince her to tell him her story.

Melanie didn't know how to spend the rest of her day. She cleaned her house, did some laundry, organized the information she brought home from White Donegal, and when she couldn't find anything else to keep her busy, she phoned Janet.

"Hey, sis, how are you?"

"Good, and you? How was your trip?"

"It was great. We got a lot accomplished and we even got in some sightseeing."

"You'll have to tell me all about it."

"That's why I'm calling. What are you doing for dinner?"

"I have no plans, why?"

"How does a greasy burger from Oxfords sound?"

"I haven't been there in at least a week. Sounds delicious. Half hour?"

"See you then."

Janet met Melanie at Oxfords Bar & Grille. Melanie often stopped on her way home having called ahead for carryout. Brant "Ox" Oxford was the proprietor of the bar and a nice guy. Melanie had gotten to know him when Gabriella played softball on St. Margaret's team.

She was greeted by the vociferous Ox when she walked through the doors. "Melanie!" He waved to her from the bar. She waved back and slid into the booth across from Janet.

"Mel, you look great. Did you have a good trip?"

"In all actuality, I did for a change. James and I were able to see the city mostly at night and we even stayed the weekend." She sipped her water. "Oh, we even saw a couple get engaged atop the Empire State Building. That's pretty romantic. Don't you think?"

"It is, but I didn't think you believed in that. Haven't you pretty much declared over and over again that relationships are for the birds and you have absolutely no intention of getting romantically involved with anyone?"

"I have but I may be softening my opinion on the matter."

"Really? That's interesting. Who's helping you soften this opinion? Could it possibly be one James Samuels?"

Melanie looked sheepishly at her sister. She didn't

want to own up to the fact that she was hoping for a relationship with him. He was the best thing that had ever happened to her. He could read her so well. Knew when she needed to hold his hand so that it would calm her fears. He was the only person that had ever helped her through a panic attack and not walked away from her. Most of her supposed friends thought she was crazy and many had ended their friendship. But so far, she believed James was here to stay.

"James is doing his best to convince me. I'd already agreed to go out with him as friends, but he wants more. He told me in no certain terms that he has feelings for me." Melanie took a sip of water. "Janet, ever since I was a little girl, I promised myself that I was going to stay single. Not fall into the trap of thinking you're in love with someone when deep down you probably aren't. I've witnessed too many situations where what you see on the surface is truly not what's going on behind the scenes. Couples that appeared to be caring and so much in love actually detested one another."

"Honey, maybe James is different. Every time I've been in his presence, he seems loving and caring of his family. He shows an interest in their friends. He seems like an all-around great guy. I think you should give it a try. You might be surprised and realize that he's the one to ultimately change your beliefs on the subject."

Janet reached for Melanie's hand. "I don't know what you went through in all of the homes you were assigned. I only know that you were moved about quite frequently. I can't even begin to help you if you won't tell me." Melanie looked away. "I know it was a long time ago, and I know that you've carried a lot of baggage from your childhood. Maybe you should see someone. Maybe a therapist would help you work your way through those times. Learn to move on and try to experience new and exciting things for yourself."

Melanie knew Janet could see that she was on the verge of crying. She did her best to control her emotions and thankfully their waitress appeared just at the right moment to take their orders. Melanie buried her face in the menu she'd already memorized from cover to cover, acting like she was trying to decide what to order. Once she'd fought back her tears, she lowered the menu ordering the special "Ox" burger. "I haven't had one of these in ages."

"That's one of our best sellers," the waitress replied as she wrote down her order.

"Originally I was going to get a burger, but that chicken club's just calling my name," Janet said then changed the subject not wanting to upset her sister.

"How was bingo?"

"I had a blast. I guess you heard Angelina got so excited after winning a game that her water broke."

"I did. She sure can be the life of a party when she wants to."

"She can. But the best thing was I won the big prize—a weekend getaway to Chicago."

"I didn't hear that. Congrats. Are you going to take James?" Janet caught the instant sparkle in her sister's eyes. "You are, aren't you?"

"I'm not sure."

"Melanie?"

"Okay, alright, I think I will. We'll have to see where this goes. I have to use the trip within the year, so I have plenty of time to decide."

Janet checked her watch after having devoured her

sandwich. "Look at the time. I better get moving. Tomorrow's a school day."

"Yeah, I have a meeting tomorrow with James and company. I'd better get moving myself."

The two were parked right next to one another. Janet pulled her sister into a hug as she said her goodbye. "I hope you'll give James a chance. I think he'd be perfect for you."

"Between you and me, I think I'm going to give it a try. What's there to lose, right? Talk to you soon." Melanie watched as her sister got into her car and drove away. She was right. He was kind and caring. What was there to lose? The worst outcome might be a broken heart. It wasn't as if she hadn't experienced that a million times as she worked through the foster care system.

Chapter Twenty-Six

THE NEXT MORNING MELANIE DROPPED her things off in her office and headed directly to Saxson's conference room. She'd received a text from him the evening before instructing her of their intended meeting with various Amcrost representatives.

As she came around the corner, she ran smack dab into James. He automatically reached out to steady her. "Good morning, James. Sorry about that I didn't expect anyone here this early."

"I came directly here instead of going into Amcrost first thing. Good morning to you too. Would you care for a cup of coffee?"

"That's where I was headed when we collided." James followed Melanie to the kitchenette where she poured each of them a cup of coffee. "Care for a bagel? I see Saxson has gone all out this morning."

"Yeah. We've got quite the contingent coming over. I guess he wanted to be hospitable."

"Usually when we have an early morning meeting, he provides breakfast, but not in this quantity. Generally, it's just bagels, but looky here he has fruit, Danish, donuts, bagels…quite the spread this morning." She grabbed a cheese Danish while James selected a bagel and cream cheese.

"I think we might be the first ones here."

"Probably. What time does this meeting start, anyway?"

"I believe eight-thirty."

"Oh well, we have almost an hour. How about coming back to my office for a bit? We can eat there. It might be a little more relaxing than sitting in that huge conference room."

When they returned to her office, Melanie shut the door. She didn't want anyone to possibly overhear their conversation as they were still working through the sale. Melanie picked at her Danish and listened to James. "Kelly came home late yesterday afternoon. Mom told me Alec seemed a little nervous."

"Alec, nervous? I don't see that."

"Surprisingly, yes. When it comes to my sister, he turns into a completely different man. He's easily rattled. In fact, I don't know if you know this, but when he went to say his wedding vows, he couldn't remember her name. He fumbled until he found his words. It was actually pretty hilarious. Alejandro burst out laughing right there on the altar. Alec loves her so much and doesn't want to ever see her hurt again. It's actually quite endearing, seeing a doctor who normally keeps their emotions in check respond to my sister's needs the way he does. She's his life and now that they have Abigail, I think he's going to get worse. He's just like Alejandro when it comes to family. Family's first and foremost with them. It's refreshing to see these days with how busy they both are."

"I'll have to get by and see them." She knew James watched her closely as she tore at her pastry.

"We could go see Angelina and the kids tonight. I'm free."

"Sorry, but I can't. I have plans." It was Tuesday and she had art therapy.

"Maybe another night then." She watched James as he finished off his bagel. Out of the blue he stood and came around her desk. He caught her off guard when he placed his hands on either side of her face, leaned over, and placed a soft kiss on her lips. He pulled away, licked his lips, and returned to his seat.

Melanie was taken aback by his actions. With a broad smile, she watched as he reached for his coffee. "I think I'll have one of those pastries when the meeting begins. That was quite tasty."

"What was that for?" She was perplexed by his kiss.

"I've wanted to do that for ages. I thought what a better way to start off our day than with a kiss."

"But."

"But what?"

"We're at the office."

"Yes, and we are also behind a closed door. Don't worry. It's okay."

"Easy enough for you to say. You're definitely going to have a job when the sale is completed."

"Who says you won't?"

"I certainly don't think your dad's going to employ two VP's of Acquisitions afterwards."

"My dad's creative, he'll think of something. Stop worrying so much. It will all work out."

She shrugged. "If you say so."

"I do. Now, let's plan our first real date? I'm sure you've heard about The Vineyard on the Hill. It's where both Kelly and Angelina got engaged. I've never eaten there, but I've heard the ambience is something pretty spectacular. What do you say? Shall I make reservations for this weekend?"

"Isn't that a little too much for us. It's just our first date."

"I know but I'd like to start this relationship off on the right foot. There's nothing to be nervous about. It's not like a blind date. We've known each other in pretty intimate ways." She was speechless remembering San Antonio, spending nights together in the same bed. "Sorry, I shouldn't have brought that up. I realize even with our friendship today that it's still a sore subject for you. Come on. Let's dress up and have a good time. I'm sure we'll have a memorable night."

"I have a cooking class with your mother."

"So, what does that have to do with it?"

"Nothing."

"Stop hemming and hawing. Just say yes."

"Okay. Yes." She watched as James stood. "Now where are you headed off to?"

"Our meeting, of course."

They had a productive meeting. All things were on target for the pending sale. Just a few short weeks and Parklayne Bank would be no more.

"So, what are your plans for the rest of the weekend?" Jackie asked as she watched Melanie roll out a pie crust.

Melanie wasn't sure if Jackie knew about her date with James. She decided not to tell her because she didn't want her interfering. "Not much."

"Have you visited Kelly and Angelina yet?"

"No, I've been pretty busy."

"The babies are both precious. I love them to pieces." Melanie knew Jackie would be putting her through some type of inquisition. She waited and waited and then it came. "So, Melanie, when are you going to get married and have a family?"

Melanie started chewing on her lower lip. She didn't want to respond. She was still trying to work through the fact that she and James were going on a real date. She tried to ignore the question and kept rolling out the dough. Then she felt Jackie's hand on her arm stopping her movement. "Melanie, honey, did you hear what I asked?"

"I did."

"And?"

"I'd rather not discuss that right now."

"You'd make a wonderful mother."

"Jackie, please stop." Jackie latched onto her arm and led her over to the table. She motioned for her to sit. "Like I said, I'd rather not discuss this."

"Melanie, I want you to know that I am here for you. If you ever need someone to talk to."

"Thank you, Jackie. I appreciate it."

"So why don't you take me up on my offer? If you're afraid someone will overhear you, we're alone in the house." Jackie was gearing up for more. "Melanie, as long as I've known you, I felt a sadness surrounding you. I know you put on a good front for everyone, but I see it. I see it in your eyes, in your mannerisms. You never speak about your family, other than Janet. You never reminisce about your childhood..."

Melanie did her best to waylay tears from forming but nothing worked. When one escaped and slipped down her cheek, she knew she was a goner. Jackie wouldn't let that pass. She wiped the tear from her face and started to stand. Jackie stopped her. "I upset you and I am sorry."

"I know you are. It's just hard for me to talk about my past, my childhood." She clasped her hands in front of her. She needed to hold onto something or else Jackie would see her trembling hands. "I really didn't have a family. My dad died when I was a baby and Janet and I became separated when I was six. We didn't see one another for a long time. I'd like to forget that time."

"I'm sorry to hear about your father. What about your mom?" Upon Jackie's last question, Melanie thrust herself out of her chair and returned to the pie crust.

"Now what do I do?" Melanie hoped that Jackie would realize that she was done with her conversation. She never spoke about her mother, ever. Not even with Janet. Janet knew that topic was off limits.

Jackie rejoined her at the counter and they went about making a cherry pie. Jackie took her cue and didn't bring up Melanie's family again.

Melanie told Jackie she couldn't stay long since she had plans for that evening. Jackie mustn't have known about hers and James' date because she didn't question her further. Jackie begged her to set-up another class, so Melanie agreed to the following Sunday and promised she'd stay for dinner too. Melanie wasn't keen on being a part of a family dinner but agreed anyway.

Melanie put Jackie's meddling, if that was what to call it, behind her. She wanted to be in a good frame of mind and also look her best because she was excited for their date, but nervous at the same time. She still didn't truly believe in the whole falling in love thing. If she went in with her eyes wide open, she wouldn't be too disappointed when it didn't work out. Melanie had been exposed too many times to people telling half-truths only to be disappointed in the end.

Since she and James were going to The Vineyard on the Hill, Melanie took care as she dressed. She pulled her hair up into a French twist with tendrils framing her face. She wore a wine-colored dress that flowed just past her knees. The dress was accented with a gold necklace and she wore gold hoop earrings. She looked prim and proper. Nothing too sophisticated. The overall look pleased her.

She'd barely finished putting in her earrings when her doorbell rang. James greeted her with a bouquet of flowers. "These are for you."

"Wow!" She smiled in surprise. "You definitely are trying to impress."

"I'm not trying to impress you at all. I just wanted to do something special to commemorate our first date. That's all."

"Well thank you. Let me get these in water and then we can go." She hurriedly put the flowers in a vase. She'd left her coat lying on the back of the couch. When she started to reach for it, their hands brushed as James beat her to it.

"Here let me help you with that." She spun around and he held the coat for her. He clasped his hands on her shoulders. "Relax, Mel."

"I am." She slightly turned and saw him give her that half-cocked look that he always seemed to have when he questioned her. She smiled. "Let's go, I'm hungry."

The Vineyard was all he'd heard about from his sisters.

It was a truly romantic experience from the moment they walked through the doors. They were greeted by a hostess who immediately led them to their table. James had heard about the special rooms that overlooked the vineyard. He'd thought about trying to reserve one, but in the end, he knew it would be way too much for Melanie.

Their waitress was waiting for them at the table. She informed them of the specials and suggested several wines The Vineyard was known for. James selected a white wine because he knew Melanie enjoyed that more than a red. They perused the menu while they waited for the sommelier to bring their wine.

"James, this is a lovely restaurant." She glanced over his shoulder taking in the ambiance. "I can see why it's so special for your family. She leaned closer with a quiver in her voice, "I can't believe you brought me here especially on our first date."

"Why not? I wanted it to be a memorable evening for you."

"Well, it definitely will be." They enjoyed their wine and placed their orders. While they waited for their first course, the music started up. "Would you care to dance?"

"I'd love to but just so you know I'm not very good. Be prepared for sore toes because I'll be stepping all over them."

Chuckling at her comment he stood and reached out with his hand. "You let me worry about my toes. Just enjoy." James clasped her hand in his and led her to the dance floor where they joined three additional couples. He pulled her into his arms and nuzzled the side of her face. No words were spoken as they enjoyed the music.

When the dance ended, he pulled away slightly. He lifted her hand brushing a soft kiss to her fingers. "That was perfect." When they returned to their table, he remained holding her hand until their salads were served. He watched her as they ate. She looked beautiful. He'd never seen her wear her hair up like this with wispy tendrils framing her face. He liked the look. "I love your hair like that. You should wear it up more often."

"I wear it up quite often. When we work together, you'll see." She stopped practically mid-sentence. He immediately read her emotions. She was worrying again, gnawing on her lower lip.

"Don't worry about it unless you have to. I'm sure everything will be fine."

"You don't know for sure. I could be one of those employees easily job discontinued. You hear about it all the time."

"Let's not think about it—tonight's all about us. We'll worry about that other if it happens." Again, he kissed her hand. "Smile and enjoy all tonight has to offer."

He knew Melanie always had her job in the back of her mind. He didn't know how he'd convince her she had nothing to worry about. Yes, she may not keep the job she was used to and comfortable with, but he was almost assured she'd still have a job.

They enjoyed their meal and even danced to several more ballads. "I love having you in my arms, Melanie. It feels right— like you were meant to be here." He drew her closer. As they swayed in time to the music, he felt her relax even more. He hoped that she was enjoying herself as much as he was.

Before he knew it, they were on their way home. As

they drove along, the streetlights cast a glow across her face. At that moment in time, he knew he was hooked. After just one date, she'd stolen his heart. He hoped in time that he'd convince her that fate brought them together that night in San Antonio. That was when he realized that Elsa wasn't right for him. It took him a few months to end their relationship, but that week was a life altering time for him. That's when he knew he'd found the woman of his dreams. Now, he just needed to convince her that they were destined to be together.

Chapter Twenty-Seven

THE NEXT WEEK FLEW BY and before long it was time for her next cooking class. She'd agreed to stay and have dinner with the Samuels, but now she was having some regrets. She originally thought dinner was just Ben, Jackie, Wyatt, and herself, but she was surprised when the whole clan arrived, including Gabriella and Ashton.

"I couldn't say no," Jackie told her as they prepared the side dishes of au gratin potatoes and green bean almandine. "I invited Angelina, Alejandro, and the kids, and of course Alec and Kelly. You know they need time away from the hospital. I think Kelly lives there with Abigail. I would have included John and Maria but they already had something planned and Joe was on call, so he declined. I couldn't leave out Gabriella."

"I understand Jackie. You have a large family. You don't want any hurt feelings."

Jackie appeared to count in her head. "Oh my, I forgot James. I invited him too. How could I forget about him? Oh well, he's coming too." She wasn't quite sure she believed Jackie had forgotten her son but smiled when she mentioned him.

As the food cooked, Melanie sat in the kitchen with

Jackie, Angelina, Kelly, and Gabriella. "I see that everyone gets here rather early."

"Of course, we do. It's time to catch up. We're all so busy now that this is better than using the phone. We get together and everyone can hear the same stories at once— no forgetting or leaving anything out." Kelly thought for a moment and added, "Abigail gained another two ounces. If she keeps up this pace, she might come home next week. Fingers crossed."

"That's wonderful news," Angelina said as she held Christian. Thankfully he was sleeping soundly because when they first arrived, he'd been screaming at the top of his lungs.

Melanie took in the scene around her. She was overwhelmed with everyone, but the moment James walked through the door everything seemed to change. His family had no idea they were dating, and she didn't plan on mentioning it. It was their life, their story, and if things worked out then they'd share their status with everyone.

Everyone ignored James once he announced himself except for Melanie. He was old school. The women were wrapped up in sharing news about the babies. She knew he was in tune to everything about her and could tell she was overwhelmed. He winked at her as he crossed to the refrigerator to get a can of soda. No one saw him except her. She knew it was his way of saying everything would be alright.

"Hey James, check your mail. I think there's an invitation to your fifteen-year high school reunion in there."

"And how would you know that, Mom? Did you open and read it?"

"Oh no, I wouldn't think of doing that." She waved

him off. "It's a postcard announcing it. You're supposed to check out a website they've set up for it."

"So, you did read it?"

"Well, how could I not? It's a postcard, for crying out loud."

James shook his head at his mother. True to form, Jackie knew everything, or at least she thought she did.

Jackie announced dinner and everyone headed off to the dining room. Melanie was surprised when she first arrived and discovered that their table was huge with all the leaves in it. It would seat everyone. There was even a highchair for Angel.

Melanie had no idea where she should sit. James caught her eye and pulled out a chair. He motioned for her to take a seat while he grabbed the chair to her right. He smiled as he sat and reached for her hand underneath the table. No one would notice because the tablecloth covered their handholding. He leaned over and whispered in her ear. "You okay?"

She nodded that she was, even though she wasn't. She had a smile plastered on her face which she knew he deciphered as fake to the nth degree. "We'll leave as soon as we can, I promise." James released her hand so he could pass the rolls to her.

Her anxiety with all the noise had picked up right before he walked through the door, but one look at him calmed her immensely. She still had issues but she felt much better with him close by.

Melanie made it through dinner and helped clean up. By the time the dishes were done, she was tired. "Jackie, I think I need to head on out. I have a few things I need to do before work tomorrow. Thank you for inviting me to dinner. I had a great time."

By the time she arrived home, she was more than ready for bed. It was only eight o'clock but the socializing had zapped her energy. She wasn't cut out for family stuff, that was for sure.

Just as she was ready to turn off her lights, she heard a knock at her door. She didn't even inquire who was there. She knew. She eased the door open. James leaned against the frame. He didn't say a word. Instead, he leaned in and pulled her into his arms. He held her for a few moments, pulled away, and walked into her home. "Sorry about that."

"What do you have to be sorry about?"

"My family. How did you end up there for a family dinner?"

"One guess." James knew immediately. "She invited me last week. I thought it would just be your parents and Wyatt, but when I walked in and saw the table set with all of the leaves in, I knew I was in trouble. I was never so glad to see you. I worried you weren't coming."

He threw his arm around her and led her to the family room where they sat down. "I knew you were a little overwhelmed."

"A little? How do you put up with all that noise? Everyone talks at once."

"Yeah. They all want to be heard, that's for sure. In all actuality, I was surprised to see you. My mom never mentioned that you were joining us." He started playing with her hair. "I don't think they know we're seeing one another."

"I never said a thing and I don't intend to."

"You realize this may work out between us. I wasn't misleading you. I have real feelings for you." He leaned closer. "I loved our trip to New York. I think it was the best thing we could have ever done. I saw another side to you."

"That's because I was relaxed and not nervous like I normally am when I travel."

"It wasn't that and you know it." He cupped her jaw. "Whether you want to admit it or not, I know you have feelings for me. Soon you're not going to be able to deny it." He leaned in and kissed her forehead. "I'm going to head on home. I just wanted to make sure you were okay." She followed him to the door. He opened it and started out, paused, and stepped back into her foyer. "I have a question for you."

"Okay?"

"What are you doing May 20?"

"Why do you ask?"

"Will you attend my reunion with me?"

"James, I don't know." He grasped her hand. "We don't even know where we will be then."

"What do you mean by that?"

"Who's to say we'll even be together then? I've never dated anyone longer than two weeks. That's almost three months from now."

"I believe in us and that's what matters. You've just got to start believing in our future too. I know we're going to have one." With that he turned and walked out the door leaving her to contemplate his words. *Is he right? Should I consider this a second chance? A second chance at having a family, a real family? I'm not going to dwell on this. I'm just not.* Melanie closed the door and headed off to bed. She had to get up early the next day.

The closing of the sale of Parklayne Bank was scheduled to be completed that Friday. So much had happened in the last few weeks.

Melanie was more nervous than normal. She still didn't know what her future held. She'd received a call from Ben late Friday evening, advising her of a meeting with both him and Saxson first thing Monday morning. She didn't mention it to James when they'd gone out Saturday night. If he were planning on being there, he'd undoubtedly have mentioned it and he hadn't. She hoped for the best but deep down felt her time was limited.

Melanie pulled into the parking garage at Amcrost just before ten for the scheduled meeting. She was doing her best to keep her anxiety in control but knew she wasn't. She hopped on the elevator. She was alone. As the elevator climbed, her claustrophobia took over and the walls began to close in on her. By the time the door opened, she was breathing heavily. She made her way to the ladies' room where she splashed cold water onto her face. She took several deep calming breaths before making her way to Ben's offices.

His assistant Delia greeted her outside. "You may go on in, Ms. Holmes." Melanie thanked her and knocked on the door. She wasn't just going to barge in. She heard Ben's voice telling her to enter, so she eased open the door, unsure who would be present. She entered the room and saw Ben and Saxson sitting at his small conference table. "Come join us," Saxson called.

Melanie ambled to the table and pulled out one of the chairs. She sat down nervously looking about the room. Ben was cordial but she knew the writing was on the wall. She was going to lose her job.

"Melanie, first of all, we both want to commend you on your work with engineering the sale. We both know how much time you and James both put in along with handling the Dalton B&T and White Donegal acquisitions." *Here it comes.* "On that note, with the closing on the sale this Friday, we wanted to talk with you about your future with Amcrost." *I'm out.* Her heart starting racing. She knew all of her hard work wasn't going to pay off. She wasn't a member of the Samuels family and definitely wasn't guaranteed a job with Amcrost.

Melanie clasped her hands and listened as Saxson outlined the transition. "As you well know, we don't have room for two VP's of Acquisitions. As of right now, James will remain in his current position. We'd like for you to assist him through the transition and then..." *Hasta la vista...* "After sixty days, we're going to move you into a new position." Her face dropped. Saxson paused. She had a blank look on her face like she wasn't understanding their plan. "Melanie, I want to assure you that you are not losing your job. You'll have a job somewhere, but I'm not exactly sure what position or department you will be assigned. I have to be honest here, but more than likely you will lose your title." *The title I worked so hard to attain. The title that means the world to me.*

"Melanie," Ben added, "I promise you have absolutely nothing to worry about. I personally assure you that you will have a comparable job—just not with the title of vice president."

She heard what each of them said but she was having a hard time understanding. She knew she'd have a job after sixty days, but what? She didn't like not knowing what her future held. Each of the men detailed the transition, but she really didn't hear what they were saying. She was solely focused on the loss of the job that she'd fought so hard to achieve. Their conversation was just a jumble of words, words that she didn't comprehend. Then she heard Ben ask her if she had any questions. "Ah, no. Not right at this moment," she replied still in a state of shock. She knew she should be thankful she still had a job. She just couldn't wrap her head around what they'd just told her.

Melanie realized the meeting was over. She stood, shaking both men's hands. She thanked them and walked out.

Melanie hurried to the elevator, which just so happened to be waiting. She shuffled past someone who exited, barely aware they said something. She jumped on, never hearing James calling out to her.

The elevator ride back down to the garage passed in a blur. The door opened and she stumbled out right into the arms of Holcomb Newson. She was rattled by her meeting but laying eyes on the man that sent her to the hospital all those years ago. The man that changed her life and made her fear having a relationship. The man that lived in her dreams— one of her worst nightmares— had her by the arms.

"Let me go! Get away from me!" She threw her hands up in a protective manner. "W-what are you doing here. Are you following me?"

He shuffled backwards raising his hands. "Melanie, I'm not going to hurt you."

"Stay away…" she shrieked as she closed her arms around herself.

He stepped forward closer to her. "Melanie, listen to me," he pleaded. "I've changed. I'm not the same man

I was."

The walls were closing in around her. She feared he was going to beat her again. The blood rushed to her head, her temples throbbed. She was going to faint. Her airway narrowed and she had difficulty breathing. She needed to get away before he injured her. She stumbled, Holcolmb reached out to right her, and that's when she broke.

She started beating her fists against him. "Let me go… Holcomb let me go…" she screamed.

"Let her go," a voice called out.

"I'm not hurting her. She tripped out of the elevator and I caught her."

"I don't care what you say you did. Let her go." Holcomb dropped his arms and Melanie sagged to the cold concrete floor.

"Mel, it's me, James. I've got you." James pulled her into his arms. She was trembling. "Sweetheart, I'm right here. You're alright. I won't let anything happen to you." He ran his hand up and down her back trying to calm her.

"Just go, Holcomb. I'll catch up with you in the office." He grabbed the elevator and left James holding Melanie on the garage floor.

"Mel, everything's going to be alright." He helped her to stand, to gain her balance on shaky legs. "I'll take you to my office where you can calm down and relax."

"No. I need to go. Just let me go." James pulled away and watched Melanie as she practically ran to her car. "Mel, you're in no condition to drive."

"Just leave me alone." With that, Melanie jumped into her car and pulled out of the garage, never once looking back. She knew James had no idea what happened during her meeting with Ben and Saxson. What she did know was that he knew Holcomb. He called him by name. How did he know him—the man that turned her life into the living hell that it was. She couldn't forget. The dreams were always with her. She was going straight home, not answering the door or the phone until she got herself under control.

James immediately went to Holcomb's office. He worked in the back-office operations of the bank. James had no idea how he knew Melanie, but what he did know was that he'd upset her. James knew the man was waiting for him. He entered the office without even knocking and closed the door. "First, what the hell happened out there and second, how do you know Melanie Holmes?"

Holcomb explained that Melanie fell out of the elevator into his arms. "My reflexes were just fast enough that I caught her before she face-planted on the concrete floor. I could tell she was upset. Then she recognized me."

"How do you know her?"

"I was one of her many foster parents. I'm surprised she recognized me. That was a long time ago."

"Why was she so upset?"

"I was a different man then. I've changed." He ran his hand along the back of his neck and sighed. "I was having marital problems, I drank a little too much, and I hit her a few times." He sagged.

"You what?" James became enraged. He clenched his hands but what he really wanted to do was take out this man. He'd hurt Melanie. She was but a little girl, defenseless. Why? How could he take his anger out on her?

"In a drunken spur, I hit her and knocked her around a bit. She had to go to the hospital. I was arrested and she was reassigned to a different family." James couldn't believe his ears. Was Holcomb the cause of her problem? Was he the reason she didn't want a relationship? A family?

"Melanie experienced some pretty horrible things before she lived with me, and I didn't help her in the least. I only added to it." Holcomb dropped into a nearby chair and hung his head. "I'm sure I messed with her psyche too. James, I regret everything I did. I'm changed. I am." With regret in his eyes, he looked up. "I've gotten the help I needed. I regularly attend AA meetings now. I've been sober for years."

"I believe you, Holcomb. I do." James turned away. He was shocked by what he heard as Holcomb had been a model employee. Melanie beaten, by him, but what else? What other horrible things could have happened to her? Wasn't this enough? She'd been just a child. He brushed his hand across his face, took a deep breath and turned back. "It's just that I'm worried about her. Thanks for being truthful with me. Now, I've got to go find her." James hurried out. He had no idea where she'd fled. In the state she was in, he was almost positive she hadn't gone into the office.

He called her office and all her assistant knew was that she'd had a meeting with both Ben and Saxson. Her assistant hadn't laid eyes on her since she'd left the office at nine-thirty.

James drove to her house. Her car wasn't outside. He rang the doorbell and she didn't answer. Two hours had elapsed since she left the parking garage. No one had heard or seen her. He contacted Janet and left a voice mail message. He was worried and was getting more upset by the minute. He was getting nowhere so he returned to his office. She'd turn up eventually but he wasn't sure where or what condition she'd be in both mentally and physically.

Melanie drove around. She first headed for her house, but James would search for her there, so she decided to go to the one place she knew she felt safe and secure.

She knocked on the door and when it opened, she threw herself into Jackie's arms. "Melanie, dear, what's wrong? What happened? Oh dear, it's alright." Jackie held onto Melanie as the tears flowed. "Come in, let's get you settled, and I'll get you something to drink."

Jackie wrapped her arms around Melanie and led her into their warm cozy family room. She eased her down onto the couch, reaching for a box of tissues on the end table. She handed one to Melanie and sat beside her as she calmed.

"Thank you, Jackie. I didn't know where else to go." Melanie sniffed as she got herself under control.

"What happened? What has you so upset?"

She explained about her meeting with Ben and Saxson. "I'm losing my job. I have sixty days and then I'm being reassigned to...what? I haven't a clue. I know I should be thankful that I still have a position, but it won't be the same. I worked so hard to get this job. I was proud of myself. I'd come so far in life and now it's slipping through my hands."

"But honey..."

"Jackie, it was my dream job."

"What else is bothering you, dear? I know it's not just your job situation."

"When I was exiting the building, I ran into my past."

"And?"

"Let's just say he caused me a lot of pain. I haven't been the same since I lived with him."

"Melanie, I'm not sure exactly what you are talking about."

"No, of course, you don't." Melanie sighed and took a deep, deep breath. "What I am about to tell you I'd rather you not share with anyone, including James."

"I promise. This is just between you and me."

Fresh tears formed in Melanie's eyes and Jackie drew Melanie's hands into hers. Melanie gained strength from the touch. She needed it to tell her story. "My dad died when I was a baby."

"I know you told me."

"Well, I ended up in foster care when I was six." Melanie knew Jackie had questions but she also knew not to ask them. "Janet and I were separated and I didn't see her for a long, long time."

"Oh, Melanie, I'm so sorry."

"Thank you, but there's nothing you can do. What happened, happened. I must have had the worst luck because I was constantly reassigned to different homes. Sometimes because of financial reasons, others because of deaths, divorces. It didn't matter. I just never had a chance to settle. Then, I was in a home. The man was an alcoholic. He didn't like me. For some reason he got off on shoving me around. I was a kid. I didn't know what to do. One day, he got really mad, hauled off and hit me, and I ended up in the hospital. I never returned to his home. I was reassigned again and had never been face-to-face with him—until today. I was leaving Amcrost after my meeting with Ben and Saxson. I'd just found out about my job status. I was upset and tripped coming off the elevators. I fell right into Holcomb Newson's arms. The man that forever changed my life."

"Melanie, I'm so sorry. What can I do?"

"You can't do anything. I just needed someone to talk to, and I thought of you. You've been so kind to me. I can talk to you and not worry about what I say. I want you to know that I appreciate our friendship. Thank you for being there for me." She ran her hands through her hair. Their conversation settled her. The tightness in her chest that had formed earlier had lessened, her hands were steadying and her tears had dried.

Jackie took Melanie's hands. "Dear, I consider you a daughter. I enjoy our time together. You can always come to me when you need to vent, or share something, or even cry on my shoulder. I love you, Melanie, and I'm glad you felt comfortable enough to come to me with this." She pulled Melanie once again into arms. "You're not alone. You'll always have me, Ben, and James. We'll be here for you."

Chapter Twenty-Eight

JAMES WAS GOING CRAZY. FINALLY, at seven, he drove by Melanie's and discovered lights on in the house. He wasn't sure if she would let him in, but he decided to try. There was no answer when he knocked, so he tried again. Just as he was ready to walk away, she opened the door.

With one look he knew she wasn't in a good place. She moved away from the door welcoming his admittance. As he stepped into the foyer, he cupped her cheek. Shyly she looked up at him. She'd been crying—her eyes were red-rimmed and puffy, her nose was red. No words were spoken as he drew her into his arms. She went, wrapping her arms around his waist.

He held her close for a few moments then pulled away slightly, but he kept her face buried in his shoulder. He reached down and raised her head so she'd look him directly in the eyes. "Sweetheart, I know about Holcomb." A surprised look crossed her face. She averted her eyes. "Come on, let's sit down and talk about what happened."

"I don't think I can."

"How about I talk and you listen, then?"

He guided her to the family room sofa where he

again wrapped his arms about her and stroked her arm. He wanted her to know she could depend on him. "I spoke with Holcomb." She tensed but he continued to caress her arm, his voice soft, calming. "I didn't realize you knew him."

Still no response so he changed the subject. "I didn't know you were coming into the office today. Why were you there?"

Melanie pulled away. "You have no idea why I was there?" James had a perplexed look on his face. She quirked her eyebrow. "You really haven't a clue why I was there?"

"If I did, I'd say I did. In fact, why didn't you tell me Saturday you were coming to the office? We could have scheduled lunch."

"After that meeting, I wouldn't have been in any condition to do lunch. Add Holcomb to the mix, and I definitely was done for the day."

"Who did you meet with?"

"Your father," she paused. "And Saxson." James' gaze shot up to her face. He hadn't spoken with his father the entire day. In fact, after she tore out of the garage, he'd spent the day worrying about her. He'd been absolutely useless as he ran around looking for her.

"May I ask what it was about?"

"Are you serious? You have no clue?"

He drew in his lips and shook his head. "Nope, no clue. After I ran into you, I met with Holcomb and then drove around the rest of the day looking for you." He reached for her hands. "Is it about your job?" She nodded, obviously on the verge of crying. "Sweetheart, it can't be that bad."

She started to withdraw. Her hands trembled in his. A

lone tear slid down her cheek. She swiped it off. He was thankful that he stopped by. He wanted, no, needed to be supportive of her.

"It's okay if you don't want to talk about it. I just want you to know that I'm here with you and I'll be here as long as you need me."

He felt her start to relax. Her tears had stopped, and overall, she seemed calmer. "Thank you, James."

"For what?"

"For just being you."

They sat wrapped in one another's arms for some time before she spoke. He believed if he waited long enough, she'd tell him about her meeting, and he was right. "Your dad called me late Friday night, that's when he invited me to his office this morning."

James wanted to know why she hadn't said anything when they'd gone on their date but refrained from asking. He wanted her to do all of the talking. He was going to be a good listener.

"I should have told you Saturday night, but since I wasn't sure what it was about, I decided not to mention it. I also didn't want to put you in the middle. If it was something you should be involved with, I was sure he would have included you. When I got there and it was just the two of them, I knew right then and there what it was about." She paused, took a deep breath and continued. "You're the chosen one."

James had no idea what she was referring to. "What do you mean?'"

"Well, let's see. You are a Samuels. You are the top dog in the department for the company that's taking over my department. You've been in your position longer than I have. Over the years, Amcrost has done way more acquisitions than Parklayne—"

"Would you quit being so cryptic in your response and just tell me exactly what happened?"

"Basically, I'm out. I have sixty days to work through the transition and then..."

"You were job discontinued?"

"More or less. In sixty days, they'll find a job for me. I'll more than likely lose the title I worked so hard to attain. I'm going to be forced into a job—"

"No one's going to force you."

"Well, of course they will. I won't have a choice in the matter if I want to stay with the bank."

He was surprised his father had decided this would be her outcome. "Mel, I had no idea."

"Really?" she said in disbelief.

"Listen to me." She turned her head away and tried to stand. He tightened his arm about her. "Please look at me. Honestly, this comes as a complete surprise. I had no idea that you were going to be removed from the job. I assumed we'd co-manage the department, but I guess my dad and Saxson thought otherwise."

She turned back to him. "You really didn't know?"

"I didn't. I wish my dad would have talked to me about this. I had a few ideas on how we could've made it work, but I guess he didn't want my opinion."

She pulled away and started to stand. "I'm exhausted and I'd like to go to bed."

"Sure. I'll leave, but we are going to have lunch tomorrow, okay?"

"Yeah, sure thing."

James didn't like the tone of her voice. Deep down he didn't believe that she'd keep their date.

He walked to the front door with Melanie on his

heels. He opened the door, turned and pulled her into his arms. "We'll get through this Melanie, together, I promise." He kissed her softly on the forehead and walked out.

James felt completely helpless. He had no clue as to his father's decision about Melanie's future. In that moment, he decided he was going to fix it all for her. He didn't want to see her unhappy. He felt like they'd made strides of late and he didn't want her regressing.

James looked at his watch as he drove towards his parents' home. Too late to stop in, so he phoned his father and left a voicemail on his office phone instead of phoning him at home. This conversation needed to take place at Amcrost and not at home where his mother could overhear. He decided to put his career on the line. He knew he'd do anything in his power to keep Melanie happy. He'd do it for the woman he loved. Yes, in that moment, he realized he was unequivocally in love with Melanie Holmes.

The next morning James arrived at the office earlier than he had in a long time. At six thirty he was already on his second cup of coffee as he reread the guidelines for job discontinuance. Everything Melanie shared with him the night before was accurate. She was being given sixty days to transition and then human resources would aid management in finding her a comparable job. This wouldn't work for her. She must continue in her current job, otherwise, she would fall apart. The strong woman he'd come to love and care for had major confidence issues. He was aware of them but now he knew where some of her problems originated. A huge chunk definitely resulted from her childhood, living with Holcomb.

James sat deep in thought when he heard a knock on his door. He looked up and saw his father standing just inside. James motioned for him to join him.

"I thought you'd be in early," his father said.

"Did you get my message?"

"No, I got your mother's?"

"Mom's?"

"Yeah, she definitely gave me an earful last night." Ben sat, stretching his legs out in front of him. "You mother was not too happy with me. In all the years we've been married, I'd have to say this was our first real argument."

"I'm sorry to hear that. What was on her mind?"

"Melanie."

"Mel? What's up with that? She doesn't have another class with her until—"

"Melanie stopped by yesterday and confided in her."

"Oh, she did. About what?"

"Like you don't already know."

"I don't. I had no idea she saw Mom yesterday."

"I'm surprised, with your dating and all."

James hadn't a clue how he knew they were dating. He hadn't told a soul.

"You think I didn't know about you and Melanie? I've seen how you look at her."

What did she see Mom about?

"Yes, I am seeing her. It's relatively new and I didn't want to say anything that would jeopardize her career, but I guess that didn't really matter, did it, Dad?"

"James, I wanted to keep you out of that decision. Anyway, the decision was made long ago almost solely on job experience."

"I see. I guess there's nothing I can say or do to

change your mind."

"Not at this time, no. Saxson was in complete agreement."

"Well, okay then. What about Mom?"

"Oh yeah. That's why I originally came in. She took my head off last night. I walked in the door and she started yelling at me about firing Melanie." James listened as his father recounted his argument with his mother. "I was surprised that she sought your mother's counsel."

"They have gotten close with their cooking classes."

"I realize that. I'm just surprised she told your mother what she did."

"And what's that, *Dad*?"

"She told your mother a little about her past. She was in the foster care system."

"I know."

"She told you?"

"No, she hasn't. I found out on my own, and I am waiting for her to tell me about it."

"Why haven't you asked her?"

"First of all, it's none of your business. Melanie needs to do things her own way. I can wait to hear her story from her. Let's just say I had a feeling and it was confirmed." James narrowed his eyes. "Dad, there's something else I'd like to discuss with you."

He spoke with his father regarding Mel's job placement. Over the next hour, James laid out a workable plan that benefitted both he and Melanie. He left his father with a lot to think over. James was resourceful and would somehow get his way.

Melanie pulled herself out of bed, dressed, and made her way into the office at nine, much later than normal. She had bags underneath her eyes, a pounding headache, and her eyes felt like sandpaper due to lack of sleep and crying.

When she arrived at her office, the light was blinking on her phone. She sighed. She didn't think she'd make it to noon let alone five o'clock. As she stared at her phone, she heard a knock on her door. Looking up through blurry eyes, she saw a bouquet of flowers. "These just arrived for you." Her assistant placed the vase on her desk. "They're gorgeous and smell so good. Are they from James?"

"Why would they be from him?"

"Aren't you two seeing one another?" Melanie stared at her assistant. She hadn't said a word to anyone except Janet. "I know you're keeping it to yourselves. I just hope you're happy Melanie, you deserve it." Her assistant turned and left never confirming whether or not they were dating.

Melanie reached for the yellow envelope that was sticking out the side of the flower arrangement. The spring flowers were beautiful and did brighten her day.

Melanie,

Thank you for coming by yesterday and opening up with me. I want you to know that I will always be that shoulder you can lean on. I feel like you're one of my own. Have a good day. Love always, Jackie.

The tears that she'd been keeping at bay since she got up spilled down her cheeks. She felt loved. For once in her life, she felt loved.

She spun her chair around and stared out her office window while she calmed herself and thought about the many what if's in her life. What if she and James worked out? What if Jackie had been her mother, her real mother? What if she walked away from everything that used to matter in her life? Melanie got lost in thought and dozed off in her chair with her back to the doorway.

She woke with a start. As she opened her eyes, she was greeted by James' intense stare. He was leaning over her and she knew he was checking to see if she were still breathing. "I'm alive," she whispered, "but barely." She closed her eyes and felt his hand cup her face. "What are you doing here?"

"I've left you three messages. Didn't you get them?"

She opened her eyes and glanced at her phone. The message light was still blinking. "No, I didn't."

He squatted down in front on her. "I'm going to be flatly honest here, Mel, but you look like you've been run over by a train."

"I didn't sleep well last night."

He reached for her hand and yanked her from her chair, into his arms. "Get your things, I'm taking you home."

"No, I can't. I've got so much to do."

"Work can wait another day." He reached for her purse that sat on the floor beside her desk. She'd been so out of it when she arrived, she forgot to put it away. Then he noticed her flowers. "What's this? From your other boyfriend?" he jokingly asked.

"No, from my other mother." James had a funny look on his face. Before he could ask her who her other mother was, she told him. "Your mother sent them. I went to see her yesterday when I left here. I guess she wanted to cheer me up. It was kind of her to think of me."

"She loves you like one of her own."

"That's what she said in her note."

He escorted Melanie to his car. "We're going to get lunch and I'm taking you home."

"Let's do carryout. I'm not in the mood for a sit-down lunch."

James placed a carryout order from Pedals Diner. Melanie closed her eyes when he went in to pick it up. She knew when he returned with their food, he'd find her fast asleep. She couldn't keep her eyes open one moment longer.

Chapter Twenty-Nine

JAMES WAS GONE ONLY FOR seven minutes but when he returned to the car, he wasn't surprised to find Melanie fast asleep. He drove the short distance to her house, pulled into her driveway, and put the car in park. Leaning over, he brushed her hair from her face. "Mel, we're home." Home— that sounded good to him. Maybe one day they'd be sharing a home. He could only hope.

When he placed his hand on her arm, she started to wake. "James? Where are we?"

"We just arrived at your house. Do you need help?"

"No, I'm good." She reached to open her door, but he stopped her. "What?"

"Wait for me. I'll get the door." He grabbed their lunch and hurried to her door.

She opened the door but waited as he presented his hand. She latched onto it and stood. Stumbling slightly, she righted herself. "Oops."

"Careful there." He reached for her arm and led her to the door.

Inside, she led him to the kitchen. "We can eat in here." She set her purse down while he placed their lunches on the table. She grabbed napkins and two glasses. "Ice tea okay with you?"

"That's perfect." Melanie poured their tea and he carried the glasses to the table and watched as she gulped down her sandwich.

"Feeling better?"

"Much. Thanks for lunch. I think I just needed to eat something." She threw the sandwich wrappings in the trash, then refilled their glasses and motioned for him to follow her to the family room where she cuddled up in the corner of the couch. He eased down beside her.

"I heard you visited my mom."

"Well, of course you know about it, you saw the flowers."

"I'm not referring to the flowers. I spoke with my dad today. Apparently, he and my mother had an argument last night."

"And?"

"My mother was quite upset about you."

She shrugged her shoulders. "Oh. I didn't think she'd say anything to your dad."

"You know my mom. When she has something to say, she says it."

"That's true."

He reached over and started to play with her hair. "Come with me to the cabin this weekend. We have a cabin, or better yet, a house in the Ozarks. Let's get away Friday after the sale is official. Just you and me. We can relax. Go for a long walk and talk. Focus on us. What do you say?"

"I don't know." She looked away and he could tell she was pondering his question, then she smiled at him. "Why not? Alone time sounds good to me."

Friday was a day filled with mixed emotions. The sale

was finalized and a celebration was held for all of the employees. Melanie reflected on her career with Parklayne. She'd come so far from a bank teller all the way to vice president of acquisitions. And now, she didn't know where she was headed. What she did know was James had joined her at the celebration, and they were scheduled to leave for his family's home at five.

Melanie's bags were all packed and sitting in her kitchen. She couldn't wait to run home and change and be with James. She looked at her watch. It was almost four. She had nothing left on her desk to worry about, so she grabbed her purse and headed home. He met her promptly at five, dressed as she was in jeans and a sweatshirt. She took one look at him, surprised at his casualness. She'd never seen him in jeans. She smiled, realizing what a heck of a good-looking man he was. His bangs had fallen over his eyes. She reached in and swept them away.

"Hi, there."

"Hi, yourself." He leaned in and placed a chaste kiss on her cheek. "Ready?'

"I am."

James took one look at her bags. "Mel, we're not going on an overseas adventure. We're only going to the Ozarks."

"I know. I just didn't know what your plans were." He chuckled, grabbed her bags, and opened the door. "I've got snacks for the car too."

He looked over his shoulder and shook his head at her.

"We've got to be prepared. You never know."

"Whatever you say, Mel. Come on let's get going. I'd like to stop for dinner on the way."

They stopped at a restaurant right outside of St. Louis. It was off the highway and mainly supported by locals, but James had eaten there for years.

She felt his eyes on her while she was eating. "Why are you staring?"

"I'm enjoying watching you relish your food."

"This is fabulous. I love a home-style cooked meal. We'll have to come here again." *Did I just really say that? Come here again? Well, I guess I meant it.* She smiled at him as he waited for the waitress to bring their bill. "So, what's on the agenda?"

"We won't get in until late. Let's sleep in and then we can go out for breakfast. I don't think there's much food in the house outside of frozen bratwurst and stuff like that. Mom stocks up at the local butcher shop. She always has that kind of stuff on hand for last minute get-togethers."

"Do you go down often?"

"Not as much as I used to, but I think that'll change now that we're dating."

"Why?"

"Because I think you'll enjoy it. Elsa hated going to the cabin. She did not like the outdoors at all." He'd barely finished his sentence when the waitress appeared with the bill. James handed her his credit card and within minutes they were back on the road again.

They arrived at the cabin just before eleven. It was pitch dark. When they pulled up, she noticed the complete darkness. "No lights?"

"What do you think this is, the back hills of Tennessee? Of course, we have electric. We just don't leave any outside lights on when we're not here. Why? Are you afraid of the dark?"

Melanie didn't react to his comment. When they'd been in San Antonio, she'd slept with the lights on. It hadn't seemed to bother James and hopefully it wouldn't now.

"I'm going to wait here until you get the lights on, okay?"

"Sure thing." He pulled out his house keys, opened the door, and before she knew it the property was bathed in bright lights. She took a calming breath, ecstatic to see the light.

She opened her car door as James approached, grabbing her bag of snacks and her purse.

"I've got our bags, just go on in," he said.

Melanie headed for the house and was pleasantly surprised. It definitely wasn't a cabin as she'd imagined. It was a beautiful home that looked like it had been dropped from his neighborhood. Wood floors ran throughout. There was overstuffed furniture with lots of pillows in pastel colors, ornate sconces lining the walls, and a gourmet kitchen with a Viking six-burner range, double oven, and stainless-steel appliances.

The kitchen was outfitted better than the Samuels' house in the city. She stood in awe and was surprised when James joined her, wrapping his arms around her. She jumped when James startled her. "I didn't hear you. I can't believe this kitchen. It's gorgeous."

"Yeah. Mom loves it here. She keeps saying she wants to remodel the kitchen in St. Louis, but hasn't yet. I think eventually they'll move here permanently once Wyatt and Colleen get out of school and my dad retires."

"He's pretty young to do that."

"He is but he keeps threatening that he's going to."

Melanie felt good standing in his arms. They really

hadn't taken the time to spend one-on-one time together since they'd started dating. Going to dinner and seeing one another in the office was one thing, but spending quality time without interruption was something else altogether.

She turned and wrapped her arms around his neck. Looking around the room she smiled. "This is definitely not a cabin, James."

He chortled. "I know. I guess we refer to it as a cabin since we're remotely located, well off the main road. It sounds more rustic, I guess."

"Rustic's a good word." She pulled out of his arms and walked around the kitchen, swiping her hand along the countertop. "So, what's all to do here?"

"Fish."

"Fish?"

"Yeah, we hold fishing tournaments here regularly. We have a small lake that my dad keeps stocked. We also have some nice hiking trails."

"How big is this place?"

"My dad owns about a hundred acres. I sometimes hunt, but not too often. It's not one of my things, but he loves to hunt."

"I wouldn't picture him as a hunter."

"He is. He's hunted all over the United States and Canada. Some of his trophies are mounted in the family room. Come on, I'll show you." He reached for her hand and she followed alongside him as he gave her a tour of the house. He led her first into the family room where he pointed out the prized trophies his father had shot. Melanie couldn't believe how real they looked.

"I feel like they're staring at me."

"Yeah, you do. Come on let me show you the rest

of the house." He pointed out the media room, a small office, and several bedrooms. She wasn't sure why he stopped outside a closed door.

"This is my room when I stay here." He opened the door, flipped the light switch, and led her inside. He opened the floor length drapes. The room opened onto a large deck. The whole wall was filled with windows. Since he'd turned on the outside lights, she could see well into the yard, to a pool and pool house. "I forgot to mention we have a pool and a hot tub too."

"This is nice, James, really nice." She walked around his room brushing her hand across the bedspread and making her way towards the windows.

"I know we haven't talked about this yet, Mel, but..." She knew where he was taking this conversation. When he'd asked her to spend the weekend at the cabin, she wondered if he intended to take their relationship to the next level. Yes, she cared deeply about him, but she wasn't sure she wanted to spend the night with him. If she did that, there was no turning back. She still wasn't convinced that she wanted something long-term with him. Her feelings for him had grown and she often thought about him during the day, but what that truly meant she wasn't sure.

She stopped him mid-sentence. "I know where you're going with this..."

"It's okay if you don't want to sleep with me. I understand, I really do." He smiled. "I didn't want you to think that I wasn't interested just in case you were." He placed his hand along her face. "We have plenty of time. I know where you stand on relationships, in general. I just have to be honest here and say that I am a little disappointed. After all I am a male, you know."

"You are?" She chuckled. "I'm thankful you understand. I have to be one hundred percent sure here. I can't commit fully because I'm still not sure that I believe in the love and marriage thing. I've been through and seen way too much in my life to question whether love really exists." When he pulled her into his arms, hugging her closely, she did feel something. Was it love? She didn't know, but she did feel a closeness that she'd never felt in her entire life. Maybe she would finally discover what love was with James Samuels.

After their conversation in James' room, he gave her the choice of three other bedrooms where she could sleep. She chose the one directly across from his. It faced the front yard and didn't have a walkout onto a balcony which she was thankful for. It was late by the time James brought her bag into her room. She was tired after the long week and grueling schedule since Saxson had announced the sale. Now, she could let her hair down and actually relax for a change.

Melanie said her goodnight and closed the door. She was elated to see two end tables that both held lamps. She even had an overhead ceiling fan that had a light. She had a bathroom, too, that had a light she could turn on. She took a satisfying deep breath. She had plenty of light in her room.

Melanie dressed in a pair of shorts and a camisole then turned on every single light in the room, including the one in the ceiling fan. She hopped into bed feeling relaxed for the first time in she couldn't remember when. She hoped to see a completely different side to James as they spent the weekend together. He was disappointed that she didn't want to sleep with him, but she knew he was well aware of her relationship fears.

Maybe, in time...

Before she knew it, she was awakened by the smell of bacon. She looked at the bedside clock and was surprised to discover that it was eight. *Eight.* For the first time in what seemed like forever, she'd slept the entire night without waking and without having one of her recurring dreams. She felt rested and alive.

She jumped out of bed, took a quick shower, and joined James in the kitchen where he was already indulging in a cup of coffee.

Melanie bent over kissing the top of his head. "It smells wonderful in here. What are you cooking?"

"Bacon and eggs. I have it warming in the oven, waiting for your beautiful face."

"Well, I'm here. Let's eat."

After breakfast, they took a leisurely walk around the grounds, hiking through the back part of the property. She was surprised that James not only cooked breakfast but also made a picnic lunch for them that they enjoyed at the lake.

By the time dinner arrived, she felt more and more relaxed. He surprised her with reservations at an area dinner theatre. They had a lavish meal and were treated to a theatrical presentation of *Annie.* Melanie hadn't seen this musical about the orphan who escaped the orphanage and it really hit home. She wasn't lucky enough to have lived with a billionaire like Annie, and she wasn't adopted. All of her past living in a multitude of foster homes came rushing back. She did her best not to let James see the emotions, but she knew he felt her tense at various moments during the play.

"I've never seen *Annie,*" Melanie commented as they drove home. "I liked the music." In fact, she really did enjoy the music, having heard several of the songs through the years. Especially "Tomorrow". Like Annie, she dreamed of better days to come.

By the time they got home it was late, almost midnight. She was tired due to the lateness of the hour and all the fresh air they'd gotten while taking their hike. She thanked James for the evening and scurried off to her bedroom. She needed to be alone. The musical had evoked many memories from her childhood.

"Night, Mel," he said as he kissed her. "I think I'm going to stay up a little while and watch some television. Have a good night. Sweet dreams," he called out as she closed her door.

She followed the same routine as the night before turning on every single light in her bedroom. With as tired as she was, she fell asleep immediately and into a world filled with nightmares from her past. She dreamed of the night Holcomb had struck her, sending her to the ER. She dreamed of the darkness. The darkness that always seemed to envelope her in her dreams. The darkness where she never saw light. The darkness that was filled with her screams. She tossed and turned, pulling her sheets from the bed.

She heard a loud bang. She'd never experienced that before in her nightmares. The bang rumbled on and on, and that's when she realized she was no longer in the throes of a dream. She cracked open her eyes to darkness. Her room was completely black. There was a flash of light and then the rumbling of thunder. They were in the midst of a severe thunderstorm. The house shook with the violent booms. Then silence. The complete darkness lasted. No light. No booms.

Melanie's heart raced. She felt all around for her lamp.

She thought she'd turned on the lights when she went to bed. She was sure of it. She looked for the clock that usually sat illuminated on the end table beside the bed. Off. They must have lost electricity in the storm.

She began to panic. She broke out in a cold sweat. Her hands shook. *No, this can't be happening. Mom's dead. She didn't lock me in…*

She struggled to stay in touch with reality, but she was losing. She wasn't sure if she was living in a dream or if what she was experiencing was real. Her body was wracked with tremors. She pulled the sheets and blankets from the bed and fell to the floor. She curled into a tight ball and covered herself. She was cold, so cold. She needed to get out. Out of this locked room. She started to cry. Sobs engulfed her.

"Melanie, what's wrong?"

Was someone talking to her? Never before had her mother answered her pleas for help.

"Melanie?" She heard her name again and then felt herself being drawn into someone's arms. *Where am I? Who's here? I'm alone. I'm always alone in here.*

"Melanie, wake up. It's just a dream." *A dream? This isn't a dream. It can't be.* The arms around her tightened. A kiss brushed against her temple as someone talked to her softly. "It's okay, Mel. I've got you." *Her mother never talked to her in that manner. Never.* "Melanie, I'm here for you. I'll always be here. Come back to me. Melanie, I love you." *Love you.* Her mother had never once told her she loved her. "Come on, Mel. It's me, James." Hearing James say her name made her aware that she was truly living in the present and not the past.

Melanie threw her arms around him.

"Hold on, Mel. I'll never let you go."

Chapter Thirty

JAMES WASN'T QUITE SURE THAT Melanie heard the words he'd spoken to her. He loved her. Yes, in that exact moment the words spilled from his lips and he couldn't stop them. He meant every word. James loved Melanie.

The sound of his voice pulled her out of her state of confusion. "The lights. What happened to the lights? James, I don't like the dark."

"Mel, it's okay, I've got you. I won't let anything bad happen to you." He pulled her more closely, rubbing his hand up and down her back. He did his best to calm her and he wanted to uncover what caused her sense of panic.

"James, I can't take this. I need light. I'm never in the complete dark."

"Close your eyes then and you won't realize the electricity is out. I guess the storm took out the power. The generator should've kicked in. Will you be okay while I check on it? I'll only be gone a few minutes. The switch is probably turned off."

"As long as I know you're not leaving me alone."

"I promise I'll be right back. Close your eyes and before you know it, I'll have the lights back on." He brushed a quick kiss to her cheek and hurried out the door.

Melanie sat with her eyes closed. If she didn't have her eyes open, she didn't realize the lights were out. She knew she wasn't locked in a closet. Thank heavens James had come to her rescue because she didn't know how long she'd have lasted before she completely lost it.

True to his word, James returned in a matter of minutes. "Open your eyes, sweetheart."

She did and the lights were back on.

"The switch was tripped on the generator. Sometimes, that happens. I checked the gas and we're good to go, so we should have lights until the electric comes back on." He reached for her hand and helped her stand. "You're coming with me." He led her to the family room where he lit the fire that had already been preset, grabbed a blanket, and covered them both as they sat down to watch the fire catch.

James secured Melanie in his arms. "You okay now?" She nodded. "Would you care to talk about what happened? Why don't you like the dark?" The expression on her face changed. She pulled her eyebrows in, gnawed on her lip, and clasped her hands tightly against her side. He wanted to comfort her but didn't truly know what would put her at ease.

He placed his hand atop her clenched fist. He slowly worked his fingers into hers and felt her begin to relax. "We have as much time as you need, but sweetheart, I think whatever's bothering you, you need to share with someone. I'm a good listener and I promise whatever you tell me won't go beyond these doors."

He could tell she was struggling with what to do. They watched the fire and listened as it crackled and caught. No words were needed. She was safe in his arms.

Finally she said, "James, I don't know where to begin. I know you think I'm crazy."

"Why would you say that?"

"Because I'm afraid of the dark."

"There must be a valid reason for it."

Shyly she whispered, "There is." Another moment of silence passed and then Melanie spoke. "I've never told anyone what I'm about to tell you. Not even Janet knows. My therapists growing up never knew my whole story, either." James brushed his hand along her forearm.

"Take your time, we have as long as you need." He tightened his arms around her letting her know that he wasn't going anywhere.

"It all started when I was a baby and my father died. Janet was six when I was born and she was lucky. She was never exposed to the treatment I received at the hands of my mother." *Her mother? What could she have done?*

"When I was about three, my life changed. My mother slowly went into a downward spiral after my father's death and became a raging alcoholic. I still don't understand why Janet wasn't aware of what was going on, but she wasn't." Melanie took a cleansing breath and continued with her story.

"To this day, I can't fathom why my mother treated me like she did. Maybe it was because my dad died shortly after I was born. I don't know, maybe she blamed me for his death. From what I understand, my dad was forced to work two jobs to make ends meet. He was a teacher during the day and drove a cab at night. One night, during a raging snowstorm, he got a call. He didn't want to be driving that night, and in truth, the cab company shouldn't have taken the call, but they did. My dad drove mainly for the tips. As he drove on the snow-covered streets, he lost control of his cab, and slid straight into a light standard. He was killed instantly."

"I'm so sorry, Mel."

"Janet told me my dad was a proud man. He wanted to solely support our family. He didn't expect my mother to work. He was the bread winner and she was the housewife responsible for taking care of the household."

"That was the mind-set back then, and for some husbands, still is today."

"Yeah, I know." Melanie paused and sighed. "My mom started to drink heavily when she couldn't make ends meet. My dad had a life insurance policy but she ran through that pretty quickly. I guess why I'm so affected by what she did to me is because I was so young. What she did to me are my first real memories. These memories never go away— they're so profound." Melanie pulled her hand from his and tightly drew them both into fists. He could feel her anxiety revving-up. Her breathing change into shallow breaths. A fine line of moisture had broken out across her upper lip.

"It's okay, Mel. Take your time." She looked at him and smiled. He reached in and cupped her jaw, showing his support. He felt like he was sitting on the edge of his seat as he waited for her to recount her story.

"The abuse, as I like to call it, started out slowly until she..." She stopped, swallowed loudly, controlled herself, and started back in again. "My mother used to get drunk and lock me in a closet. Sometimes for hours at a time. There, I said it." She sighed.

James didn't comment he just listened. "It was dark, so dark in there. I couldn't see or hear anything most of the time. She'd leave me there for hours and hours. Sometimes, it felt like days. On occasion, I could hear her moving about, stumbling around her room. I'd hear her throw her empty bottles on the floor. Sometimes, they'd crash against the closet door. There were times when she let me out, she'd hit me, yell, slap me around some more, then banish me to the dark again."

James noticed a wisp of hair had fallen into her face. He carefully reached over to secure it behind her ear. He didn't want to frighten her as she spoke. She was in a fragile state and didn't want to do something that would throw her further over the edge.

"This treatment went on for years. When I think about it, I seem to remember the reason why Janet wasn't aware of my mother's treatment was because she wasn't there. She had a really good friend that lived next door and I think she was probably playing with her or spending the night. That's the only reason I can rationalize that she wasn't cognizant of my mother's treatment of me.

"One night when I was around six, she was really drunk—staggering all about the house. I remember she tried to push me into the closet and I fought back. She continued with her onslaught. I lost my balance and fell against her dresser. And then there was nothing.

"The next thing I remember is waking up in the hospital. I knew no one. I recall a nice lady that kept telling me over and over that everything was going to be fine. That I wasn't going back home. She'd found a home for me.

"My mother died that night. Apparently when she was fighting with me, she too in her drunken stupor lost her balance and hit her head on the side of the bedframe. She suffered a brain trauma and died within hours of the incident." Melanie stopped talking and looked at her shaking hands. "I didn't see Janet again for years. I was moved from foster home to foster home. Some were good, others not. That's how I know Holcomb. He was one of the homes that are a part of my bad memories. He abused me too. I ended up in the hospital after an incident with him. That's why I detest hospitals so much. I hate the smells, the bright lights. They bring back too many bad memories."

James hated her mother. How could she have locked her in a closet? She beat her too just like Holcomb. He moved his head from side-to-side to release the tension.

He didn't know what to say, so he listened and supported her. "Now you know why I hate to fly. I detest being closed in. I'm fine until the doors close and then... I hate elevators too. I don't like the confined feeling. I get claustrophobic. I often do my best to avoid them by taking the stairs whenever I can."

Now it all made sense to him.

Melanie paused again and then looked at him. "Now you know why I shouldn't be in a relationship. I'm damaged. Damaged to the core. I can't have a family because I wouldn't know where to start. That's why I was so dead set against going out with you— starting something that I know I can never have."

"I don't believe you, Mel. I think with the right person, you could have a relationship, learn to be a family. I know you feel something for me, I just know you do. I'm not going anywhere. I can help you overcome the memories. I know we're a strong unit. Together, if you choose, we can do absolutely anything. You just need to believe. Believe in us." He squeezed her hands.

She contemplated his words. He believed she would find the will to make their relationship work, he just knew it. "May I ask you a question?"

"Sure," she croaked.

"You mentioned you went to a therapist. Why didn't you tell them about all you went through? They could have helped you overcome your fears."

"I don't know. I felt ashamed, maybe. I believed that I had done something wrong. I believed that I caused my mother's death. I have so much baggage, James." She shook her head. "So much."

"Now that you've told me, how do you feel about seeing someone again? You've released the memories. I would think now it would be easier to share them. Maybe get some help."

She sighed. "I don't know. I'll have to think about it. Right now, I just want to sit here and watch the fire. It's calming."

"That's what we'll do, then. We'll sit and watch the fire." James held her against him. He was having a difficult time processing what she'd just shared. Why hadn't someone seen that she needed help? Why was she kept from seeing Janet? The questions kept surging through his mind. He wanted to wrap her in his cocoon and never let her go. He wanted her to be happy, forget about her past. He needed to figure out what he could do for her to see that he could help her through the dark times. Now that he was aware of her past, he would be with her every step of the way until she found it in her heart to have a family with him. He wasn't going to let her go.

Melanie woke to a brightly lit room. The lights were still on and the sun was shining through the windows. She was wrapped in James' arms. She felt safe. Safe for the first time in her entire life.

Melanie was thankful that she'd finally released all of her traumatic memories. James had been a real trooper as he sat listening to her story. He'd never interrupted or said a word. He quietly listened as she recounted her childhood. She hoped he didn't believe she was crazy. He now understood why she hated the dark, elevators and closed in spaces in general. He understood why she disliked going to the hospital. And she hoped he understood why she believed she could never have a family. She felt damaged to the core and she didn't want him having to deal with all of her issues.

There were still a few things about her past that she neglected to share. She didn't tell him about the wonderful families that she'd temporarily lived with, and she definitely didn't share her art therapy with him. In time, she thought. She'd dumped enough on him. For the most part, what she had left to share were the good times. Although few, she did have a handful of happy times.

She felt James stir. She watched him closely as his eyes fluttered then opened. "Morning, Mel." He smiled at her. "How'd you sleep?"

"Pretty well. It helped being in your arms." She looked towards the fire that had died several hours earlier. "Thank you. Thank you for listening and for understanding."

"Of course, why wouldn't I?" He reached out to cup the side of her face. "Mel, I love you."

"James..."

"I know you're not ready to hear it, but I do. I love you. I just wanted you to know. I'll always be here for you, in good times and bad, so please learn to trust me, rely on me, because I'm not going anywhere— that is, of course, unless you walk away from me, and then, I'll do my damnedest to convince you otherwise."

"I know you care for me. You've shown your feelings over and over again. I don't know why you'd want to have anything to do with me after what I confessed last night."

"Why wouldn't I? Your past makes you who you are today. That's the person I love."

"I realize that. It's just ..." She elected to change the subject. She was tired of dealing with her past and who she was today. "I'm starving, what about you?"

"Yeah. I could eat something. I'm going to shower first." Right before he stood, he leaned over and kissed her softly on the lips. "We'll figure this all out— in time. Will you promise me one thing?" She nodded. "Please, just give what we have a chance. That's all I'm asking. A chance for what I know will be something that will last a lifetime. I know you, Mel, and I know that you can overcome all of the adversity you've experienced in your lifetime. You owe yourself the opportunity to have a relationship and maybe have a family that you can give all the love I know you have locked up inside that heart of yours. Think about what I've said because I know you'll see I'm right." He jumped off the couch and headed in the direction of his bedroom.

Maybe he was right. Maybe she should give them a

try. *I really want to, I really do.*

Chapter Thirty-One

JAMES AND MELANIE HAD A pleasant Sunday. They lunched at a local diner near the cabin, then set out for the return drive to St. Louis. He wasn't surprised when she fell fast asleep. He was sure she hadn't slept well after reliving her childhood with him. As he drove, he replayed what she'd told him the evening before. How could her mother have done that to her? He couldn't even begin to imagine the physical and emotional trauma she'd endured at such a young age. He was also surprised that Janet had been unaware of everything her sister had experienced.

Melanie wakened shortly before five, right as James pulled up at her home. He grabbed her bag and went to open her car door, but she'd already started making her way out. In that moment, he felt like she was detaching herself from him. As she put her key in the door, his hand brushed hers. "Hey, is everything alright?"

"Yeah, why wouldn't it be?" James knew her better than she gave him credit for. Something had changed on their drive. He started to come in when she stopped him. "James, I'm pretty tired. I'll see you at the office?"

"Ah, yeah sure, whatever you say." He leaned in and brushed a kiss on her cheek, placing her bags right inside the door. "I had a good time, Mel. I hope you did too."

"I did. Thanks for inviting me." She walked inside and closed the door.*ow How*

What the hell just happened? James was clueless as to her change in demeanor. He shook his head as he returned to his car. Tomorrow was another day. Maybe she would be in a different frame of mind.

Melanie made her way into her house and sat on her couch. She didn't know what to do. After sharing her past with James, she felt lost. She knew she should have felt a weight lift off her shoulders, but she didn't. She wondered if that had to do with the fact that he loved her. She didn't want to hurt him, but how could she get through to him that she wasn't made to be in a relationship or, better yet, have that family he so wanted, seemed to need?

She spent the rest of the night pondering her life. She was in a relationship with a man who truly loved her, but she couldn't seem to find the emotions to love him in return. Everything was buried so deep in her psyche. Her job was changing in the next sixty days, though to what she hadn't a clue. She guessed she'd take one day at a time and see what happened. Maybe she'd find it in herself to open up her heart to James. She didn't know if she had it in her to have a true relationship, one filled with love.

Monday was uneventful. She went into the office as usual and was surprised when she didn't receive a visit or call from James. Tuesday brought severe storms and an overall feeling of the doldrums. Even though she'd spend her evening at her art therapy class, nothing seemed to brighten her day.

Melanie hurried home as usual and barely made it to her class. Jared seemed in a happier mood, more like the child she'd gotten to know over the months he'd been in the class. She worked beside Jared, painting a picture of the Samuels' cabin and remembered the rustic feeling it gave her. As she painted in the large lake and even a few ducks floating across the waters, all her worries of the past months seemed to vanish. She was calm and felt a sense of peace. She wasn't sure where these feelings came from. Maybe it was from the scene she was painting.

As the class came to an end and everyone went home, Melanie cleaned up the room. When she gathered her things to leave, she realized she was no longer alone.

James stood right inside the door.

"What are you doing here?"

"I came to see you."

"But how, how did you find me?"

"I knew you were here on Tuesdays. I inquired about what you were involved in. This is an art therapy class for kids. Right?" He lifted his eyes and approached her.

"Yes, it is. I don't understand how you knew I was here. Did you follow me?"

James had a sheepish expression on his face. He shrugged. "I did several weeks ago. Remember when you saw me? It wasn't just a coincidence."

I can't believe he followed me. Why didn't he tell me the truth? She questioned his motives. "But James, why? I don't understand. This is my personal life, my own time. I wasn't slacking on the job."

"I know." He gestured with his hands, "I wondered why you left early on Tuesday's."

Doesn't he trust me? She didn't understand. She didn't need that in her life. "I don't leave early. I leave when I'm supposed to." She became defensive. *Why do I need to defend when I leave work and what I do?*

"Come on, Melanie. We know that's not true," he chuckled. "You normally leave at six, seven, eight o'clock. I thought it was odd that you always left by five on Tuesday's, so I decided to follow you."

Melanie's temper flared. Her voice raised. "You followed me. You really followed me. I can't believe you'd do that, James." She clenched her hands, her knuckles turned white. "You could have just asked me where I was going. I would have told you."

"Really, now. You'd have told me?"

Now he's questioning me?

"I find that hard to believe. I also find it hard to believe that you're working with children. Children, Melanie. You're the one that keeps telling me you can't have a relationship, can't have a family, and that you weren't comfortable with babies. Here I find you working closely with children and even enjoying yourself." He threw his arms up in frustration. "So, what is it Mel? Do you or don't you like kids?"

Melanie was taken aback by his attack of her.

"Is it just that you don't want to have a family with me? What is it, Mel? Huh?" He stepped into her space and she started to feel claustrophobic.

"James, I can't do this right now. Please." Melanie grabbed her things and started from the room when he latched onto her arm and pulled her towards him.

"Don't you dare walk out on me now."

She looked at his hand wrapped around her upper arm. The panic started to set in again. She tried to pull away, but he wouldn't let her go.

"Let me go." Her voice trembled. "Please let me go."

James dropped his hand and spun away from her, dragging his hand through his hair, a pained expression on his face.

"Consider this the end. I'm done with you, with our *relationship*, or whatever you want to call it. I can't do this James. I just can't." She left James standing in the middle of the room.

She made it safely to her car, but didn't know where to go. She couldn't go home because she knew he'd follow her. She couldn't go to Janet's house, so she went to one of the few places that she felt safe. She returned to her office.

It was almost nine when she pulled into the parking garage. She was more confused now than she'd ever been in her life. She sat staring at her hands that were clenched to the steering wheel. She needed to make a few decisions. Instead of going inside, she put her car in reverse and headed home. By now, if James planned on stopping by, he'd have realized she wasn't there. She took her time driving, stopping at a drive-thru ice cream parlor. Ice cream always made her feel better and she realized she really needed that sweet right now.

She sat in the parking lot underneath a light standard while she ate her lusciousness. Her sweet cream flavored ice cream was smooth and thick and quickly satisfied her. By the time she got home, she was exhausted from not only her day but her confrontation with James. James, the man whom she thought she could trust, was not what he seemed. *How could he have followed me? I trusted him.*

Trust was one of the reasons why she didn't have relationships. Tonight, she'd lost any and all trust she had in James. She couldn't believe he'd investigate her whereabouts after work and then follow and confront her.

Melanie plopped down into bed. All of the emotions had taken their toll. She felt like she'd been hit by a Mack truck. When all was said and done, the sixty days she had remaining in her job may not lead to a job she wanted. She needed to face reality. Yes, she'd have an income, but if she didn't enjoy her job, a job she would be forced to take, why should she even stay with the bank? Because it was the easy way out? She decided to ponder that outcome. She'd been forced to face her childhood memories. Maybe now she'd find the strength to do something she'd never thought possible six months ago.

James was ashamed of himself. He couldn't believe their conversation. He didn't know what had overcome him. For all the love he had for Melanie, why had he treated her like he had? Maybe because he loved her too much and wanted her to heal? Face all of her demons head-on and then she'd love him too? If he was looking at the situation through her eyes, he'd wonder if in fact, he did love her. He definitely didn't treat her like he did, and he was sure she felt that way especially with the way he turned on her.

Yet, he was upset with her. He watched her through the glass door and saw how she interacted with the children, a little boy in particular. She'd pointed out things in his painting. She smiled openly at him and even hugged him when he threw his arms about her. She liked children he could see it in her eyes as she interacted with them. Why did she say one thing and do something totally out of character? She told him repeatedly she didn't want a relationship or a family, and he assumed that meant children too. He'd thought she didn't like children with the way she reacted to Angel's crying fit when they babysat the kids while Angelina was in labor. Melanie was the complete opposite of what she claimed. Did she act as though she didn't like children to make him walk away? He knew she had her issues but now he speculated how deep they really ran.

James went to bed unsure of where their future was headed. In her eyes their relationship was over before it really began, and in his eyes, he questioned if this was a little blip on the radar. And then, he wondered if he should have even gone to the Y. Maybe he should have let her tell him about her art therapy sessions. James had hoped she would explain to him why she was involved in the program. Now, he didn't think that would ever happen.

He slept fitfully and somehow made it into the office. When he arrived, he was greeted by his father. "You're late."

"Oh hi, Dad."

"James, you're late. Just what is going on with you?"

"I had a rough night. I'm only fifteen minutes late. What's the problem?"

James hadn't noticed the slip of paper in his hand. Ben slapped it down on his desk. "I'd like to know the meaning of this?" James looked at his father. He had no idea what he was referring to. "Read it, then you'll understand."

James perused the letter. The first two paragraphs were meaningless until he got to the end. "So, effective immediately, I am tendering my resignation. I've cleaned out my desk of all personal belongings." James snapped his gaze towards his father's.

"I don't understand. What's the meaning of this?"

"I thought you could read."

"Well, I can, but I still don't understand."

"How can you not understand? It's written in plain English. Melanie has terminated her employment with Amcrost effective immediately."

"How, when?"

"I found this letter in my inbox this morning. From the time stamp on the email it looks like she sent it about three a.m." Ben slapped his hand on James' desk. "What the hell happened, James? I thought she was on board here."

"I did too." James stopped for a moment. "Dad, this weekend she told me about her childhood, and then I did something really stupid last night. Melanie helps out at the Y in an art therapy class. I confronted her about it. Let's say things didn't go as I planned and we had a little fight. She walked out. End of story. Never did I imagine that she'd quit because of that."

"Son, I'd say you better go find her and talk some sense into her."

"I will."

"Now. I mean right this minute. Go. Go talk to the woman of your dreams. Make this all right and then convince her to come back to Amcrost. She's needed here."

James looked at his father and then rushed out the door. He needed to get to Melanie. Talk to her. Apologize and make things right.

James hurried to her house. When he got there,

the drapes were all closed. He rang the doorbell. No answer. He ran around the back only to see that her house was locked up tight. He could see her car in the garage. *Where is she? I've got to find her.*

Melanie had made her decision almost as soon as she returned home from her detour to the ice cream parlor. She grabbed her go-to bag, added a bunch of clothes and returned to the office. It was almost three in the morning by the time she'd finished cleaning out her desk. She drove home, called a cab, and made her way to the airport. She didn't know where she wanted to go. The only thing she did know was that she wanted to get out of town as soon as possible.

She saw that a plane was leaving for San Francisco at seven. Her mind went crazy with the possibilities. As she walked past one of the bars in the airport, it hit her. She'd go to Napa. She'd always wanted to tour the Napa Valley. There was nothing to stop her now. On a whim, she made her decision and booked her flight. Napa was her intended destination.

While she waited for her flight, she pulled up all the information she could find on the Napa Valley. There were over 500 wineries in the region. She could easily get lost out there for quite some time.

With her decision firmly made, Melanie boarded her flight to California. She'd never done something this impulsive in her entire life. She decided she was going to live a little, turn this into a vacation. She hadn't taken a vacation in years. And she would use this time to make some decisions about her future. A future that had endless opportunities if she only let herself believe.

Chapter Thirty-Two

Two weeks later…

JAMES WAS FRANTIC WITH WORRY. He hadn't heard from Melanie in over two weeks. He'd left her numerous voice mails, emails, stopped by her house to no avail. He'd even phoned Janet. She acted like she had no clue as to Melanie's whereabouts, but he knew better than that. He was sure she knew where her sister was.

James had barely slept since their argument. He looked ghastly. He hadn't shaved and had begun to grow a beard. His hair was a mess after having run his hand through it countless times over the weeks since her disappearance. He had dark circles and puffiness beneath his eyes. He'd hardly eaten and had lost at least five, maybe ten, pounds.

He couldn't think, let alone work. He was constantly trying to locate her. He'd taken vacation practically with no notice. His father wasn't happy with his behavior missing work especially after the acquisition of Parklayne. There was an enormous amount of work still merging their brands and personnel.

At the end of the second week, James' doorbell rang.

He barely had enough strength to cross to the door to open it. Whoever was at his door was impatient; they kept ringing the bell. After the fourth ring, he ambled to the door and threw it open. His mother stood with her hand poised over the bell. "My God, James, what's happened to you?" She pushed her way in and headed to his kitchen. She automatically went to his refrigerator only to discover it filled with beer and bottled water. "Where's your food?"

"Don't have any."

"James?"

"I'm not hungry anyway." He closed the refrigerator and sat down at the table. "What do you want, Mother?"

"I came to see you. According to your father, you haven't been to work in days. You don't answer your phone. I was worried. What's happened?"

"You haven't heard?"

"No, I have no idea what you're referring to."

"Melanie."

"What's wrong with Melanie?"

"She's gone."

"Gone? What do you mean by gone? I just talked to her the other day." James' eyes flew open. "She called to cancel our cooking class."

"Where was she?"

"I assumed she was at home."

"You're wrong there. I've gone by at all times of the day and she's not there. She's skipped town, that's what she's done."

"I find that hard to believe. You must have just missed her." She looked at her son closely. "Haven't you seen her at work?"

James looked at her. "I haven't been to work in days, weeks..."

"What's going on here? What do you mean you haven't been to the office? Your father hasn't said a thing to me."

"I guess you'd better ask him about Melanie's letter of resignation."

"Letter of resignation..."

"Mother, will you quit repeating what I say. Yes, Melanie resigned."

Jackie was flabbergasted. "Wh—Wh—Why would she do that? I thought she liked her job. She was looking forward to the merger."

"I guess she pulled a fast one on you, too."

"But she was. I know she was."

"Mom, do you know about her background?"

"I know some, not much, why?" James proceeded to tell her about Melanie's horrific childhood. "That's awful, James. I had no idea."

"No one did, including Janet. And then I made matters worse." He stopped and jumped up from the table. He made his way to the door where he looked out to his expansive backyard. He turned. "Mom, I really messed up. First of all, I confronted her about her work at the Y." He stopped mid-thought. "I never thought she'd react the way she did." He looked over his shoulder. "Did you know she works with children in foster care?" His mother shook her head. "She actually helps out in an art therapy class." James turned, running his hand through his hair for the thousandth time since Melanie had left him. "To top off everything, while we were at the cabin, after she told me everything, I told her I loved her. I knew she wouldn't say the words herself, but I needed to let her know she was loved and definitely not alone."

"Wow, that's a surprise. You sure kept that under wraps."

"Yeah, we'd been dating. At least that's what I called it. Mom, I've tried everything to find her. I'm at my last wits. I'm going to call Jonas Sounds and see if he can track her. I love her and I can't lose her."

"You also loved Elsa."

"This is different. I feel like a totally different person with Melanie. She's my soulmate, I just know it. I have to find her and convince her that she needs to give me— us a try. She's fearful of building a relationship, relying on another person. She tried to convince me she didn't want children, but after what I saw how she engaged with the kids in that class, I think she's lying to herself. She made a pact with herself when she was a child that she'd never get married and have children. I was slowly breaking her down. I know I was. I needed a little more time, but I..."

"James, Melanie's had an awful lot going on in her life. From what you've said, she exhibits panic or maybe anxiety attacks. I think she was overwhelmed with what happened at Parklayne..."

"Mom, there's more."

"More? What else could there be?"

"The day she discovered she was going to be changing jobs she ran into her past."

"How could that be? You said her mother's dead."

"Yeah, she is. She ran into one of our employees. He turned out to be one of her foster fathers from hell."

"Oh, my." She placed her hand on James' arm.

"One that sent her to the ER." James sighed loudly.

"Mom, I don't know what to do. She's been through so much..."

"You need to find her. Convince her that she can have a relationship with you. Reinforce her interaction with the children in the art therapy class, help her realize that if she can have that sense of fulfillment, she'd only have so much more with a family of her own. Melanie's special. I've known that for a long time. She feels like a daughter to me. You need to find her and bring my daughter back to me."

James chuckled at her daughter reference. "I'll do my best, Mom, but I'm not sure I'll be able to."

She pulled her son into her arms. "You're a good man, James Samuels. You can do anything you set your mind to. The first thing you need to do is contact Jonas, and the second is clean yourself up." She yanked on his beard.

"Ouch!"

"Get rid of this. I expect you to come over for dinner this evening, and I expect a clean-shaven face." She tugged on his hair. "You need to do something with this hair, too. Go get a haircut."

James knew his mother meant well. "Okay, mom," he said dejectedly.

She kissed him on the cheek. "Six," she called over her shoulder as she headed for the door.

His mother's visit was exactly what he needed. After she left, he phoned Jonas who agreed to begin a search for her. Then, James went to have a haircut and rid himself of his beard. By the time six o'clock arrived, he felt renewed. He felt like he was on the right path now. A road that would lead him to the woman he loved.

Melanie had spent the last two weeks traveling all over Napa Valley. She'd texted her sister that she was taking an extended vacation and had left it at that. She checked in every couple of days via text but that was all the communication she'd had with anyone from St. Louis—that is, except for her phone call to Jackie to cancel their next cooking class. By the way Jackie spoke, she had no idea she'd resigned or left town.

Melanie surprisingly felt really good. After leaving St. Louis, she'd flown into San Francisco, rented a car, and drove up to Napa. She'd found a reasonably priced bed and breakfast and was actually having a blast staying there. Susanna Altepeter, the owner of Sweet Wine Bed & Breakfast, even let her into her kitchen. She showed her how to make her famous croissants and various breakfast dishes. Melanie almost felt at home in the kitchen, yet she dearly missed Jackie.

"You're pretty good at this, Melanie. Do you like to bake?"

"I've just started. My mother…" Melanie caught herself. Yes, she thought of Jackie as her mother. "I mean, my friend has been giving me lessons lately. Actually, Jackie is my friend's mom. I like to refer to her as Mom. That's what our group of friends refers to her as— Mom."

Melanie was telling a lie, she knew it, but that's just how she felt about Jackie. She was easy to talk to and after she learned how to deal with Jackie's need to interfere with her children's lives, Melanie got along with her really well. Deep down she wished Jackie were her mother. If things between her and James had worked out, she more than likely would have been.

Each day after spending time with Susanna, Melanie took the time and visited a different winery. Several of the wineries had self-guided tours that she enjoyed. Often, she was treated to their gorgeous grounds with views of row after row of grape vines sprawled across the rolling hills. She absolutely loved the region. She even thought about relocating to Napa Valley.

She enjoyed visiting the Oxbow Market. There she could visit various artisans, shops, and restaurants. They even had a chocolatier and a bakery that specialized in cupcakes. She also enjoyed hiking in the Skyline Wilderness Park. It was a peaceful way to spend her day, meandering the various trails, taking in the breathtaking views.

An actual thirteenth century inspired Tuscan castle could be found in the region. Castello di Amorosa was located in Calistoga, California. She learned that the owner spared no expense when he built it. He'd used over one million bricks from defunct palaces and employed medieval techniques to hand-craft them. She was amazed at the detail and expense, especially after seeing the hand carved stone crests of the owner's family. After touring it, she felt like she'd been a part of the Middle Ages. It was a gorgeous structure and hoped to return.

Each and every vineyard was unique unto itself, inspired by something whether it be a different era, country or culture. She was amazed at the differences between each one she visited. Some were referred to as châteaux, while others were styled as missions. Some were contemporary in nature while others were inspired from a different era altogether.

She often thought of James throughout the day but

mostly while she enjoyed a glass of wine. She wondered what he was doing, if he was overwhelmed at work with her leaving. She remembered their dates and conversations— how he'd held her hand when they flew. She thought about San Antonio and that whole debacle of a trip having to stay in the same room at Night's Landing. She thought of their trip to the cabin and her confession. But most of all, she missed him. She missed the way he held her hand, the way he looked at her when she was argumentative. She missed looking into his brown eyes that sparkled when he got excited over something stupid. She missed his chuckle and the way he scrunched his face. She missed working beside him, traveling, and experiencing a new city through his eyes.

When all was said and done, she missed James more than she ever thought possible. Several times she found herself grabbing for her phone when she heard the ringtone she'd assigned to him go off. He'd called her every day, several times a day, and she never answered, nor did she listen to his messages. She'd saved them but that was as far as it went. She needed to find herself and avoiding him was her way of doing it.

Melanie had accumulated tons of literature about the Napa Valley area. She intended to file it away to make a scrapbook of her vacation. It would be a memory she'd never forget.

As she pulled the materials from her purse, she came across the fortunes she'd held onto. She reread them and realized they told a story. Hers and James' story. The first fortune she picked up read: "Life's path doesn't always lead you in the right direction. Follow the stars." She realized the path she'd chosen had been all wrong for her. She needed to open herself to new possibilities.

She wasn't sure what follow the stars meant, but she understood a little more about her fortune.

James had two unique fortunes. "Take one day at a time. There's light at the end of the tunnel" and "Love is in the air staring you in the face." Wow, how true. There was light for him after his break-up with Elsa, and he did confess his love for her on more than one occasion.

Then Melanie read her last fortune: "Be careful of those around you. Trust no one. They're not who you think they are." Melanie stared at the words for a time and then came to a conclusion. She believed the fortune referred to their argument, to James following her to the Y. He hadn't trusted her and in-the-end, she'd lost her trust in him. She was amazed that these fortunes actually told their story almost from beginning to end.

As she contemplated everything they'd endured over the last several months, she realized what kind of impression he made on her. He loved his family more than anything. Although he didn't babysit his niece and nephews much, he wasn't turned off by it. He enjoyed every moment he spent with them whether they were crying, spitting up, or in need of a diaper change. Nothing fazed him in the least. He was a giving, caring man who loved his family dearly. He had a heart the size of the largest state in the Union. James was her savior, her lifeline, her friend. Not her friend, but her best friend. He was her sounding board. He was her other half. Yes, her other half. James was the love of her life. She finally admitted it to herself. Melanie Holmes was in love. She was in love for the first time with a wonderful, special soul. James Samuels was it for her.

The revelation took her breath away. She didn't know what to do. She couldn't return home and throw herself at his feet. She'd walked away from not only her job but from him too. Part of their disagreement had been his fault, but the other half had been hers. She'd been awful to him when they argued.

A sense of calm overcame her. A smile filled her face. She'd found her answers and now she had to find a way back to James.

James spoke with Jonas, who had a lead on Melanie. He knew she'd taken a flight to San Francisco and he believed she was still in California. At the same time James received the news from Jonas, his father informed him he was being sent back to Dalton B&T to perform another due diligence. James was thankful to return to California, but it also held memories for him—memories of their trip to San Francisco and their tour of the city.

The next day James was traveling back to the region he'd first fell in love with Melanie. He recounted their entire trip. How she'd relaxed with him by her side. He thought about their tour of San Francisco Bay, and how her eyes sparkled with excitement. He remembered the look on her face when she first boarded the cable car. She seemed scared at first and then laughed with excitement. How her hair blew into her face and how he brushed it aside. Happy memories, he thought.

James successfully completed his due diligence and had a free day on his schedule before returning to St. Louis. The night before, he had returned to San Francisco from Monterey since he was flying out of San

Francisco International airport. He woke that morning to a beautiful cloudless day. Instead of staying in the city and revisiting the wharf and the onslaught of memories from their trip, he decided to take a drive. It had been some time since he'd been north, so he put the car in drive and headed off towards where he didn't know.

The gradual change in landscape fascinated him, and he pulled off the road at a park. He decided to take a walk, so he parked and, hoping to see more of the countryside, headed off down a trail. He didn't know where he was going, just that he needed to clear his head of his memories with Melanie. He didn't know where she was, and she definitely didn't want to be found. She'd covered her trail well. Except for her airline reservation, Jonas hadn't been able to find her yet.

James paused to take in the views. Trees soared in front of him almost touching the sky. Everything was green, fresh, and surprisingly clean. He couldn't believe he lived in such a beautiful country. He was lost in thought observing the scenery when he swore he heard his name. He had to be wrong. He knew no one in California other than his business contacts. He must be hearing things—and then he felt a presence and heard footsteps approaching from behind.

Slowly he turned and there before him was the love of his life. He thought he was seeing things. He blinked several times trying to clear his eyes, but every time he reopened them, she was still standing before him. He was speechless. Fate had intervened and she was standing right in front of him. Should he reach out to her? He didn't know if he should acknowledge her presence. For once in his life, he was clueless as how to proceed.

"Cat got your tongue?"

"I… Melanie," he smoothly whispered her name. The next thing he knew, she was throwing herself into his arms.

James held her tightly, afraid his imagination was playing tricks on him. She placed her hands on either side of his face and he looked into her beautiful hazel eyes. She was smiling that winsome smile he'd come to love. He still thought he was seeing things until the moment he felt her lips on his. Melanie was kissing him. She wasn't a figment of his imagination. His hopes at finding her again had come to fruition.

James pulled away. "How, why?" Melanie started to laugh at him. "I'm serious, how did you find me? In all of the places I could be, you just show up. I don't understand."

"I called your dad."

"But how did that lead you here to this park? He didn't know what my plans were for today."

"Thank Jonas Sounds."

"How do you know him?"

"I don't but your dad does. I knew you were leaving town today. So was I. I was at the same hotel as you. Forgive me, but Jonas tracked your cell. He texted me your location."

He ran his hand along her cheek. "I can't believe you're here. God, how I've missed you." He hugged her closely again, fearing she'd disappear. He pulled back cupping her cheek.

"Where have you been? I've been trying to find you. I even had Jonas looking for you. All I knew was that you had flown to San Francisco."

"I needed time to myself, time to think, and make a few decisions about my past and my future." She reached for his hand and led him to a nearby bench.

"James, I was in a bad place when I left. I felt like you'd betrayed me. I was trying to come to terms with our relationship and then you followed me to my safe place."

"Safe place?"

"Yeah, my safe place. When I was going through everything as a child, I was entered into an art therapy class. There I was able to express myself. I could draw or paint what I felt. If I was having a good day, I painted something that made me happy. If I was having a bad day… Well, I'm sure you get where I'm going. Painting is my sense of relief. My safe haven where I can get out whatever's on my mind. It helped me deal with my mom and my foster life."

"I've never heard of art therapy."

"It's not a new concept. It's been around since I was a child. At one point in my life I wanted to be an art therapist. I took many of the classes, but the internships were one of the reasons that stopped me from pursuing it. I just didn't have the time working at the bank and all.

"Several years ago, the Y started up a program just like I had been involved in. It's to benefit kids in foster care. There they can let out their emotions. Right now, I'm working closely with two children."

"Mel, may I ask you a question?" She nodded her approval. "Why do you claim that you don't like children when you work so closely with them? When I saw your face when that little boy hugged you, I saw love. You looked so happy and fulfilled."

She closed her eyes and when she reopened them tears pooled in the corners. "I do love them." She openly cried. James pulled her into his arms. "I always thought with my childhood I wouldn't make a good mother. I had so much happen to me. I thought if I couldn't love myself, how could I love someone like you? How could I love our children?"

She pulled away and stood. "James, I've been thinking a lot while I've been here, and I've probably drunk too much wine in the process, but what I realized through all of this is that I love you. I love you with all my heart, and if you'll take me back, I'd love to be with you."

James didn't know whether to laugh or cry. His dreams were about to come true. He'd found the woman he'd spend the rest of his life with. He just hoped that she'd agree, in time. He wasn't going to launch into a proposal right this very minute. They both needed time to recover, but one thing James did know—he wasn't returning to St. Louis alone. He'd have his love right beside him.

Chapter Thirty-Three

JAMES AND MELANIE RETURNED TO St. Louis the following day. He still couldn't believe his lucky stars. On a trip that he'd been less than thrilled about taking, he'd rediscovered his love.

That afternoon, after Melanie had time to settle in, they headed over to his parents' house. Neither his dad nor his mother knew he'd reconnected with her. James walked into the kitchen. He certainly thought that's where he'd find his mother, but he was wrong.

He called out, "Mom?"

"In the family room," she replied. "I'm watching my soap." James motioned for Melanie to stay just outside the room. "James, what are you doing here? It's the middle of the day. Come to think of it, I thought you were out of town."

"I was and you'll never believe who I ran into."

She shrugged her shoulder. "I haven't a clue." She looked away from James and turned her focus back on her soap opera.

He took that as his key to gesture to Melanie. "Look what the wind blew in."

She looked at her son and was flabbergasted. He'd never seen his mother speechless.

In the blink of an eye, she bolted out of her chair. She ran to Melanie and pulled her into her arms. "Oh, my gosh! Melanie, is it really you?" She pulled away and looked at her again. "It is. My eyes aren't deceiving me, are they?"

"Ah no, Jackie, they're not. It's me." Melanie laughed.

Jackie pulled her in close again. "I can't believe my eyes. You're here, right in front of me."

"I am." She smiled brightly at James as Jackie squeezed her tightly.

"Come, sit down beside me. We have so much to catch up on." Pointing to James, she called out, "Get us something to celebrate with. How about a sparkling water?" Melanie giggled at Jackie's mode of celebration. "Go, James, go get our drinks." Jackie hugged her again. "Melanie, I am so happy you're home." Whispering to her afraid James would overhear, "James was lost without you. You should have seen him. He looked like death warmed over. He fell apart in your absence. I had to insist he get a haircut. And that beard he grew."

"James grew a beard? I've never seen him but shaved."

"Yes, and it looked atrocious. Thankfully, he listened to his mother and cleaned himself up."

"I wasn't gone that long. What? Two weeks, maybe a smidgeon longer."

"One day was too long for him. Dear, my James loves you."

"I know," she replied.

"No, I mean he really loves you, Melanie."

"I know he does, Jackie. And you know what? I love him too."

Jackie threw her hand across her heart. "I'm so thankful I just heard those words coming from your lips. I knew you loved him and have for a long time."

"Maybe I have. I just needed that time alone to realize what he meant to me. I also needed to deal with my past. James has been the only person to help me through it. Maybe with him by my side, I'll outgrow my panic attacks, if that's possible. He's also the one who helped me realize that I wasn't damaged beyond repair. I learned to fall in love and maybe someday I'll be able to have a family."

"Oh, Melanie."

"Don't get your hopes up, Jackie. James and I have a long way to go in this relationship. One thing I do know is that I love him with all my heart. If we can get through my past, I think we can deal with anything." Jackie hugged her again. "Jackie, you've been a godsend to me. Thank you for being the mother I never had. You've taught me so much."

Tears started to form in Jackie's eyes. "Melanie, thank you for saying that. I want you to know I consider you one of my daughters. Whether you or James make this relationship work, it's up to you. But, know that I'll always be here for you."

The three of them spent the rest of the afternoon chatting. Melanie told them about her adventures in Napa. "I even had a cooking class. Susanna, the owner of the B & B where I stayed, taught me how to make croissants from scratch."

"Huh, I've never made them before. I think now you'll have something to teach me." Jackie laughed.

Before long, Ben interrupted their conversation. "Melanie," he called out. "Where did you come from?" Ben pulled her into a hug. "It's good to see you."

"Thank you, Ben. I'm glad to be home."

"Have you told her, yet?" Ben looked directly at his son then at Melanie.

"No, I haven't."

Ben jerked his chin to his wife. "I know you would do your darnedest to overhear our conversation, so, James, do you want to do the honors?"

"Sure." James went to her side and reached for her hands. "Melanie, how would you like your old job back?"

Melanie raised her eyebrows and her eyes grew bright. "I don't understand. I resigned my position."

"Yeah, well, I didn't process the paperwork," Ben chimed in. "I was working with James about another position. The vice president of investor services has decided to retire at the end of the quarter. I thought it would be a good stepping stone for James, so I offered the position to him. That left your position available. Now, why would I want to hire and train someone new when we had someone perfectly capable for the position— that being you, Melanie?"

A broad smile broke out on her face. "I couldn't tell you until we were sure Helmich was going to retire. Once he turned in his paperwork, I knew I had his replacement. So, Melanie Holmes, how about coming back to work?"

"I guess I never really left." She snickered.

Ben got a good laugh out of her statement. "No, I guess you didn't. I'm paying you vacation time while you were gone. You deserve it. So, what about it?"

Melanie closed the gap between her and Ben. "Yes, I accept," she said as she hugged Ben tightly. "Thank you for this chance. I promise I won't disappoint you."

"I never thought you would."

James knew he'd blown his mother's day out of the water. It clearly had done an about face on her. He knew she was thrilled that he was in love with a fabulous woman, and she was happy that Melanie was gainfully employed again and in love with her son.

James and Melanie sat with his parents for a bit longer and then he turned to her. "Mel, I think you need to go see Janet. Let her know that you've returned safely."

"I guess you're right. Will you come with me?"

"Of course, I will. That's why I suggested it." James watched as Melanie was enveloped in hugs from both his parents. He smiled. This was definitely what family was all about and he hoped Melanie had the same feelings as he did.

James drove her to her sister's house. She'd called Janet on the way just to make sure she was home. Hand-in-hand, they walked to the door. Melanie rang the doorbell then smiled up at him. "Thanks for coming with me."

Janet opened the door, immediately pulling her sister into her arms. "I missed you. It's so good to see you."

James and Melanie followed Janet into her family room. He and Melanie sat side-by-side on the couch and waited as Janet got them both glasses of iced tea.

"Here you go," she said as she handed them their glasses. "So, tell me about your trip."

"First things first, Janet. I need to share something with you."

"Okay," Janet replied as she looked between the couple.

"Before I get down to why we're here, I want you to know that James and I are…"

"Engaged?"

"No, at least not yet." Melanie looked at him and reached for his hand, squeezing it. She smiled at him and continued. "I came here to tell you about my childhood."

"Oh, Mel, that's not necessary."

"It is and you'll understand why after I finish telling you my story." She went into explicit detail of how she felt when their mother locked her in the closet. "There were times I was so scared, I was afraid to breathe. Janet, I don't know where you were when she was doing this to me."

"I bet I was at Nelly's house. I was there all the time."

"That's what I've recently come to believe." Melanie gnawed on her lower lip. "I should have told you how she treated me, but I was afraid. Afraid that she'd permanently lock me in there. I don't remember much from the night she died. I just remember her shoving me and then nothing. I remember waking in the hospital being told I was never going home. I recall crying for you, but you never came."

Janet knelt in front of her sister. "Melanie, I'm so sorry I wasn't there for you."

"There was nothing you could do. You were taken and forced into foster care just as I was, except my experiences were so different from yours." Melanie went on to tell Janet about Holcomb and the many families she'd lived with.

"I think what saved me was being involved in an art therapy program. I could vent all my emotions into my art." She stopped and gave James a sideways glance. "Even to this day, it helps me overcome my anxiousness. I can get out my feelings onto a canvas."

"Melanie, I wished you would have shared this with

me a long time ago."

"Yeah, me too, but I didn't. Now we just need to look forward." She squeezed James' hand again. "Now that I've got you and James in my corner I think I can overcome all of the anguish I endured. One day at a time, right?"

"Yep, one day at a time." James said as he leaned in and kissed her brow.

Melanie and James left Janet's house shortly before eight. "How about we get something to eat? Imperial House?" He asked.

"I'm really not in the mood. Actually, I'm exhausted from our travels and sharing my past with your mother and Janet. I'd like to go home."

James listened to what she said. "That's fine. Come on, I'll take you home." When they arrived, he held her inside the door for several moments, cherishing the feel of her in his arms. "It feels so good to have you in my arms. I feared I'd never feel this way again." He kissed her softly. "Listen to what my dad said and stay home tomorrow. I'll call you later in the day."

"I'm not sick, and, after all, I did just have a two-week vacation."

"I know, but you went through something emotional today. Take time to yourself and we'll figure out what to do next."

"Huh?"

"I think you should consider counselling, but that's entirely up to you. I believe it would give you a different perspective on everything now that you're an adult, but it's your call. Now, you head off to bed, and I'll see you tomorrow." James kissed her one last time and headed out the door.

Just a week ago, he thought he'd never find her, never feel her in his arms again, and today, he'd been able to hold her, kiss her, and begin to make plans for their future.

Melanie returned to work and fit right into the Amcrost culture. Two months after the sale, Ben decided to relocate Melanie's office. In fact, he relocated many of the high-level executives that once worked for Parklayne to the Amcrost building. Melanie packed her supplies and files and headed over to Amcrost, where James planned on showing her around and taking her to her new office.

Melanie parked her car and entered the elevator. Since returning to St. Louis, her anxiety had lessoned and she was feeling much better. She believed by sharing her childhood, she'd released the horrible memories and was able to function better. She'd also begun to see a therapist that was helping her through her experiences. She knew she wouldn't overcome her issues overnight. It would take time but she was finally focused on getting past her childhood and on with her life. She guessed she owed her sense of calm to that as well.

With James' help, Melanie's fear of elevators and closed spaces had waned somewhat. Whenever she felt the walls closing in, she thought of his smile and everything seemed better.

As the elevator climbed towards James, it stopped at a floor and opened. She hadn't been paying attention as she'd been looking at her phone. Immediately, she recognized the voice. For once, her anxiety didn't kick-in. She raised her gaze and found herself looking directly into the eyes of Holcomb Newson.

"Melanie," he said.

She surprised herself. For once, she didn't flinch or begin to tremble when faced with her past. She didn't feel as if a panic attack was coming on— she felt calm, normal. "Mr. Newson," she replied. She didn't know what to say to him. Outside of the day she ran into him in the parking garage, the last time she'd seen him face-to-face had been right after the incident that sent her to the hospital. He'd been jailed but had somehow gotten out, she didn't know how, but he did.

He started to approach her but decided against it. "I heard you were working for Amcrost now."

"Yeah, I'm the VP of acquisitions. I came over when they bought out Parklayne."

"I know." He clenched and unclenched his fists. She could tell he was nervous. For once, and she didn't know why, his presence didn't bother her. "I know this isn't the place to do this, but I'd like to apologize to you. Melanie, I wasn't in a good place when you lived with us. In all actuality, I don't know how Social Services allowed you to be in our care, but they did."

"I guess times were different back then."

"They were. Anyway, I want you to know this—I was, and still am an alcoholic. What I did to you forced me to take a good look at myself. I couldn't live with what I'd done. I entered rehab and I've been sober since the moment I caused your pain." He paused momentarily. "I hope you can find it in your heart to forgive me. I know you'll never forget what happened, but I pray that you can forgive. I'm not the person I used to be. Since Mr. Samuels took a chance on me, I've changed. I'm responsible now. I come to work every day on time. I earn a good living." For all the anguish she lived with, she was glad that he'd gotten his life on track. Holcomb turned away. "I wish you'd say something, anything."

"Mr. Newson."

"Holcomb, please."

"Holcomb. Just recently, I've been able to come to terms with my childhood. I'm nowhere near where I need to be, but some things are a little clearer. I understand fully what alcohol can do to a person. I have to commend you. You've changed your life. Not many people recognize the need to do that." She couldn't say that she'd forgiven him for what he did to her, but she was glad he'd gotten the help and support to turn his life around.

"Thank you." With that, the elevator doors opened for Holcomb's floor. "I guess I'll see you around."

"I'm sure you will." And with that the doors closed on another part of her past. She realized that to overcome her past, she also needed to forgive. She'd never forget what happened to her when she was a child, but she could forgive.

The weekend of James' reunion was upon them. This was an event for the entire school. There were class-specific events for the various reunion classes along with general activities for all alumni. Since James' class was celebrating its fifteenth reunion, special events had been planned for his class alone. In addition to a golf tournament, a cocktail reception and dinner were on the schedule for Saturday. Sunday brought about his class's special family activities. A barbeque was planned at Piers Park. It had several park pavilions and was a well-known area for hikers. He'd often hiked the trails with Gabriella and Ashton.

James elected to attend the reception and dinner. He also wanted to visit with his friends' wives and family and signed up for the barbeque.

He wasn't sure if Melanie would attend the barbeque since it was all about families, but he kept his fingers crossed, hoping she'd decided to go with him.

Saturday evening, they both dressed up. James pretty much dressed as he would for the office, in a suit and long-sleeved shirt. He wore a purple tie that perfectly matched the color of her dress. Melanie wore an A-line dress. It had a crew neckline, three-quarter length sleeves, and lace that overlay to her waist. It was the perfect dress for her. She appeared chic and elegant. She complemented it with plain gold jewelry.

When James arrived to pick her up, he was overtaken by her appearance. She was stunning. Her hair had been pulled up into a French twist with tendrils framing her face, a style he loved. Her make-up was flawless. She looked like a princess.

"Wow, you look gorgeous," he stated as he stepped into her foyer. "Turn around. I want to see your dress." He motioned with his finger for her to twirl. Melanie snickered as she spun around.

"James, you see me all the time. Nothing's different here."

"Yes, there is. You have a certain glow about you. You look happy."

"I am happy." She reached up, kissing his cheek. "And it's all because of you. You believe in me. You take me just as I am. You don't care if I'm having a bad day or not."

"Why wouldn't I believe in you? I love you."

"I know you do. You're the best thing that's ever, and I mean ever, happened to me. Even though I wasn't crazy about how we actually hooked up, I can look back on it now and see that fate played into us finding one another. Maybe finding is not the right word..."

"Yeah, I have to say that was the deciding factor for me. Staying with you at Night's Landing brought me to the conclusion that Elsa and I weren't right for one another. While we shared that room, I felt a certain pull towards you."

"All the way from the floor?"

James smiled broadly at her remembering her banishing him to the floor.

"Yep, but you'll remember I didn't stay there very long. Remember how my back starting giving me fits and you finally gave in, allowing me to sleep on the bed. I can still see you stringing a blanket up down the middle of the bed attaching it to the bedposts. I'm not sure how you pulled that one off, but you did."

"I used my pantyhose. I always travel with more pair than I'll ever use—five."

"Five pair?"

"That's what I said. You can never be too prepared." He pulled her close. "Mel, that trip is when I knew you were meant for me. You challenged me in ways Elsa never did. Over the years when we've run into one another, I always knew there was a vulnerable side to you. Somewhere along the way, I decided I wanted to be the one there for you. My mom played big into my plans too."

"Jackie?"

"Well, yeah. If you could get along with her, I knew

you were meant to be a member of our family. My mom gets under everyone's last nerves, including her children, but you just seemed to roll with the punches. When she said or did anything you didn't like, you stood up to her. That's more than we do. When she didn't take offense to you, I knew you'd definitely won both of us over."

"I love your mom. I really do. James, I mean it when I told her that she was my mom because in my eyes she is. I know she'll always be there for me whether you and I make it or not."

"Hey, there!"

"It's true. I believe we'll make it, but you never know."

"We have to communicate always. We also need to listen to one another. That's what's going to make us survive."

They enjoyed Saturday evening's reception and dinner.

When James picked her up the following morning for the picnic, he was a tad bit concerned. The day was all about family. He was anxious to see how she fared being around children, but most especially around babies.

She had visited both Kelly and Angelina when she returned from Napa Valley. She was still apprehensive being around babies, but he hoped she became more comfortable as time went by.

James was surprised with how well she did at the picnic. She interacted with his friends and their wives and children. He was amazed when he watched her hold his friend's baby while she dealt with another of her children.

James observed her from afar noticing the smile that

crept across her face as she played with the baby's feet. She laughed as the baby latched onto her finger, giggling in the process. He could feel her as she relaxed around his friends and their families. He knew she was still dealing with her past but he was extremely proud of how far she'd come in only a few short months.

That evening as they sat outdoors listening to music, he brought up their weekend. "It was good seeing everyone from my class. I can't believe how many of my friends are married with toddlers." He watched her intently as she listened to him discuss the children. "That little girl who ran around with the bowl on her head…"

"You mean Jack's kid."

"Yeah, what's her name?"

"I don't remember but wasn't she a hoot? I laughed every time she ran over to me. She was definitely a cutie."

"So was Langston's baby. You seemed like you enjoyed holding her."

"I did." She paused and smiled broadly at him, her eyes glistening. "She was precious, wasn't she? She was so aware of her surroundings and at such a young age. I was amazed."

"She loved holding your finger."

"Yep, and pulling my hair too."

As their conversation progressed, James knew he'd made the right decision all those months ago when he was lying in that bed in San Antonio. Breaking up with Elsa had been the right thing to do because James discovered Melanie in the process. She made him happy, happier than he'd ever been. The funny thing was he thought he'd been happy with Elsa, but he'd been definitely wrong about that.

They enjoyed the rest of their evening rehashing the weekend. A new workweek was upon them and James had plans. They had a long weekend ahead since Memorial Day was coming up. Kelly and Alec were having their summer kick off barbeque on Saturday. Everyone on both sides of the family would be there including friends and staff from Alec's practice. James also discovered that he'd invited Jonas Sounds and his sister, Elizabeth. She was a widow. Her husband had been a Navy SEAL who lost his life while fighting in Afghanistan. James dropped Melanie off at her house. He needed to hurry home and finish working through arranging what he hoped to be an unforgettable week.

Chapter Thirty-Four

JAMES BARELY SLEPT SUNDAY EVENING. As he lay in bed, special moments from their weekend flashed before him. He was almost giddy with excitement. Monday and Tuesday were extremely busy days. He'd tried to get over to Imperial House both days, but every time he turned his back he'd been faced with another crisis. Wednesday, he made up his mind. Nothing was going to prevent him for having lunch at his favorite Chinese restaurant.

He arrived late for lunch. He'd phoned ahead and spoke with Debbie. He wanted to have her undivided attention. He enjoyed his lunch and then he, Debbie, and Yan had a nice conversation. He hadn't seen them in some time and missed talking to them.

That evening, he spoke with Melanie. She'd left Monday afternoon on a short business trip and expected to return Thursday morning. "I just got off the phone with your mother."

"I told her you were on a business trip."

"Yeah, I know. I'm really not sure what she wanted. She talked mainly about nothing…"

"That's how she is sometimes. I think she likes to hear herself speak. More than likely she was checking up on you since you're out of town and alone."

"Yeah, that's what I thought too."

They spoke for a little longer. He could tell she was exhausted. "I'm going to let you go. I know you're tired. See you tomorrow. I love you, Mel."

"Love you too," she replied before hanging up.

James lay in bed planning the rest of the week. Friday he would take Mel to Imperial House for dinner. He knew she'd been craving Chinese. Saturday was Kelly and Alec's barbeque. Sunday, his parents were having everyone over, and Monday he'd reserved for just the two of them.

Friday afternoon, James stopped by Melanie's office. "Now, don't forget tonight's Chinese for dinner."

"Oh, I won't. I've been dreaming about hot and sour soup all week, especially since you told me you had lunch there the other day."

"I know you have. I'll pick you up at six. I've already called ahead and Debbie's reserving our table for us."

"That is a special table."

James smiled at her knowing how special it really was. He couldn't wait to pick her up. He ordered a special flower arrangement for her. He wanted to show her how much she meant to him. The florist surprised him when they had in stock just what he wanted.

He arrived at her house promptly at six. She was definitely taken aback by the floral arrangement. "Peonies. How did you know? They're my favorite flower." She inhaled their sweet scent. "These smell so good." Melanie set the flowers down on the table in her foyer, grabbed her purse, and motioned for him to head out the door.

"Are you in a hurry?"

"I am. I'm starved and can't wait to have a bowl of hot and sour soup."

"Well, okay then, let's go."

The two walked hand-in-hand into Imperial House, which was packed for a Friday evening. Debbie welcomed them with open arms and led them to their favorite table where they had a little privacy from the huge crowd.

While they waited, they discussed their week. She recounted her trip, the first she'd taken alone in months. "I missed you traveling with me."

"It seems like you did okay. Didn't you, Mel?"

"Yeah, I did. I just closed my eyes and thought about you. It made all the difference in the world. I wasn't anxious at all."

He reached for her hand and kissed the top of it. "I missed you more than I ever imagined. The office wasn't the same without you in it."

"It's not like we see each other all that much during the day."

"I know, but just knowing you're one floor away…"

"James, Melanie, welcome," Yan interrupted. "Deb just told me you arrived and I thought I'd come out from my playing the role of chef. I don't get to see you as much anymore since I'm back in the kitchen. I hope you enjoy your meal."

"I'm sure we will," responded Melanie. "I've been looking forward to a bowl of hot and sour soup for days now."

"Well, then, let me get you one." Yan returned a few minutes later with not only their soup, but an array of appetizers. "I know you love the egg rolls, pot stickers, and crab Rangoon, so I made-up a plate for you."

"These look luscious," Melanie said, grabbing one of the egg rolls.

"Enjoy your dinner,"Yan called as he headed back to the kitchen. He'd taken a few steps away, turned back towards James, and winked.

By the time James and Melanie had finished their meal, the restaurant had pretty much cleared out. Only a few patrons remained and they were on the other side of the room.

Debbie finished boxing up their leftovers and left the bill along with the fortune cookies.

They always had a good time with this part of their meal. "You know when I was in Napa, I reread our fortunes."

"You did? I had no idea you kept them."

"Yes, you did," she teased. "And when I read them, I realized they did foretell our future. Do you remember what they said?"

"Me? Nah, I really don't pay attention to them. I'm just in it for the cookie. You should know that by now." James watched as she fished around in her purse.

"Okay, see if this isn't us to a T." Melanie read each of their previous fortunes. "'Life's path doesn't always lead you in the right direction. Follow the stars'— that was mine. I figure that refers to us. I also had 'Be careful of those around you. Trust no one. They're not who you think they are.' I think that refers to when you followed me to the Y. I didn't trust you after that because you couldn't trust me."

"I do remember that one." He winked.

"Your fortunes were: 'Take one day at a time. There's light at the end of the tunnel.' I think that refers to your break-up with Elsa. And finally, 'Love is in the air staring you in the face.' James, I can't believe you forgot that one."

"I guess I did." He looked down at their bill. "Look, Deb gave us extra fortunes tonight. She gypped me when I was here the other day. I didn't realize I didn't get a fortune until I was on the way back to the office."

"Huh," was all she said in response.

James passed her a fortune. "Here take one." He sat nervously waiting while she opened the slip of paper. He hoped she chose the correct one. "What does it say?"

"It says 'Life's about new adventures.'"

"That's interesting. Here take another." James nerves were slowly picking up.

"This one says 'The past is your past— it's time for your future." She tapped the fortune on the table pondering the slip of paper. "It's your turn, you take one."

"You're the one that enjoys reading them. I'll take the cookie." James reached for one of the cookies and began to nibble on it. He watched as she reread the fortunes.

Melanie reached for the next one on the tray. Loudly, she cracked it open and the paper fell to the floor. James reached over and grabbed it. He glanced at the saying before handing it to her. He rested his head in his upturned palm as he watched her read it. She was opening them in the exact sequence he'd hoped. "Your family is all around you. Reach out and follow the way." He could see the wheels spinning in her head as she analyzed each saying. "This is crazy, James. I understand each of these."

"You do? I'm having a hard time following the logic." He was doing his best not to bust out laughing.

"Yeah, I do. Don't you think it odd that they seem to be addressed directly to me?" Again, he focused on her as she reread each one again. "The first one, to me, was about opening my life to new things. The second tells me to leave my past behind, and this last one makes me believe in family. You know I only have Janet as my family."

"I know." He reached for the last fortune, split open the cookie and handed her the message. "What's it say?"

"Take your Life's Second Journey with me…"

He knew she was onto him. "James, what's this all about?"

"What did you just read?"

"I know what I read…" With that, James slid from his chair and knelt down beside her.

"This is what it means, Mel." He reached for her hands. "I love you and I want you to start your life over again by my side. Life's a journey that we're on. Your first one didn't go as planned, but together I know I can lead you along your second journey. You'll have me and my entire family by your side." He squeezed her hands and, looking up into her eyes, broadly smiled. "Melanie Holmes. I love you more than life itself. I want to go on this journey with you. I want you to experience what living in a family is all about. Mind you, my family isn't small, and as you know, my mother loves to be involved in everything." She laughed at his comment.

"Will you take this journey with me? Will you be by my side for the rest of your life? Melanie Holmes, will you marry me?"

James watched the relaxed expression change on her face as he spoke. He watched as the tears formed in the corners of her eyes, as she began to chew nervously on her bottom lip. His eyes never left her face and he saw a smile, the biggest he'd ever seen, cross her face.

"James, you know my opinion on marriage." His heart dropped out from under him. She was going to say no. Then he saw the tears begin to fall as she launched herself into his arms. *If this is the way she's letting me down...*

"Are you okay?" He felt her head nod against his shoulder. "Do you have an answer for me?" Again, he felt a nod. He waited for a second. "Mel, you're scaring me here..."

She pulled away and placed her hands on either side of his face. She drew in her lips and then felt her hand shaking against his skin. "You're not going to pass out on me, are you?"

"No. I'm not." She wiped the tears from her cheeks then returned her hands to his face. "I never, ever thought I'd hear those words coming from anyone." She paused again, taking a deep breath, and continued. "You know where I once stood on the idea of marriage. I made a promise to myself that I'd never, ever, fall in love and get married. Then you came into my life when I needed you the most. I was falling apart, fearing that my life was coming undone around me. My comfort zone at Parklayne was unraveling right before my eyes. My anxiety was at an all-time high. Looking back on San Antonio...I never would have imagined that experience would develop into me..." She stopped and pointed to herself. "Me, giving you a chance. That week was hell for me, especially when I allowed you to begin to sleep on the bed with me."

James roared with laughter. "Yeah, that was pretty interesting. Anyway, go on..."

"You've become my whole world. You're on my

mind from the moment I wake up until I go to sleep at night." She stopped speaking. "Changing the subject momentarily..."

"Melanie, you're killing me here."

"Did you have anything to do with these fortunes?" She gestured towards the papers lying on the table. "It is rather suspicious ... You wrote these, didn't you?" She picked up the fortunes. "I also assume that Deb and Yan were in on this little plan of yours."

James looked at her sheepishly.

"Don't look at me that way..." James cleared his throat. "It was you... You wrote these."

"Yeah, I did."

"I can't believe you went to all of this trouble. You know me too well, and knew what I needed to hear."

"Did you hear what you needed to?"

From the moment she started to read thc fortunes, James saw her change right before his eyes. Her eyes sparkled, her smile was effervescent almost contagious. He hoped he'd hear the one word that would come from her lips. She was taunting him. He could feel it.

He reached for her hand that held the fortunes. "So, will you go on a new adventure with me? Will you put your past in the past and let me be there for you in the future? Will you join my family?" He snickered. "You know mom would love it. But most importantly, will you, Melanie Holmes, take your life's second journey with me? Will you marry me, have babies with me, and will you share whatever life has to offer on our journey? I love you and want to take that trip with you."

Tears cascaded down her face, her smile grew and she nodded her head. "Yes, James, I'll marry you and become a part of your family. I'll follow you on that lifelong journey. I want to let go of my past. I look forward to a future filled with hopes, dreams, and most importantly filled with love. A love that I know will last a lifetime."

Epilogue

SATURDAY WAS UPON THEM. AS James drove over to Melanie's, he didn't know when they should tell his family about their engagement. Janet would be at Kelly's party, so he thought they should do it then. They'd be amongst family and friends.

Their announcement would be a little unusual for the family. The last several big announcements occurred on the patio at Alejandro and Angelina's. This time their engagement really only affected his family as Melanie's family consisted of her sister. He couldn't wait to share the news. He knew his mother would be overjoyed.

James knocked on Melanie's door and waited for her. He couldn't forget the look on her face when he presented her engagement ring to her. She raised her hand to her mouth in surprise. "You have a ring and everything," she'd said through her tears.

"I couldn't go through the motions without one. This is a big deal," he'd said as he opened the jeweler's box. "If you don't like it, I can return it."

"Oh, James," she'd said. "It's beautiful."

He'd pulled the ring from the box and slid it down her finger. He had designed a one-of-a kind engagement ring. A large two carat emerald-cut diamond was surrounded by sapphires. While designing the ring, he researched various stones. He'd chosen the sapphire to surround the diamond because its mental and emotional properties spoke volumes to him. A sapphire was known for its mental clarity. It lessened confusion and helped bring hope where there was hopelessness. It relieved depression, eased anxieties, and helped bring clarity to a situation. It was also known as a healing crystal.

He didn't know if any of the lore of the sapphire meant a thing, but just knowing that the stone was known to bring joy, peace and beauty through meditation gave him the inspiration to believe in its possibilities.

In the midst of his thoughts, Melanie threw open the door. James had never seen her happier. She drew him inside where she leapt into his arms, kissing him soundly on the lips. "I've missed you. I barely slept last night thinking about this," she motioned to her ring. "It's stunning. I can't believe you designed it."

He held her close listening to the sheer joy in her voice. "Well, I did, and I enjoyed every minute of it. Now, do you want to share our good news today or wait a bit?"

"Let's do it today. Everyone will be together and you know your mom will definitely guess something's up with the smile that's plastered all over my face."

On their way to Kelly and Alec's they discussed how they'd share their news. "Everyone in the past always made a big announcement at a family affair: Angelina and Alejandro started it off with their engagement, then Kelly and Alec, Gabriella and Ashton. Are you sure you want to announce it today?"

"I do. Should I hide my ring?"

"Nah, let's see how long it takes someone to notice it."

He made it difficult for anyone to spot the ring because he held her left hand from the moment they arrived. At one point, he left her side only to return seconds later with bottles of water. If anyone really knew Melanie, they would have immediately noticed the change in her demeanor.

They'd just finished eating. James had led her over to a few chairs that had been set up under the huge tulip tree in the backyard when Jackie approached. She hadn't spent more than a few minutes talking to them before she was drawn to the sounds of a crying baby. He had laughed at his mother because she hadn't a clue whose baby was crying.

"I don't know how they do it," Jackie commented referring to her daughters and their crying children. "I know I did it when you kids were young, but I don't know if I have the energy to keep up with them today."

James smiled as Melanie leaned over, placing her elbow on her knee and her chin in the palm of her hand, and looked at him. Jackie kept up her pace talking, going on and about her grandchildren, until she let out a scream that would wake the neighborhood. Before either of them knew it, she was pulling on Melanie's hand. She pulled so hard, and Melanie was so relaxed, she yanked her off the chair. Melanie landed on the ground at James's feet.

"Melanie," he cried. "Are you okay? Mom, what is wrong with you?" He helped Melanie from the ground while Jackie ogled her ring.

"What's this?" she cried. "Is this what I think it is?"

James wrapped his arm around Melanie. "Are you engaged?" James watched the smile on Melanie's face grow. "It is, isn't it?" Melanie nodded her head.

"Yep, Mom, we're engaged," James said.

"How could you keep this from me? When did this happen?" James chuckled as his mother threw one question after another at them.

Before James knew it, he and Melanie were surrounded by family. Janet approached Melanie pulling her into her arms. "You're happy?"

"I am, Janet. I am."

James watched the exchange between sisters. He needed to quiet his mother's excitement. "Gee, Mom, you sure took the fun out of our announcement." He snickered, knowing their announcement played out just as they'd intended. In fact, he was glad she was the first to see Melanie's ring.

"I asked Mel to marry me last night. We planned on telling everyone today, but you went ahead and spoiled it with your screams."

"James, it's not like you haven't had time today to tell everyone. You did socialize with us and we just ate."

"Yeah, I know."

"So, when's the big day?"

"We haven't even begun to think about that." James watched as Melanie was pulled into hugs by every member of his family, then Melanie pulled his mother aside.

"You're happy, right Melanie? I know you had some doubts about marriage and having a family."

"I did, but James helped me work through all of that. I'm still getting used to being in a family and all... What I wanted to ask you is this... May I call you Mom?"

James watched as Melanie and his mother spoke. He

saw the tears begin to fall from both of their eyes. "Of course, you can dear," he heard. "I've wanted this for so long. I knew you and James would end up together. I saw how he'd changed when he returned from San Antonio."

"Ah, you heard about that?"

"I did and from the moment he broke off his engagement with Elsa I knew you were the one."

"So, that's why you insisted on teaching me to cook?"

Jackie thought for a moment. "Yes and no, but what does it really matter now. I'm going to have you as a daughter, and I can't wait."

"I've always longed for a mom and now I'm going to have one. Thank you for James." Jackie looked at her questioningly. "You taught him how to treat a woman. He recognized my fears and helped me deal with them. He never left my side and saw things in me I'd never seen in myself. You raised one hell of a son."

Jackie wrapped her arms around Melanie. "Thank you for saying that. You're one lucky woman, that's all I can say."

"I am and I know that too."

James watched the two women that meant the most in his life cry and laugh at the same time. He'd stuck by Melanie and taught her that she could move on from a past that was filled with pain. He would take her on a journey. One filled with love, hope, and a happily ever after. She was his now, and he'd never let her go. San Antonio had brought them together— led them on a journey that neither one of them expected. Life was about having a past, present, and a future. He was ever thankful that he'd come to realize during his stay at Night's Landing that Melanie was his future.

Author's Note

Thank you so much for reading Life's Second Journey. For news and updates from Anne Stone, subscribe to her newsletter. You'll be treated to sneak peeks, give-aways, free books and bonus material just for signing up.

If you enjoyed reading Life's Second Journey, please consider leaving a review. Reviews are always appreciated!

CONNECT WITH ANNE ONLINE:

Facebook:
https://www.facebook.com/AnneStoneAuthor/

BookBub:
https://www.bookbub.com/authors/anne-stone

Goodreads:
https://www.goodreads.com/author/show/14730179.Anne_Stone

Email:
Anne@Annestoneauthor.com

About the Author

Anne Stone was born and raised in St. Louis, Missouri but now lives in the cold state of Wisconsin with her faithful Cavalier King Charles Spaniel. She writes heartfelt sweet contemporary romance and is the author of the following series: Black Gold Management Agency, The Show Me, and Williams & Company. She loves to tell a story and that's what you'll definitely get in an Anne Stone novel.

Anne's degree is in education but she has worked in the corporate sector managing a large number of staff. Now, she works from home where part of her day is still spent in the corporate world and the other part is dreaming of her heroes and heroines.

Learn more about Anne by visiting
www.AnneStoneAuthor.com.

Also by Anne Stone

The Show Me Series:

Book 1:Life's Second Chances

Book 2: Life's Gateway to Happiness

Book 3: Life's Turned Upside Down

Book 4: Life's Second Journey

The Show Me Series Boxed Set:Volume 1 (Books 1-3)

Williams & Company:

Never Lose Hope

Black Gold Management Agency:

Book 1: Love's Final Match

www.ingramcontent.com/pod-product-compliance
Lightning Source LLC
LaVergne TN
LVHW041106080826
845145LV00007B/1694

* 9 7 8 0 9 9 9 7 8 6 0 3 1 *